David Dickinson was born in Dublin. With an honours degree in Classics from Cambridge, he joined the BBC, where he became editor of Newsnight and Panorama, as well as series editor for Monarchy, a three-part pro-gramme on the British royal family.

**Titles in the series
(listed in order of publication)**

Death Comes to Lynchester Close

David Dickinson

CONSTABLE • LONDON

CONSTABLE

First published in Great Britain in 2016 by Constable

This paperback edition published in 2017

1 3 5 7 9 10 8 6 4 2

A CIP catalogue record for this book
is available from the British Library.

ISBN: 978-1-47212-121-9

Typeset in Palatino by TW Type, Cornwall
Printed and bound in Great Britain by Clays Ltd, St Ives plc

Papers used by Constable are from well-managed forests and other
responsible sources.

Constable
An imprint of
Little, Brown Book Group
Carmelite House
50 Victoria Embankment
London EC4Y 0DZ

An Hachette UK Company
www.hachette.co.uk

www.littlebrown.co.uk

For Annie, and for Jane and Krystyna

Part One
Overdose

1

Some wives never give up. They plough on with their requests through the deserts of indifference and the fogs of uncertainty that engulf their husbands. The most determined will sail on across uncharted seas, their voice the only one disappearing into the silence.

For the husbands the daily newspapers, sometimes raised above their face like a parapet, are the first line of defence. Close inspection of the City pages or the sports reports can hold a wife at bay for a time. Business may have to be attended to, necessitating an early retirement to the study if the husband is lucky enough to have one, or even out through the front door to the office, if he is lucky enough to have one of those. Others may find sanctuary in the garden shed, last defensive position of the husband under siege.

It has to be said that in the case of Lady Lucy Powerscourt the normal charges did not apply. Throughout her twenty years of marriage to her husband Francis she had never nagged him about anything. She was not a harridan or a bully or a domestic tyrant. But this cause was different.

It was different because she regarded it as special. It was different because she had an ally in her camp, their son Thomas Powerscourt, whose views on the matter were even stronger than her own.

'I know we went to the Deep South of the United States last year, Francis, and I know we stopped off for a night or two in New York, but I want to see New York properly: a week or ten days, something like that. I'd really like to go on a cruise round the world. There's nothing to stop us. And I know I've been going on about it, but I would like it very much. So would Thomas. He reminded me about it only this morning.'

Lady Lucy seemed to have amassed a small library of brochures from English and German shipping lines.

'Look at this, for instance. You can now sail right round the world, if you like. On this one here, the SS *Cleveland*, they've got electric lifts connecting the various decks. You can make telephone calls from one cabin to another. The ship's got a darkroom for amateur photographers and a library stocked with books in English, French and German. That should please you, Francis. There's a gymnasium with electrically operated machines including several in the form of a saddle. You could, as it were, take a ride in the middle of the Atlantic Ocean. If you go all the way round the world, India, Burma, the Philippines, those sorts of places, you go back to New York by train from San Francisco. If they ever finish that Panama Canal on time, we'd be able to complete the entire journey by sea.'

All that Lady Lucy could see were the front and back pages of *The Times*, held high like a defensive wall.

'Wouldn't that be a good thing to do, Francis?'

There was no reply.

4

Lady Lucy glanced at her selection of transatlantic and round-the-world literature.

'This one here has got a dinner menu, Francis. You start with caviar on toast. Doesn't that sound good? Then you can have Chesterfield soup, or salmon in parsley sauce, followed by oxtail au gratin or duckling salad. For the main course you can have all sorts of things: roast spring lamb with mint sauce, calf's head vinaigrette – I'm not at all sure about the calf's head – or roast turkey with cranberry sauce, all served with a choice of vegetables like green peas and cauliflower. Then there's a course of baked ham with Madeira sauce. I'm beginning to feel quite full up now so I'll just give you the dessert course: apple tart or plum pudding, Mont Blanc jelly or lemon pie, Neapolitan ice cream to follow. What do you think of that, Francis?'

Lady Lucy looked at the dense layout of the print on the front and back pages of the newspaper. Slowly, very slowly, her husband's defensive wall began to come down. He spoke before she could see him.

'I've been wondering about the fish, my love.'

'The fish?'

'Do they have fishermen sailors on board, lines permanently spread out at the back, perhaps, to replenish the supplies at the tables?'

'You're being absurd, Francis, and you know it. What do you say to this plan?'

'I'm afraid I didn't hear most of it. Some very interesting stuff in here about the situation in Ireland.'

'You're being unreasonable and you know it.'

'I tell you what, Lucy. This is what I'll do. You give me those brochures full of electric lifts and fish courses and I'll read them all. How's that?'

'That's very kind of you, Francis,' said Lady Lucy, bundling up her brochures and handing them over. She wondered as she did so if this might not be another delaying tactic, insufficient time for reading available, other matters needing attention, pressing articles in *The Times* or *The Economist*. She just didn't know. She would have to wait for a couple of days or more before she could reopen negotiations. Of one thing she was quite sure. She wasn't going to give up.

Many of England's country cathedrals look as if they have been dropped down direct from heaven and secured with celestial clamps. They sit in their surroundings of well-mown grass as if they have been here for ever. Occasionally the divine architects may have made a mistake in their calculations, or some of the clamps could have worked loose, segments of steeple or internal arches collapsing under their weight and discovered lying in an unsuspecting nave. Others, like Lincoln at the top of its steep hill, seem to have been despatched from the heavens as a single unit when God was in a hurry.

Lynchester, in England's West Country, was blessed with the usual collection of chantry chapels and clerestories, chapterhouse and cloister, lady chapel and ancient stained glass, choir stalls and transept. It was not one of the great glories of the English cathedral collection like Salisbury or Wells or Winchester. Only the most discerning of architectural pilgrims made their way to see it, guidebooks in hand, comparisons to be made with the other cathedrals of England.

The font – customs point and border crossing for the new arrivals, bathed in the waters of Jordan – was by the

West Door. Through the same door the dead departed after their funerals, possibly passing the font that had christened them, their souls washed in the tears of those who loved them. The nave and the choir stalls were not particularly distinguished. Above the High Altar and the magnificent stained-glass window behind it, true believers maintained, there hovered the presence of the Holy Spirit: immortal, invisible, God only wise.

The West Front was filled with sculpture. At the bottom Christ and his disciples kept grave watch over the congregations as they came and went, checking perhaps that the visitors were not going to change money inside or take the name of the Lord in vain. Above them Moses kept guard on the success of his commandments, crook in hand, back bowed from the strain of carrying the tablets down from the mountaintop single-handed. He was staring balefully at the crowds beneath, as if some of them might have been caught worshipping the golden calf. Throughout the centuries many had. The four evangelists were there, scroll or tablet in hand, wondering maybe about which, if any of them, would be read in the education of the faithful or the conversion of the ungodly. Above and beyond them a whole range of auxiliary statues acted as sentinels, telling of different aspects of the Christian faith and the sufferings of God's chosen people.

Lynchester was very proud of its Close. It was most often compared with the great sweeps and terraces of Bath, some forty miles away. At the north end was a long curved row of houses, nearly as grand as the Royal Crescent. On either side were two handsome terraces. Other buildings – a grammar school, a former Bishop's Palace, residences for clergy and chantry chapel priests, a small cottage hospital – were dotted about in the gaps between the terraces and the crescent. A river ran round the back and was occasionally used for water transport to the railway station when the traffic in the town was very dense. At the heart of the Close was a great sundial, clearly visible from the buildings and the West Door of the cathedral.

Passing through the great gate that linked the cathedral to the town and its railway station very early one January morning was a tall man, deep in thought. He was looking round about him as if he did not wish to be seen. His worn but well-cut suit proclaimed that he was probably on his way to a government department in London or to a solicitor's quarters, maybe to one of the great banking houses of the City. He looked behind him from time to time, as if he thought he might be observed or maybe even followed. The man bought a first-class ticket to London and settled down behind his newspaper. He was going to a meeting where he had no appointment and had no idea if he would be welcomed.

2

Lord Francis Powerscourt was reading his letters in the upstairs drawing room looking out over Markham Square. There was a knock at the door followed by an apologetic cough. This had to be Rhys, the Powerscourt butler, who was incapable of entering a room without the cough, as if he might be the bearer of bad, if not cataclysmic, news.

'Excuse me, my lord, there's a gentleman below who wishes to speak to you as a matter of some urgency.'

'Thank you, Rhys, do we have a name?'

'The party says he is the Bishop of Lynchester, my lord.'

'You sound uncertain. Better show him up.'

As the Bishop came into the room, Powerscourt realized what had made Rhys sound slightly doubtful.

'Lord Powerscourt,' said the Bishop, 'how very kind of you to see me without an appointment. I was quite prepared to come back later in the day. Trevelyan is my name; Percival Trevelyan, Bishop of Lynchester, at your service.'

Powerscourt could see now what had concerned the

butler. Bishop Trevelyan did not have a single item of ecclesiastical clothing on his person. There wasn't a purple shirt or a crucifix or a dog collar or even gaiters to mark him out as one who strode out into the world clad in the whole armour of God. This Bishop was a plain clothes Bishop. It was as if Archdeacon Grantly had come to London to smite Barchester's enemies dressed like a City solicitor. The Bishop looked very strained, as if he had received bad news that very morning.

'Could I make one thing absolutely clear at the beginning, Lord Powerscourt. I'm not here. I haven't been here.'

'I beg your pardon, My Lord Bishop. You are here. I can see that you're here. I don't understand.'

'Forgive me. The matter of which I am about to speak is private. That is why I am asking you for complete confidentiality. A mutual friend suggested I call on you for advice. I do not feel able to tell you his name.'

'Very well, I am used to keeping secrets. This meeting has not taken place. Now, won't you please sit down.' Powerscourt showed the Bishop into his own favourite chair by the fireside. The sitting position seemed to relax him. He still knotted his fingers together all the time, but some of the earlier strain had gone from his face.

'Thank you, Lord Powerscourt. Let me say that I have been thinking about my narrative in the train.'

'Like preparing a sermon, perhaps?'

The Bishop managed the ghost of a smile. 'It is a matter of life and death. In every sense. Perhaps I should begin at the beginning.' He ran his fingers through his hair now. He paused for a moment to marshal his thoughts.

'Our cathedral owns a great deal of property in the little city of Lynchester, especially in the Cathedral Close itself. Some of the buildings have been sold off in the past. Now we prefer to maintain them to a high standard and rent them out. In one of these, Netherbury House, to the rear of the crescent, there lived an old man called Simon Jones. He was very old, he was very ill. He had one of those terrible illnesses old people get. His hands shook. He could scarcely walk unaided. He'd been this way for years; sometimes as clear in his mind as you and I, sometimes raving like a lunatic, if you'll forgive the phrase. He used to say some years ago that being old was like an exam where they didn't tell you the questions, never mind the answers. Last year he changed his description. He said it was like being struck dumb and blind in the middle of crossing a busy main road. You didn't know what direction the blow was going to come from.'

'Forgive me for interrupting, Bishop. Did he live alone, Mr Jones?'

'I should have said. He did live alone apart from his housekeeper, Mrs McQuaid. She is in her early sixties but was well able to cope with the cooking and cleaning and all-round support. She had a room of her own in Netherbury House and a little cottage round the corner. I knew him well, Simon Jones. I used to call on him once a week or so. I like to think I was a person he could confide in. He was always very frank with me. He always maintained that however great his trial – I think he had been a successful lawyer in an earlier life – he would see it through to the end. He gave the impression that he would never take his own life; he knew that was a sin against God's holy law and commandments. It does show, I suspect, that he had been thinking about it – taking his own life, I mean.'

'Did he stick to that, the not taking his life?' Even as

he spoke, Powerscourt knew that there must be some ambiguity about the poor man's end, an ambiguity that brought a Bishop to Markham Square in plain clothes, almost as if he were ashamed of being a Bishop.

'I'm coming to that, Lord Powerscourt. I must stick with the timescale of my narrative. Last Monday must have been a difficult day for poor Simon. One of the neighbours reported him trying to walk with his two sticks out of his front door. He never made it. He turned back indoors. One of the neighbour's children said that they heard him crying and shouting later in the day towards suppertime. He went to bed. He took his sleeping pills. He was found dead in the morning by Mrs McQuaid. As I said, she has a little cottage of her own round the back but she sleeps on the top floor sometimes when he's bad. She spent the night in Netherbury House and said she heard nothing in the night.'

'Did he take the pills himself? Had he ended up taking an overdose?'

'There are many things in this troubled world I am not sure of, Lord Powerscourt, but I am absolutely certain that he could not have taken his two normal pills himself, let alone any more.'

'How do we know that he took an overdose in some fashion or other? I presume there was an overdose?'

'There was. I now turn to the doctor who examined Simon Jones – the late Simon Jones. He came to see me immediately after his examination of the body and arranging for the undertakers to take the body away. Dr Willoughby is quite young, and new to the practice. He was very brief, almost curt with me. He told me that the poor man had died of an overdose. There should have been twenty to thirty pills left from his last prescription.

Now there were half a dozen. He himself had taken the bottle of pills away. He had stressed to Mrs McQuaid that she should say she gave Mr Jones his normal ration of pills. Dr Willoughby said he had told her, as he was about to tell me, that Simon Jones had died of natural causes. That was what he proposed to put on the death certificate. That was the simplest thing to do. I was about to ask him some questions but he left, pleading an urgent engagement elsewhere.'

'Have you tried to speak to him since?'

'I tried and failed on a number of occasions. He seems to be especially busy at present. When I did track him down he said that he had given his opinion and he wasn't going to change it.'

'That doesn't seem very polite for a young doctor not long in his post.'

'I don't think he's a believer. I don't think he approves of us very much. I've never seen him at any of our services and neither have any of my colleagues.'

'I see,' said Powerscourt, noting that an expression of anguish seemed to have replaced anxiety on the Bishop's face. 'I can see that it is a very difficult situation all round. Have you spoken to Mrs McQuaid since these events?'

'I have. She is quite sure about the pills. She gave him two as usual. No more. Two would not have killed him.'

'Did you ask her if she gave him any more than his usual dose? By mistake, perhaps?'

'Of course I did. She swore she did not. She is a very religious woman, Mrs McQuaid, unlike the doctor, and she is a regular at cathedral services. I asked her if Mr Jones could have gone to the bathroom and taken the pills himself to put himself out of his misery after such a terrible day. She said she thought that was what must have happened. You can never tell what these diseases are going to do next, she said. Maybe he felt well enough or stable enough to go and do it himself. One minute you're down, the next minute you're up, the minute after that you might be dead. She wouldn't say any more. I didn't believe her.'

'Had she been with Mr Jones long? Did she know him well?

'She had been with him for eight years or more. She was extremely fond of him. She used to say that looking after him was a bit like caring for her own father in his last months.'

'Is she also a patient of Dr Willoughby's?'

'She is.'

'I see.' Powerscourt waited for the reply. The Bishop was staring very hard at his shoes and wringing his hands again.

'Now I must tell you my fear, or fears, Lord Powerscourt. I must bring them out into the open.'

The Bishop began running his hands through his hair again.

'It seems to me that the most likely thing to have happened is that Mrs McQuaid killed him. She had watched him suffer for years. She knew he wasn't going to get any better. He was only going to get worse. She gave him an overdose of his pills, quite a large one. Maybe he asked her to do it. She killed him out of kindness, if you like, but she killed him. That is against the teachings of the Ten Commandments. I'm sure I don't need to remind you, Lord Powerscourt, that the Sixth Commandment says: Thou shalt not kill. I believe the motive is irrelevant. She killed him as surely as if she had put a pistol to his head and pulled the trigger. Whichever way you look at it, it's murder. I cannot live up to my vows as a churchman and Bishop and condone – or be seen to condone – such an act, carried out in sight of my own cathedral.'

'What happens if Mr Jones asked her to give him an overdose?'

'I have thought about that, too. I believe it's still murder.'

Powerscourt wondered if he too should run his hands through his hair. This conversation was now in very difficult territory.

'I can see your difficulties, Bishop. What do you intend to do about them?'

'I hope you will be able to assist me in my deliberations, Lord Powerscourt. Our mutual friend said you were wise.'

It's Rosebery – my old friend Rosebery, former Prime Minister and Foreign Secretary – he's talked to, Powerscourt said to himself. I'm sure of it. The man has tentacles stretching out round the worlds of Westminster and Whitehall. No reason why they shouldn't reach deep into the Church of England as well.

'I will give you the best advice I can, Bishop. But I think you may already know what you intend to do.'

'Your friend pleaded with me not to do anything until I had spoken to you. But I intend to make an appointment with the Chief Constable next week.'

'Would that be to ask his advice, or would it be to lay a charge against Mrs McQuaid for murder?'

'As I said, I intend to lay the facts before him. As a churchman I can do no other. I cannot be an accessory to murder, can I, Lord Powerscourt?'

'Let me try to give you a summary of your position, if I may, Bishop. You believe that Mrs McQuaid, acting no doubt out of kindness, gave the unfortunate Mr Jones a fatal dose of his pills to put him out of his misery. In your book that is murder, and Mrs McQuaid should be charged with murder and brought to trial.'

'That is correct.'

'I am going to give you my response in three parts, if I may, Bishop.' At the moment when he said that, Powerscourt had no idea what the second and third parts were going to be, but he trusted that his brain would have worked them out by the time he had finished the first one.

'I would like to call my first part "A Life for a Life", Bishop. Suppose you tell the relevant people – the Chief Constable, the doctor, perhaps – about your views and about what you think should be done. Suppose the doctor changes his mind, which I rather doubt, as he too has higher powers like the Hippocratic Oath to remember. Suppose Mrs McQuaid sticks to her story. Suppose you stick to your belief that Simon Jones would never have taken his own life and that, therefore, somebody else must have taken it from him. Suppose the case goes to court and ends up at some great theatre of the law like the Old Bailey, with Mrs McQuaid on a charge of murder.'

The Bishop was looking uncomfortable. He had not come here to be reminded of places like the Old Bailey. Powerscourt pressed on.

'There would be wave after wave of publicity about such a case. An elderly housekeeper, a dying man, a young doctor, a Bishop of the Church – all on parade in one place and at one time. The doctor would have the full weight of the medical profession behind him. You would have to go into the witness box, Bishop. Whatever respect is due to your position, you could be sure that the defence counsel would give you a pretty hard time.

But Mrs McQuaid would have an even harder time from the prosecuting counsel. If Simon Jones has mentioned her in his will, I am sure that money would be used as a motive for murder.

'Suppose the verdict is guilty. No allowance is made in law for the question of motive. Murder is murder is murder, even if the instincts of the perpetrator are totally virtuous in their own eyes. Mrs McQuaid could be led back to the cells and hanged by the neck until she was dead. The law must take its course. A life for a life. Is that what you want, Bishop?'

Powerscourt didn't wait for an answer. He was relieved to find that his brain had served up the two other points he wished to make.

'My second point hangs around what I propose to call "In the Public Interest". If it came to court, the newspapers would be all over the case and the players in the drama. Churchman holds elderly housekeeper responsible for death from an overdose of pills. A Bishop's evidence might be enough to sway a jury, even if Mrs McQuaid denies all charges and the doctor sticks to his guns. She would have been sacrificed to save a Bishop's conscience. And think what the reaction might be in your own community, Bishop. The people of Lynchester would be gripped by the story and its terrible end. Whatever the court decided, people would take sides. The same would probably happen with your own clergy. Do you really want hostility on the streets and in the shops of your city? Do you want faction in the chapterhouse? Your own position might become untenable. You could feel that your own role as Bishop had become impossible. The Archbishop of Canterbury and his people might have to spirit you away to a teaching position in some remote

Anglican theological college, far from the controversies of Lynchester and the tragic death of Simon Jones.'

The Bishop was drumming his fingers on his knees. He looked as though he would much rather be somewhere else. Powerscourt hadn't finished yet.

'I propose to call my final section, "The Way of the World". This, I feel duty bound to tell you, is pure speculation, like so much of what I have said already. This is what I think could have happened. Let us begin with Dr Willoughby. I would stress that this is hypothetical. He sees at once what must have taken place. He decides to do nothing about it and treat the death as due to natural causes. He makes off with the only evidence that might hold good in a court of law. I doubt if anyone will ever see that bottle again, with or without the remaining pills. In his judgement, that is the most sensible course of action to take. Doctors, in hospitals especially, must come across cases like this all the time, where a killing by mercy may be the best thing to do. In those cases doctors administer the dose themselves, or simply discontinue the courses of treatment necessary to keep their patients alive. Dr Willoughby may have told the senior doctor in his practice. He may have talked to a senior policeman, in confidence, about what he has done. I am sure the police and the Chief Constable would have agreed with the doctor. Far better to keep the whole thing under wraps and leave Mrs McQuaid alone with her conscience. If she wants to confess at a later stage, stricken with remorse perhaps, she will be able to do so. As long as she sticks to her story and denies all imputations of murder, it will be very difficult to bring a case anyway. You weren't there. She was. That, I think, is how the way of the world would have worked in this case.'

Powerscourt stopped. He rose from his sofa and began pacing up and down the room like a sea captain on his quarterdeck. 'Forgive me, Bishop, if I have been somewhat intemperate in my choice of language.'

'Not at all,' said the Bishop, 'you have been most helpful.' He was rubbing his hands through his hair again. Powerscourt thought this was the signal for maximum distress, closely followed by the fingers drumming on his knees.

'Could I make a suggestion, Bishop? You need more time to consider your position. You need time to pray, I expect. I would not think it appropriate for you to say anything at all at this stage.' The man needs some sort of lifeline to get him out of here. Powerscourt was sure of it. It couldn't have been the most comfortable time Percival Trevelyan had had in his life, however many trials and tribulations come a Bishop's way. 'I propose that we should meet again or talk on the telephone, whichever you think is more appropriate, in three or four days' time. I may have had further thoughts myself by then. I would be more than happy to come to Lynchester or somewhere close by if that would suit. In earlier times, Bishop, I wrote a book on English cathedrals, but I have to confess I did not pay sufficient attention to Lynchester. I would love to see it again. Of course, if you would rather not meet or talk again, that is fine by me.'

The Bishop rose slowly from his chair. 'Lord Powerscourt, I am more grateful than I can say for your words of wisdom.'

Politeness, Powerscourt realized, could take you a long way if you were a Bishop. Poor man must have to be polite to all sorts of people every single day of the week, with a double helping on Sundays.

'Thank you. I agree with your proposal, Lord Powerscourt. Four days should be ample. I find if you leave these questions spinning round in your head, they turn into a sort of primeval soup after a while.'

Rather like the Virgin Birth, Powerscourt said to himself, or the miracle of the loaves and fishes – extra caterers discovered suddenly on the mountainside.

'I must return to Lynchester, Lord Powerscourt. I can see myself out.'

With that the Bishop and his sea of troubles returned to the railway station and his cathedral.

3

Four days later, the Bishop of Lynchester called Powerscourt to tell him that, for the time being, he had decided to let sleeping dogs lie. He said, rather ominously, that he needed more time to think. But Powerscourt's association with the diocese of Lynchester was only just beginning. Events called him back a couple of months later.

The cathedral had evolved its own special way of dealing with the houses in and around the Close when they became empty or their leases ran out. The properties were advertised in the normal way by the oldest and most respectable firm of estate agents in the town. The oldest and most respectable firm of solicitors looked after the details of the transactions. In calculating the rental, the estate agents took account not just of the house itself but the likely cost of any repairs that might become necessary in the course of the lease. Netherbury House, where Simon Jones had breathed his last, was advertised for a sum of £7,000 for a lease of twenty years. When they had established a list of potential buyers, the estate agents presented this to the lawyers and cathedral authorities so they could draw up a shortlist and make the final decision. It was now up to the Dean and a small committee of churchmen, including the Bishop, to decide which of the applicants was going to win the prize. Residents were informed but not formally consulted about the process.

The lawyers and the Dean's committee took many factors into account: who would fit in well with the other residents, whose children might find others of their age in the Close, who would be a pleasant and helpful neighbour. Occasionally they took something of a leap in the dark and brought in somebody of national distinction. There was at present a former Home Secretary tending his bees in his garden by the river, a retired Bishop writing what he hoped would be the definitive account of the four gospels, a successful author, famed throughout the Close for the splendid parties he threw at Christmas and New Year, and an art historian from Oxford who was writing a biography of the Renaissance painter Giorgione and was feeling his way towards a highly unorthodox interpretation of one of his most enigmatic paintings.

It was also the practice for the Dean to invite the shortlist to dine and sleep on the day of their interview.

It was the custom of the cathedral to start a process of consultation with the residents about who should become their new neighbour after a death or a premature departure. There would be little gatherings in the two terraces and the crescent. The spokesmen then held meetings of their own and came up with the candidate they preferred. They usually included a second choice in case the Dean and the Bishop had already turned down their first preference. The cathedral authorities undertook to take note of the residents' views but were not bound by them.

Sandy Field was the spokesman for the West Terrace. Four of his neighbours had joined him early this evening to run through the list of candidates, kindly sent over by the Dean earlier in the day. Sandy Field was a solicitor in the town and had a finger in many of its important pies, including the conveyancing and administration of this particular lease. This was the first time his firm had entrusted this task to him. His guests included Roderick Chase, formerly a senior civil servant in the Treasury. Close gossip had it that he had been appointed because the Dean and Chapter hoped he would be able to help with their finances, only to discover that he was an expert in public expenditure, or rather in keeping it under control – the stopping rather than the spending of taxpayers' money. Mrs Agatha Rowthorn was a widow and the chief force behind the running of the Close's charities. Ambrose Harrison was a prosperous author who had time to spare if he felt the cause was worthwhile. Brook Giddings was a businessman from the town who always had strong views about the candidates.

'Have you all got a glass of Bordeaux – you have, I see,' Sandy Field said. 'Let me begin.' He pulled a sheet of paper from his pocket.

'This is the list I was given yesterday by the Dean. The first name on it is Sir Edward Talbot, the great retail man.'

'Is he the man behind Talbot's Stores down in the market square?' asked Mrs Rowthorn.

'It is he.'

'God bless my soul.'

Ambrose Harrison was stroking his beard very slowly, as if it might be some mystic rite.

'What does the fellow want to come and live here for? He must have plenty of houses elsewhere. If he doesn't he could bloody well afford to go and buy some. I don't see why we need to offer him refuge here. Chap probably wants to open a new branch in the middle of the Close, for all I know.'

'I don't see why we should be prejudiced against a prosperous businessman,' said Brook Giddings, who ran a hardware store and a building firm. 'I think that's quite uncalled for, I really do.'

'Very well,' said Sandy Field, 'we'll take that into account. Roderick, you've been very quiet so far.'

Roderick Chase was usually the last to offer an opinion on these occasions. It was a tactic he had deployed, sometimes with deadly effect, in the Treasury.

'I just wonder if the fellow would fit in,' he said. 'I'm not thinking of the slight difficulty of buying one's groceries in the morning and meeting the owner in the afternoon. There are no other tycoons for him to pass the time of day with, begging your pardon, Brook. I feel there is a slight risk that he would feel out of place.'

'Don't worry about that for now,' said Sandy Field. 'There are more runners and riders to come. What do you say,' he looked down at his list again, 'to Captain Johnny Chapman, in command of HMS *Indefatigable*? The Dean thought it was related to a dreadnought. Is that true, Roderick?'

Chase had spent his last years in the Treasury opposing the construction of dreadnought battleships and all other members of the dreadnought family on grounds of cost.

'You're taking me back to the Treasury, Sandy. It is indeed a relation of the dreadnoughts, a vessel with enormous guns and considerable speed. The official name for them now is battlecruisers. They've got a squadron of their own under Admiral Beatty.'

'Never mind the ship, Roderick, what do you say to a sea Captain?'

'I imagine he is so busy that he would never be here. He wouldn't have time to be among us at all.'

'I think it would be jolly nice to have a Captain, actually.' Agatha Rowthorn was smiling to herself, as if the hidden delights were already with her. 'Would he wear his uniform all the time?'

'I'm afraid we don't have the answer to that yet, Agatha. Who knows? Brook, have you anything to say?'

'Only this,' said the businessman. 'I haven't been here very long, but I've had time to observe all those who have, as it were, passed the Dean's examination. Every now and then we invite a very distinguished man, one who will bring a measure of distinction – maybe even fame – to the Close. I think this Captain could be one of those.'

'I agree. I agree wholeheartedly,' said Ambrose Harrison. 'I have nothing further to say about this candidate.'

'Good,' said Sandy Field. 'We have another military man now, from land rather than naval divisions. Colonel Colquhoun, aide-de-camp to a Sir Henry Wilson of the Imperial General Staff, and various other military positions.'

'Do you think they know something we don't?' said Mrs Rowthorn. 'Are they keen to come here because we are, so to speak, remote from the coast and far from any German invasion forces?'

Mrs Rowthorn was well known for a phobia about German invasions, regularly informing the authorities about posses of unknown postmen or telegraph maintenance personnel who were – undoubtedly in her view – German spies or double agents come to Lynchester to do the Kaiser's bidding. The local police Inspector kept an ever-growing file on this correspondence.

'Not that again, Agatha, please,' said Ambrose Harrison. 'Can't we consider the fellow for what he is, rather than treating him as one of your fantasies?'

'If we have to choose between two military men,' said Roderick Chase, 'I would plump for the naval gentleman myself. There's a great deal of intrigue and plotting in those top military circles, as you probably know.'

'I presume,' said Brook Gittings, 'that the Colonel would be able to spend more time here. I presume he does most of his intriguing and planning up in London.'

'Are we to expect regular parades?' asked Ambrose Harrison. 'March pasts from one end of the Close to another?'

Sandy Field laughed. 'I don't think there is any danger of that. Any armies at the Colonel's beck and call will probably stay at their posts in Aldershot.'

'I've been told on very good authority,' said Roderick Chase, 'that the main problem with soldiers and sailors in peacetime is how to keep them busy. What do you do with them all when they're not actually fighting? This is the reason for all that drill and those endless naval exercises. Sorry, Sandy, that's not strictly relevant.'

'Don't let it ever be said that the views of a Treasury man are irrelevant, Roderick. Any further thoughts on our Colonel?'

'I've always thought,' said Agatha Rowthorn, 'that it's

a pity the Dean never tells us about these men's families. It would enable us to come to a better understanding of how they might fit in.'

'In one or two cases,' said Ambrose Harrison, 'I suspect that the only people we would see would be the wives and families. The husbands would be away all the time.'

'I think it's time to move on,' said Sandy Field. 'I suspect some if not all of us know our next candidate, Paul Jenkinson, who teaches history in the grammar school here in the Close.'

'Do you mean the Paul Jenkinson who looks as if he's just over twenty years old?' At least Agatha Rowthorn wasn't accusing the man of being a German spy, despatched years ago to infiltrate the grammar school.

'We do,' said Sandy.

For once Roderick Chase was among the first rather than the last to speak.

'I know I'm getting old, but isn't this candidate too young?'

His colleagues from the terrace turned on him.

'The man must be in his thirties. Heavens above, Roderick, we can't fill the houses here with old people. The Close would die out as a place of human habitation.'

'You're not suggesting that we turn the Close into an old people's home, are you?'

'I should say the Close needs all sorts of people from all sorts of ages to keep it going.'

'Surely there must come a time for youth to have its day? Renewal, refreshment, all those sorts of things. As far as I can recall, all the successful candidates recently have been in their fifties or beyond. Isn't it time to even out the balance?'

'All right, all right,' said Roderick Chase, holding up a

hand to ward off the imaginary blows. 'I take it back. I withdraw that comment. I shall confine any future observations to the costs of dreadnought construction and the likely effect of Mr Lloyd George's measures on old-age pensions and the like. I shall turn into one of those saints who sat on top of pillars and never spoke a word.'

'Our last candidate,' said Sandy Field, 'is a philosophy don from Oxford called Gervase Crutchley. Do we have any views?'

'Very impractical people, philosophers,' said Roderick Chase. 'I don't think he would fit in. Who wants to have to pass the time of day with a philosopher, for God's sake?'

'It might be rather interesting,' said Mrs Rowthorn.

'What's wrong with Oxford, for heaven's sake?' said Brook Giddings. 'Place is full of bloody philosophers.'

'Maybe he wants somewhere different,' said Roderick Chase. 'Maybe he'll be able to think better here.'

'Well,' said Sandy Field, 'we'll leave things there for now. I suggest you give the matter some more thought. Perhaps we could meet again in a few days' time to reach our conclusions. Then I could hand them over to the Dean.'

Netherbury House was built in the reign of Queen Anne and was a splendid example of the architecture of the period. There were three storeys with a series of attic rooms on the top floor. It had a number of reception rooms and a study on the ground floor, the principal drawing room running right through the house, with views of the Close at one end and the garden that ran down to the river at the other. It was regarded as one of the most beautiful houses in Lynchester. There was a service wing on one side with all the usual offices.

The Dean's dining room was the place for the interviews about the vacant house in the Cathedral Close. The table was highly polished, so an observer positioned opposite the fireplace and its mirror could see the four clergymen in their full regalia twice. The Dean was there, of course, and the Bishop himself, and the Precentor and, the youngest by a long way, Timothy Budd, the librarian and archivist who was still in his late twenties. Together they looked like one of those seventeenth-century paintings of the *consiglieri* of some Roman cardinal plotting another coup in the curia. From the open window they could hear the schoolboys from the grammar school playing a noisy game of football.

The first man to be interviewed was Sir Edward Talbot, founder and owner of Talbot's Groceries, a chain of shops that spread out from London like dragon's teeth. Lynchester's branch was the most distant from the capital, and it was virtually certain that each of the clergy on parade today would have consumed its wares in one form or another. The Dean opened the batting.

'Good afternoon, Sir Edward. How kind of you to come and see us today. Let me make the introductions. On my right we have the Bishop, the Right Reverend Percival Trevelyan. I am the Dean, Aylmer Fettiplace Jones. To my immediate left is Rupert Digby, the Precentor, who looks after the services and the music in our cathedral, and on my far left is Timothy Budd, the librarian and archivist, who is trying to make sense of our large collection of ancient manuscripts.'

Sir Edward nodded gravely to each in turn, as if they had all come to his till and paid their bill.

'It is our custom that the Bishop should begin the first interview.'

Sir Edward was a small man with a shock of grey hair. He was wearing a dark blue suit with a white shirt and a pale blue tie. His shoes were as highly polished as the table. He might have felt nervous but he didn't show it. He had decided on his way down to Lynchester to treat the clerical gentlemen as if they were major shareholders in his company, assembled for information about the recent past and the expectations for the immediate future.

'Good afternoon, Sir Edward, just a few questions if I may.'

Sir Edward nodded.

'Am I right in thinking that you are not a local man?' the Bishop continued. 'Apart from your own business, you have had little to do with Lynchester?'

'That is correct, Bishop.' Sir Edward looked slightly uncertain at this point. His homework had not included the correct way of addressing these clerical worthies.

'But you wish to come and join us now? You would like to come and live in the Cathedral Close? Might I ask why?'

'Of course you may ask that question, Bishop. The answer is simple. Your Close is – to my mind – one of the most beautiful of its kind in England. It is possibly even more beautiful than its only competitor in Salisbury.' This was what one of the two bright young men from Cambridge who worked in Sir Edward's private office had suggested as an answer to this question. 'When I was growing up I lived in Salisbury, and would cross the Cathedral Close every day on my way to school. I fell in love with those houses. I promised myself then that – if I ever had enough money – I would buy one of those houses, or one like it in another Close. Here I am. I would be honoured to live here. I should add – ' this next was something that the young men had suggested he might hint at towards the end of the interview, not the beginning – 'that I would like to make an initial offering, exceeding ten thousand pounds, for the general improvement of the Close, a new wing for your grammar school maybe; whatever you gentlemen might think would be most appropriate.'

The Precentor was so astonished he dropped his pencil on the floor and had great difficulty retrieving it. The librarian and archivist stared at Sir Edward open mouthed. Sir Edward dealt in money. He had done so all his life. That was the currency he used, the currency of his life. These churchmen did not deal in money, but in the worship of God, the care of souls, and the maintenance and the glory of their cathedral. It was difficult at this stage to say if this offer would be treated as a bribe or as an opportunity.

'Thank you, Bishop,' said the Dean with a smile. 'The baton now passes, as it were, to our Precentor, Rupert Digby. He is a great believer in the power of church music to bring people together, to provide a little glue to help the unity of the little community in the Close.'

'Thank you, Dean,' the Precentor began. 'Sir Edward, could I ask you if you are a regular churchgoer? It is not a prerequisite of the lease, of course, but it helps our thinking.'

The two young men had warned their master that this question was bound to come up. They recommended vagueness, imprecision, hopes for the future. Above all they stressed that there was no point at all in pretending that he went to church every Sunday. He didn't.

'Alas, gentlemen, I have to confess that I am not a regular at our local church.' Sir Edward realized to his horror that he couldn't even remember the name of the place. St Andrew's? St Mark's? St Peter's? Surely his young men must have reminded him of the name. It was no good. He couldn't remember. He pressed on.

'Of course, if I came to live here that would all be different. Isn't there something in the Bible about great rejoicing for the sinner that repenteth . . . ?'

'My own responsibilities,' the Precentor carried on, 'as well as the organization and running of the services, lie with the music of the cathedral, Sir Edward. I am glad to say that the standard and the range of our choir are improving all the time. Would that be of interest?'

'It would, of course it would, Mr Digby. With such a wealth of music on offer, how could I refuse?' The bright young men had insisted that he should not mention that he regarded Christmas carol services with loathing, and that any performances of Handel's *Messiah* were to be avoided like the plague.

'And church services in general, Sir Edward? If you were to come here?'

'As I have said before, gentlemen, surely it's never too late to start.'

The Dean moved to bring in the archivist and librarian. Timothy Budd was a young man devoted to scholarship as well as the rites of religion. He knew that there was no point in asking Sir Edward about the medieval manuscripts that punctuated his days. The Dean and the Bishop found him useful on these occasions because he had a habit of asking unorthodox questions.

'Your turn now, Mr Librarian,' said the Dean, writing furiously in his notebook.

'Thank you, Dean. Sir Edward, thank you for coming to talk to us.' There was one awkward question the librarian wanted to ask. Would all the inhabitants of the Cathedral Close receive discounts at the local branch of Talbot's Stores? And if so, how much? He restrained himself.

'I see from the paperwork, Sir Edward, that you give your address as London. Is that correct?'

'It is.'

'Might I ask if you have a secondary residence as well? In the country perhaps?'

'I do have a little place in Hampshire as it happens.'

The great retailer did not admit that his little place had twelve bedrooms and a live-in staff of four.

'And would you intend to keep the little place going if you came to live with us here?

'I must say I hadn't thought of that at all. I would need time to consider. Our Hampshire place is very easy to reach by train.'

'Do you mean that Lynchester isn't? Easy to reach by train, I mean.'

'It's just a question of the timetables.' The young men hadn't mentioned houses in the country at all. Maybe they didn't know about them.

'Forgive me, Sir Edward, if I just try to sum up the situation about your various places of residence. You have a house in London. You have, as you say, a little place in the country. If you came to live with us here, you would have a house in the Cathedral Close as well – a third home, unless you disposed of one or both of the others? Or are there any more places of residence you haven't had time to tell us about?'

Sir Edward smiled. 'I have no hunting lodges in

Scotland or ski chalets in the French Alps, if that's what you mean.'

'Thank you,' said Timothy Budd, 'thank you so much.'

The Dean stopped writing in his notebook. He smiled at the great retailer.

'I would like to ask about your family, if I might, Sir Edward.'

Sir Edward smiled.

'Of course.' The bright young men had warned him about this line of questioning.

'We pride ourselves on our Close being a place for families and family life in general. Your wife now – would you expect her to come and live with us here full time, as it were?'

'I fear not, Dean. She has a lot of charitable commitments in London. She would, of course, come as often as possible, like myself.' Both young men had recommended playing the charitable commitment for all it was worth.

'And the rest of the family? You have two sons and two daughters, I believe.'

'Like my wife, they would come as often as they could.' Sir Edward chose not to mention that his daughters would not like to leave London for the rural and religious delights of life in the Cathedral Close. It was all he could do to persuade them to come to Hampshire once in a while.

'Could I ask, Sir Edward, what you and your family would bring to us here in Lynchester?'

'As I mentioned before, there is the question of a financial contribution. I say no more about that in present company.' For God's sake, don't go on about the money, the young men had emphasized. They might start asking if you want to open a money-changing service in the nave of the cathedral.

'I have no doubt that I would bring a different experience to that of most of your residents. I feel it would be good for the people who live in the Close to meet and befriend a man of business. And I have no doubt that I would benefit from coming into contact with the wide range of people who live here already.'

'One last question, Sir Edward, and I should say that we ask this of all those who would come and live with us here. Are you a believer in our religion? Do you acknowledge that Jesus Christ is the Son of God who came and suffered on earth to save mankind?'

There was a pause. Sir Edward appeared to be inspecting a portrait of a nineteenth-century Dean who appeared to be keeping a grave eye on the proceedings from a space next to the mantelpiece.

'I can only say, gentlemen, that I have spent more time serving Mammon than serving God. But surely, as you gentlemen would no doubt be the first to say, it is never too late?'

'Thank you, Sir Edward. Any further questions?' The good impression caused by the last answer was about to be swept away.

'I wonder, Dean,' said Timothy Budd, the librarian, 'if I could just ask one question?'

'Of course,' said the Dean, suspecting that some unpleasant query was about to come Sir Edward's way.

'In an average year, Sir Edward, how many weekends do you think you would be able to spend with us? I am assuming that your work would keep you in London during the week. Four? Six? Eight?'

The young men had not warned him about this. Sir

Edward was beginning to think that his shareholders might be easier to deal with than this collection of clerics.

'I don't feel it would be helpful to make promises I would not be able to keep. But I am sure that the more often I came, the more I would want to return.'

'Thank you very much, Sir Edward, thank you for coming.'

The great retailer was shown to Netherbury House, the one whose lease he wanted to buy, and fortified with a cup of tea followed by a very large whisky. Later that evening he made his way back to the Dean's house for dinner. This was a pleasant meal, untouched by theological controversy or financial inducements. Sir Edward made an appointment to see the Bishop in the morning.

4

'Well, gentlemen,' said the Dean, when Sir Edward had been shown to his lodgings for the night. 'What did you think of Sir Edward?'

The Dean would have been the first to admit that he enjoyed these sessions. Senior officers of the Church can be as interested and as preoccupied with the exercise of power as their counterparts in civilian life. 'I know we have an unwritten rule that we don't discuss candidates until we have seen them all. But he was an unusual applicant in some ways. What do you have to say? Precentor?'

Rupert Digby said he was not concerned about Sir Edward's attitude to church music. If he had been, he said, the cathedral would be half empty. 'I was concerned about his offer of money, Dean. It was almost the first thing he mentioned, as if he were conducting some financially sensitive negotiations with his suppliers.'

'Forgive me for butting in,' said Timothy Budd, 'but I couldn't agree more. It was almost as though he wanted to exaggerate his wealth. It looked to me as if he was trying to buy his way in. There are lots of places where he could buy his way in, indeed he may have already done so, but I don't think our Cathedral Close should be one of them.'

'Don't tell me that there aren't a lot of places where we could use that money,' said the Dean. 'I can think of half a dozen projects, apart from the one he mentioned in connection with the school.'

'Come, come, Dean, you can't be serious,' said the Precentor. 'We all have our little fantasies from time to time – and quite right, too. But that doesn't mean we have to act on them. And another thing. I can't see Sir Edward fitting in with the people who live on the Close now. I just can't see it.'

'Well, gentlemen,' the Bishop intervened, anxious to close this particular door as soon as possible before hasty decisions were made. 'I think we can leave it here for now. There are still a number of other candidates for us to interview, after all. I feel that this discussion can be postponed until then. There's plenty of time left.'

The Dean was breaking into his second poached egg of the morning when a distraught parlour maid burst in.

'Sorry for bursting in, Dean, but something terrible has happened. It's that man who came down for inter-view yesterday, sir, he's dead, sir. The porter looked in the house to see if he wanted anything. When there was no answer, the porter checked upstairs and there he was, lying on the bed – dead.' The girl broke down into floods of tears.

'There, there, Emily, don't worry. Take your time. How do we know Sir Edward is dead?'

'Sir, the porter went and found that doctor who lives

near the end of the crescent, sir. He said the man was dead and sent for the police. There's a Constable on duty by the door now, sir. Nobody's allowed in at present, sir.'

'Thank you, Emily, thank you very much. You've done very well.'

In private moments, the Dean would probably have admitted that he rather liked crises, plenty of decisions to be made, being not necessarily at the very epicentre of events but close to it. As the titular head of the cathedral, he should hear of developments quicker than the Bishop. Sometimes when he said his prayers last thing at night, the Dean reproached himself for too great a love for the affairs of this world. It seldom troubled him during his waking hours.

'I shall walk over there in a moment, Emily, to represent the Church's interests. Could you arrange for somebody to tell the Bishop?'

Ten minutes later, the Dean was strolling across the Green to Netherbury House, last resting place of two men inside a couple of months. The Dean's initial reaction was that the poor man must have suffered a heart attack and died in the night. The Constable was still in position outside the front door. Early roses were in bloom in the beds on either side of it.

'Good morning, Constable, this is a sad business.'

'It is, Dean. I'm afraid you're not allowed in the house at present.'

'Whyever not? This house is Church property. Surely I have the right to go in?' The Dean didn't like not getting his own way. To be baulked by a mere Constable, lowest of the low in the police hierarchy, would be a poor start to his day.

'I'm sorry, sir. It's Inspector Vaughan's orders. He's the

officer in charge, sir. He says nobody's allowed in until he gives the word.'

'I see,' said the Dean, deciding that retreat might be the best policy in the circumstances. 'I'm sure your Inspector has a lot on his plate just now. Perhaps you could ask him to call on me as soon as he can. We need to discuss the arrangements for the body and so on.'

The life of the Close continued at its normal sedate pace. The cleaners were polishing the brass and the silver near the High Altar of the cathedral. There was a service of Holy Communion at half past ten, attended by the old and the faithful. The Dean refused to cancel it, saying that the services of the cathedral carried on every day of the year through death and warfare and flood and famine. The Bishop was walking in his garden, thinking of a sermon he was due to deliver at Gloucester Cathedral that coming Sunday. The Precentor was looking through some new arrangements of church music to teach his choir. The librarian was poring over an ancient manuscript with a magnifying glass, identifying the tiny letters and transferring them into his large black notebook. In the almshouses and the school, the staff were beginning the preparation of lunch, with the Dean's housekeeper originally wondering if she would have to feed the police as well.

It was nearly lunchtime before the police Inspector called on the Dean. Inspector Jack Vaughan was in his middle thirties, although he looked younger. He was clean-shaven, with a full head of light brown hair and a newish suit in subdued dark blue. He was in a sombre mood when he was shown into the Dean's study.

'Good morning, Dean. I fear you have to brace yourself for some bad news.'

Looking at the young man, the Dean felt sure that some terrible tidings were coming his way.

'We are used to bad news here, Inspector. It seems to come all the time.'

'I'm afraid Sir Edward Talbot passed away in the night, Dean. At this stage we do not know precisely how he died. We shall have to wait until the post mortem for that. In the meantime Netherbury House will remain closed. A police Constable will remain on duty outside until we are sure what we are dealing with.'

'Are you saying that the poor man died in the night? A heart attack, something like that?'

'I am sure that a man like yourself, Dean, will understand that we have to keep to the rules. You have rules and procedures for your behaviour here. So do we. For the moment there is nothing I can say. The body has been removed to the morgue, pending the post-mortem examination. The next of kin have been informed. We have yet to contact the dead man's business partners. One of my men is due back from the store in the town to tell us who to get in touch with up in London. There can be no discussion as yet about the funeral and where it is to be held. I presume, as his time here was very short, that his family will wish him to be laid to rest closer to home.'

'I see,' said the Dean, rather sadly. There seemed very little for him to do for the time being.

'What a terrible business. We shall remember Sir Edward in our prayers, of course. I presume, Inspector, that you would not want us to refer to the death in any of our services in the cathedral until the position becomes clearer?'

'That is correct, Dean. Thank you for being so understanding.'

'I've just been thinking,' said the Dean, suspecting that he had been rather backward in grasping the essential facts of the matter. 'Post mortem, did you say? Would I be right in thinking that the poor man did not die a natural death?'

'As I said before, Dean, I cannot comment on any speculation at this moment.'

Something in the way he answered the question told the Dean all he needed to know. He scurried round to find the Bishop.

Lynchester was too small a place to keep a secret long. The undertaker told his wife after lunch in the strictest confidence. She worked on the kitchen staff at the grammar school. Word began to move round the staff of the school and the cleaners in the cathedral. From then on it was unstoppable. Murder most foul had come to desecrate a place of worship and contemplation. The master masons, on repair duty three-quarters of the way up the spire, paused for a cup of tea while they discussed the implications. The gardeners talked about it in the quiet of their greenhouses. It was Irish nationalists, bringing the troubles of their wretched country across the sea. When word reached her via her butler, always keen to feed her fantasies, Mrs Agatha Rowthorn announced to all and sundry that it was the work of German assassins, out to damage the retail and industrial fabric of the country. Alone among the clergy of the cathedral, the Bishop made a positive move. He placed a telephone call to an address in central London. He told the Dean and nobody else. There was nothing he could say until he knew if the man he wanted was available and could come to Lynchester, hopefully on the next train.

Lord Francis Powerscourt was still holding out on the question of the trans-Atlantic expedition and the voyage round the world. He had discovered a useful delaying tactic in the question of lifeboats. He had brought the fatal shadow of the *Titanic*, sunk the year before, into Markham Square. Most of the big companies had hurried to increase their provision of lifeboats, but they had not yet troubled to include this news in their sales literature. Lady Lucy had written to them all asking for clarification on questions of safety and lifeboat numbers, but they were very slow in replying. Her husband felt that when the lifeboat redoubt had fallen, he had little left in the question of defences. He would have to refuse or give in. So when Rhys the butler called him to the phone to take a call from the Bishop of Lynchester, he wondered if another line of defence might be opening up.

'Lord Powerscourt? Trevelyan here, Bishop of Lynchester. We met a couple of months ago.'

'Indeed so, Bishop; good to hear from you. I trust that there have been no unfortunate developments in the matter we spoke of earlier?'

'Nothing has changed on that front, I am glad to say. But I think we are about to have another problem down here which is in need of your attention and expertise.'

The Bishop explained the events of the morning. 'So you see, Lord Powerscourt, although we have no definite proof yet, a number of indications seem to be pointing towards murder in the Close, if I could put it that way. Sir Edward Talbot would appear to have been the victim.'

'Quite so, Bishop. Could I ask one or two questions if I may? Is the house where the dead man spent the night still guarded by a police Constable? I know you may not know the answer to this question, but where did the rumours start that it might be murder? It may be a reliable source or it may just be a succession of hysterical footmen or parlour maids.'

'The Constable is still there, Lord Powerscourt. I saw him myself a quarter of an hour ago. I suspect the rumours began with the undertaker talking to his wife. For all we know he may have taken a look at the body.'

'And the police, Bishop? Apart from the Constable on duty? Have they put in an appearance yet?'

'Oh yes, I should have told you. An Inspector Vaughan gave such details as he could. The Dean thought he looked very young. The Dean also thought that it was more than likely that a murder, or foul play of some sort, had taken place.'

'I fear, Bishop, that the presence of an Inspector is significant. Is your Sir Edward Talbot the man who owns and runs all those shops? The arrival of your Inspector suggests to me that there may indeed have been foul play, and that he is the man in charge of the case.'

'You mean that if it had been a simple affair of death by natural causes, the police presence would have been less prominent? I can confirm that Sir Edward Talbot is indeed the proprietor of all those shops across southern England. Perhaps I should have said he *was* the proprietor.'

'That could account for the presence of the Inspector. Important men usually receive special treatment in these matters. Is there something you would like me to do, Bishop? I am fairly free at the moment; nothing that won't wait.'

'Would you be able to come down and look into the matter, Lord Powerscourt? Acting on behalf of the cathedral, of course.'

'I'd be happy to, Bishop, thank you for asking me. I would prefer to wait until the morning before I set out. Perhaps you or one of your staff could ring me first thing tomorrow to report any overnight developments? The position might be clearer then. I could be with you about midday.'

After his phone call, Powerscourt sat in his study for some time, staring at his shelves of political biographies. Ten minutes later he picked up the receiver and asked to be connected to the police headquarters in Lynchester. He left a message asking for Inspector Vaughan to call him as soon as he could.

The Dean spent a frustrating afternoon in his study. He knew he should be in charge of events. This, after all, in a manner of speaking, was his cathedral, in that he was responsible for running it. He wondered if he should summon a meeting of all the clergy to fill them in on events. Only the thought that he might look a fool if he was proved wrong prevented him. The Bishop, concerned as ever about the poor and the destitute, who showed no sign of going away, continued his work on his sermon for Gloucester Cathedral. He decided to take as his text 'Blessed are the meek'. The schoolboys of the grammar school wrestled with their homework in history and maths and geography and science.

* * *

Powerscourt's phone rang at five minutes past eight the following morning. The Sergeant at the other end reported that there had been no new developments overnight. Inspector Vaughan looked forward to meeting him later that day. He had taken the trouble to book Powerscourt into the King's Arms hotel. It was, Powerscourt was told, very close to the cathedral, and the place used by the Bishop and the Dean when they needed to put up important visitors. As his train sped southwest towards Lynchester, Powerscourt recalled the phone call from the Inspector the evening before. He had been proper and circumspect, Inspector Vaughan, careful to give as little as possible away. He hadn't actually used the word 'murder'. He had talked of 'unfortunate events', which Powerscourt took to mean murder, and an intervention by the medical gentlemen, which Powerscourt suspected might mean the post mortem. He wondered if the Inspector was concerned about the possibility of other people like telephone operators listening in on his call.

Inspector Vaughan met Powerscourt at the station and escorted him to the scene of the crime. A solitary police Constable was still on duty. The Inspector took Powerscourt on a brief tour of the house, the grand reception rooms and the dining room on the ground floor, the principal bedroom on the first floor where the dead man had been found.

'Sir Edward was called down here for an interview, Lord Powerscourt. Netherbury House became vacant after the death of the previous tenant. It is the custom of the cathedral to advertise such properties extensively. When they have a shortlist of persons willing to pay the price of the lease, the Dean and various clerics

– including, I think, the Bishop, but I'm not sure – interview the potential candidates. They have the final say in who comes to live in the Close. Sir Edward was the first of five such candidates to come down here for the Church of England inquisition. Now he's gone.'

'Forgive me,' said Powerscourt, 'for what must seem to be a stupid question, but do we know if this was the first time Sir Edward had been to Lynchester?'

'As far as we know at the moment, it was.'

'Is there a Talbot's Store here? They seem to be almost everywhere.'

'There is.'

'And is there any record of Sir Edward coming to open it, or coming down to show the flag and enthuse the workers?'

'My Sergeant went down there yesterday, my lord. There are no records of any such visits.'

'My word, Inspector, this is a pretty problem. Did the murderer follow him down on the train? Did he know Sir Edward was coming? If so, how? And did he then loiter around the town till he saw his victim retiring for the night? It sounds very improbable to me. What do you think?'

'All those questions have occurred to me too, my lord. There is yet one more conundrum to throw into the mystery. How did the murderer get away? Did he walk back and hide somewhere in the city? Did he take an early morning train? I have to say that my Chief Constable is a man of eccentric views, and he has decided that there should be no interviewing of the people who live in the two terraces and the crescent here until we know how Sir Edward was killed. They are a curious lot, these Close people; well educated, most of them, and bound to be consumed with curiosity at a time like this. The Chief doesn't want word flying round the Close that there has been a murder before the appropriate time. I have plans for those interviews to start later on tomorrow morning.'

'Does that mean that you can't start interviewing people at the station and the hotels?'

'It does, but we haven't long to wait. The post mortem is tomorrow morning at ten o'clock over at the hospital. I would be grateful if you could join me.'

'Thank you. I have to go and pay a courtesy call on the Bishop. It was he who asked me down here, after all. May I use the word "murder" to him?'

'You may indeed. I believe the Bishop and the Dean know there has been a murder, but they don't know how the poor man died.'

5

'My dear Lord Powerscourt, how very kind of you to come. And at such short notice, too. If there is anything you want to know that is in our power to deliver, you mustn't hesitate.'

'Thank you, Bishop,' said Powerscourt, wondering briefly about eternal life and sinking into an armchair with a view of the two terraces and the spring daffodils reaching out across the lawns. 'I shall take you up on that as I learn more about the case.'

'I presume you must talk to the police, Lord Powerscourt.'

'I already have.'

'Good. Their interviews with the inhabitants of the Close will prove fruitful, I'm sure.'

'They might and they might not, Bishop. Inspector Vaughan and I are in difficult terrain. The murder – there is no doubt that it was murder apparently – was carried out on a man who had never, as far as we know, been here before. How did the murderer know that Sir Edward was going to be here? Who could have told him he was coming? It would be useful to be able to remove all those people from our inquiries.'

'You might want to drop in on Sandy Field in the West Terrace, Lord Powerscourt. He is a sort of unofficial spokesman for some of the residents. We consult them about the new people who might come to live here. We take their views seriously, as you would expect, but the final decision remains with us.'

Dr Willoughby, the local doctor, had summoned reinforcements. 'Please allow me to introduce my colleague from London – Dr Brightman, gentlemen. He has more experience than I in cases of this kind.'

They were in a small interview room next to the morgue where the post-mortem examination had taken place. A couple of respectable prints of Lynchester and the main street of the town adorned the walls. This must be where the relatives waited before they identified the dead.

Dr Brightman was a tall man wearing a green surgical coat. He was fiddling with his surgical gloves as if he couldn't get them off.

'I will be brief, gentlemen. You have a murder on your hands. I am sure you must have much business to attend to. Sir Edward Talbot was poisoned with a lethal dose of strychnine. The dose was disguised in an alcoholic drink of considerable potency. I can tell from this first examination that it was stronger than whisky or brandy. It might have been some form of foreign vodka of considerably high proof. There is no evidence that there was any violence around the time of his death, apart from the poison. I presume that Sir Edward must have taken this fatal cocktail downstairs and then taken himself up to bed. The symptoms usually begin after a quarter of an hour – maybe even sooner with a dose of this power. Do you follow me so far, gentlemen?'

'Yes, thank you,' said Inspector Vaughan. Powerscourt nodded.

'It's not a pleasant way to go, being poisoned by strychnine. The man was repeatedly sick, trying, I suspect, to reach the upstairs bathroom. Breathing would have been increasingly difficult. He would have suffered from nausea. There would have been convulsions of all muscle groups and spasms of the facial muscles. Before we cleaned him up, as it were, there was evidence of convulsions on his face. Eventually the convulsions would have killed him. I think that death would have come fairly quickly. He would have been unable to breathe.'

'Thank you very much,' said the Inspector. 'What a terrible way to go.'

'It is for me to try to establish the nature of the drink that contained the poison. I shall have to take samples of various kinds back to London. It is for you, gentlemen, to find the container that held the strychnine. I'm fairly sure it was some kind of spirits bottle, but I cannot at present help you with what it was meant to contain. And now, if you will excuse me, I must return to London. I shall be in touch when I have some answers. A very good morning to you all.'

As Dr Brightman made his way out towards the railway station, the Dean was shown in.

'Dean,' said Dr Willoughby, 'you have come to make the formal identification, I presume.'

Powerscourt and the Inspector heard low voices coming from the next room.

When the Dean came out he confirmed that the body was that of the late Sir Edward Talbot.

'Thank you for that, Dean,' said the Inspector. 'You can expect a number of policemen in the Close this afternoon. They will be working their way up and down the terraces and along the crescent.'

Powerscourt and Inspector Vaughan left the morgue deep in conversation.

'Tell me, Inspector, do you have high hopes that your interviews with the residents of the Close will be fruitful?'

The Inspector laughed a bitter laugh. 'We'd have had a better chance if we could have started when I wanted,' he said. 'To be fair to him, the Chief Constable will have wanted to do everything by the book – or even by more than the book. The men and women of the Close have known about the murder for some time now. If they had anything suspicious to report, they would have come forward. They're not ones to hide their lights under bushels, if you see what I mean. I'm fairly sure that the killer came in the dark and departed in the dark. And now, apart from the quest for traces of the murderer, we have to find the container that held the poison. It'll be like looking for a bottle in a haystack.'

'I fear our task is more difficult yet,' said Powerscourt. 'This thought occurred to me on the train. It seems to be extremely unlikely that the murderer lives in the Close. How did the Close people know he was coming? How did they know which house he was staying in? They could, I suppose, have guessed that he might stay in Netherbury House as that was the one whose lease he hoped to buy. But it might be that the murderer doesn't come from the Close at all.'

'I agree with you that such may be the case. But we have

to begin with the other people who live in the Close. My men will start this afternoon.'

Powerscourt walked twice round the Close. He passed the school and the little hospital and the various houses dotted around and behind the terraces and the crescent. He watched Inspector Vaughan's policemen work their way up and down the streets. 'Were you here in your house yesterday evening? Can you remember what you were doing? What time did you go to bed? Did you hear anything, any strangers perhaps, moving about in the Close? Did you hear anything suspicious this morning? Have you heard of Sir Edward Talbot? Did you know that he was coming to Lynchester for an interview? Thank you so much for your time. If anything occurs to you, could you let the police know at once?'

Powerscourt called on Sandy Field as the church clock in the town was striking six o'clock.

'So you are Lord Powerscourt. We have heard a little about you. Come, please take a seat. How can I help you?'

Powerscourt settled himself at a great Georgian window looking out over the grass and the flowerbeds of the Close. 'I understand that you, Mr Field, and a number of your colleagues are consulted by the Dean and the Bishop when they are choosing a new candidate to come and live here in the Close. Is that correct?'

'Absolutely correct, Lord Powerscourt. We had our first informal meeting just before Sir Edward Talbot came down to see the clerics. The Dean gave me a list of suitors that afternoon. I have mentioned this to Inspector Vaughan, but I wondered if I should come and tell you as well.'

'I appreciate that. Are you saying that you and your colleagues knew twenty-four hours in advance who the candidates were?'

'I am, but I do not think it is as important as all that. We didn't know which of them was going to come first, if you see what I mean. It could have been any one of the five people trying to come and live here. I can give you the list of names and the names of the people who were here when you leave. I try to keep notes of our little meetings, you see. It helps to know at the end what you thought at the beginning.'

'Could I ask what the sense of the meeting was? Did you come down on the side of any of the candidates?'

'It was a general discussion. We aren't going to make any particular suggestions to the Dean and the Bishop at this stage. That can come later.'

'You are obviously a man of some experience in these matters, Mr Field. Was there, perhaps, a favourite candidate, a man who appealed to you more than the other?'

'Well there was. But I wonder if I shouldn't consult my colleagues before I tell you that.'

Democracy seems to have penetrated deep into the Cathedral Close, Powerscourt said to himself. They'll be electing the postman next.

'I should point out, Mr Field, that we are dealing with a case of murder here. The local constabulary are working their way round the terraces and the crescent, as we speak, with a list of questions. They should be with you shortly.'

'I'm sorry about that, Lord Powerscourt. I was out of order. As I said, there was no particular recommendation at this stage. There were a number of strong candidates.'

'Thank you very much, Mr Field. I'll take that list if I may. Is there anything else you wish to bring up?'

'Only this,' said Sandy Field. 'Are all of us in the Close suspects, Lord Powerscourt? That is the question people round here have been asking all day.'

'It's a very fair question, Mr Field, and thank you for drawing it to my attention. It is a question for Inspector Vaughan, rather than me.' Powerscourt was sure that the locals had checked out Inspector Vaughan as well as himself. They probably knew where he went to school by now, and the date of his wedding. 'I would say for the moment that we are in the process of eliminating people from our inquiries. It may be possible to clear all the people in the Close at some point in this investigation, but we haven't reached that point yet.'

One thought struck Powerscourt very firmly on his way back to the hotel. The people in the Close were unlikely suspects. The answer might lie in Lynchester, but it was much more likely to be in London. He placed a call to his brother-in-law, William Burke, a mighty figure in the world of finance, who had often helped Powerscourt with his investigations in the past.

'William?' asked Powerscourt, as the telephonist finally put him through.

'Francis. Good evening to you. I was just leaving. I presume you are looking for information? Are you calling from Markham Square?'

'I'm calling from a place called Lynchester.'

'Cathedral?' said Burke. 'Chapterhouse? Cloisters? Bats in the belfry, that sort of place.'

'You are absolutely right, William. I've always thought

a career in finance should give you a well-rounded education. But my mission here is serious. Sir Edward Talbot, the grocery tycoon, came down here a few days ago in the hope of leasing a house in the Close. The night after his interview and dinner with the clergy, he was murdered. The Bishop has asked me to look into it.'

'And you want me to find out what I can about Sir Edward Talbot and his stores, spread out across the southern parts of England. Is that right?'

'It is.'

'I do know a certain amount about Sir Edward as it happens. But I'm not happy discussing it on the phone. Could you tear yourself away from the choir stalls and the prebendaries to come and talk to me here tomorrow? I am sure that as usual you want the answer the day before yesterday. Two o'clock tomorrow? Would that do? You should still be able to catch the last train back to Lynchester.'

A gloomy Inspector Vaughan was waiting for Powerscourt in the foyer of the hotel. They took a glass of beer in the bar, garishly decorated with dramatic scenes of fox-hunting, bloodthirsty cries from the Master of Foxhounds, the unfortunate animal cornered by the hounds, the hunt in full cry across the fields.

'I suppose I should have expected it, my lord. My men are getting their reports typed up back at the station. That's another of the Chief Constable's little foibles, typing up all the notes. It's going to waste an awful lot of time. We've covered well over half of those houses now. Nobody saw anything. Nobody heard anything. They all seem to go to bed early. Not one single solitary lead, I'm afraid.'

'There may be better news in the morning. I have decided to go to London tomorrow, Inspector. I have asked my brother-in-law William Burke to find out all he can about Talbot's Stores and the late Sir Edward. He owns banks, my brother-in-law, rather like you or I might own shirts or shoes. One end of this investigation obviously lies here. The other may lie in the professional or personal life of Sir Edward.'

'From what we discovered this afternoon,' said the Inspector, ordering another couple of beers, 'the answers are as likely, if not more likely, to be in London. I just hope the Chief Constable doesn't decide to hand the whole case over to the Met.'

William Burke was one of those people who seem able to absorb enormous amounts of pressure without showing it. He was cheerful as he showed Powerscourt to a seat by the marble fireplace in his enormous office. Burke was in charge of a consortium of banks that were slowly advancing up the map of England. His latest acquisition had been a group of banks in Nottingham. Cynics in his organization said that he aimed to reach the Scottish border by the end of the decade.

'Things are a bit bumpy here in the City right now,' he said, ordering some coffee. 'Nothing for the general public to be alarmed about for the moment. The City is just having one of its fits of irrationality. It's as if certain sections of the place want to be somewhere else. Imagine Lombard Street flying off to Essex, the Royal Exchange gone to Hampshire. They'll all come back in the end.'

'You seem to be very calm about the whole business, William.'

'I'm paid to be calm in these situations,' said Burke with a laugh. 'It's remarkable how often doing nothing is the best course on offer. But come, tell me how Sir Edward Talbot – the late Sir Edward, as I should call him – met his end.'

'He died of strychnine poisoning. He had gone to Lynchester for an interview about taking over an empty house owned by the cathedral in the Close. They advertise the vacancy. It is a most desirable residence: Queen Anne, and well preserved. A shortlist of suitable candidates is drawn up. The final five are interviewed by the Dean and the Bishop and a couple of the members of the Chapter. The clergy's decision is final. The interview with Sir Edward took place in the late afternoon a couple of days ago. He attended a dinner with the gentlemen of the cloth. He went back to the house he was trying to live in – the clergy let them stay overnight as a kind of trial run. He was found dead in the morning. He died a rather horrible death. So far, house-to-house inquiries have turned up nothing at all.'

'The poor man,' said Burke. 'It seems inappropriate to talk about his business affairs at a time like this, but I suppose we have to. That's why you're here.'

'I fear we do,' said Powerscourt. 'As far as I can tell, the person who killed Sir Edward is still at large, possibly carrying about his person lethal doses of strychnine to dispose of any more victims.'

'Let me start at the beginning, Francis. Sir Edward is, or rather was, a self-made man. There are plenty like him these days. He started up with a grocery stall in one of the North London markets. Then he opened his first shop, up in Haringey. He worked hard. The shop was a success. He bought another. And another. He worked his way round London as if he was following the expansion of the capital. At some point, about fifteen years ago, he floated his chain successfully on the Stock Exchange. As the only shareholders were himself and his family, this made him – and them – very rich indeed. He could have retired and lived the life of a country gentleman, but he didn't. Once a grocer, always a grocer, it would seem. He just went on expanding. He moved into the country-side, and his kingdom now extends as far as places like Lynchester. Are you with me this far, Francis?'

'Keep going, William, it's fascinating.'

Burke paused to light a very large cigar. 'There are a couple of things he did, or didn't do, on his way to the top. He never moved out of groceries. Others in similar circumstances have expanded into furniture or house-hold goods. He never did. And he was always very careful about where he put his shops. They aren't to be found in the places where the poor lived. They wouldn't have the money to buy enough groceries. He didn't put them in places where you and I might live – we have other arrangements and other suppliers catering to our needs. He puts them in what I call Pooter Land, after the character in the Grossmiths' book, *Diary of a Nobody*: clerks, insurance workers, teachers, nurses; respectable people who want to get on.'

'You said on the phone, William, that you were reluc-tant to talk about Sir Edward and his shops on the phone. Is there some crisis in the world of Sir Edward Talbot; something, I mean, that happened shortly before he was killed?'

'I'm not sure I would use the word "crisis" myself. A couple of weeks ago it was rumoured that Talbot's Stores were about to mount a takeover bid for one their biggest rivals, Scott's Stores. They only have about half the number of shops. It's thought that their owner, Horatio Scott, wants to cash in his grocery stores and travel across Europe before he's too old and too decrepit. This, you must understand, is the first time Sir Edward has come out of his shopfront and talked about buying anything at all. He's a novice in this field, but I will say he is said to have some very sharp advisers on board.'

'What will happen to Scott's and the people who work for them, William?'

'That's a very good question. Some of them, maybe all, will be left alone. Those that overlap with the existing Talbot's Stores may be amalgamated.'

'This is no doubt a stupid question, William. I am not a man of finance. Why doesn't he close them all down?'

'All what, Francis?'

'Why doesn't he close all the Scott's Stores down? Remove the competition from the playing field. Increase prices a little bit because some of the customers have nowhere else to go. It's a bit hard on the Scott's people, of course, but the owners will have the money from the sale to keep them going.'

'God bless my soul, Francis, I haven't thought about that. I mean I hadn't thought about Talbot buying and then selling the whole lot and shutting them down. Sir Edward doesn't have to say what he is going to do with the stores after he's bought them. He might need to borrow some money to buy them all, but I can't see that being a problem.'

'Would there be complaints in the City, William, if people knew that was what he was going to do?'

'God bless my soul, you need to know some of the operators in these parts, Francis. Or maybe you don't, now I come to think about it. Nobody would turn a hair. People round here are concerned with profit, not philanthropy. Lots of big concerns nowadays have progressed by buying up their competitors and putting them out of business. Sir Edward wouldn't be the first and he won't be the last.'

'But suppose you worked for Scott's. You hear that the shops are to be shut down. You are going to lose your job. Your family will have no income till you find another position. If you were really angry, I mean *really* angry, you might go and remove Sir Edward from the equation, might you not? You would probably hold extreme left-wing views, like people say a lot of these trade unionists do. I agree it's a pretty long shot as a motive for murder, but I've known feebler motives than that. Is it possible?'

'It's certainly possible. But I think you are getting ahead of yourself, Francis. We need to find out if that is what Sir Edward intended to do. And if his heirs intend to carry out his wishes now he's no longer here.'

'How difficult would it be to find out if they intend to buy the Scott's shops and then close them down?'

Burke turned to stare out of his window. The tops of a couple of London's buses were making their slow progress through the tangled streets of the capital. 'I think I should be able to find out. It may cost me a seat on one of my boards but that's no matter. I would ask you to hold off any further inquiries in this direction until we have talked again. I think that would be for the best. Rumour would not be helpful to our cause. But come, Francis, you are looking depressed.'

'It's simply this, William. When I came here I was dealing with a murder in Lynchester where the victim was unknown to almost all the inhabitants. I very much doubt if any of them knew that Sir Edward was thinking of going on a takeover spree. Now I may be faced with the prospect of hundreds and hundreds of irate workers who might well have a motive for murder, but I do not know who they are or where they live. They could come from anywhere in London and the Home Counties. And that assumes that one of them might actually decide to commit a murder. They don't sell strychnine in most grocer's shops, do they, William? He could have got it by pretending to be a farmer with rats in his barns and outhouses.'

'That's true, Francis.'

6

Inspector Vaughan checked all the reports that had come in so far. There wasn't a single clue to be found. He felt he was like one of those fishermen in the Bible who had toiled all night and caught nothing. They might as well be living in a bloody monastery over there in the Close, he said to himself. Soon they'll all be getting up for those prayers in the middle of the night, still seeing nothing, as they made their way to church or abbey. Tomorrow, he said to himself, tomorrow, surely, we shall catch something.

Sitting on his train, Powerscourt wondered if there was anything in Sir Edward's private life that might have precipitated his wish to buy out his rivals. He felt sure Burke would have mentioned it had he known of some family row, a son gone to the bad with gambling debts, a pushy mistress anxious to get her hands on the money. But then, that didn't make sense either. If Sir Edward needed large amounts of money, he wouldn't be buying; surely he'd be selling some of his shares or a fixed number of his shops.

He decided to call on the Dean when he got back to Lynchester. He was sure the Dean would be about the Lord's work at a quarter past six in the evening.

'Lord Powerscourt, how kind of you to call. Is there any news to report? Any useful information from the police on their rounds?' The Dean had felt more and more frustrated as the day went on. This was his cathedral, in a way, and his Close. He certainly felt that it was his. Men were clambering all over it, collecting information, and nobody told him anything. Here, at last, there might be some intelligence from the front.

'I had to go up to London, Dean, I've only just got back. I don't have any news yet about the interviews around the Close. I rather wanted to ask you about your interview with Sir Edward Talbot the day he died. You talked to him in the late afternoon, I believe.'

The Dean mounted his high horse at record speed.

'I am afraid, Lord Powerscourt, that at this stage that information must be regarded as confidential. We are all expected to keep our comments to ourselves until the final candidate has been interviewed, and that is still some time away.'

The Dean smiled, as though he had won a major skirmish on the battlefield. He would guard his territory to the end.

'I think murder is pretty confidential, actually, Dean. The dead man is not here to judge what he would like to be made confidential about his affairs. He is, as far as I know, going to be taken to London in his coffin with the screws already in place.'

Powerscourt was actually feeling pretty irritated about this confidentiality, but he knew he would have to offer a lifeline of some sort to this troublesome Dean.

'You know as well as I do, Dean, that there is a murderer on the loose, possibly with a bottle of strychnine in his pocket. He could strike again at any time. The more we know about Sir Edward's last hours and his interview with you gentlemen of the cloth, the greater our chances of apprehending the killer. I and Inspector Vaughan and his men are well used to dealing with sensitive material. So, I ask you, please tell me something about that interview.'

The Dean was on the back foot now. 'You have made your position very clear, Lord Powerscourt. I do, however, feel that I should consult my colleagues. That would be the proper thing to do.'

'Very well,' said Powerscourt, picking up his hat and preparing to leave. 'If that's what you want to do, there is nothing I can do to stop you. But I am going to call on the Bishop this minute. I have no doubt he will tell me what I want to know.'

Way off at the far end of the Close, Powerscourt could hear the faint sound of a trumpeter beating the retreat.

'There is a solution, now I think about it,' said the Dean with a rather forced smile. 'If you would allow me to inform my colleagues of our conversation here this evening, I am sure we could proceed.'

'I have absolutely no problem with that, Dean. Thank you for being so understanding. Please feel free to tell your colleagues.'

'I speak from memory here, Lord Powerscourt. I shall consult my notes later and bring you up to date, should that be necessary.'

'Please proceed.'

'I think you would have to say that Sir Edward brought quite a lot of negatives with him. He's not a believer. He doesn't go to church on a regular basis. Church music seemed to mean nothing to him. He has a place in Hampshire as well as a house in London. He didn't seem to want to give it up. His wife is kept busy with charity work in London. He was unable to put a figure on the number of weekends he and his family would actually spend here. It was in some ways like interviewing a man who wants to be an absentee landlord.'

'There must have been some positives somewhere, Dean, surely.'

'There were, or should I say there was. He offered, very early on in the interview, to donate a sum of ten thousand pounds for the cathedral coffers. Something for the school, perhaps. I do not need to tell you, Lord Powerscourt, that such a sum, to us, would be like manna from heaven. It would take generations before our own humble fundraising works for the fabric of the buildings and so on could ever reach such a figure.'

'Forgive me if this seems rude, Dean, but did you and your colleagues think of this as a bribe? You give me the house, I'll give you the money?'

'I think our librarian, the youngest of our number, was certainly of that view. But we didn't discuss it afterwards. You may find this hard to believe, Lord Powerscourt, but we try not to talk about the virtues or defects of any of the candidates until we have seen them all. We did have a brief chat after the interview but it decided nothing. So our final conversation is still four candidates away.'

'Could I ask if this happens often? A candidate offering money?'

'Not on this scale; we've never had anything like ten thousand before. Some small gesture perhaps, once the candidate is safely installed. But always after, never before, if you see what I mean.'

'Did you think of it as a bribe, Dean? I hope you don't find that an inappropriate question.'

'There is always a trade-off in these matters, isn't there, Lord Powerscourt? Nobody knows better than I how much we could do with that money. But there are the other residents of the Close. They would be furious to hear that somebody had, in effect, bought their way in. That close-knit community, if not quite rent asunder, could certainly turn hostile both towards the newcomer with the money and to the Dean and Chapter who authorized it. If you pushed me up against the wall, I would have to say that I do think it was a bribe.'

'And would you have supported Sir Edward's application?'

'I do not intend to repeat this last section of our conversation to my colleagues, Lord Powerscourt. But no, I don't think I would have supported him at the end. I'm not sure any of my colleagues would either, but I cannot speak for them.'

'Poor man arrived on a fool's errand, don't you think? If he hadn't bothered to come, he would still be alive.'

Powerscourt found Johnny Fitzgerald waiting for him in the hotel bar.

'Good evening, Francis, I called in at Markham Square while I was in town and Lady Lucy told me I'd find you here. She said she thought you might be in need of reinforcements.'

Johnny Fitzgerald was Powerscourt's oldest friend. They had been companions in arms in the army in India and South Africa, and in all of Powerscourt's investigations ever since.

'You'd better fill me in, Francis. All I got from Lady Lucy was a dead fellow who used to run a lot of grocery stores by the name of Talbot.'

Powerscourt filled him in with the details of the case so far.

'I see,' said Johnny, ordering another round of drinks. 'The murderer could come from anywhere at all. Let me take a guess at what you want me to do.'

'I made a mental note on the train to send for you this very evening, Johnny. You've come a day or two early, that's all.'

'You haven't answered my question, Francis. Here am I, fresh to the situation, just waiting for orders like a good subordinate officer.'

'Well, I think the first thing we need to do is to take you in a walk round the Close and Netherbury House itself – that's where the murder was committed. Then you'll have a proper appreciation of the geography of the situation.'

'I'm sorry to disappoint you, Francis, but I don't believe you wanted me here to behave like some passing tourist. Should I pop down to the town first thing and buy a couple of guidebooks? There's a shop just next to the hotel here that sells all that stuff.'

'I'm sure you would find that very illuminating, Johnny, getting the guidebook and that sort of thing.'

'For God's sake, Francis, out with it for heaven's sake. I'll tell you what I think you want me to do. I always get the dirty and difficult jobs while you're sitting here taking tea with the Dean and Chapter and admiring the carvings in the chapterhouse.'

Johnny took a large swig of his beer. 'I think you want information about the late Sir Edward. The only thing is that this isn't the kind of stuff you can read in the newspapers. You said you'd been to see William Burke and wondered why the man might want to buy these other shops all of a sudden. I think you want more information than he might have. The man's private life, for example. Any hint of a scandal in the family. And you want to know more about his business. All of which leads me to the conclusion, which will have occurred to you, no doubt, some time ago, that Sir Edward may have been killed here, but that the motives for his murder are almost certainly in London or, possibly, in one of those grocery stores of his. How's that?'

'I would have to say spot on, Johnny. But please don't go back to town without the guided tour of the Close and Netherbury House.'

'Have no fear,' said Fitzgerald, 'I'll do that first thing tomorrow. Only after I've bought my guidebook, mind you.'

Inspector Vaughan met Powerscourt at his hotel in the morning. Johnny had enjoyed his tour and promised to read his guidebook on the train.

'Any news, Inspector? Any thin shafts of light so far?'

'Not a single shaft, my lord. All that time collecting those statements so far has been a waste of time.'

'I wonder, Inspector, if you and I haven't been looking in the wrong direction. I know you are familiar with the Close. But look here for a moment.'

Johnny Fitzgerald had insisted on buying his friend a guidebook. It included a map of the Cathedral Close.

'If you came in the main gate, looking for Netherbury House in the dark, you wouldn't necessarily be seen from the terraces or the crescent at all. You could creep along the back here. The only people apart from those in the Close who might have seen anything at all would be the people who live across the river. They might have seen our man coming or going from the house. Come to think of it, he could have come by water. Hopped into a boat further upstream and made his way down. In that case somebody living in one of those houses on the far side of the river might have seen or, more likely, heard something. Do you see?'

'I do, I do, my lord. That is very promising. Why didn't we think of it before? My brains must be going soft. I'll get my men on to it straight away. We've managed to persuade that new Chief Constable that it's a waste of time typing up the interviews immediately. Notebooks are all we need for the present. That should save a lot of time.'

'I wonder,' said Powerscourt, 'if we couldn't jog the memories of those people on the far side of the river.'

'I'm not sure what you mean, my lord.'

'I was just wondering if it would help if we staged a re-enactment of what might have happened. You and I arrange for the lights in Netherbury House to be exactly as they would have been on the night of the murder. You and I take an evening row down the river, pausing to get off at the bottom of the garden. After about ten minutes we pop back into the boat and row back the way we came. That might jog a few memories.'

'Capital,' said Inspector Vaughan. 'I like this plan, I like it very much. The only question is whether we postpone the questioning until after the river expedition, if you see what I mean. We only ask the questions after we've rowed down the stream. That would mean tomorrow rather than today.'

'I think today's interviews should go ahead as planned,' said Powerscourt. 'We might find out something that would make the re-enactment unnecessary. And there's another thing. Imagine there is a key discovery after the rowing event. The residents would have been questioned twice. Think of the trouble a barrister could cause in court asking the witness if he is sure which day he spotted a boat on the river in the middle of the night. Are you sure which day you saw this boat on? Are you absolutely sure it was not the second occasion when the Inspector and Powerscourt were playing about on the river?'

'Very well,' said Inspector Vaughan. 'I take your point. Let's cross that bridge if and when we come to it. I'll send my men off at once. They're going to have to make two visits, I think, to be sure everybody is at home. Never mind. By the way, my lord, if you see a man in naval uniform heading for the Dean's house, he's not the murderer. He's the second interviewee for the vacant position at Netherbury House – a naval gentleman, I gather.'

Johnny Chapman, Captain of HMS *Indefatigable*, a modern battlecruiser, was the second applicant to pass before the interviewers in the Dean's dining room. He was in his middle forties, of normal height, wearing a dark blue suit with a cream shirt and a pale blue tie. Immediately after the introductions, he asked permission to say a few words.

'Before we begin, gentlemen, could I just say how delighted and proud I am to be here today. My parents used to bring me to this cathedral for services sometimes when I was a boy. I never guessed that one day I might have the chance to come and live in your beautiful Close. That's all.'

With that he smiled broadly at the men of the Church, a body considerably smaller than the ship's company he was used to addressing.

'Thank you, Captain, thank you very much.' The Dean had changed the batting order from the previous interview. 'Mr Budd, please, would you like to start the proceedings?'

Timothy Budd had been warned that he was to go first. As usual he tried to begin with a slightly unorthodox question.

'Good day to you, Captain. My work here is with ancient religious documents. It's like trying to decode the past in a way. It could not be more different from your own duties. But perhaps you could answer me this, Captain. Every year now, we are told we have to build more battleships of one sort or another. Why do we need to spend all this money?'

Captain Chapman's bright blue eyes flashed round the table once more. 'I'm afraid this arms race in battleships is caused by the Germans, on their side, building bigger and better vessels every year. We have to outstrip them with bigger ships of our own in response. If they stopped their building programme tomorrow, we would stop ours. Heaven knows, we've offered often enough. It has always been the navy's intention to have a fleet superior to whatever the Germans or anybody else could throw at us. For our trade and our commerce across the oceans of the world, it is vital that Great Britain is the leading naval power. Does that answer your question, sir?'

'It does and it doesn't. I don't feel it is a satisfactory answer for the leapfrogging in boat construction that seems to have been going on for years now.'

'I know precisely what you mean.' The Captain glanced round the table and spotted a tray of pencils next to the Dean's blotting paper.

'Might I borrow three of these pencils, gentlemen?' The Captain arranged them in the shape of a triangle. 'I don't think I'd be revealing any state secrets if I use a few pencils here. These are the three things that define a modern warship.' He pointed to the bottom pencil of the triangle. 'This, if you like, is the armour, the steel protection bolted onto the frame. The more of that you have, the less likely you are to sink if you're hit by enemy shells. But it makes the ship very heavy and slower than she would be without it.' The Captain pointed to the top left-hand corner. 'This pencil here represents the guns. The bigger they are, and the further they can send their shells, the better.' His index finger now turned to the last corner of the triangle. 'This one represents the power of the engines, the speed at which the ship will travel. Modern warship design is a compromise between the demands of those three variables.'

He looked up again at his little audience. 'Sorry about this, gentlemen,' he said, smiling, 'naval construction lesson nearly finished. I come to the reason for the arms race.' He removed all the pencils and placed them by his right hand. Then he placed one on the middle of the table.

'Let us, for the sake of argument, suppose that we have here HMS *Lynchester* on patrol in the North Sea. Her speed is twenty-three knots, she is carrying lots of armour and her five-inch guns will carry to a distance of five thousand yards. She doesn't need to get any closer to sink an enemy ship. She can sit five thousand yards away and blast off her guns to her heart's content. That is because,' he placed another pencil parallel to the first, 'her opponent HMS *Kaiser* here has got smaller guns and doesn't travel so fast. Her guns only reach three thousand yards. So the advantage is with HMS *Lynchester*, as long as she doesn't get too close. But the Germans see what the problem is. So they produce a larger, more lethal vessel, *Frederick the Great*, that is faster and has bigger guns than the *Lynchester*.' The Captain moved the second pencil further away from the first. '*Frederick the Great* can fire her eight-inch guns at the *Lynchester* from seven thousand yards away and blow her to bits. The *Lynchester* can't run away as she is slower. She is now out of date. So the British build a ship that is faster and carries heavier guns than the *Frederick the Great*. The Germans respond in kind. So do the British. And so on and so on and so on. It looks at present as if the naval arms race could go on for ever.'

'I see,' said Timothy Budd. His medieval manuscripts had never seemed so attractive. 'Thank you very much.'

'I'm sorry that took so long. I think I got carried away. Please forgive me.'

'It was most illuminating,' said the Dean, staring hard at the naval vessels cruising round his dining-room table. 'Our Precentor, the man in charge of music in the cathedral, Mr Digby.'

'Captain Chapman, I presume that you have had little time for church music in your career. Does it mean anything to you?'

'If you mean by that, would I attend the sung services and the concerts given at this great cathedral, the answer is yes. We do a certain amount of singing at sea, you

74

know. Well-known hymns and that sort of thing at our Sunday services, whenever we can hold them."For those in peril on the sea" is always a great favourite, and most of the men know all the words by now. There is always something uplifting about a ship's company singing. How much more uplifting it would be to hear hymns and the oratorios of Bach and Byrd sung by a great choir in a great cathedral.'

So far the advantage was entirely with the navy rather than the Church. But Captain Chapman knew there was one question he would have to address sooner rather than later. He was fully aware that it could sink his application from a range of rather less than ten thousand yards.

'Thank you, Captain,' said the Precentor. The Dean handed the baton over to the Bishop.

'We are fully aware of the dangerous and vital work you do, Captain. I can assure you that we are in your debt. We shall pray for you here from now on, whatever becomes of the vacancy. I turn now to two questions that lie at the very heart of our deliberations. They won't surprise you, I'm sure. The first is this. Would you be able to live among us if your application is successful? Your ship is based far away in the north of Scotland, I understand.'

Captain Chapman smiled. 'You have found my Achilles heel, Bishop. I can tell from part of your question that you already know the answer. I cannot put my hand on my heart and say that I would be coming to live here full time. I just couldn't do it, not as long as I remain Captain of my ship. It is, as you so rightly say, too far away. If you asked me now how much leave I have between now and next Christmas I couldn't tell you. If I did I would be lying. It could be a couple of months, it could be a month, it could be a fortnight. If there is a war, life would be more complicated still. There mightn't be any shore leave at all for a time. A war might take a year or so.

'However, gentlemen, there is one factor I would like you to consider. I'm referring to my wife and children. We have two boys aged six and eight. If this application were successful, they would move in here at once and use this as their full-time residence. At present we are living in London in rented accommodation. I am sure we could shorten the lease if required. Think how happy it would make me if I knew they were here in the Close while I was on duty somewhere out there in the cold and stormy waters of the North Sea. I have no doubt that they would be happy here. I know my long absences are a disadvantage in the question of this lease. I would ask you to think as well of my wife and the two little boys. Perhaps they could go to the school in the Close.'

'Thank you, Captain. We shall of course take heed of what you have said.' The Dean was thinking that this was going to be one of the more difficult appointments of his time in office at the cathedral.

'Let me move on to another important issue. The question of faith is not that important to us here – there are people living in the Close who never darken the cathedral doors from one year to another – but we do like to know. Would you describe yourself as a believer, Captain?'

Captain Chapman was trained to leave as little as possible to chance. He had enlisted two fellow Captains to conduct a rehearsal of the likely questions. They had very different approaches to the matter. One had recommended a policy of total honesty at all times. This, he claimed, was more likely to produce a victory in such surroundings. The other, as much a politician as a sailor, had recommended a few little white lies to see him safe to harbour. This was one of the questions where they had recommended completely different answers.

'Well, Dean, I find that a very difficult question to answer. Part of me would simply say that religion is part of the fabric of my life. It always has been. Hymns and Bible readings have accompanied me on my life's journey, from lessons and hymns and the occasional sermon at school and at naval college and at the gunnery school. I've never thought about it; it's just part of the routine in the navy. I and my family go to church on Sundays. I have no doubt that, with or without me, they would continue to do so here.

'Because it's always been a part of me I don't think I've ever thought very much about exactly what I do believe. It didn't seem necessary. I certainly believe most of it. But if you asked me if I believed every single word of it, I'm not sure. I am the Resurrection and the life doesn't seem very credible when you're tipping some dead sailor, his coffin wrapped in the Union Jack, into the Pacific Ocean hundreds of miles from anywhere. I'm not sure about anybody coming back to judge the quick and the dead. I'm not persuaded that Christ came with a return ticket for us all, if you see what I mean. I have always had difficulty about the Holy Spirit, who has always seemed to me to be the rabbit produced from some ecclesiastical hat to solve the problems which were insoluble without him. I hope you understand my position, gentlemen; there must be plenty of people in your pews who feel the same.'

'That's a very honest answer, Captain. Thank you for that. Now, is there anything you would like to ask us?'

'I don't think there is. It's been a pleasure.' He leant

forward and put the three pencils back in their place. 'I'd better put the *Lynchester* navy vessel safely ashore, if I may. And the *Frederick the Great*. Thank you very much indeed.'

7

The four men looked at each other after the Captain had left. The Dean looked across to Rupert Digby.

'What did you think, Precentor? Any first impressions?'

Rupert Digby smiled. 'He was, I thought, very nearly the perfect candidate. Except that he'd never be here. I'm sure his family would come, of course, but we're not in the business of selecting families. It does worry me. Even without a war we'd hardly ever see him. If, heaven forbid, there was a war, we might never see him for years.'

'Librarian?'

Timothy Budd was looking at the pencils in their tray. 'I was most impressed with his account of the naval arms race, I must say. I agree with the Precentor. An admirable candidate in every way, with the proviso of how often he would be able to live here. It seems odd to advertise a place for rent and then give it to somebody who will hardly be in the house at all.'

'Bishop?'

Bishop Trevelyan looked at his interviewers one by

one. 'I tell you what I think, gentlemen. I think there are three other candidates yet to come.'

The water in the little River Lynn was cold to the touch. It was just after half past nine in the evening, the day after Inspector Vaughan's men had drawn a blank in their interviews in the houses across the river. The moon was just a sliver in the night sky. They were passing under the Northgate Bridge, a low hum still coming from the little city. Inspector Vaughan was rowing slowly, on the assumption that any murderer who had been this way before would want to make as little noise as possible. He had arranged to borrow a boat from the school in the Close. Further ahead, at their destination, a police officer had been deputed to turn the lights on in Netherbury House with particular attention to the upstairs bedroom where Sir Edward Talbot had breathed his last. There were distant cries from owls and other night creatures over to their right.

Inspector Vaughan almost missed the landing stage at the bottom of the garden. Powerscourt could hear him swearing quietly under his breath. The two men made their way into the house as quietly as they could. The police Constable stood to attention to one side of the front door. Inspector Vaughan kept watch downstairs while Powerscourt manned the upstairs. He walked to and from the bathroom, a short journey that must have been Sir Edward's last walk on earth, coughing and gasping for breath. He peered out of the bedroom windows and saw the lights from the houses across the river. As far as he could make out, all the curtains were closed.

'I reckon we should leave in about five minutes'

time,' said the Inspector as they conferred in the drawing room. 'Do you think we should make a noise to let people know we're here?'

'I don't think anybody would hear anything from the far side of the Lynn, Inspector.'

The Inspector rowed them back the way they had come. No one spoke in the boat. They passed a couple of foxes on patrol along the riverbank; they took no notice of them at all, as if nocturnal rowing parties were a regular feature of the landscape.

'I'll get my men out with their notebooks first thing in the morning, my lord.'

'There is one thing we haven't thought about, Inspector.'

'What's that?' said the Inspector, making the boat fast for the night.

'The murderer's boat. If the murderer came by boat, that is. Where did he get it from? Did he steal it? Did he leave it back where he got it? I don't suppose anybody would know if their rowing boat had been pressed into service for an hour in the middle of the night. Could we ever find out?'

'I shall have to think about that, my lord.'

'And there's another thing. This night air must have sharpened my wits. Am I not right in thinking that if you carried on rowing in this direction, you would reach the railway station? Are there any late trains our murderer could have caught? Should we be making inquiries with the railway people?'

'We should take these night-time trips more often, my lord. I shall get in touch with the railway people in the morning. I must say, having just rowed down the river, that it would have been the most unobtrusive way to get to Netherbury House.'

* * *

Johnny Fitzgerald was trying to count the number of fishing expeditions he had carried out on behalf of his friend. He reached seven before he reached his destination. Today would be another in a long list.

William Reed, the editor of the *Grocer* magazine, was a tall, slim young man with the beard of a Victorian patriarch. Johnny Fitzgerald thought it was meant to make him look older and more serious. His trip to the magazine's offices in High Holborn had been inspired by a discarded copy of the magazine on the top floor of a London bus. He had presented himself as a colleague of Lord Francis Powerscourt, currently investigating the death of Sir Edward Talbot.

'Already you are bringing me news I did not know,' said William Reed. 'I did not know there was a distinguished investigator looking into the poor man's demise.'

'I think it would help if this entire conversation could be regarded as off the record, Mr Reed.'

'Of course. Believe it or not, the world of grocery has its own secrets to keep. I promise you that nothing we say here this afternoon will go any further. What can we do to help, Mr Fitzgerald?'

'It would help if you could tell me what you know of Sir Edward Talbot and his stores. In general terms, of course. I have a couple of particular queries relating to the last six months or so which we could discuss later.'

'In some ways,' said Reed, filling a pipe, 'Sir Edward is the classic story of rags to riches. You probably know all that. It has passed into the living legend of Talbot's Stores, the humble beginnings and so on. His chain of grocery shops is now one of the leading players in London and the Home Counties. He is like Sir Thomas Lipton, if you like, only on a slightly smaller scale.'

'Thank you for that, it is most helpful,' said Johnny, as small clouds of smoke began to flow across the room. 'Has there been anything remarkable going on in recent months, would you say?'

'I would say so. For a start he has been conducting what could only be described as a price war with his nearest, although smaller rivals, Scott's Stores. Sir Edward has cut his prices on a number of lines, to the point where we have actually wondered if he was making any profit at all. This has been going on for some months. Scott's themselves have been faced with a devil's alternative: cut your own prices or lose a lot of profit; leave your prices where they are and watch the customers walk out the door. It's a fickle business, grocery. People will do anything they can to find lower prices.'

'And is there any sign of the price war ending? Is there some sort of a truce in sight?'

'There certainly is not. Part of the problem is that nobody knew Sir Edward's intentions. That is why his death came at such an unfortunate time. It may be that his intentions will become clear in his will, though I rather doubt that. He was rather a secretive man, always refusing interviews, even with us. There have been, as I am sure you know, a number of rumours floating around, most of them nonsense.'

'Perhaps you could fill me in on the rumours, Mr Reed.'

'Of course.' There was another burst of smoke round the top of his beard. 'I find them all hard to believe. We have, I hate to say, even published some of these rumours, without knowing if there was any truth in them. There is one that he is driving such a hard bargain with Scott's because he wanted to take them over. Close down some of the stores where they were in direct competition with him, then keep his own prices high. Maybe even hand them over to his son, who knows? But why? Sir Edward has had innumerable chances to swallow smaller competitors down the years and has never bothered. Why should he start now? It is possible, I suppose, that he carried out the price war to increase the value of Talbot's. Maybe he intended to sell Talbot's at the end of the day?'

'Could you see the man selling the stores he had spent his life acquiring and making profitable and then living a quiet life in the country?'

'I could not, Mr Fitzgerald. You can imagine some of these very rich men taking to the grouse moor or sailing round the world, but not Sir Edward. May I ask you one question?'

'You may indeed, Mr Reed. You have been most helpful.'

'My question is this. We know Sir Edward Talbot passed away in Lynchester. Why have a top London investigator and his distinguished colleague been called in to investigate the death? That is not the normal practice in cathedral cities, any more than it is in London. What, pray, might the answer be?

'A very pertinent question, Mr Reed. Can I just say that there were certain irregularities about Sir Edward's death. The Church authorities were anxious to have the matter cleared up as soon as possible.'

'Was he murdered, Mr Fitzgerald?'

There was a brief pause while Johnny considered his options. He remembered the beginning of the conversation, where they had both agreed to keep their discussion off the record.

'I'm afraid I shall have to say no comment to that, Mr Reed. My apologies.'

'I quite understand. I am assuming from your answer that Sir Edward was murdered. But I promise you that I shall not breathe a word of it to a single soul. Not for the time being, at any rate. There must be an inquest, if there hasn't already been one.'

'Thank you for that, thank you very much indeed.'

'Could I make a suggestion? I suspect – remember that I, unlike you, have no experience of murder investigations. I can fully appreciate the need for silence at this stage. But at some point, I think, the benefits of publicity might outweigh the appeal for secrecy. Various factors we know nothing about might come into play. We are not a national newspaper, as you can see. But the nationals read our magazine every week it is published. Sometimes they steal our stories without attribution. We are well used to that. But if you wanted a discreet channel to announce the murder, I think we could serve. I think we could serve very well, actually.'

'Thank you, Mr Reed. I shall pass that on to my colleagues. We shall be in touch.'

Constable Thomas Sweet was making his final calls of the day. He was the youngest Constable in his force. He had been working his way round the houses on the far side of the river. So far his inquiries had produced absolutely nothing. It was now a quarter to six in the evening and the Constable was looking forward to playing badminton with some of the girls at the sports club. So he was cheerful when he rang his last doorbell of the day.

'Lynchester Police here, madam. I have some inquiries relating to irregular behaviour round the Cathedral Close a few nights ago. I see that the back of your house looks out into the gardens. Did you or your husband see anything unusual out of your back windows?'

'I certainly didn't, young man. I've better things to do than to spend the evenings peering through my curtains.'

'What about your husband, madam?'

'I'll see if I can raise him. He's a bit deaf these days. Bert?' The message was shouted into the interior.

'Lay off, woman. I'm reading the paper!'

'There's a policeman here wants to speak to you.'

'I told you, woman, I'm reading the paper!'

'I'm telling you, Bert. There's a police Constable here wishes to speak to you!'

'Why didn't you say so? I'm on my way.'

Bert might have been reluctant to come to the witness stand, as it were, but he was to provide the only piece of fresh evidence that day. He had looked out of the curtains last thing at night a few days back, he said. 'I often do to have a look at the stars and stuff like that. I did see something on the river a couple of nights back, though it was so dark I couldn't see what it was.'

'What did you think it was? And was it a couple of nights back or last night that you are talking about?'

'I said it was a couple of nights ago. It might have been a boat, a rowing boat, that's what I said to myself at the time,' he told the Constable.

'Could you make out anything of who was rowing the boat?'

'It was very dark that night. I thought there might have been one man inside, but if there was, he was dressed entirely in black. And I thought he might be wearing a hat.'

'Which way was he going, Bert, could you make that out?'

'No, I couldn't. I'm not absolutely certain about any of this.'

'Was there anything else you noticed?'

'I told you, Constable, it was dark, bloody dark. That's all.'

'That's very useful,' said the Constable. 'One of my colleagues may wish to talk to you tomorrow.'

'I'm usually home from about four o'clock, young man.'

'Thank you very much.'

Inspector Vaughan was with Powerscourt in his hotel when the Constable came with his news.

'Well done, young man, well done indeed. That is the first real lead we have had so far, even if it is slightly tenuous. Could you go back to the station and ask Sergeant Jones to look out the train timetables? I shall be back directly. We're going to launch a manhunt across Lynchester and the neighbouring counties for the man in black.'

'Inspector,' said Powerscourt, 'before you go. I presume the inquest cannot be delayed much longer. Johnny Fitzgerald has told me that there is already a magazine editor who knows Sir Edward was murdered, but he is sworn to silence. Do you know when the London scientists will have finished their work?'

'My latest information, as of this morning, is that we

should have the results in the next few days. Then we shall hold the inquest.'

'Very good, Inspector. While you are communing with the train timetables, I shall go and commune with the Bishop. I don't think they have any idea what is coming their way when the Press get word of the mystery murder of a millionaire and the phantom boat seen in the river at the back of the Close.'

8

The Bishop was in his study putting the final touches to his sermon for Gloucester Cathedral. He smiled at Powerscourt and showed him to a chair by the side of the fire. Rank upon rank of theological volumes ran up and down the walls of the room. There was even a small pile of them, some with markers in particular pages, on the Bishop's desk.

'I don't have any dramatic news to give you, Bishop. But I do come with a warning. It concerns the gentlemen of the Press.'

The Bishop looked as if he would rather not hear about the gentlemen of the Press just now.

'The inquest has been delayed, as you know, but Inspector Vaughan tells me that it will take place in a couple of days. At that point the knowledge that Sir Edward Talbot was murdered on cathedral premises will come into the public domain. It will be reported in the local paper. Word will reach London very fast. In no time at all there will be reporters down here, clambering all over the Close and interviewing the statues on the West Front. You need to have a policy, Bishop. There is nothing we can do about what they're going to print, nothing at all.'

'What would you have me do, Lord Powerscourt? I would do anything to preserve the good name of the cathedral. So would the Dean and the rest of the clergy here. Should I shut the Close for a couple of days?'

'With respect, Bishop, I can see the appeal of such a course of action. However, I fear it would only convince the newspapermen that you had something to hide.'

'I see, Lord Powerscourt. But I am due to give a sermon in Gloucester Cathedral this coming Sunday. Do you think I should abandon my plans?'

'I don't think the storm will break on Sunday, Bishop. I'm sure you should go ahead with your trip to Gloucester.'

'But what do you suggest we do? The cathedral is built as a bulwark against sin and wickedness and the hosts of the ungodly. It was never designed to withstand an onslaught by the British Press in pursuit of a good story.'

'This is what I would suggest. It may be tempting to close the doors and lock the main gate. I think you should do the opposite. I think you should be as open as possible. They always want interviews, these newspapermen. It fills up the space available for their story in the paper. I think you and the Dean should be available during the day for interviews. Welcome these people like the Prodigal Son. They are all children of God, after all. Offer whatever help you can give. You may tire of giving interviews or arranging with the junior clergy to give guided tours of the Close, but I think you have to bear it. The more open you are, the quicker it will be over. I suspect that things will be pretty busy for a day or so and then the reporters will be summoned away to different murders in different parts of the country.'

'Very good, Lord Powerscourt. We shall do our duty. But what about the remaining candidates for Netherbury House?'

'I hadn't thought about that. I'm afraid that makes the story even more attractive. I think you should be honest about those interviews being carried out, but stress that they are a confidential question between the cathedral and its lawyers. They won't want to bother the lawyers, I suspect. I presume you will talk with the Dean about the timetable for the rest of the interviews and whether it should be changed. Two have been completed, I think, with three still to come?'

The Bishop nodded.

As the Lynchester shops opened the following morning, Inspector Vaughan sent his men into battle. They fanned out from the police station into Northgate, Westgate, Compton Street, Salisbury Street, and all the other places where people might be found. There were three of them at the railway station, to be relieved at six o'clock in the evening. From lunchtime there would be a detachment touring the local pubs and hotels. Always they asked the same questions.

'Did you see a man of average height, wearing a dark coat and a black hat in the town during the day or during the evening a couple of days ago? If you did, what was he doing and where was he going?'

When asked the inevitable question why, the police-men all had the same response, written in large letters that morning on Inspector Vaughan's blackboard. 'The man was needed to help the police in their inquiries.' If anybody dared to ask the further question, 'What sort of inquiries?', they were told to mind their own business. In town centres and at railway stations within a twenty-mile radius of Lynchester, other policemen were asking the same questions.

'Have you much hope of your manhunt, Inspector?' Powerscourt had joined Inspector Vaughan in the police station.

'Do you want the answer I should give to my superiors, or the real one?' the Inspector replied.

'The real one, please.'

'In that case, my lord, I should have to say that I hold out little hope. It's police procedure. The rules are there to be followed. But, speaking for myself, I do not hold out much hope at all. A great deal of police time is probably going to prove to be wasted. I haven't been responsible for many murder inquiries – we don't get a lot of that sort of crime down here. I've always had to put this kind of police presence on the streets. It's never helped me solve the crime. I always wish I could bring the victim back to life for half an hour, just half an hour of life, so we could find out who killed him or her.'

'Even the gentlemen over at the cathedral couldn't pull that one off, I fear. Lazarus might have been brought back from the dead, but he was the only one.'

'Apart from Christ, of course, but I don't think he's going to show up any time soon.'

Powerscourt suddenly stood up and began to pace up and down the Inspector's office.

'Something's just occurred to me, Inspector. You will remember our rather unreliable witness?'

'Of course.'

'Well, he just told us that he thought he saw what might have been a boat with a man dressed in very dark clothes and a dark hat, didn't he? He didn't say which direction the boat was going. He didn't say anything about that at all. We have assumed that the boat would come back to the town, to the landing stage at the school or the one behind the station. But we don't know that. What would have happened if he'd gone in the other direction, away from Lynchester altogether? Where would he have got to?'

'That's a very interesting question, my lord. I haven't considered that until now. I'm not an expert in the twists and turns of the River Lynn, but I think he would have passed through open country for five or six miles before he came to Winchampton. That's just a village; there's certainly no railway station. I doubt there's even a bus stop. If this theory is good, there's one problem with it. There aren't any houses or cottages along that stretch at all. We'd have to interview the bloody cows.'

Powerscourt was making his way back to the hotel across the Close. He was approached by a shambling man who looked as though he might have been the worse for drink. His clothes would not have won a prize in the best-dressed scarecrow of the year competition. His trousers were dark and looked as if they might have begun life as part of a suit. The shirt had once been white, now a patchy grey. The hat had a large hole in one side. The teeth looked to have little future. He was carrying what might have held his worldly goods in a tattered black suitcase. The scarecrow smelt very strongly of drink. Powerscourt thought he was at that state of advanced drunkenness where the words come out properly but the thoughts are jumbled up. The apparition peered closely at Powerscourt.

'You are the one from London, the man who sorts out crimes and puts men in jail.'

'My name is Powerscourt,' he replied, shaking a grubby hand with blackened fingernails.

'They call me Simon,' said the scarecrow. 'Some peoples call me Simple Simon. I'm not simple any more than they are, I can tell you that, man from London.'

'I see,' said Powerscourt.

'I sometime travels by night when the stars are in the right order.'

'Really?'

'Sometimes I hears things on the wind. Sometimes I sees things in the wind, so I do. Nobody knows what you can see when you travel in the dark.'

Powerscourt was wondering how good the scarecrow's memory was. And whether the drink was doing the talking. With that amount of drink on board, the memory might be rather faulty. The scarecrow prodded him in the chest.

'There are more things that move in the night than are dreamt of in your philosophy, my friend. Foxes on patrol, looking for sinners. Owls; there's enough owls round here to run a ring of bells.'

'That's from *Hamlet*, that first bit,' said Powerscourt, wondering if this was one of the better-educated scarecrows, brought low by the demon drink.

'When shall we three meet again, In thunder, lightning, or in rain?'

'So it's *Macbeth* this time, Simon. Were you fond of Shakespeare at school?'

'I didn't care for school, nor for them teachers neither. I ran away so many times they gave up looking for me. I got locked up once in a library for the whole weekend by mistake. I read some of that Shakespeare fellow in there in a back room where they couldn't see me. He didn't half write a lot of plays, the man. He can't have stopped for a moment, if you ask me.'

'Do you travel round the Close in the dark, Simon?'

The scarecrow's brain was still running on Shakespeare.

'Fair is foul and foul is fair: Hover through the fog and filthy air.'

Powerscourt was hoping now that the library visit hadn't included *King Lear* or the storm scene, or that The Fool might be about to come to Lynchester. He particularly didn't want to know about the blinded Gloucester at this time.

'When the hurly-burly's done, When the battle's lost and won: that's what I say,' said the scarecrow. 'What happens to those that die in the dark? What indeed?'

The scarecrow was searching for something in his pockets. Supplies might have been running low.

'After the daylight comes the dark, the people sleep, the dogs don't bark.'

Powerscourt wondered if Simon had been about on the night of the murder.

'Do you come this way often in the dark, Simon?'

'Happen I do and happen I don't. Creatures dressed in black come out here in the night when the good people are abed. Sometimes they soar up into the sky. Sometimes they travel on the water, waves splashing in the night air.'

'Simon, this is important: can you remember where

you were a couple of nights ago? Were you here? In the Close?'

The scarecrow paused and looked carefully at Powerscourt. 'That's a personal question, a very personal question, if you don't mind me saying so. What is it to you?'

'I just wondered, that's all.'

'I don't want you getting all personal on me. What goes out at night, by land or water, comes out at night. I sees the things that come out in the darkness. Round here there are many different kinds of dark.'

'I can see that. But I'm talking about a couple of nights ago now.'

'You're trying to trap me. Then you'll take me off to one of those hard prison cells. They don't have no Shakespeare in there. I know your sort. Locked up. Locked up all night. Horrid policemen's eyes peering at you through the slit in the door. Prison food. Have you ever tasted prison food? Macbeth's witches could have made something tastier in their cauldron, if you ask me.'

The scarecrow sounded as if he might burst into tears at any moment. He was scratching violently on his shirt and swaying from side to side. Powerscourt suspected that the scarecrow might indeed have something to tell about events on the night of the murder. But now was not the time to ask. He wondered which time of day was the most sober in the scarecrow's lifestyle. Late morning? Early afternoon?

They had reached the entrance to the Close. Simon was turning round to return to its wide spaces. Powerscourt was heading for his hotel.

'We shall speak again, I'm sure, Simon. It's been a pleasure talking to you.'

'Farewell,' said the scarecrow. 'When shall we two meet again? Please remember, that the answers are lying about in the dark, waiting to be found. Seek out what moves in the Close in the hours of darkness, and you will see much that is not now revealed. Double, double, toil and trouble; Fire burn, and cauldron bubble.'

'Till we meet again,' said Powerscourt.

The scarecrow looked as though he was performing some mighty feat of memory.

'When the hurly-burly's done, When the battle's lost and won.'

Inspector Vaughan joined Powerscourt for breakfast the following morning. 'I can't pretend that it's been a triumph, our questioning yesterday, my lord, but it's not been a complete disaster. We got nothing of interest from the two terraces and we're halfway along the crescent. There were two reports of our man, if he is our man, at the railway station. He took a train to Reading; from Reading, as you know, you can go almost anywhere in England. I have telephoned my opposite number there to ask him to carry out some more inquiries tonight. I think our man could have caught a train to London, if not last thing at night, then first thing in the morning.'

'Well done, Inspector, that's all better than nothing. Any further descriptions? Age? Colour of hair, that sort of thing?'

'Our man, if it was our man, positioned himself right at the end of the platform and spent his time staring up the track. Apparently he never looked round.'

'The man in the ticket office? Did he remember anything?'

'No, he was rather rude, apparently, the ticket office fellow. He said it was not part of his job description to provide detailed information about passengers wearing dark clothes. That's about it, my lord. I've got to go to give evidence at the inquest. I presume you're coming too. That Coroner's a stickler for punctuality.'

There were six reporters at the back of the court. Inspector Vaughan whispered to Powerscourt that four of them were strangers, come presumably from the London papers. The witnesses were impressive, the Bishop telling the story of the interview about the vacant house in the Close, the Dean retailing the dinner later in the evening. Both confirmed that Sir Edward Talbot had been in sound health and of sound mind. Inspector Vaughan was grave as he gave details of the discovery of the body the following morning. The gentlemen of the Press muttered to each other as the word 'strychnine' made its appearance in the medical evidence. The Coroner concluded that Sir Edward had been murdered by person or persons unknown. The journalists fled into the open air to plan their campaign.

The Bishop and the Dean were both on parade after the legal proceedings. They each gave separate interviews to the four men from London, the Bishop remarking afterwards that it was a bit like having to take the same oral exam four times in a row. Members of the cathedral staff gave a guided tour of the relevant parts of the Close.

'I thought of offering the gentlemen a guided tour of the cathedral itself,' the Bishop reported, 'the more interesting architectural features, the statues and so on the West Front, but I didn't think there would be many takers.'

'What do you think they will print in the papers tomorrow, Powerscourt?' The Dean felt that he had acquitted himself well in his interviews. He was not to know that the journalists referred to him as the stuffy one who wasn't the Bishop. They had quite liked the Bishop.

'Heaven knows what they will print,' said Powerscourt. 'It may even do us some good – jog a witness's memory, that sort of thing. I'm sure they will have interviewed people in the town for their reaction to the murder. Come to think of it, they may not have interviewed anybody at all, except for the people at the local Talbot's Store. It's only a couple of hundred yards from the courthouse after all. Or they may have just made their quotes up on the train back to London.'

The headlines the next morning were certainly dramatic. 'Grocery King Murdered in Cathedral Close.' 'Death Comes to the Cathedral. Sir Edward Talbot Slain.' 'Sir Edward Talbot Poisoned in Cathedral City.'

There were quotes from the workers at his store. 'He will be sadly missed.' 'Sir Edward was an ornament to the grocery trade in this country.' 'How tragic to think that he met his end in a way like this.' Two of them had checked in their cuttings files to find the details of Sir Edward's rise from rags to riches. There was speculation about the future of his grocery empire. The most enterprising of the journalists had infiltrated the estate agents and discovered the details of Netherbury House, the property Sir Edward hoped to buy and ended up dying in. Both the Dean and the Bishop were quoted, 'A man who will be greatly missed in the wider community beyond Lynchester,' from the Dean at his most worldly wise. 'A great man who would have been an ornament to the Close if he had come to live here,' from the Bishop. The reporter did not discover that there were three more candidates yet to come.

'I must say, I'm rather disappointed,' said the Dean to Powerscourt, perusing his collection of the day's papers the following morning. 'I took great pains with those reporters. I must have spent twenty minutes or more with each of them. And I get one miserable quote from the whole pack of them. Don't they realize how significant a dean is in our great cathedrals?'

'I'm sure the reporters will have included more of your comments, Dean. Maybe the subeditors, the people who make the paper ready for the presses, might have had to cut some of the quotations for reasons of space. That happens all the time.'

'Does it really?' said the Dean. 'I never knew that. That's not so bad then.'

'Tell me, Dean, if you would, about the plans for the other interviews regarding Netherbury House. You're not going to change the timetable, are you, in view of the murder and so on?'

'The Bishop and I have considered it,' replied the Dean, 'But it would be very hard to arrange. Our second interviewee was a Royal Navy gentleman and we have an army fellow yet to come. If we start to unravel the timetable, it could take months before we are through. At least the journalists didn't get wind of those interviews. I dread to think what they could have made of them.'

As Powerscourt went off to see Inspector Vaughan, he didn't think the newspapermen would have had any trouble coping with Netherbury House. He didn't like to think what might happen if they bumped into Simple Simon.

The Inspector was on the telephone when Powerscourt arrived after his conversation with the Dean.

'Yes, Chief Constable, I did say a second murder. What's that? It's a bad line. No, it's not another candidate for Netherbury House. It is a man who lived on the Close, by the name of Sandy Field. He was found lying on the rough ground at the back of the Close late last night. The doctor thinks he might have gone out for a breath of fresh air. Do we think we can cope, did you say? Yes, we can cope. Do we need reinforcements from London? Not at the moment, sir. I'll let you know when we do. The medical gentlemen say he was shot. No, he didn't die in the same way as Sir Edward. Yes, sir, Lord Powerscourt is still here. You want me to talk to the cathedral people, is that right? Very good, sir. Thank you, sir. Goodbye, sir.'

9

'I do wish Chief Constables would leave you in peace first thing in the morning, my lord. You will have gathered most of the main points. Sandy Field is dead. Autopsy tomorrow. Dr Willoughby says he was shot in the heart, and death would have been instantaneous.'

'I talked with Sandy Field the other day. Wasn't he a well-known figure in the Close?' asked Powerscourt.

'He was. Cricket club, football club for the children, good works about the Close.'

'And he was a solicitor, am I right?'

'You are. He worked for a local firm called Ardglass, Puckeridge and Ross. We told them first thing this morning. Could you go and talk to them, my lord? So we can get a sense of his business life. Not that they'll tell you very much. Brandon Puckeridge, one of the partners, talks to people as if they were members of some inferior tribe most of the time.'

'I shall do that,' said Powerscourt. 'Is there anything more you can tell me about the death?'

'Sorry, my lord. The body was found by the milkman

early in the morning in the long grass by the edge of the Close. Death would have been more or less instantaneous. There are no reports as yet of the shot being heard by anybody else. No doubt the Chief Constable will be asking for the links between a country solicitor and a captain of the grocery trade fairly shortly. Personally I have no idea – no idea at all.'

Brandon Puckeridge was tall and thin with a small, well-trimmed moustache. He looked, Powerscourt thought, like everybody's idea of how a country solicitor should look, wearing a dark grey suit with waistcoat and fob, white shirt and a dark blue tie. Powerscourt wondered if he kept a supply of black ties in a cupboard in his office. Somewhere in London, near Savile Row perhaps, there could be a shop specializing in discreet and well-tailored garments for the soliciting trade, where grey and dark blue material were the order of the day.

'Good morning to you, Lord Powerscourt. Please take a seat.' Powerscourt was ushered into a chair on the far side of Puckeridge's enormous desk.

'You are here to assist the police force in these terrible murders, so the Dean told me the other day.'

Powerscourt thought that the solicitor's intelligence service was probably as good as you could get in a place like Lynchester.

'You are right, Mr Puckeridge. I feel it would be worthwhile if we could establish what sort of professional life Mr Field had here. I don't need to tell you that in cases like this we need to amass as much information as we can. Not all of it, in fact hardly any of it, will prove to be relevant in the end, but there we go.'

'I understand. Do you know, I don't think I have ever been involved in a murder case before. I have been involved in all sorts of cases, of course, but never one like this. How unfortunate that we should end up with one on our own doorstep.'

'Quite so, Mr Puckeridge, it is indeed most unfortunate. Could you tell me about Mr Field as a colleague? I presume you were his commanding officer, as it were, would that be right?'

'It would be. Sandy must have been in his late thirties. He came to us seven years ago from an Oxford firm he didn't care for. The thing you have to remember about Sandy is that he is – sorry, he was – a very cheerful soul. He came to the office in a good mood and he left the office in a good mood. His good humour was infectious. The office was always a happier place when he was in it. When he was out on business our clients always remarked that he seemed to be cheerful all the time. It was contagious.'

'Can you by any chance remember the name of the solicitors in Oxford? The firm Mr Field worked for before he came here?

'Of course, we still have dealings with them from time to time. Harrison, Moreland and Crooks. Their main offices are on the High Street.'

'Thank you very much for that. And could you tell me, in broad terms, the nature of your business here?'

'Of course.' Brandon Puckeridge paused to flick an unwelcome speck of dust from the corner of his desk.

'We do some conveyancing work, as you can imagine, Lord Powerscourt. We have always had close links with our neighbours, the estate agents and the local bankers. If I could give you an example. When Netherbury House in the Close is sold, the advertising and so on will be done by the agents; we shall handle the legal side and the money will be looked after by the bank. Leases, we do a lot of those, with shops changing hands and people looking for somewhere to live. Wills, plenty of wills, large and small. We encourage all our clients to make wills, Lord Powerscourt. It was Sandy Field who hit on the policy of telling all actual or potential clients how much money they would save if they left a will before they died. Divorces are very rare, as you can imagine. Arbitration is a regular feature. You'd be amazed how often farmers and shopkeepers can fall out with each other.'

'And was Mr Field a specialist in any of those fields?'

'You could almost say he was a specialist in all of them, Lord Powerscourt. It falls to me to assign cases to individuals. We have six solicitors here, including myself. I always try to make sure that each man has a mixed portfolio of clients and problems. You might become very bored and very boring if you had nothing to do but sort out leases every day of the week. So I try to keep each menu as varied as possible.'

'You have spoken very warmly about your colleague, Mr Puckeridge. What would you say were his bad points?'

'You phrase the question to imply that he did have bad points, Lord Powerscourt. He had very few. Overenthusiasm, perhaps? I'm not suggesting that he was a man who would have started singing popular songs in the nave at a funeral, far from it. But sometimes – and I am sure the fault is with us, not with him – such cheerfulness can be too much.'

'And would you say he had any enemies?'

'Not that I know about. Obviously I know much more about his professional life than I do about his personal affairs. But, on the whole, I would say he had no enemies that I was aware of.'

Was there some hidden meaning attached to the way Puckeridge said personal affairs? Powerscourt wondered. 'On the whole, Mr Puckeridge? On the whole? That implies something you may not have mentioned so far.'

'A slip of the tongue, Lord Powerscourt. Pay no attention to it.'

'Thank you very much, Mr Puckeridge, thank you for your time.'

The offices of the *Lynchester Press and Journal* were directly opposite those of Ardglass, Puckeridge and Ross. Powerscourt was shown straight in to the editor's office, a small cramped department that contained back copies of the paper.

'Jenkins, Sylvester Jenkins at your service, Lord Powerscourt.' Jenkins was a small man of about five feet six inches tall, clean-shaven and dressed in a rather shabby suit. He seemed to be a chain smoker as a couple of overflowing ashtrays threatened to fall off the edge of his desk.

'Mr Jenkins, I was talking to Mr Puckeridge across the street, and when I saw your nameplate I thought I would pay you a call. Thank you for seeing me so promptly.'

'Could I ask you straight away, Lord Powerscourt, if the two murders are linked: the one in Netherbury House and the poor man Field found on the edge of the Close?'

Powerscourt could see the headline 'Double Murder' in enormous type flashing across the front page of the *Journal*.

'All I can say, Mr Jenkins, is that there have been two murders. I cannot confirm for the moment whether they are linked or not, I'm afraid.'

'That means they are, in my book. We should know more after the post mortem.'

'Mr Jenkins, you know this little city far better than I do. I have only been here a couple of days. I am sure you are well acquainted with the local branch of Talbot's Stores, but I would not expect you to know much about the business affairs of its managing director. But do you have any idea what might have caused the second one, the lawyer Field? Was there anything suspicious about his life?'

'Very popular man, that Sandy Field, particularly with the ladies. Always had a good word to say about everybody. Almost too good to be true.'

'Were there any exceptions to this golden rule? Mr Field seems to have been one of the most popular men in Lynchester.'

'There's only one concrete example I can give you, I'm afraid, and that isn't very significant.'

'Tell me more.'

'Sandy Field was a key member of the cricket team over at the Close. They play a lot of matches in the summer. He didn't complain most of the time, but Sandy Field had the reputation of arguing when he was given out to what he thought was an unfair decision: dodgy leg before wicket, a catch behind when his bat hadn't touched the ball, that sort of thing. Last July he completely lost his temper when the umpire gave him out on a doubtful call for leg before wicket. It came to blows right there in the middle of the pitch, with the spectators looking on and all. Children watching, too.'

'So what happened next?'

'The wicketkeeper and the other umpire intervened. They had to frog-march him off the pitch. They say he hit his bat so hard on one of the benches in the pavilion that it broke into two pieces.'

'That's a very good story. Did people forget all about it?'

'Well, they did, especially when his teammates rallied round and said it's just Sandy in one of his funny turns. But as I say, it's not significant.'

Sylvester Jenkins was lighting another cigarette from the stub of the old one, which went to join its fellows on the edge of the desk.

'Mr Jenkins, can I make a suggestion? You know more about this little place than almost anybody else, you and your reporters.'

'Two reporters, Lord Powerscourt.'

'The more the merrier, I say. Could I ask you to think of anything, however insignificant, that might have a bearing on these murders? Mr Field must have touched many parts of this little city. And could you let me know? I'm not asking you to incriminate anybody or accuse anybody of murder, I just want information that might help to solve this case.'

'And what are you going to do for us in exchange, Lord Powerscourt?'

'In return, I offer you the following, Mr Jenkins. You come to me when you are about to print an important story about the murders. I will tell you if it's true or not. I'm not going to tell you the inner secrets of the police investigation, mind you. That wouldn't be right.'

'Very good, Lord Powerscourt, it's a deal.'

Powerscourt found Johnny Fitzgerald reading *Country Life* in the hotel reception.

'As I told you when I got here the other day, Lady Lucy said you might be needing reinforcements, Francis. I'm back. What's next?'

There was endless speculation in the Powerscourt household about the affair Johnny was supposed to be having with a rich widow in Warwickshire. But not a word – not even the lady's name – was ever mentioned, so the affair lay between them all like a family secret.

Johnny filled Powerscourt in on the details of his inquiries so far. 'I haven't finished with Sir Edward Talbot yet, but I can tell you that there is not a sniff of anything suspicious about his private life. No illegitimate children, no mistresses, respectable children, the man is only interested in three things: his money, his shops and his family, and the main one of these is money. I have one or two people I haven't talked to yet, but I thought I should report on the story so far.'

'Thank you very much for that, Johnny.'

Powerscourt told him about the second murder, apparently unconnected with the first. He passed on the information about Sandy Field, a man of good cheer, occasionally laid low by fits of temper on the cricket pitch.

'I think he probably did the right thing, having a go at that umpire, Francis. Have you ever noticed the age of the umpires at these country games? They're often retired players from before the Boer War. Blind as bats, some of them.'

'I have no idea if these two murders are linked in any way, Johnny. Neither does the local Inspector, a man called Vaughan.'

'If the first was strychnine, why didn't the first murderer try that again? Once you've seen the bloke take the dose, you can fade out of sight and be far away when the poor man has died.'

'I don't know, Johnny. There are far too many things I don't know in this case. Maybe the first murderer had run out of strychnine. Maybe he couldn't work out a way of getting the victim to drink the bloody stuff. Maybe he thought it would be too obvious.'

'You'd expect there to be some link between them, wouldn't you? But from what you tell me, these two victims mightn't have known each other if they passed in the street.'

'That's true. It's hard to imagine what the connection was, if there was one. Sir Edward wasn't going to buy up a load of shops round here, was he? With Sandy Field as the solicitor? I think that's as good as I can manage for the moment.'

'It all sounds very improbable, Francis. What would you like me to do?'

'Well, Johnny, that depends . . . '

'You're going to send me off somewhere, Francis. I can tell. I've only just come back, for God's sake. Where do you want me to go now?'

'It's all in a good cause, Johnny. I know you're the best man for the job.'

'Where are you sending me this time?'

'I'd like you to go to Oxford, Johnny. Starting with the

solicitors Sandy Field worked for before he came here. They're called Harrison, Moreland and Crooks. They're on the High Street.'

'And I presume you want the normal bag of tricks, Francis? Hand in the till? Clients defrauded? Dubious accounting practices? Work not carried out properly?'

'All of that. And one more?'

'What in heaven's name is that?'

'Women,' said Powerscourt. 'It's only a hunch, mind you, based on something somebody said. But some women find people who can make them laugh very attractive.'

'By God, Francis, that's opening the field out a bit. Carrying on with the customers' wives? Carrying on with the colleagues' wives? Carrying on with wives in general? Is that it?'

'It might be; that's what I want you to find out.'

'Very good,' said Johnny Fitzgerald. 'That's a pretty tall order, if you ask me. I'll try my best, Francis. You know me. There's one other thing. I presume you want the answer the day before yesterday, as usual. I forgot to tell you one thing the day I got here. Lady Lucy sends her love. She says not to take any drinks from strangers, especially in the dark.'

Powerscourt found Inspector Vaughan staring hard at a very large notebook. The page was nearly full.

'Good morning, my lord. I do have a certain amount of information. My men have been fanning out from the Field house at number seventy-four, nearly at the top of the terrace. Now then. The neighbours on either side went to bed and to sleep shortly after ten last night. Field's wife went to bed an hour or so before that. I should

111

tell you that she has some terrible wasting disease and is confined to a wheelchair. Her husband told her not to wait up for him as he had some work to do in his study. She never saw him alive again. She was very matter of fact about the whole thing. Nobody heard the shot; nobody heard a thing. Mind you, there's an awful lot of houses still to call on in the Close. My men must be tired of knocking on the same doors over and over again. One of them offered to bring a tent and sleep out overnight. He said it would save time the following morning.'

'There are always moments in investigations like this,' said Powerscourt, 'when you feel you're never going to get to the bottom of it.'

'That's true, my lord, very true. Now, I have more news. I went to see the manager of the local Talbot's Store down the road. I remembered what you had told us from your time in London about the rumour that some, or all, of the shops might be sold. If that were the case, it might be that Ardglass, Puckeridge and Ross could have been approached to handle the legal side of things, and perhaps that Sandy Field was the solicitor at this end. A long shot, my lord, but I thought it worth a try. It would at least provide a link between the two dead men.'

'And what did he say, the man from Talbot's?'

'The manager there is called Williams, Robert Williams. I think he sings in one of those choirs they run up at the cathedral. Not a word of a possible sale had reached him; not a hint, not even a rumour. He did point out, however, rather sadly, I thought, that he and his staff would have been the last to hear if the shop was going to be closed. "We'd arrive at work one morning and find the whole bloody place locked up" was how he put it. He wasn't complaining, he said. The Talbots were good people to work for on the whole. They paid well. They were just very secretive. Mr Williams said that – as far as he knew – Sir Edward hadn't visited the store the day he came for the interview at the cathedral. Mind you, he also said that he didn't think any of the staff would have recognized him if he had.'

'So,' said Powerscourt, 'they had heard nothing of a plan to sell the store?'

'Yes and no, my lord. You see, he also said that if anything like that was going to happen, all the legal work would be done by the people at head office. He said they were buying stores all the time up there, as he put it.'

The offices of Finn and Company were on the edge of the ancient part of Lynchester. Inspector Vaughan had given the name to Powerscourt that morning. Michael Finn was bent over his desk, making notes with a pencil on a long legal document in front of him. He looked, Powerscourt thought, as though he had been to the second-hand department of the solicitors' clothing shop patronized by Mr Puckeridge. The suit was respectable but well worn. The collar on his shirt was starting to fray. His dark blue tie had seen better days. He shook Powerscourt by the hand and showed him to a chair.

'Lord Powerscourt, how good to make your acquaintance. I believe you are here to investigate these terrible murders. Is that right?'

'It is. I am here at the invitation of the Bishop.'

'And how can we be of assistance here? As you probably know, the solicitors who look after cathedral affairs are Ardglass, Puckeridge and Ross up the street. We have no dealings with them here.'

Was there a hint of something – envy; resentment, perhaps – in the way he said Ardglass, Puckeridge and Ross?

'Mr Finn, I will be frank with you. I hope we can regard this conversation as off the record.'

The solicitor nodded.

'In my profession we are used to looking for the dark side of the moon and the planets. Sometimes we entertain the most extraordinary conjectures. It is in that spirit that I would ask you to hear me out.'

Michael Finn nodded. He began twirling a pencil round in his fingers.

'I am not only here about the murder of Sir Edward Talbot, Mr Finn, but also with the case of your fellow solicitor, Sandy Field.'

'I see.' Finning to look rather uneasy.

'Is there anything you can tell me about your rivals here, the firm of Ardglass, Puckeridge and Ross?'

The pencil was turning faster and faster now. Finn began looking at the door, as if some unexpected visitor might burst in at any moment.

'Yes,' he said. 'I see.' There was silence in the little office.

'Is anything the matter, Mr Finn?'

'Forgive me, Lord Powerscourt, I just don't feel comfortable talking about it here.'

Powerscourt thought he could see the problem. The secretary or one of his colleagues might burst in at any moment. Locking the door could only arouse suspicion.

'Why don't you come to my hotel, Mr Finn? I have a private sitting room and nobody will disturb us there unless we send out for some tea. Perhaps you would like to come round this afternoon, after you have sorted out your affairs here? Maybe we could say four o'clock?'

'Thank you, Lord Powerscourt. Thank you for being

so understanding. I don't feel at all comfortable talking about Sandy Field and his firm here, and that's a fact. I look forward to seeing you this afternoon. Four o'clock would be fine.'

Powerscourt had the tea, complete with scones and chocolate cake, ready for Mr Finn at four o'clock. He wondered if Finn would bring his twirling pencil with him. On the hour he was shown in and took a seat by the window.

'Do you know, Lord Powerscourt, I've never been in this room before. There's a little cubbyhole of a place for hotel legal work they put you in downstairs, which is just about adequate for business but no more.' Powerscourt presumed that the offices of Finn and Company didn't run to a boardroom.

Powerscourt helped Michael Finn to a cup of tea and a slice of chocolate cake. He suspected suddenly that this wasn't going to be easy. He thought it might be like drawing teeth.

'Now then, Lord Powerscourt,' Finn began, 'I've been thinking about the matters we discussed this morning. I've decided to tell you the truth, although I'm not sure what good that will do.'

The pencil was out again. Powerscourt wondered if he took it to bed with him.

'It may well be that there is a perfectly innocent explanation for what I'm about to tell you. You see, there is something not quite right about Ardglass, Puckeridge and Ross. I'm not saying there's something illegal about them. But there is something wrong all the same. I checked on my client lists before I came up here this afternoon. In the past two years I have looked after eleven clients who had previously been with Mr Puckeridge and his colleagues. Eleven means that it is unlikely to be a coincidence.'

'Did they give a reason for coming to see you instead of the other firm?'

'Not in so many words, they didn't. They just said that they were no longer happy with their treatment. It was as if they were all leaving their doctor for unspecified reasons. Now I was placed in a difficult position. Naturally I would have liked to ask for more details of what had gone wrong, but I have obligations to my fellow solicitors as well as to my clients. One of them muttered about financial irregularities. It had to do with a will.'

'Did you ask what that meant?'

'I'm afraid I did. I'm not sure I did the right thing there. The fellow muttered that he thought the charges were very high.'

'Did you ask what the charges were, Mr Finn?' The pencil now looked as though it was in training for some acrobatic pencil contest.

'I did not; I thought that would be going too far.'

'I see,' said Powerscourt. 'Mr Finn, I do not think you would have come to see me this afternoon if the matter only concerned some financial overcharging. Ardglass, Puckeridge and Ross are an old-established firm with a considerable reputation here in the city. Maybe they felt justified in doing that. Experience tells me that there are a number of ways in which a solicitor can make money out of wills. And, no doubt, they would ensure that they are the executors. They wouldn't even have to tell anybody about the odd three or four hundred or three or four thousand pounds left to the solicitors. How does that sound, Mr Finn?'

Michael Finn smiled. 'What devious minds you

investigators must have, Lord Powerscourt. I don't know exactly how they do it, but it certainly sounds plausible. The key, I think, lies in their being the executors. And they could simply include a very high rate of charges on all the wills they handle. The bereaved aren't going to be in the mood to argue.'

'How many wills do you suppose Ardglass, Puckeridge and Ross look after in an average year?'

'I don't know the answer to that,' said Michael Finn. Powerscourt noted that the pencil had stopped moving. 'Thirty or forty? I'm afraid I don't know the exact figure.'

'In the course of a year, they could make a considerable sum of money; more, I suspect, than any of the solicitors would make from his salary. Would that be right?'

'I suspect it may be right, but I don't know. You see, Lord Powerscourt, I think they may just overcharge for everything: conveyancing, dealing with leases, handling disputes and so on. It won't be too large for a row, but it will produce a great deal of extra income. I have to say that I could not appear in court and breathe a single word of this.'

'I understand, Mr Finn. I am most grateful to you. Can you think of any way in which this malfeasance might have a bearing on the murder of Sandy Field? We are still off the record, as you know.'

'I'm afraid I can't see any connection at all. Can you?'

'Not at the moment, Mr Finn. Now then, I must let you get back to your business. If anything further occurs to you, perhaps you could leave a message here at the hotel?'

'Of course.' Michael Finn put his wandering pencil back in his pocket and went back to his offices. Powerscourt wondered if he had just witnessed a large bunch of sour grapes.

10

Johnny Fitzgerald was buying drinks for the chief reporter of the local Oxford newspaper in the King's Head in Summertown. Charlie Johnston looked as though he was close to retirement. He was of normal height, with hair turning white at the temples, and was smoking a pipe.

'You said that you wanted some information, Mr Fitzgerald. How can I help?'

'It's rather a long shot, Mr Johnston. I'm looking for information about a solicitor called Sandy Field who worked for a time here in Oxford for a firm called Harrison, Moreland and Crooks. My information is that he left here for Lynchester about six or seven years ago.'

'There's nothing unusual about that, surely?'

'The thing is this,' said Johnny. 'Our friend Field was murdered in Lynchester several days ago. I wonder if news had reached Oxford yet. And I should say that I am a colleague of an investigator called Lord Francis Powerscourt who has been asked to look into the matter by the Bishop. The Lynchester Police will be in touch with their colleagues in Oxford in the next few days, if they haven't done so already.'

Charlie Johnston frowned. He sent a small cloud of smoke just past Johnny's left ear. 'Did he play a lot of cricket, this Sandy man?'

'I believe he did.'

Charlie Johnston laughed. 'I've got him now, Mr Fitzgerald. He's the man they called the Casanova of the Cotswolds. He was caught in bed with one of the other solicitors' wives. This information never reached the paper through official channels, Mr Fitzgerald, and we wouldn't have printed it even if it came from more orthodox sources. We only heard about it because one of our reporters was brother-in-law to one of the solicitors at Harrison, Moreland and Crooks. Not the one with the misbehaving wife, I hasten to add. We kept asking this man – I can't for the life of me remember his name for the moment – out for lunch to get the latest news.'

'How was he caught? Mr Field, I mean.'

'He was a very charming man by all accounts, this fellow Field. Always able to make people laugh and smile, that sort of thing. He was caught by accident. I believe these sorts of affairs often end through unforeseen and unforeseeable events. Field could tell which partner was out of the office on business at any time of the day. He just had to ask the secretary, who would usually let him know when the other fellow was coming back. Prothero, that was the name of the man. Like Field, he wasn't a partner or anything like that. Once Field knew Prothero was out of the building for the next two hours, he knew the coast was clear and popped round to Prothero's house for a spot of Casanova-style activity.'

Charlie Johnston asked for a refill, blowing smoke clouds at the bar to indicate it was time for another double whisky. He blew an extra-large cloud when Johnny brought back the drinks.

'Thank you, Mr Fitzgerald. As I was saying, it was all an accident. Prothero received a call one morning to go and see the bursar of one of the colleges. It doesn't matter which one. On the way, his bike took a puncture. He wasn't very far from home. He popped in to collect his kit to repair the thing. He heard noises upstairs. Sandy Field fled through the front door, buttoning up his shirt as he went, but it was no good. Prothero, so we were told, went slightly mad, shouting at his wife and bashing his bicycle against the wall of his shed. Sandy Field went back to the office and tried to pretend that nothing had happened.'

'So how did the firm react to this domestic difficulty? Did they all try to pretend nothing had happened?'

'Well, they tried at first to play it all down. People's private lives are none of their business, that sort of thing. But the tension in the office grew unbearable. Prothero found it virtually impossible to be in the same room as Field. Field tried to take some time off but they wouldn't let him. After a few days of this, Prothero said he was going round to Field's house to tell Field's wife about the affair. That seemed to bring matters to a head.'

'What do you mean, Mr Johnston?'

'Well, they didn't want to lose Field, you see. They'd much rather have lost Prothero – and probably Mrs Prothero, too, if it came to it. Field was very good at bringing new business into the practice. Prothero wasn't as good a solicitor; more of a journeyman, who wouldn't make a mistake but who would never set the Cherwell on fire. But there was no doubt who was at fault. So they asked Field to resign. And he did.'

'Do you know if there were any conditions attached to his departure, Mr Johnston? Did they say they would recommend him to other firms without mentioning his Casanova-type tendencies?'

'I'm afraid I don't know the answer to that. If you asked me to hazard a guess, I would say that Sandy Field made that silence a condition of his departure. Otherwise he wouldn't have got another job in the legal profession, would he? No senior partner is going to take on a man with a track record in sleeping with other people's wives, especially the wives of his own staff. Solicitors are meant to be above suspicion.'

'And who should I speak to at Harrison, Moreland and Crooks?'

'I think you should speak to Mr Harrison himself, Mr Fitzgerald. He is the senior partner. I'm fairly sure he was senior partner at the time of the Casanova Field affair. Please don't, for God's sake, tell him that you've been buying me large whiskies in the King's Head here in Summertown.'

William Burke found Powerscourt on the point of leaving his hotel in Lynchester. He was, he told his brother-in-law, checking out a chain of small country banks that his firm was thinking of buying.

'My God, William, you're just as bad as the Talbot man – buying up the opposition, growing ever larger in the process.'

Burke laughed. 'I can assure you, Francis, that those

banks would become much more efficient if we were to take them over.'

'I'm sure that's what Talbot's people would have told Scott's Stores as they moved in for the kill.'

'Not so fast, Francis, if you please. I haven't dropped by for a discussion on the merits of acquisitions in the commercial sector. I came to tell you the latest rumours in the world of finance and groceries, that's all. You should be grateful.'

'I am, William. Sorry about that.'

'The latest news is that there is as yet no indication about what, if anything, Talbot's are going to do. There are strong rumours, mostly from unreliable sources, that Jonathan Talbot, eldest son and heir, is going to buy the Scott's Stores that compete directly with Talbot's and close them down. But for the time being he is in mourning, and not thought to be returning to business for a week or more.'

'Do you mean that all those people who work in the Scott's Stores selected for early closure do not know what is going to happen to them? And that they may lose their jobs within a month?'

'I do mean that, Francis.'

'It would make me pretty cross,' said Powerscourt, wondering if the loss of one's job could be a sufficient motive for murder.

Edmund Harrison looked like the Master of one of the Oxford colleges. He was tall and clean-shaven with a Roman nose. He was wearing a dark blue suit with an almost invisible pinstripe. His office, right in the heart of Oxford, was lined with books and prints of Oxford landmarks. He showed Johnny to a chair by the fire.

'Fitzgerald, did you say? A colleague of a certain Lord Powerscourt? Did you not serve in Intelligence in the Boer War?'

'We did, Mr Harrison. I did not think our fame had spread so far.'

'I have a brother who served in that conflict. He still speaks of you both and the trials of war against the Boers. Now then, how can I help you today?'

Johnny Fitzgerald decided to take advantage of his temporary military glory. He would lay his cards on the table straight away rather than peeling them off one by one.

'Mr Harrison, I have come about your former partner here, Sandy Field. He was found murdered a few days ago in the little cathedral city of Lynchester. He was working there for a firm called Ardglass, Puckeridge and Ross. I suspect he went there with a reference from you. And I have to say that I have been told about the affair between Mrs Prothero and Mr Field that led to his departure from here.'

'You are remarkably well informed, Mr Fitzgerald. I trust that none of that information came to you from an employee of mine here.'

Johnny thought the punishment for bad behaviour might be pretty severe. 'No sir, none of my information came from inside your firm.'

'So what would you like me to tell you, Mr Fitzgerald? I presume that our conversation is confidential.'

'Of course,' said Johnny. 'I would like to know what you feel you can tell me about Sandy Field, as a lawyer and as a colleague. I would like to know if there were any other matters, apart from the business with the wife of Mr Prothero, that led to his departure.'

'Very well,' the solicitor said, folding his arms over his waistcoat. 'I will do what I can to help. Seven years it is since Sandy Field left us. I have to say, Mr Fitzgerald, that I grew very fond of him while he was here. He was energetic, he was cheerful, he seemed to work hard; he had charm that could bring the birds out of the trees and the wives out of their marriage vows. If there was a tricky case involving complicated disputes over ownership of land, the charm was sometimes so powerful that the parties signed up to an agreement before they remembered how much they hated each other. The affair with the wife of a colleague, that was very sad. He should never have done it. It was playing with fire, if you like. I have often wondered, looking back on it, if Sandy wasn't a man who liked playing with fire.'

'Could I just ask one question? You imply that there were other affairs – apart from the one with Mrs Prothero – that might have come to your attention? Was the man a compulsive womanizer? One of those who can't stop themselves?'

'I don't know the answer to that, Mr Fitzgerald. Certainly there had been other affairs. He must have had a tolerant wife if she knew the half of what was said to have been going on. Word of these encounters only reached me by hearsay, Mr Fitzgerald. I'm sure there are plenty of people in Oxford conducting illicit affairs all the time. It's just that we don't get to hear about them. But an affair with the wife of a colleague went too far. He had to go.'

'Forgive me for asking you this, Mr Harrison, but do you think it possible that any of these aggrieved husbands could have gone down to Lynchester to kill him?'

'Seven years later? I doubt it, but it's not absolutely impossible. It may be that there are a whole lot of deceived husbands down there – new ones, as it were – who would like to see him dead. Sandy Field might have been a chastened character, but I doubt if he had changed very much.'

'I see.'

'There is one other thing I should let you know about, Mr Fitzgerald.' Harrison was looking rather embarrassed now. 'What I am about to tell you is, potentially, even more incendiary than the adultery.'

'And what might that be?'

'Sandy Field was a most accomplished forger. I do not think he ever used that ability to defraud our clients, but there it was. He made no secret of it. He used to forge the partners' signatures in front of them to raise a laugh.'

'God bless my soul, Mr Harrison. So he could forge the signature of some unfortunate old lady on a will, perhaps?'

'I think that would be taking things too far, Mr Fitzgerald. The forging was more of a conjurer's turn, a party trick if you like. People are quick to jump to conclusions about greedy doctors or solicitors influencing old ladies and their wills. But forging their signature, though superficially attractive, would be a very hard thing to pull off.'

'Really?'

'Let me explain,' said the solicitor. 'Suppose we're talking about a will. Just think about the various obstacles in your path. You could certainly forge the signature of your victim. That would not be difficult. To have any hope of success you need to find an old lady or an old gentleman with no relations left alive. If there are members of the family still living, they will probably have been told of their relation's intentions before he or she passes away. If not, they will certainly contest the will in court, if, say, half or a third of the money goes to the family solicitor. Even if you think the deceased had no relations, you could be wrong. Long-lost nephews, genuine or not, could appear on the scene, crying foul. Suppose you attempt to dilute your criminality, as it were, and leave some money to the housekeeper and the domestic staff and the doctor concerned, and the hospital and the home for stray cats and dogs. Some relation could still appear and challenge you in the courts. If a housekeeper is advised by some mercenary lawyer to sue because she has been left five hundred pounds rather than the promised five thousand, the forgery will appear in court and may be examined by people claiming to be handwriting experts. That could prove to be the end of you. Anybody intending to forge wills in their favour would need nerves of steel. You could be undone at any moment. The really insurmountable problem is ignorance of the relations who may come out of the woodwork to say they have a better claim on the money than you do.'

Harrison paused and took some snuff out of his waistcoat pocket. 'It was for those reasons that I did not mention the forging facility when I wrote to Ardglass, Puckeridge and Ross about Sandy Field.'

'I beg your pardon?'

'I did not mention the forging facility when I wrote to the Lynchester solicitors.'

'God in heaven,' said Johnny Fitzgerald.

Part Two
Cherchez la Femme

11

Powerscourt was with the Bishop, sitting opposite him in front of the fire. It was still cold in Lynchester, in spite of the early spring sunshine. He had come about a question that had been bothering him for some time.

'Bishop, my apologies for troubling you. You have a diocese to run and I don't want to take up too much of your time.'

'Please continue, Lord Powerscourt, I always have time to talk to you.'

'My question does not require an answer, Bishop, and I shall not be offended if you decline to answer. It concerns the death of Simon Jones, the old man who lived in Netherbury House and then died of an overdose. It is, of course, the matter you came to see me about in London some time ago. You were worried that the housekeeper, Mrs McQuaid, might have given Mr Jones the overdose to put him out of his misery. The last I heard from you was that you were still considering what to do for the best. Is that still your position, or have you seen fit to talk it over with the Chief Constable?'

'I should certainly have consulted you before speaking to the Chief Constable, Lord Powerscourt. My position remains in the undecided column. I have not made up my mind what to do. I do not need to tell you about the impact on opinion in Lynchester of another death, even if it was a mercy killing. I shall certainly consult you before taking things any further.'

There was a terrible refrain running through Powerscourt's brain as he made his way across the Green. Two murders or three? Two murders or three? Were they all related? Was there one central thread that ran through them? The question would not leave him alone. He had a sudden urge to speak to Lady Lucy. He would ring her up and invite her down to Lynchester as soon as she could get away. He resolved to point out that this was not an embarkation point for round-the-world cruises. Apart from the little river, the place was entirely landlocked.

Johnny Fitzgerald was staring at Edmund Harrison. 'Let me make this clear, Mr Harrison. You knew that Sandy Field, apart from his adulterous activities, was a skilled forger, capable of replicating the signatures of anybody in your office. Yet you chose not to mention the fact when asked to provide a reference by the Lynchester solicitors. Is that right?'

'It is.'

'Why not?'

'I didn't think it relevant to his abilities as a solicitor, which were considerable.'

'So what did you tell them?'

'I said that he was leaving us for personal reasons. That was all.'

'You didn't mention the affair with your colleague's wife?'

'No.'

'Did you discuss the letter of recommendation with Mr Field?'

'I did, as a matter of fact.'

'Did he ask you to ignore the business with Prothero's wife? Or the forging?'

'I do not propose to answer that question. I should point out to you that there have been no reported cases of forged wills or forged cheques in Lynchester since Mr Field went there. That would seem to support my earlier arguments.'

'Let me put the question another way, Mr Harrison. If a solicitor came to you, looking for work here, with a reference that stated he carried on with colleagues' wives and was an accomplished forger, would you have given him a job?'

'Now that you put it like that, I don't think I would.'

'And would you have expected the Lynchester solicitors to have given him a job?'

'I do not propose to answer that question, Mr Fitzgerald. It is not for me to speak on behalf of another firm in another city.'

'Mr Harrison, you have been very patient with me, and I am grateful for that. Let me try to phrase my question in another way. You liked Sandy Field, I think. Most people did. But he could do your firm a great deal of damage if he talked. Nobody is going to be in a hurry to place their most intimate affairs in the hands of a firm of solicitors where the solicitors or a solicitor are involved with their colleagues' wives. It doesn't feel right. You were worried about the reputation of your firm if the affair became public knowledge. I only heard about it by accident. You were anxious to get Sandy Field out of the way. So I think you did a deal with him. If he promised never to speak of the events which led to his departure from your firm, you would minimize his faults to any prospective employers. Would that be right, Mr Harrison?'

There was no answer from the other side of the desk.

'Thank you, Mr Harrison. Your silence says it all. I suspect that the precise terms of any deal or any understanding between yourself and Sandy Field may not have been exactly as I described, but there was a deal of some sort. Let me ask you another question if I may? Have you kept in touch with Mr Field since he left here?'

'I have, as a matter of fact. We correspond a couple of times a year. I think he was grateful for the way his departure was handled. That, after all, enabled him to secure another position. And not a whiff of scandal has there been since in the seven years since he left us.'

'Not unless you include being murdered, Mr Harrison.'

'I don't need to tell you that murder victims seldom choose to get themselves killed, Mr Fitzgerald.'

'I take your point. Could I ask when you last heard from him?'

'It was a couple of weeks ago.'

'And did he mention anything that might be relevant to Lord Powerscourt's inquiries?'

'He did, as a matter of fact. I was going to mention it to you before you left. Mr Field was looking after the sale of Netherbury House for the Dean and the Bishop. He would have looked after the legal side of things. He was also involved with the drawing up of a shortlist and the final selection of the candidates for interview. He said it was very interesting work. Perhaps I could ask you a question, Mr Fitzgerald?'

'I have asked plenty of questions, so please carry on.'

'Do you think that may have led to his death, his links to Netherbury House?'

'If I could answer that, Mr Harrison, I wouldn't be here. It could well be relevant – but how it might be relevant, I have at present no idea at all.'

Ambrose Mills, the captain of the Lynchester Close cricket team, lived in a house right in the middle of the crescent, with a view straight down to the cathedral. He was in his early forties with curly brown hair and a small beard.

'Lord Powerscourt, I have been expecting you. I presume you have come to talk about Sandy, God rest his soul.'

'Thank you, Mr Mills, I'm grateful for your time.'

'Let me tell you what I know about Sandy as a cricketer. You won't be surprised to hear that he was a flamboyant player. He batted at number four, which I'm sure you know is one of the key positions in the team line-up. His best score last season was sixty-nine not out against Winchampton, who are a good side. Many people in that slot accumulate their runs slowly, accelerating as they get the measure of the bowling. Sandy wasn't like that at all. It made no difference what the score was, he attacked the bowling with verve and vigour from the very first ball. A great many of his runs came from boundaries. The problem came when he had scored twenty or thirty. It wasn't quite as if he had a rush of blood to the head, he just grew overconfident. I know he's apologized to me often enough for getting himself out going for an over-ambitious six over the bowler's head. He couldn't help himself.'

'Did he bowl as well?'

'After a fashion, Lord Powerscourt; he bowled rather erratic off-breaks. Some days he would get two or three wickets; on the bad days he'd be hit all over the ground and have to be taken off before he lost the match because he was so expensive.'

'Anything else, Mr Mills? What else should I know about him as a cricketer?'

'Just one thing, Lord Powerscourt. He was a remarkable slip fielder, easily the best in the team. He could catch people out low down near the ground or high above his head, it didn't seem to matter. The ball stuck to his hands like a piece of glue. He was no good anywhere else. But he was superb in the slips.'

'And what was he like as a teammate? People in your position usually get a pretty good idea of the character of their teammates.'

Ambrose Mills paused for a moment. 'He was flamboyant; always cheerful, always anxious to win whatever the quality of the opposition. He was a popular member of the team. His fault was this recklessness, the death-or-glory ride, if you like. I've often wondered how he coped with it in his profession. But that's not my problem.'

'There is one other matter, not connected with cricket, on which I would welcome your opinion, Mr Mills.'

'You're going to ask me about women and girlfriends, aren't you? You seem to have your ear pressed pretty close to the ground here in Lynchester, Lord Powerscourt. I'm afraid I can't help you there. I only knew him as a cricketer. You're not likely to tell anyone your secrets when you're on duty as first slip. I am the wicketkeeper, you see.'

'I'm sure you understand, Mr Mills, that there can be no secrets in a murder investigation. Often they turn up all sorts of information that proves to be irrelevant in the end. But we have to find out as many of the facts as we can before we decide to throw them away. Is there anybody else in Lynchester who might be able to help me?'

'I thought you would ask me that, Lord Powerscourt. This is a bow drawn at a venture. Sandy had a friend who teaches history at the school here. He too plays for the eleven, though he is as cautious a batsman as Sandy Field was flamboyant. His name is Perry, William Perry. If you're quick you could just catch him before he packs up school for the day. I think he's the only teacher I know – and there are a number of them in our cricket teams – who doesn't complain about marking.'

'Thank you so much for that, Mr Mills. I'm most grateful for your help.'

'Please come back if there's anything more I can tell you, Lord Powerscourt. We're just as keen on finding Sandy Field's murderer as you are. You see, he was one of our own.'

Inspector Vaughan was working on the final draft of the evidence collected round the houses of the terraces and the crescent. He shook his head when he had finished. It was hard to believe that so much effort had produced so little hard evidence. It was almost as if they needn't have bothered at all.

* * *

Twenty minutes later, schoolmaster Perry had been rescued from the delights of common-room tea and installed beside the fire in Powerscourt's private sitting room in the King's Arms. He must have been about the same age as Sandy Field, with brown hair and blue eyes and a weary air about him, as if the education of the young was proving rather a burden.

'Tea should be here presently, Mr Perry. As I said on the way over, I have been asked by the Bishop to investigate recent events in Lynchester.'

'I think everyone in the city knows who you are by now, Lord Powerscourt. I suspect the local cats discuss your progress in night meetings at the back of the cathedral.'

Powerscourt smiled. 'I don't think Ambrose Mills will mind if I take his name in vain. It was he who suggested I talk to you.'

'And what would you want to talk to me about?' asked the schoolteacher warily.

'Ambrose Mills talked to me about Sandy Field the cricketer. I would ask you to talk to me about Sandy Field, the ladies' man.'

'I thought that would be it. You could say in a sense that I knew you or somebody like you would be coming.'

He paused for a drink of the tea that had just been delivered.

'I know this is difficult for you, Mr Perry – much more difficult than if you were just talking about cricket or the latest history curriculum. I wouldn't be asking if I didn't think it could be central to the question of who killed Sandy Field.'

There was a further pause for another drink of tea. 'I know that, Lord Powerscourt. I must say that I do find this very difficult. Taking a group of senior boys through religious legislation under Henry the Eighth is a much easier proposition than this. I should say from the start that I only know what Sandy told me. There could be scores of other women he has been involved with whom I have never heard of.'

'I understand, Mr Perry.'

'I think I should say something at the start about Sandy's wife. You probably know that she fell victim to some wasting disease some time ago, just after they came here. She's handicapped now, Beatrice Field; she can only get around in a wheelchair. She's taken to religion in a big way, reading the collect every morning and the Bible every afternoon. Sometimes she gets herself wheeled over to evensong and the clergy always make a great fuss of her. I'm not saying that's an excuse for bad behaviour, but I thought it could be relevant.'

'You have my word on that.'

'As I said, there are only two ladies I can talk about, because Sandy told me about them. I don't think he was boasting when he told me, he just wanted to get it off his chest. Rose Deacon was married to a banker who spent a lot of the week up in London. I don't know how the affair started. Rose was always very discreet. Sandy said to me once that he was thinking of instituting a system of smoke signals so he would know when the coast was clear. This went on for a couple of months. Then she broke it off. I suspect that she finished the affair in case she fell seriously in love with Sandy. She was getting out while she still had time. That's what Sandy hinted to me when he told me the affair was over. I think they still see each other even now, but it's purely platonic.'

William Perry paused. 'I think you said there were two ladies, Mr Perry?' said Powerscourt, as gently as he could.

137

'There were, Lord Powerscourt. The second one is more difficult. Some people like danger. I'm sure they're the first over the difficult fences on the hunting field. They will try to hit a dramatic six when a regular four might also be available. Julia Brooks was one of these people. She is probably the best-looking woman in Lynchester – quite small, black hair, eyes that seem to dance at you when she is animated. It was as if she had the same temperament as Sandy. They were both drawn to danger like moths to a flame. Julia's husband is a rising lawyer, appearing regularly now at the Old Bailey. So he was away a lot.'

'Did they have any children?'

'Do you know, I don't have the answer to that. What I do know is that Sandy and Julia would flaunt themselves around the place, dinners here and in the other hotel down the street. They didn't seem to care. It was as if they were daring somebody to tell the husband what was going on.'

'And did they? I'm sorry, did somebody tell the husband what was going on?'

'Not as far as I know. Sandy and Julia were seen together at a concert in the cathedral only last week. Maybe the husband still doesn't know about it. I hope nobody bothers to tell him now. You could tell they were lovers when they were together, Lord Powerscourt. You know how it is – it's as if you could almost touch the electricity flowing between them.'

'I don't suppose you know the answer to this question, but do you know if Sandy Field told them about his wife?'

'I don't know the answer to that, Lord Powerscourt. It wasn't as if Sandy and I had regular heart-to-hearts about these affairs. He only let slip a few clues every now and then. I don't think he liked talking about his private life very much. There was one interesting cricket match this summer, here on home ground. Julia had come to watch and was sitting with the others outside the pavilion. Sandy scored a dashing fifty before he was caught on the boundary. When he got back to the pavilion, he laid his bat down in front of her, as if he was some medieval knight at a jousting tournament. It was like writing a message in the sky that they were lovers.'

'What did Julia do with this tribute?'

'She laughed it off and told him to stop being ridiculous. Secretly I suspect she was rather proud. They'd flown very close to the sun again and lived to fight another day. I think part of her wanted to be Queen of the May. She rather liked it when he came before her with vine leaves in his hair, as it were.'

'This has been very helpful, Mr Perry. Is there anything else you could tell me?'

'I don't think there is, Lord Powerscourt. I presume I can find you here if anything further occurs to me. I must get home to my family and my marking.'

As the schoolteacher made his way home, Powerscourt reflected that, at last, he had one, maybe two, candidates, with very good motives for murdering Sandy Field.

Inspector Vaughan and his Sergeant, Thomas Pendry, were waiting for Powerscourt in their little office at the police station. Powerscourt passed on the information from Perry about Sandy Field's love life.

'My word, he's been a very busy boy,' said the Inspector. 'We'll come to that later when I've run through the statements made to the Constables in the two terraces and the crescent.

'Though I can't say I've found this assembly of evidence very fruitful. On the contrary, it's almost no use at all.'

Inspector Vaughan peered closely at the sheet of paper in front of him. 'I've divided it into two parts, the evidence relating to the murder of Sir Edward Talbot. Enter here, the man in black, possibly seen on the river, destination of travel unknown. The man could have been going up or down, towards or away from Netherbury House. The witness thought he was dressed in black, possibly with a black hat. That is all we have on the Talbot murder. There was no reaction at all when Lord Powerscourt and I took a boat ride down the river a couple of days later. I have to admit that I suspect the two murders may not be linked at all. Sir Edward knew nobody here. It was his first visit. One conclusion from the evidence, or lack of it, would be that his killer or killers came down from London. Any comments so far, gentlemen?'

Neither Powerscourt nor Sergeant Pendry had anything to add at this stage.

'Right,' Inspector Vaughan continued, 'we now come to the murder of Sandy Field. Here we have a man in grey, spotted at about ten o'clock, though the witness at number sixty-two West Terrace wasn't clear about the time. She thought he might have been walking his dog. The man at number eighty-two heard a door bang at about a quarter past ten. He thought it might have been a gun, though whether he thought that at the time, or after he'd heard about the murder, I don't know. It could have been somebody shutting their back door very loudly.

'The woman at number fifty-six thought she'd heard a

scream, though she admitted it could have been one of the neighbours having a row. She explained to Constable Sweet that the people in number fifty-eight were always having noisy rows, and gave it as her opinion that it was time the police did something about it.

'Number forty thought she heard footsteps on the cobbles shortly after ten. Number twenty-two thought he heard a back door being closed by the drawing of the bolts at about ten past ten. He was sure of the time, he said, because he looked at the kitchen clock.

'There was nothing from the crescent, and only one report from the other terrace at number thirty-eight, where the owner heard piano music. It transpired after a conversation with number forty that this was only the husband practising. He is, apparently, a newcomer to the piano and waits for his wife to go to bed before practising – she refers to his playing as "that infernal noise".

'So there we have it, gentlemen,' the Inspector concluded.

'I suppose,' said Powerscourt, 'that after the man in black, it would be too much to hope for a woman in white.'

'I fear she could take some time to appear, my lord. I think we should consider the new evidence about Field's women that Lord Powerscourt brought us at the beginning of this meeting. My lord, do you have any thoughts in the matter?'

'Obviously somebody should talk to the wives and husbands concerned.'

'Absolutely, my lord. The question is, who should talk to them? I fear that they would be more likely to talk to you than to us. Even in plain clothes, words like Inspector and Sergeant carry a lot of baggage. People may feel they are about to be arrested and clam up. I fear we shall have to ask you to talk to the women, Lord Powerscourt.'

'Thank you very much,' said Powerscourt, who had suspected for some time that this was coming. 'It's damnably difficult. The husbands will all see straight away that if they say they knew about the affair, they will be instantly promoted to the top of the suspects' column. If I were them, even if I did know about the affair, I still wouldn't say a word. Not to me, anyway. Certainly not to me, because talking to me is just the same as talking to a policeman.'

'But what if they both had cast-iron alibis, Lord Powerscourt? Then we could remove them from the list of suspects.'

'The problem, as you can see as well as I can, is that it's very difficult to ask the one question that brings you there in the first place. "Did you know your wife was having an affair with Sandy Field?" You might get thrown out on the spot. And we have to remember that even if they knew of the affair, that doesn't make them a murderer.'

'I wonder if it's possible to tell whether they knew or not from the way people talk and behave,' said Sergeant Pendry.

'I'm sure it is,' said Powerscourt. 'Do you gentlemen have an address for the Deacons, Inspector? I thought I might get one of them out of the way this evening. Half past six is not too late to call.'

'Number eighteen The Crescent, my lord. I shall await your return with interest.'

'Wish me luck,' said Powerscourt, and set off on his mission.

* * *

The parlour maid opened the door. 'Mr Deacon is still in London, my lord. Mrs Deacon is in the drawing room.'

It was easy to understand what Sandy Field had seen in Rose Deacon. She had dark brown hair on top of a very pretty face with bright brown eyes. She was re-arranging the flowers in her drawing room as he came in. She hadn't had the curtains drawn yet, and there was a clear view of the front of the cathedral.

'How do you do, Lord Powerscourt. The flowers look better now, don't you think?'

'They look lovely, Mrs Deacon,' said Powerscourt, taking a seat by the window. 'Forgive me for calling on you so late in the day.'

'That doesn't matter at all; my husband is working late in London. So I will at least have someone to talk to.'

Powerscourt wondered suddenly if this might have been a time for Sandy Field to drop by in the days when they were having an affair. 'I should tell you, Mrs Deacon, that I am an investigator, here at the invitation of the Bishop to look into these terrible murders.'

'We never met that poor man Talbot with the grocery shops, Lord Powerscourt. But I suspect you have come to talk to me about Sandy Field. Such a tragedy. So young to die too soon in such horrible circumstances, don't you think?'

'Absolutely, Mrs Deacon. Could I ask you how well you knew Mr Field?'

'Of course,' she said. Was that a faint blush on her cheeks? 'I knew him very well for a time, but it didn't last very long. I don't suppose anybody is suggesting I killed him, are they?'

'Certainly not, Mrs Deacon. I only met Mr Field very briefly. Perhaps you could tell me what sort of a man he was?'

'He was good looking,' said Mrs Deacon, that faint blush still visible on her cheeks; 'he was quick, he was funny, he made everybody laugh. I don't think anybody would deny that the staff of a cathedral are a pretty serious lot. Sandy brightened the place up – not that he worked at the cathedral, of course, but he had a lot of dealings with the people there. He made everybody feel better the minute he walked into a room.'

'Did all the ladies fall a little in love with him, Mrs Deacon?'

Rose Deacon laughed. 'Of course, Lord Powerscourt – certainly all the ladies in the Close.'

'You implied earlier that you were lately not as close to him as you were once. Could I ask if there was a reason?'

'Reason, as I'm sure you know, Lord Powerscourt, is not always the most infallible guide to the female heart. I don't know why we drifted apart; perhaps we'd seen too much of each other. Perhaps I got tired of the jokes, who knows?'

She's doing pretty well, Powerscourt said to himself. 'Even though you were not as close as you had been, you still saw Mr Field from time to time. Is that right?'

'I did.'

'Would you have said there was anything worrying him in recent weeks?'

'I don't think so. I believe there was something worrying him about the selection of the new tenant for Netherbury House, but I thought that was just some legal problem. He didn't carry the cares of his office round with him as a rule.'

'Could I ask you, Mrs Deacon, to get in touch with me if anything occurs to you that might be useful in our investigation? You can find me at the King's Arms. And when would be a good time to talk to your husband? Will he be home in the morning, or does he have to go off very early?'

Rose Deacon looked rather cross at the mention of her husband.

'He'll be here until eleven o'clock tomorrow morning. Perhaps you would like to call about ten? Shall I tell him to expect you then?'

'Please do, Mrs Deacon. That would be very kind. And thank you for your time.'

12

The next candidate for the vacant property in the Close was late, very late. The Dean pulled a large notebook out of his bag and began making entries. The Precentor drifted off to a mental rehearsal for his latest anthem, a complicated work by Johann Sebastian Bach. The librarian and archivist thought about his latest problems with the ancient manuscripts, some of which, he suddenly realized, might have been written a couple of hundred yards from where he was sitting. The Bishop was staring rather sadly at the Close.

There was a knock at the door. 'Colonel Colquhoun, gentlemen.'

'Come in, Colonel, come in,' said the Dean. 'So glad you could make it.'

The Colonel sat down in the interview chair. He was wearing full military uniform. Even his medals were on display. He laid his cap on the table in front of him.

'Gentlemen, I am so sorry. My train was late. There was some trouble, I gather, with a strike further down the line. My apologies.'

There was something about the way the Colonel said the word strike that made the librarian Timothy Budd think that he would have been happy to put them all in irons. The Colonel was of average height, with a prominent nose and a small, well-clipped moustache. There was a small red blotch on one side of his face and a corresponding pink one on the other side. The Bishop wondered if the man was a drinker. He shuddered slightly as he thought of one of the Dean's predecessors who had fallen into the bottle in a big way. It became so bad that he had to be removed from his post. The last straw came when one of the vergers found him preaching an alcoholic sermon late at night in the empty cathedral, his text a biblical one: 'Thou shalt have no other gods before me.' Whether the text referred to the Almighty, or to the whisky bottle he was holding in his right hand, was not clear.

The Dean introduced the other clerics. The Colonel made a slight bow to each one. 'Precentor, perhaps you would like to open the batting with our Colonel here.'

'My position here relates to the music of the cathedral, Colonel. Would that mean anything to you, if you were to join us, I mean?'

'I would be more than happy to attend any concerts or other musical entertainments in the Close, sir. I do not have a singing voice and I gave up the piano when I reached the age of twelve. I'm sorry about that.'

The Colonel smiled a wintry smile. The Bishop thought there was a very slight air of menace about the man. Maybe, he said to himself, it had to do with the military temper, the violence necessary for armed forces sworn to defeat His Majesty's enemies.

'Perhaps you could tell us, Colonel, a little bit about your own position in the army.'

'Of course,' said Colonel Colquhoun. 'I am ADC, an aide-de-camp, to Sir Henry Wilson of the Imperial General Staff. Sir Henry is at the centre of planning for a possible war on the Continent of Europe. My work takes me regularly to France and, in the last few years, to Ireland. I know that civilians' – he made them sound like some lower form of reptile – 'find it difficult to understand why military men spend so much of their time planning for war. Our enemies do not advertise their intentions six months in advance in the Court Circular. We have to be prepared.'

'Quite so, quite so,' said the Dean. 'I'm sure that's all very sensible . . . Mr Budd, our librarian and archivist.'

'I was interested to hear you talking about going to Ireland, Colonel. I presume that has to do with the question of Home Rule and the possibility of Ulster being allowed to opt out of the arrangements for some form of Irish Home Rule or even rise in revolt. Would that be a fair assessment?'

'It would,' said the Colonel.

'And do you see the army playing a role in this difficult and sensitive situation?'

'The army will do whatever it thinks is called for in the circumstances. I don't see, I'm afraid, how that impacts on the vacancy here.'

'You're quite right,' said the librarian with a grin. 'It's just that I have a grandmother who lives in Portadown.'

'I'm sure your grandmother will be perfectly safe in Portadown, Mr Budd.'

The Dean thought the Colonel sounded rather tetchy on the question of Ireland, as if there were things he knew but could not speak about. He handed him over to the Bishop.

'Thank you, Dean. Colonel, you are most welcome here. Believe me, the answer to this question does not have a direct bearing on the vacancy here. We just like to know the answer. Do you believe in God?'

The Colonel paused for a moment. 'Of course I do, Bishop. I always have. It's like the army regulations. It's always been part of my life. I believe now as sincerely as I did when I was a little boy. Our military services lock that belief ever more firmly into place. Even on service abroad, the army takes its religion with it. I have listened to the words of the Book of Common Prayer in some very unlikely places in India, or out on the high veldt in South Africa. I sometimes fear that I may hear those words again in battlefields rather closer to home.'

'Thank you, Colonel. That's very clear. Another question, if I may. It says in your papers that you are single. Is that so?'

'I'm afraid it is.'

'I don't think there is any need to apologize, Colonel. It takes all sorts. Would you intend to live alone? With a housekeeper, perhaps?'

'My younger sister has agreed to come and look after me. She too is unmarried and obviously has no children.'

Timothy Budd wondered if there was something about these Colquhouns that accounted for their single state. To have one Colquhoun unmarried might be within the law of averages. But two?

The Bishop pressed on. 'There is one other question we ask all those who wish to come and join us in the Close, Colonel. How much time would you be spending down here in Lynchester? I mean, would your work take you up to London during the week? So you would only be with us at the weekends? Would that be right?'

'My plan, Bishop, would be to go up to London in the morning and come back here in the evening. I could catch up on my reading on the train. If the pressure of work was too great, I would have to stay at my club, the Army and Navy. The place is full of refugees from domestic life.'

The Dean came in with a question to which he knew he would not receive an honest answer. Indeed, he might have been disappointed if he had.

'Colonel, our questions are nearly over. Could I ask you one thing, though it has no bearing at all on the vacancy here. Do you think there will be a war?'

The Colonel smiled. 'I can only give you one answer, Dean. I do not know. I spend my days planning for a war in every way we on the Imperial General Staff can think of. Every night I pray on my knees that it may not happen.

'Sometimes I feel that the temper of the times has changed. Ever since that book *The Riddle of the Sands* came out a decade or so ago, there has been a flood of books that take as their subject a war with Germany. The newspapers are full of ridiculous stories about German spies disguised as delivery boys, or telegraph workers reporting direct to the Kaiser in Berlin. I believe wars often start by accident. I suspect that the next war, if there is one, may come about in circumstances we have not thought about. I've always believed that war games, so beloved of staff officers, are largely a waste of time. I could bore you gentlemen stiff speculating about the prospects for war. But that is all they are – speculation. To repeat my original answer, Dean, I just don't know if there will be a war or not.'

'Thank you very much for that answer, Colonel. Is

there anything you would like to say before we come to a close?'

'Thank you for that, Dean. There is. I feel my answers to your questions at the beginning may have been too brief. I was somewhat thrown by the delay to the train and the lateness of my arrival. This is what I would like to say. I know that on the surface I am not an ideal candidate. I have no wife. I have no children. All I would bring with me is a single sister. Don't get me wrong. My sister is an admirable woman and would bring many qualities to the Close. But she is not a wife. In the time I have been here – I came down last week in civilian clothes on a sort of reconnaissance mission – I have realized how happy I could be living here. I would ask you gentlemen to ponder on the succour and support your Close could give to one who spends his days and too many of his nights in the service of King and country.'

Mr Jeremy Deacon looked like the banker he was. Clean-shaven, a dark blue suit with a white shirt and an anonymous tie. He was carrying a bundle of papers in his left hand.

'Lord Powerscourt, I understand you wish to speak to me.'

'I do, I'm afraid. It's about the death of Sandy Field. I presume you knew Mr Field?'

'Everybody in the Close knew Mr Field, Lord Powerscourt. Are you intending to talk to everybody in the Close? I gather you were round here yesterday speaking to my wife.'

'I just wondered if you knew anything that might be

relevant to his death; whether he seemed unhappy or concerned about something.'

'I am not in the habit, Lord Powerscourt, of keeping a check on the mental condition of all the inhabitants of the Close. I presume you can find gossip where you look for it. For myself, I was working late at my office in London. The staff there will be able to confirm it.'

'That's very helpful, Mr Deacon. Could I ask you another question?'

The banker looked pointedly at his watch. 'If you must.'

'Can you think of anybody in the Close who might want Sandy Field dead?'

'No, I cannot, Lord Powerscourt. Do you have any more impertinent questions you wish to ask?'

'Not at the moment, Mr Deacon. Thank you very much for your time.'

As he made his way back to the hotel, he wondered how long it would take to arrive at Christian-name terms with Jeremy Deacon. Months? Years? Most of all he wondered why Rose had married him in the first place. Perhaps Mr Deacon had just got onto his high horse to see him off the premises.

Lady Lucy was waiting for him at the hotel.

'Lucy, my love, how very nice to see you, I didn't expect to see you here so soon.'

'Very good to see you too, Francis. I'm not sure this country air is agreeing with you. You look rather strained to me. Anyway I've just received some more literature about sailing to America and going round the world. I've left the brochures in the bedroom.'

'That's very kind of you, Lucy. I shall give them my full attention as soon as I can.'

'Would it be fair to say that the investigation is not going well?'

Powerscourt told her the main points: the lack of witnesses; the lack of any visible motive, apart from the husbands of the two women who lived in the Close and had been attached to Sandy Field; the difficulties in finding out whether Sir Edward Talbot had been meaning to buy Scott's Stores before his death; Sandy Field's abilities as a forger, though Powerscourt declared he found it hard to see what that had to do with his murder; the mysterious man in black who might or might not have disappeared into the railway system in the middle of the night.

'This Sandy Field person, the late Mr Field, as I'm sure one should refer to him, what sort of things did he forge?'

'All I have been told is that he could forge people's signatures perfectly. It was a sort of party turn, like a conjurer at a fair.'

'But do we know if he forged anything else, Francis?'

'What sort of anything else, Lucy?'

'Well, suppose he was a sort of freelance forger, able and willing to produce the required signature at the drop of a hat. I mean for money, obviously. And if he was sensible, he wouldn't do any of this forging here in Lynchester – people might notice. He'd go to nearby towns, perhaps, or up to London. I'm sure there's a ready market for forgers in London, cash available in banknotes right on the spot.'

Lady Lucy paused and stared abstractedly out into the

street. 'There's another thing about our forging friend, Francis. Was it only signatures he could forge? Was he perhaps producing Old Master drawings, or some other form of fine art? There's always a ready market for those.'

Powerscourt shrugged his shoulders. 'I'll have to speak to Inspector Vaughan about that thought, Lucy. He's pretty hard pressed at present. His Chief Constable wants results and he wants them quickly.'

'Did you say you had been to see one of the two women who were said to have been having affairs with Sandy Field?'

'I did.'

'And how did she strike you?'

'Well, she didn't deny it, Rose Deacon. She sounded as if she was really rather proud of it. The whole conversation was conducted in a sort of code, as I'm sure you will understand. Looking back on it, I suspect she thought that I had talked to more people in the Close than I actually had, so she assumed I must have been told about the affairs already. There was little point in denying it.'

'And did you say you spoke to her husband?'

'I spoke briefly to Mr Deacon, husband of Rose, the last conquest but one. I got very little change out of him, apart from the fact that he had been working late in London.'

'Do you think the husband did it, Francis? Murdered Mr Field, I mean.'

'I have no idea, my love.'

'Cast your mind back, Francis. You've looked into lots of cases where a jilted husband might have committed the crime. But they never have. Or they never get caught.'

'People used to fight duels about this sort of thing.'

'That was too long ago now. One other thing, Francis, and I'll leave you alone. You say you have been to see one of the two mistresses, as it were. Have you been to see the wife yet?'

'Oh my God,' said Powerscourt, 'she has completely slipped my mind. I'll go and see her straight away. Thank you for reminding me, Lucy.'

'I shall go and unpack now. I have to warn you that I shall be making many complaints about the curtains in the bedroom. They're so hideous they make you want to remove them at once.'

Powerscourt presented his card at the Fields' house in the terrace. He felt that Beatrice Field should have the chance to refuse to see him. It was still only a matter of days since her husband had been murdered. He was shown into a large drawing room with a superb view of the Close and the cathedral. Mrs Field was sitting in her wheelchair by the window, dressed in black.

'Beatrice Field,' she said, holding out her hand.

'Powerscourt, Mrs Field, how very kind of you to see me.'

'You are well known to all the people who live in the Close, Lord Powerscourt. Everybody has heard of you by now.'

'I'm not sure whether that is a compliment or not, Mrs Field. I was originally called in by the Bishop to look into the murder of Sir Edward Talbot. My inquiries now take in your husband's death as well.'

'How can I help you, Lord Powerscourt?'

'It would help me a great deal if you could tell me a little about your husband, Mrs Field.'

'About Sandy?' said Mrs Field. 'Well, there was his work at the solicitors' firm. He worked very hard; he

155

enjoyed it most of the time. He was very cheerful. I think everybody would tell you what a happy soul he was. He was like that at home, too. He had started to bring a lot of papers home with him these last few weeks, but he'd done that before. I think there might have been something at work that worried him. He loved cricket; he started looking forward to the new season well before Easter every year. Oh dear, I suspect you have heard this already, Lord Powerscourt. I'm not doing very well at all.'

'There's nothing like hearing it at first hand, Mrs Field. There's one thing I would like to ask. I have been told that he could forge signatures at will. It might have been a sort of conjurer's turn. Did he do any drawing at home, that sort of thing?'

'Do you mean was he running a sort of forgery business up in his study? Not as far as I know, Lord Powerscourt. It was just a party trick, as far as I was aware. I had seen the signatures, of course, but that was only a game.'

She turned to look at the view from her drawing room. A couple of porters were pushing a wagon with an enormous cupboard towards the houses by the river.

'I know Sandy would want me to help you as much as I can,' she said. 'Let me try to tell you what he would have wanted me to say.'

She was fingering her row of pearls very slowly.

'Six or seven years ago, I contracted this wasting disease. I hadn't any children then and I can't produce any now. I've still got it, the disease I mean, and they can't cure it. Quite what I'm going to do for the rest of my life, I just don't know. I know now, as I knew then, that Sandy would seek some sort of satisfaction elsewhere. Some of his away fixtures, to borrow a cricketing analogy, meant that we had to leave the practice in Oxford and move here. I don't believe Sandy has been involved in any way with his colleagues' wives since. Perhaps he'd learnt part of his lesson. In a way I didn't mind. He even asked me at one point if I wanted him to tell me what was going on. I refused; I thought it was beneath our dignity. But the one thing he swore to me from the beginning was that he would never leave me. I believed him then and I still believe it. He hinted once that one of his women wanted a more permanent position than he was prepared to give her. I didn't ask who she was and he didn't mention it again.'

Mrs Field looked as though she might be on the verge of tears.

'You don't have to tell me anything that might upset you, Mrs Field. You've enough to bear at this moment without my questions.'

She managed the ghost of a smile. 'I promised myself that when you came, and I was sure you or somebody like you would come, I would answer your questions, Lord Powerscourt. I shall do my best.'

Powerscourt realized that he didn't need to ask about the two most recent conquests. He had met one of them already and would see the other very soon.

'Did he talk about his work with you? The solicitors and all that side of his life.'

'Hardly ever. He used to say that he left the office in the office. By the time he came home it was time to speak of other things – what kind of day I'd had, that sort of thing. We did manage to go out once a month, to a restaurant or to the theatre sometimes. He always planned these outings very carefully in advance.'

'You said, Mrs Field, that he hardly ever talked about his work. Do you remember him saying anything about it in the days and weeks before the end?'

'No, I don't think I do. I said that I thought something might have been worrying him, but he never said what it was. He was rather quiet for a couple of days before he was killed, but I presumed he had a lot of things on his mind. That's all.'

'And as far as you knew, there wasn't any crisis in his private life at that time?'

'He didn't tell me. And I wouldn't have asked. That was just the way we handled it.'

'Mrs Field, you have been very frank with me and I am very grateful to you. Is there anything you would like to ask me?'

'Thank you for that, Lord Powerscourt. There is one question I would like to ask. Are you close to finding out who killed my husband?'

'I could tell you a pack of lies, Mrs Field, but that wouldn't be fair. It's only fair to say that we are no nearer an answer than we were when we started. Inspector Vaughan of the local force is a most capable man. I hope we shall be able to clear things up fairly soon.'

'And if you can't clear things up fairly soon? Do I just have to wait for the answer?'

'You just have to trust us, Mrs Field. We shall do our best. It is more than likely that I shall have to come back and talk to you again. Could I just ask you in the meantime to see if you can remember anything out of the ordinary that happened in the weeks before Mr Field's death?'

'Of course, Lord Powerscourt. And come back whenever you feel the need. You will be more than welcome. I'd much rather talk to you than to a policeman, after all.'

13

Julia Brooks lived at the end of one of the terraces. Powerscourt was shown into an airy living room looking out over the Close and its sundial. He had sent a note the previous evening saying that he proposed to call at eleven o'clock.

'Lord Powerscourt, how kind of you to call. How can I help?'

Julia Brooks had black hair and blue eyes that looked rather red this morning. Had she been crying? She looked, Powerscourt thought, like one of those beautiful but rather sad Madonnas by Giovanni Bellini, where the Virgin looks as though the task she has been chosen for is too difficult to bear.

'I've come to talk about Sandy Field, Mrs Brooks.'

'I rather thought you had. I've been expecting somebody to call. People always talk too much in closed communities like this one. My husband is away in London for a few days on a rather difficult case at the Old Bailey.'

'How well did you know Sandy Field, Mrs Brooks?'

'Oh, I knew him very well. That's what they're saying

about the Close, I expect. I was very close to Sandy in the months before he died.'

Powerscourt wondered if 'very close' was as near as he was going to get. He rather thought it was. He was to tell Lady Lucy afterwards that it was like playing cards blindfold. Julia Brooks didn't know what he knew or where he found his information. He didn't know if her husband knew about the affair and the husband wasn't here to be asked.

'You say you were "very close" to Mr Field, Mrs Brooks. Would you say you were closer to him than anybody else in the city?'

Something seemed to snap in Julia Brooks's mind.

'What a horrible job you must have, Lord Powerscourt, asking people these horrible questions. I have to presume that you will be discreet as regards what I tell you.'

There was a pause. Powerscourt waited.

'I suppose it's easier to tell a complete stranger than somebody who actually lives a couple of doors away.'

There was another pause. She ran her hands through her hair. You could hear the granddaughter clock ticking in the corner.

'I'll tell you then,' she said, staring straight in front of her. 'Yes, I had an affair with Sandy Field. Yes, I was madly in love with him. Just now I don't think I will ever get over it, but something tells me I will in the end. But not yet.'

'Thank you for being so honest, Mrs Brooks. Could I ask you if your husband knew what was going on? Did you tell your husband?'

'No, I didn't tell him. But I'm sure he knew. Husbands and wives can usually tell when somebody is having an affair. Or the local gossips will have kept him up to date.'

'I see,' said Powerscourt. 'These last few days must have been very difficult for you, Mrs Brooks.' He thought she might be going to cry, but she recovered herself.

'I loved Sandy Field, Lord Powerscourt. There. I'm not ashamed of it. If I had my time over again I would do exactly the same thing. Nobody can take what we had away, nobody. I sometimes felt these last few weeks that Sandy and I were like that boy in the story – Icarus, was that his name? We were flying too close to the sun. But I never thought it would end like this. It's too terrible. But there's one thing you should be sure of, Lord Powerscourt. I didn't kill him. You can't kill the people you love unless you've gone out of your mind.'

'I'm sure you didn't kill him, Mrs Brooks. Have no fear on that score. There is, I'm afraid, one last question I have to put to you, if I may?'

'If you must . . .'

'In the days and weeks leading up to his death, was there anything worrying Mr Field? Something that he might have talked to you about, perhaps?'

'I don't think there was. I know he was very busy with all those interviews at the cathedral and the sale of the house. But he never talked to me about his work and I didn't ask him about it. Perhaps I should have done.'

'Thank you very much for talking to me, and at such a difficult time. I'm so sorry. Rest assured that nobody else is likely to come and talk to you about these matters. You shouldn't have to go through this again.'

There was a large congregation for Sandy Field's funeral in the cathedral at half past two in the afternoon.

Powerscourt thought that he had seen a number of these people going about their business around the Close and the city. Inspector Vaughan and his Sergeant had positioned themselves discreetly at the back. Powerscourt and Lady Lucy chose an unobtrusive position next to a pillar on the far side of the nave.

'I'm not sure we should be going to this service at all,' Lady Lucy had said as she adjusted her hat in the bedroom mirror. 'I've never met the man in my life.'

'I know,' said Powerscourt. 'I've thought of that. I did meet him once, but that was very brief. I just feel I should go to put in an appearance. I'm meant to be finding out who killed the man, for heaven's sake. It's the least I can do, to turn up for his funeral. It's a mark of respect, that's all.'

The organist was playing very softly; one of those sad and mournful dirges people always had at funerals. Powerscourt wondered if the composer had known when he wrote it of the melancholy circumstances it would usually be heard in; the black hats and ties; the tears of funerals.

Six members of the Lynchester Close cricket team carried the coffin into the cathedral and placed it down at the front.

'"Jesus said unto her, I am the resurrection and the life: he that believeth in me, though he were dead, yet shall he live: And whosoever liveth and believeth in me shall never die."'

The Dean was taking the service. To his right, Powerscourt could see Mrs Beatrice Field sitting very still in her wheelchair. Was she going to be all right? He had no idea how long their lease lasted. Could they find her a smaller house? He knew it wasn't his business, but should he mention it to the Dean? He felt sure that the Dean would find an answer to the problem.

Two rows back from the widow he could see the massed ranks of Ardglass, Puckeridge and Ross, clad in their most impeccable suits. The Dean was in fine voice this afternoon.

'We have come here today to remember before God our brother Sandy Field, to give thanks for his life; to commend him to God our merciful redeemer and judge; to commit his body to be buried, and to comfort one another in our grief. God in your mercy, turn the darkness of death into the dawn of new life, and the sorrow of parting into the joy of heaven; through our Saviour, Jesus Christ.'

The congregation rose to their feet.

'Hymn Number 185, "The Lord's My Shepherd".'

There was a rustling as the mourners rose to their feet. Powerscourt hadn't yet managed to spot Julia Brooks, but he felt sure she was here. Surely neither she nor Rose Deacon would give the Close gossips the satisfaction of saying that they couldn't be bothered to come to the funeral.

> The Lord's my Shepherd, I'll not want;
> He makes me down to lie
> In pastures green; He leadeth me
> The quiet waters by.

Way over to his left, Powerscourt could see Inspector Vaughan sitting at the very back of the nave, taking notes of those who were present. He wondered if the husbands of the two wives who had loved Sandy Field would be there. And if not, why not? Business in London?

My soul He doth restore again,
And me to walk doth make
Within the paths of righteousness
E'en for His own name's sake.

Sergeant Pendry, sitting next to his Inspector, Powerscourt noticed, was also writing in his notebook. Maybe he and the Inspector had divided the congregation into men and women. Certainly he and his Inspector would know more than half the congregation by sight.

Goodness and mercy all my life
Shall surely follow me;
And in God's house for evermore
My dwelling place shall be.

One of the cricketers read a lesson from St John's Gospel. Powerscourt wasn't sure Sandy Field would receive an ecstatic welcome in heaven. He doubted if there would be a place for him in the celestial cricket team.

"'Let not your heart be troubled: ye believe in God, believe also in me. In my Father's house are many mansions: if it were not so, I would have told you. I go to prepare a place for you. And if I go and prepare a place for you, I will come again, and receive you unto myself; that where I am, there ye may be also . . . I am the way, the truth, and the life: no man cometh unto the Father, but by me."'

The Dean was giving an address now, with a few words in memory of Sandy Field. Powerscourt was searching the congregation for Mrs Brooks. Eventually he found her. Mrs Brooks was not accompanied by a husband. Where was he?

'Above all, Sandy Field will be remembered for his

work in the community here and for the good cheer that never left him.'

There was Mrs Deacon, sitting halfway up the nave with a demure black hat. At this range he could not see any expression on her face at all. He was struck by a whole new approach to the case. Mrs Brooks and Mrs Deacon had been involved with Sandy Field this year. What about the previous year? And the year before that? And the year before that? Sandy Field had lived in the Close for seven years; assuming he had made two conquests a year, that meant there could be a total of twelve further companions to discover. Even though he doubted that any angry husband would be likely to commit murder for an affair that happened five or six years ago, the same might not apply to the husbands of the last two or three years. God in heaven. How on earth was he meant to find these women?

'That good cheer,' the Dean carried on, 'brightened up not only his place of work, but all of those who came into contact with him here in the Cathedral Close. That will make him welcome in heaven as it will make him remembered here on earth. His spirit will live on above all on the cricket field, and in the game he loved so well.'

Powerscourt wondered if Sandy Field had told his current lover who her predecessors were. He doubted it very much. Was that significant? Somehow he could not imagine Sandy Field mentioning any such thing to Julia Brooks.

'Let us pray,' said the Dean. 'Our Father, Who art in heaven, hallowed be Thy name; Thy kingdom come; Thy will be done, on earth as it is in heaven.'

Somewhere, way above his head in the cathedral stone-work, Powerscourt had been told that there was a stone rabbit and a stone snake, left there by the masons centuries before. He wondered what they made of the service.

'Give us this day our daily bread, and forgive us our trespasses, as we forgive those who trespass against us. And lead us not into temptation; but deliver us from evil. For Thine is the kingdom, the power and the glory, for ever and ever. Amen.'

The six pallbearers were taking up their position once more.

'Our final hymn,' boomed the Dean. 'Number 365, words by John Bunyan, "To Be a Pilgrim".'

> He who would valiant be 'gainst all disaster,
> Let him in constancy follow the Master.
> There's no discouragement shall make him
>   once relent
> His first avowed intent to be a pilgrim.

Lady Lucy was also wondering about the other women in Sandy Field's life. Were they all here in the cathedral, paying their last respects? Were there some her husband didn't know about?

The Bishop was wondering about Netherbury House and the various applicants for the vacancy. In the past he and the Dean had always agreed on who the successful candidate should be. Of the three applicants so far, there was one clear frontrunner. He suspected there would be little point in conducting the last two interviews, but the rules said otherwise.

> Who so beset him round with dismal stories
> Do but themselves confound – his strength the
>   more is.

> No foes shall stay his might; though he with
>   giants fight,
> He will make good his right to be a pilgrim.

Powerscourt was wondering if the discovery and inter-viewing of the last year's mistresses had diverted them from the real motive for the killing. But what might that be? Money, he said to himself; we need to find out more about Sandy Field's financial affairs. He presumed that his estate had been left to the widow.

> Since, Lord, Thou dost defend us with Thy Spirit,
> We know we at the end, shall life inherit.
> Then fancies flee away! I'll fear not what men
>   say,
> I'll labour night and day to be a pilgrim.

The coffin resumed its melancholy journey down the nave and out of the cathedral. 'I don't think we should go to the committal, Lucy. I'm sure that wouldn't be right. I think we should go back to the hotel. We can meet up with Inspector Vaughan there.'

Powerscourt took Lady Lucy to say hello to the Dean. He would, after all, be keen to be appraised of all new arrivals in the Close. Powerscourt was called away to talk to Inspector Vaughan.

On his way back from the funeral service, Powerscourt was hailed by the human scarecrow making his way unsteadily along the pavement by the hotel. He was wearing what appeared to be his regulation outfit.

His trousers were dark, with great holes by the knees. The shirt had once been white; was now a patchy grey. The hat had a large gap in one side. Simple Simon was still carrying what might have been his worldly goods in a tattered black suitcase. As before, he smelt very strongly of drink.

'Good day to you, Simon,' said Powerscourt.

'Good day to you too, Lord Powerscourt. You haven't solved the murder yet, I see. You are still here.'

The scarecrow leant forward with a leer. '"Who killed Cock Robin?"

'"I," said the Sparrow, "With my bow and arrow, I killed Cock Robin."

'Cock Robin has been flying around all over the place round these parts. I see him one day, I see him the next day. You don't know the answer, do you? You haven't a clue.

'"Who saw him die?" "I," said the Fly, "With my little eye, I saw him die."

'Only you can't talk to the fly either, no way, can you? If you could, you might have solved the murder mystery. Poor Cock Robin.'

'I'm obliged to you for your thoughts, Simon. I must get back to my hotel, I've got work to do.'

'Not so quickly you don't. Ain't heard the last of Cock Robin, have we?

'"Who'll be chief mourner?" "I," said the Dove, "I mourn for my love, I'll be chief mourner."

'There you go, put that in your pipe and smoke it if you like. The Dove mourning for her love, have you found her yet? Is there one dove or a whole flight of doves? Simple Simon has seen plenty of doves round these parts, so he has. Here we go round the mulberry bush, washing our face and combing our hair.'

'This is all very interesting, Simon, but I must get on.'

'Precious good, precious good getting on has done you so far. Would you be good enough to lend a poor scarecrow a few pennies for a drink now?'

Powerscourt handed over some money.

'"Who'll toll the bell?" "I," said the Bull, "Because I can pull, I'll toll the bell."'

The scarecrow was beginning to dance a little jig now, swaying from side to side in a rather alarming manner.

'All the birds of the air fell a-sighing and a-sobbing, When they heard the bell toll for poor Cock Robin.

'We seek him here we seek him there, that damned elusive Cock Robin.'

Powerscourt escaped into the King's Arms.

Remembering the church service he recited the last verse to himself as he fled up the stairs.

'All the birds of the air fell a-sighing and a-sobbing, When they heard the bell toll for poor Cock Robin.'

The scarecrow didn't follow him inside.

Half an hour later, Powerscourt and Lady Lucy were taking tea with the Inspector in their private sitting room on the first floor of the King's Head.

'I have told Lady Lucy the story so far, Inspector, and in telling it I realized how little progress we have made. Let's begin with the first murder. We have no idea what happened to Sir Edward Talbot when he went back to Netherbury House from his dinner with the Dean and the Bishop. We don't know who came to see him with the strychnine. We don't know how they got away. The man in black seems to have disappeared.'

'Forgive me for interrupting, my lord, but we heard from London that the substance that contained the strychnine is called cider eau-de-vie. It's almost impossible to obtain the stuff in this country, let alone down here in Lynchester. The London people suggested that somebody must have brought it back from France. And one other thing. You will remember the man who might have been walking his dog the night Sandy Field was killed. He has been found; he was walking his dog. He lives at the end of one of the terraces.'

'That cider eau-de-vie, Inspector. We don't know who the murderer was so we can't find out where he might have bought it. But could you ask the people here at the station if anybody has inquired about going to France this past year? They would probably have to write to London to get the tickets and so forth. That might give us a lead.'

'Very good thought, my lord. I'm not sure I'd have thought of that myself.'

'There are,' said Powerscourt, 'two areas we need to talk and think more about. This first one concerns Sandy Field's mistresses. We know that Mrs Deacon and Mrs Brooks were just the latest incumbents in this position. They cover this year. But what of the previous years? If the man got through these affairs at the rate of two a year, there must be about a dozen women out there, going about their business in the city or the Close. Perhaps they could start a club. How on earth do we find them? We can hardly send a questionnaire round the terraces and the crescent.'

'Could you ask the Dean or the Bishop?' asked Lady Lucy.

'I'm sure we could try, but I very much doubt if they'd tell us anything. They may not enjoy the sanctity of the confessional, but I'm sure the same rules would apply. Never mind, I'll try it anyway. The Dean is vain enough to want to be known as the man who solved the mystery of the murders in the Close. Maybe I could just ask him who would know about the mistresses. I'll try it. And I might go back to William Perry, the schoolteacher who was a friend of Sandy Field.'

'Do you think some of the other teachers over at the school might know?' asked Inspector Vaughan.

'We've got to try everything, Inspector. I'm not convinced that the murderer is a husband who feels he has been betrayed, but I have no rational grounds for saying so. And there's another thing. We haven't considered money at all. Was Sandy Field in debt? He must have spent a lot of money entertaining all these women. Did he have lots of money? Where did he get it? Is there anything suspicious about the man's financial affairs?'

'I can try the bank manager, my lord, but I don't hold out a great deal of hope. They're usually as cautious as the Dean and the Chapter, but there are special rules in murder cases. It would be different if I could say that the key to the crime was the money. But I can't say that. Not yet at any rate. I shall just have to play it by ear and say it might hold the key to the mystery.'

'At least we have a possible motive in the case of Mr Field,' said Lady Lucy, 'even if we don't believe that was what caused the murder. We don't have anything very much in the case of Sir Edward Talbot of Talbot's Stores. We don't even know yet if the rumours are true – that he was going to buy up his rival Scott's and shut the stores close to his own.'

'If you were a militant trade unionist,' said Powerscourt, 'and you thought your job and the jobs of your fellow workers were going to be taken away, you wouldn't feel very kindly disposed towards the great industrialist.'

'I'm not sure, my lord,' said Inspector Vaughan, 'that

those gentlemen carry round bottles of rare cider from France.'

'Who knows?' said Powerscourt. 'Maybe I should go and talk to the trade union involved.'

Powerscourt found the Dean writing busily at his desk. A pot of tea and a plate of scones were waiting for him at a side table by the window.

'Lord Powerscourt, how good to see you. You will take some tea and a couple of scones, I hope? How can I be of assistance to you this afternoon? I saw you at the funeral service earlier, I believe. I don't think you went to the committal. Is that right?'

'I didn't think the committal would be appropriate for one who only ever met Mr Field once, Dean. I thought the funeral would be a mark of respect for the dead man.'

'Quite right, my lord,' said the Dean, helping himself to a generous dollop of strawberry jam. 'I'm sure your attendance at the main service will have been noted here in the Close. Now then, have a scone, they're very good. How can I be of assistance to you today?'

'I come with a difficult request, Dean. I shall not be at all upset if you ask me to leave.'

'Please carry on,' said the Dean, polishing off the last of his scone and its strawberry jam. 'Please feel free to carry on. We are here to help, after all.'

'I'm afraid it has to do with Sandy Field and his lady friends. I have spoken to Mrs Deacon and to Mrs Brooks, who were involved with him this year. But the thought occurs to me, Dean, and you must remember that my mind is tuned to rather more worldly concerns than your own, that there may well have been other women in his life here in the years before that. And there may be other jealous husbands out there in the Close whose names are not known to Inspector Vaughan or myself. And that those husbands, in a fit of jealousy or fury, might have decided to kill Sandy Field.'

'God bless my soul,' said the Dean, 'and to think I only buried the poor man earlier today.'

'I know that, Dean, but the sooner we can find these other people, the sooner we can eliminate them from our inquiries.'

'I do hope, Lord Powerscourt, that you are not expecting me to furnish you with a list of names?'

'I am not expecting you to do anything at all, Dean. As I said, the earlier we can identify those people the better.'

The Dean took temporary relief in another scone. 'I do not need to tell you, Lord Powerscourt, that I am responsible for the living as well as the dead. If such people exist, it is not for me to tell you who they are. I have responsibilities to all those who live here in the Close and in the city beyond. I do not feel it would be proper for the Church to pass on information that might be harmful to members of their own congregation.'

'That is what I expected you to say, Dean, and I respect you for it. But could I ask you for advice about where I could find out this information? We don't want Inspector Vaughan and his men knocking on every door in the Close and asking if the wives have had an affair with the late Sandy Field.'

It must have been the mention of knocking on every door in the Close that really alarmed the Dean. He dropped his scone and was dabbing at the remains of the strawberry jam on his trousers.

'My goodness me, that would never do, Lord

Powerscourt. Tell me, you have talked to William Perry up at the school, have you not?'

Powerscourt wondered if the Dean's local knowledge of this case was better than his own. How did the man know that?

'I have, Dean. But he said his knowledge in these matters was confined to this year, as it were. He could not speak of earlier times.'

'I see, Lord Powerscourt. There is always the local newspaper. I believe you have seen the editor. He once told me that they always knew far more than they could actually put into print.'

'That is most helpful, Dean. I'm much obliged to you for your assistance.'

As he made his way back to his hotel, Powerscourt felt sure that the Dean knew exactly what and whom he was talking about. The Dean, he thought, could have written the names down on a piece of paper and handed them over. But then, had he done so, he would not be a fit and proper person to be the Dean of a cathedral.

14

Inspector Vaughan felt slightly nervous the following morning as he went to call on the bank manager. Being a fair-minded man, he also wondered if the bank manager felt the same when policemen came to call on him.

The local bank manager in Lynchester looked after the affairs of the cathedral and its clergy, as well as the affairs of the city. Alfred Temple had been in the service of his bank for over thirty years. He had lived through two changes of ownership, neither of which seemed to have made the slightest bit of difference to his way of doing business. He was about fifty years old, clean-shaven and wearing a dark blue suit. He smiled rather more often than was prescribed for bank managers.

'Inspector Vaughan, how nice to see you again. Come in and have a seat. What can I do for you today?'

'I've come, Mr Temple, about the financial affairs of the late Sandy Field, who's just been buried in the cathedral.'

'I thought you would say that. I looked up the details of Mr Field's account earlier today. I have to say there was nothing untoward about his financial affairs; no irregular payments in or out of the account.'

'Would I be right in saying that his sole source of income was the solicitors' where he worked?'

'You would, Inspector Vaughan, that's absolutely right. Mr Field was a valued member of the firm. I think that was because of the large number of clients he brought in. The lawyers who aren't partners, like Mr Field, receive a supplementary payment twice a year, their share of the profits for the previous six months. There are other arrangements for the partners. It's fair to say Mr Field kept a generous balance on his finances, even though he wasn't a partner.'

'Would you be able to hazard a guess as to why that was the case, Mr Temple?'

The bank manager paused and looked at the bundle of documents on his desk. Inspector Vaughan suddenly thought that the financial lifeblood of the little city probably passed through this office every day of the year.

'Mr Field had a reputation for entertaining a lot. Whether all of it was down to business, I could not say. But I think he was a careful man, no fancy holidays, no trips up to London for the weekend, no expensive cars. Off the record, if I may, I think I would say that he was building a nest egg for his wife. I do not know the medical details myself, but there must have been at the back of his mind that her illness, poor woman, could entail the expenditure of considerable sums. He has already converted the ground-floor dining room into a bedroom for Mrs Field, with a bathroom to one side.'

'So, Mr Temple, you would give the late Mr Field a clean bill of health financially, would that be right?'

'It would.'

'Could I ask you one other question? Was Mr Field paid the same amount as the other solicitors? He wasn't a special case in some way, was he?'

'No, no, they were all treated the same way.'

'And the special payments twice a year? Was there anything unusual about that?'

'I would have to say they seemed to be remarkably large. But the firm did a great deal of business in the town for the cathedral and the citizens.'

'Thank you very much, Mr Temple, I'm obliged to you.'

Powerscourt took William Perry the schoolteacher for a walk around the Close. He explained that he was looking for information about the predecessors of Mrs Deacon and Mrs Brooks.

'I didn't think I'd heard the last about Sandy Field's women since our interview. Look here, Lord Powerscourt, I'm terribly sorry, I can't help you. I just don't know the answers, I'm afraid.'

'You made it clear the last time we talked that your information was recent and didn't go back into the past. But who do you think might know the answer? I'm assuming that Mr Field wasn't in the habit of impressing his current conquests with the names of their predecessors.'

'I don't know the answer to that one either, I'm afraid. I'm sorry; I would help you if I could. Could I ask you a question, if I may?'

'Of course.'

'Do you think it possible that the husband of one of Sandy's conquests from years past might want to kill him now?'

'I don't know, Mr Perry, I just don't know. It seems

perfectly possible that the husband might not have known the affair was over, or didn't believe his wife when she told him it was. We just don't know. What I do know is that we need to clear this up if we can. We might clear up the murder at the same time, who knows?'

'All I can suggest, my lord, is that you try some of the cricket people again.'

Lady Lucy Powerscourt was taking tea with the widow Field in her pretty house overlooking the lawns and the cathedral.

'You must be the wife of Lord Powerscourt. It is very kind of you to call. I saw you at the funeral yesterday. Such a beautiful service.'

'I thought I would like to present my condolences in person, Mrs Field. Such a beautiful house you have here. That must be some consolation at a time like this.'

'It would be if I knew how much longer I should be able to stay here.' Mrs Field smiled a rather sad smile. 'I know nothing, nothing at all, of my late husband's financial affairs. He was always telling me that I didn't need to worry about money, but he never explained how that happy state might come about.'

'I presume one of his fellow lawyers from the practice will come to sort all that out.'

'There's one of them coming round this afternoon to begin sorting out the papers.'

'I must confess that I have come this morning with a question, Mrs Field. I haven't told my husband I was coming. I haven't told anybody at all. I thought you might find it easier to talk to me than to a police officer or to my Francis.'

'That is very considerate of you, Lady Powerscourt. What is your question?'

'I don't need to tell you who has been married to a solicitor all these years that the authorities are always keen to eliminate all the possible suspects. Once they have done that, they can direct their investigations elsewhere. They already know about your husband's recent friendships with Mrs Deacon and Mrs Brooks.'

'And they are wondering about any previous friendships? And if any other previous friendships might have produced jealous husbands who might want to kill my Sandy? You want to know about the earlier friendships? The ones before those two? Is that what you came to ask?'

'It is. I'm sorry this conversation has become so difficult.'

Mrs Field poured herself another cup of tea. 'I knew somebody would come and ask this question. I thought it would be a policeman and not a lady like yourself.'

Lady Lucy waited.

'You won't be surprised to hear that I would have found it almost impossible to talk to a policeman about this. So I have discovered a way of handling this question that doesn't involve my having to be interrogated at all.'

'Really?' said Lady Lucy.

'I have to go backwards to explain. I knew all the time about Sandy and his friendships with other women. They could, after all, offer him something I am no longer able to provide. He was hopeless about privacy, Sandy; always leaving letters and assignations lying about. I think I know all the names since we came here. I've written them all down, you see. That way I wouldn't have to discuss them with anybody.'

'Do you mean to say that you have a list of all these friends?'

'I do.'

'God bless my soul,' said Lady Lucy.

'I shall give you a copy when you leave, Lady Powerscourt. I have the envelope all ready for you. I would just ask one thing in return, if I may?'

'Of course.'

'Could you make sure that no policeman comes to me to talk about them? I would find that very painful. Maybe you could come again yourself if there is some query or other, but I don't think there will be.'

'I should be more than happy to do that if it proves necessary. I hope it won't be. And let me tell you how much I admire your courage in telling me about this. It can't have been easy for you.'

Twenty minutes later, Lady Lucy was back at the hotel with Mrs Field's letter safely concealed in her bag. Powerscourt and Inspector Vaughan were exchanging notes about their interviews.

'Not much joy at the bank, I'm afraid. Sandy Field's account is in good order apparently, healthy balances all round.'

'I think the statues on the front of the cathedral could have probably told me more than the Dean,' said Powerscourt. 'He was very proper and very circumspect. He did manage to drop a scone with strawberry jam all over his trousers, mind you. A commendable sign of human weakness. I'm sure he must know far more than he was saying. The way gossip can sometimes operate in places like this makes me think it perfectly possible that

Sandy Field was supposed to be involved with all sorts of women he hardly knew.'

'I think I might have something to interest the two of you.' Lady Lucy dipped into her bag and produced the letter from Mrs Field. She handed it over to her husband. He flicked down the list of names and passed it to the Inspector.

'Whose handwriting is this, Lucy? Where did you get this letter?'

'I got it from Mrs Field, actually. I've just been round to her house.'

'What did you say?' asked Powerscourt.

'I said I've just been round to her house, Francis. The conversation turned to the fact there had been other women in the past. Then she said that she had kept a record of all the previous candidates.'

'I see that four of the couples have moved away since their affairs,' said Inspector Vaughan. 'We are left with five still in place.'

'Mrs Field did have one proviso about handing the list over,' said Lady Lucy. 'She made me promise that no policeman would come to talk to her about it, or about any of the people named in it. I said that if there were any further queries, I would go and talk to her myself.'

'This is pure gold dust,' said Inspector Vaughan. 'My Sergeant and I will call on all the people mentioned here in the next few days. Your husband has done his duty with the most recent ones. We are in your debt, Lady Powerscourt.'

Powerscourt and Lady Lucy were just finishing their supper in the King's Arms when they were interrupted

181

by a panting Sergeant Pendry. 'There is a report of a boat going down the river, my lord. We don't know if the report is accurate, but Inspector Vaughan is waiting for you at the school landing stage, my lord. He says to come as quick as you can before the fellow gets clean away.'

Three minutes later, Powerscourt was climbing into the back of a rowing boat. The Inspector was in the front. He picked up his oars and they made their way downstream.

'We'd better talk as quietly as we can, my lord. And if you can help me with the rowing, we should catch up with him faster. All we know is that a witness reported seeing a boat moving in this direction. The fellow couldn't give any idea of who might be inside. And he's not what you would call a reliable witness. But I felt we couldn't take any chances.'

It was years since Powerscourt had been in a rowing boat. The water was black and very cold to the touch. He realized that the Inspector was much more proficient than he was. He was hardly able to move his oars in tune with the Inspector's. They were coming up to the gardens that backed onto the Cathedral Close. Weeping willows obscured the view. The moon was hidden behind banks of dark clouds. A stray dog was trotting along the far bank. It took no notice at all of the rowing boat and continued on its business.

'It seemed to me,' whispered the Inspector, 'that whoever was going down the river in a boat at this time of night was probably up to no good. It could be a burglar with criminal designs on one of these houses by the river.'

They were passing the first of the Close gardens. There was an empty landing stage that seemed to mock their progress. There were occasional lights from the backs of the houses now.

'Where is the bloody man?' whispered Inspector Vaughan. 'We've been making pretty good progress, I must say. Let's stop rowing for a moment and see if we can hear anything.'

They heard nothing. Way over to their right, a couple of owls seemed to be having a long-distance conversation.

'Damn it, not a single splash that might be other oars in the water further up,' muttered Inspector Vaughan. 'We'd better keep going. We're nearly halfway along the Close gardens by now.'

Powerscourt's arms were aching. He felt that his wrists might be going limp. Fifty yards ahead was another empty landing stage.

'Would our friend have had the time to tie his boat up somewhere and disappear before we arrived?'

'He might have done,' said the Inspector. 'It's so damned dark we might never have seen him do it.'

Powerscourt's shoulders were beginning to ache. He was starting to think of the glories of a warm bath on his return.

'Bridge coming up, my lord. We'd better take the centre arch. There may be a bit of a current round both sides.'

They negotiated their way through. Powerscourt noticed that there were no pedestrians or vehicles crossing it. He wondered if the boat was a phantom vessel, sent to torment him and Inspector Vaughan. Maybe there hadn't been a boat at all. Maybe the fellow, if there was a fellow, had simply turned round and gone the other way.

'Not far to go now, my lord, until we reach the end of the Close houses that back onto the river. You could still stop further up and make your way back on foot.'

'Do you think there is a boat out on the river this evening? Apart from us, I mean,' asked Powerscourt, wondering if the ache across his shoulders would ever go away. He suspected it would be reaching the top of his back soon.

'I've always thought it might be a false alarm, my lord. I just thought we couldn't take a chance. We'd never forgive ourselves if we could have caught up with the villain.'

They were coming up to the last of the houses now. The clouds cleared for a moment or two and Powerscourt could just see the great bulk of the cathedral, like a ghost ship rising out of the darkness. He wondered if Sandy Field used to row his lady friends up and down the river in the summer sunshine, the girl's hand trailing in the water, occasional breaks under the weeping willows. The Inspector kept up a good pace until the houses were some distance behind them. He signalled to stop rowing once more and bent his head down to listen closer to the water.

'I can't hear a bloody thing, my lord,' whispered the Inspector. 'I think our friend's got clean away, if he ever came this way in the first place. I think we should carry on for another five minutes before we call it a day.'

'Very good,' said Powerscourt, wondering if his shoulders would ever be the same again. There was a thick layer of weed lying across the river now. It caught in the oars and slowed their progress to a crawl.

'This is all we need, my lord,' whispered Inspector Vaughan, 'bloody weed right across the river. I think we should turn around once we're on the far side of it. God knows what would happen if we tried to reverse course in the middle of this lot.'

Powerscourt was wondering if the weed was a

metaphor for this investigation: useful paths of inquiry blocked, no clear route available for a conclusion.

'I can row us back on my own, my lord. I'm still pressed into service for the police rowing eights, so I keep my hand in.'

Back at his hotel, Powerscourt reported to his wife. 'That was a complete waste of time, Lucy. Either the fellow was never there at all, or he simply went so fast we never caught up with him. We have rowed along the river in the evening and caught nothing.'

'My God, Francis, never mind the vanishing villain, you look just like a scarecrow that's been on naval manoeuvres. I think you'd better have a hot bath. And you'd better have it right now.'

Half an hour later, the Powerscourts were taking a cup of tea in their sitting room.

'That's better, Francis; at least you look like a member of the human race now. I take it your rowing mission was not a success.'

'It certainly wasn't. It was like so much of this case, Lucy. I feel as if I am about to touch a piece of string but it turns out to be a cobweb. Everything seems to disappear when you get close to it.'

'Surely some of these inquiries will come good, my love. You mustn't be too hard on yourself.'

'I wish I shared your optimism, I really do.'

'Those names from Mrs Field may come up with something, surely?'

'They may and they may not. If any of those people are responsible, they've had a clear run at working out their alibis by now. Inspector Vaughan has had the London police check out the alibis of Messrs Deacon and Brooks. They're in the clear. They were both where they said they were. There are witnesses. He is now talking of going to London himself to check out the truth of any others who say they were in London on the night in question. I'm still not convinced that Sandy Field's women are the key to this business, Lucy. There's something somebody told me lurking at the back of my mind, but I can't remember what it was.'

'Cheer up, Francis. You always feel like this at some point in an investigation. How many times have I heard you say that you'll never get to the bottom of things, only for you to solve the whole case a day or two later.'

'Let's hope so,' said Powerscourt gloomily. 'I wish I could share your optimism. The best piece of work so far in this case has been your session with poor Mrs Field that produced all those names. Are you sure that she hasn't missed any out?'

Lady Lucy thought for a moment of the woman confined to her wheelchair in her lovely house in the Close.

'I can't be sure, obviously,' she said, 'but I don't think she would have made any mistakes. She's his wife, for heaven's sake. She knew him better than anybody.'

'The police are going to question the people Mrs Field told us about, the ones who are still here. We'll see what the Inspector has to say after the interviews.'

Early the next morning, Powerscourt called on Michael Finn, the other solicitor in the little city who had talked to him about dubious charging from Ardglass, Puckeridge and Ross. He had come with a request.

'Do you think, Mr Finn, remembering that this is a

murder investigation, that you could give me the names of some of the people who complained about the behaviour of Ardglass, Puckeridge and Ross? It could prove very useful in our investigation. We would, of course, be very discreet.'

Michael Finn paused and stared at Powerscourt. Powerscourt wondered if this was going to bring about another trip back to his hotel sitting room and more cups of tea. But Mr Finn seemed comfortable in his own quarters for now. His pencil, Powerscourt noted, was already in rehearsal for another pen-twirling competition.

'We touched on this last time, my lord. I'm afraid my answer has to be the same as it was then. I have a duty of confidentiality to my clients as well as to my legal colleagues in their grand offices up the road. My clients tell me things, secure in the knowledge that I will not pass it on to anybody. I am not willing to break those understandings. I have to stay loyal to my clients or I may as well shut up shop.'

'Even in a murder case?'

'You talk of a murder case. I do not believe that a bit of overcharging for legal services ever led to murder. The courts of England would be full to overflowing with solicitor suspects if that were true. I'm sorry, my lord, I know you have a job to do, but I cannot help you this morning.'

15

Johnny Fitzgerald was waiting for Powerscourt back at his hotel.

'Well, Francis, your Oxford correspondent has returned here for fresh instructions. I wrote to you about Sandy Field's skill at forging and his affair with one of his colleague's wives, Mr Prothero – or Mrs Prothero, to be precise. I have conducted further inquiries about the university town. They still remember him well in Oxford, you know. None of them knew about the forging as far as I could tell. Many of them knew about affairs in general, but not about the wife of Prothero. Sandy Field was remembered for his endless good cheer and his charm – both of which, as far as I know, are useful when it comes to conquests of the opposite sex. There was a deal struck with the senior partner when he left. Field was to keep his mouth shut. The senior partner would write him a reference, for use with any other firm of solicitors, which did not mention the business with Mrs Prothero at all. Or any mention of the forging.'

'Nobody down here has mentioned the forging at all, Johnny. Do you think he turned over a new leaf?'

'I very much doubt it; he doesn't seem to have turned many leaves over in the question of other people's wives. Maybe he was more circumspect in his choice of partner this time round.'

'Thank you very much for that, Johnny, it's very helpful. Do you remember that case years ago with a forger who could run up an Old Master in a couple of weeks?'

'Orlando Blane, that was the name of the fellow. Do you think Sandy Field's been taking lessons from him – knocking up the odd Rembrandt drawing in his back room?'

'I think you should find out, Johnny. Consider this, if you will. He always said that he would never leave his wife. Poor woman is in a wheelchair, after all. I'm sure he is well paid at that solicitors' firm. The bank manager told Inspector Vaughan that his account at the bank was very healthy. But suppose you were to make a killing in the art market. That might pay for better treatment, or some miracle cure in one of those expensive places in Switzerland. I have to say it is a very long shot. I'm not even sure how it would fit in with the murder. But it would be useful to know if Sandy Field had been doing any quiet forging on the side.'

'So what would you have me do, Francis? Forgery would make a welcome change from adultery, I must say.'

'I think you should talk to the local auctioneers. See if Sandy Field has brought them any works for valuation or for transfer to London. Any drawings or paintings – I feel drawings are more likely – could have been found in the house of some recently deceased person whose affairs are being sorted by Ardglass, Puckeridge and Ross. They could have been in the family for generations – maybe since Great Uncle George brought them back from the Grand Tour. Maybe you should talk to some of those big artist suppliers up in London. I doubt if you could have bought what you needed for forgery down here in Lynchester.'

'You don't think he might have played away, as it were, with any forged drawings; gone to some other auctioneers where he would not be known?'

'That's possible, but I think he might have had some advantages by going to the local people. They would know him, after all. He must have been bringing stuff in every now and then to be sold as a member of a firm of well-known and highly reputable solicitors.'

'Very good, Francis. Old Master drawings here we come.'

'There is one other thing, Johnny. This one really is a shot in the dark. There's a local woman – early sixties, I should think – called Mrs McQuaid. She is the housekeeper at Netherbury House, the one the cathedral are in the process of letting. She lives in a little place round the corner. She's been in post for about twelve or fifteen years. This is a very long shot. I want you to find out if her path crossed at any time with that of Sir Edward Talbot, the first victim in this melancholy affair, or if she has had professional dealings with Ardglass, Puckeridge and Ross, or those other solicitors. I sometimes wonder if there aren't two murderers at work here, since it is almost impossible to establish any links between Sir Edward and Lynchester, however hard I try.'

'Any other little jobs you have in mind, Francis? Finding one of the descendants of the five thousand who got fed on the mountainside? Shakespeare's younger brother? Queen Victoria's secret son with John Brown?'

'I think that should do for now, Johnny. I leave the auctioneers and Mrs McQuaid to you. I'm sure you'll sort it out in a couple of days.'

Lady Lucy had a long conversation with the hotel head porter before she set off on her mission of mercy. Her destination was Mrs Field's house in the terrace.

She found Mrs Field sitting by the great window in her living room.

'Forgive me for troubling you, Mrs Field, when it's hardly any time at all since my last visit. But I've come with an invitation. I'd like you to join me at the hotel for lunch. I've talked to the porters and they will take you from here to there. It needn't be today if this is short notice. I'm sure it would do you good to have a change of scenery.'

'How very kind of you, Lady Powerscourt. That's very thoughtful of you. I think tomorrow might be better than today. I shall have more time to compose myself.'

'Could I just ask you one question while I'm here, if I may?'

'Please do.'

'We understand from his time in Oxford that your husband was an accomplished forger. It was a party trick rather than something he used in his work. Do you remember anything of that sort from your time here?'

'I knew he could reproduce other people's signatures any time he wanted. I don't recall him forging anybody's signatures in his work. He wouldn't have thought that proper at all.'

'And he didn't have a special room here where he practised various people's signatures, that sort of thing?'

'Lady Powerscourt, my husband used to see me last thing at night when he was here and while he was alive. Since his death, the cathedral authorities have been sending a man over to look after me. My bedroom is on this floor now. It makes life so much easier. There are a couple of floors above where I never go these days. It's perfectly possible that Sandy spent a lot of time up there practising his forgeries, but I don't think he did.'

'Thank you very much for that, Mrs Field. I'm sorry to have brought it up. I shall see you for lunch at the hotel tomorrow. I look forward to it. Shall we say one o'clock?'

Johnny Fitzgerald spent some time inspecting the premises of Gillespie and Crowther, auctioneers. They were situated near the railway station in a tall building that looked as if it might once have been an army barracks. Mr Gillespie welcomed him to the fold, an enormous area packed with sofas, chests of drawers, single beds, cupboards large and small, cooking utensils, chairs, garden furniture, double beds, coffee tables, carpets, rugs, cutlery sets, discarded lights and kitchen equipment. The next auction was due in three days' time.

'How can I help you today, Mr Fitzgerald?'

Gillespie was a big man in his early fifties, who looked as though he could lift most of the goods in his hall single-handed. He was wearing a dark grey suit that had seen better days and a rather bedraggled tie.

Johnny explained that he was a close colleague of Lord Francis Powerscourt's, who had been called in by the

Bishop and the cathedral authorities to investigate the murders in the Close.

'Never heard of that first fellow – big grocer, wasn't he, who ran Talbot's Stores? I wouldn't know him if he came back to life and walked through the door this minute. But Sandy Field – we all knew Sandy Field here, Mr Fitzgerald. He was a very popular man in these parts, I can tell you. I hope you catch the murderous bastard who killed him, so I do, and that's a fact.'

'Did your paths cross often, Mr Gillespie?'

The auctioneer looked round his great assembly of unloved goods.

'He was here about once a fortnight, I should say, Mr Fitzgerald. Always cheerful, always ready with a funny story. Everybody liked him. He handled most of the stuff from his firm that had to be sold at auction when people died. It's astonishing what people think will sell when their relations pass away. Only yesterday some chap brought in a salt and pepper set that you could have bought brand new for a song. I ask you.'

'What kind of goods came your way from Ardglass, Puckeridge and Ross, Mr Gillespie?'

'Mostly they were quite high class. A lot of antique furniture, plenty of books, some carpets and rugs, one or two paintings, that sort of thing.'

'And who comes here to buy your material, Mr Gillespie?'

'Well, there are always a few old ladies who come for the excitement. There's one old dear who hasn't missed an auction here for the last five years. She's never bought anything here either – not even a bloody salt cellar. The Dean told me once that they were probably the same old ladies who always go to matins or evensong every day in the cathedral. We get a fair number of people who are moving house and come to see what they might pick up here. There are always two or three other auctioneers from the firms round about, come to see if they can pick up a bargain for their own businesses or sell it on to the London men.'

'You say Sandy Field was a popular man, Mr Gillespie. Did he ever buy anything here on his own account, as it were?'

'Not that I can think of.'

Johnny suddenly realized that Sandy Field could have dropped any item at all into the Ardglass, Puckeridge and Ross section and nobody would have been any the wiser.

'Tell me, Mr Gillespie, do you recall any drawings – maybe old ones, maybe even Old Masters – that came your way via Mr Field?'

The auctioneer scratched his head. 'Yes, I do. I'm trying to remember the details. There were two lots of two: four in all. Mr Field asked me to display them along with everything else, but not to sell them in open auction. He said he thought they might be very valuable. When the bidding stopped because the reserve had not been reached, he had a word with the man who wanted to buy them, a youngish fellow called Freebody from another auctioneers in Salisbury up the road. Then he gave the commission to Mr Freebody, and quite what happened after that I simply don't know. Sandy said he was doing the best for his clients, trying to get them a higher price for their stuff.'

'And did the same thing happen the second time? Did Mr Field entrust his drawings to the man from Salisbury?'

'He did. And we never saw any more drawings from

that day to this. Maybe there weren't any more. Maybe he took them straight over to Mr Freebody in Salisbury. We didn't mind at all. This place wasn't really meant for works of art, as you can see.'

'I understand,' said Johnny, looking at a stuffed bear that looked quite happy in its new surroundings. 'Please forgive me this question, Mr Gillespie. We investigators always have to look out for strange behaviour in our victims. Was there anything unusual about Mr Field? Was there ever a time when you thought he might not have been completely straight with you?'

'God bless you, Mr Fitzgerald, I know you have to ask these difficult questions. It's part of your job. There was never a time when I thought Sandy Field wasn't trying to secure the best deal for his clients. Never. He was always straightforward in his dealings with us. And good luck to you, I hope you find the killer soon.'

With that Mr Gillespie negotiated his way past a wobbly lamp and a Georgian chest of drawers to resume his command post behind the auction hall.

Lord Francis Powerscourt was sitting at the desk in his sitting room composing a letter. He was writing to a Mr George Chambers, General Secretary of the National Amalgamated Union of Shop Assistants, Warehousemen and Clerks, formed by the union of a number of smaller unions fifteen years before. He didn't find it an easy letter to write.

Dear Mr Chambers
  Please forgive me for writing to you out of the blue. I am an investigator. The case on which I

am working at present concerns the recent death of Sir Edward Talbot in the cathedral city of Lynchester. I was asked to look into the matter by the Bishop and the Dean of the cathedral.

Sir Edward had no links with Lynchester, apart from one of his stores in the town, which he had never visited before and which he did not inspect on his one and only visit. He had come down for an interview about the lease on a house.

Certain rumours have reached us about Sir Edward's plans, or what might have been his plans, in the days before his death. There were suggestions that he was planning to buy up some – or even all – of Scott's Stores, his main rivals in the south and west of England. There were also rumours that he was planning to close all the Scott's Stores that were in the same territory as his own shops.

I would like to know if you have heard any or all of these rumours, and whether you believe them to be true or not. At present we are operating in the dark, particularly about Sir Edward's intentions.

I should be more than happy to call on you in your offices in London. Or, if it would be more convenient, you would be more than welcome to come and see me at my house in Markham Square in Chelsea.

Yours faithfully,
Powerscourt

Johnny Fitzgerald – he always dropped his title in these situations – had turned himself into an investigator for a firm of solicitors. 'I have been charged,' he told the post-master nearest to Mrs McQuaid's house, 'with the task of discovering where she lived before she came here to the Close.' There was a question of an inheritance. He was not allowed to say any more than that.

'Mrs McQuaid, you say?' said the postmaster whose name was Biddulph, 'the old body who looks after some of the old gentlemen down in the Close? Well, I've been here for ten years now, and I've no idea where she lived before. I've always thought of her as a permanent fixture here.'

'Tell me, Mr Biddulph, who else should I talk to? Are there any shops round here who might be able to help me?'

'Well,' said Mr Biddulph, 'there's the greengrocer's – they've been here for ever – and Johnson's the butcher's. People say they had a branch open here when the cathedral was built all those years ago.'

'I'm much obliged, Mr Biddulph, thank you very much.'

Hyde's the greengrocer's gave him no help at all.

'It's never been our policy, Mr Fitzgerald, to hand out information about our clients to complete strangers. If you'd care to write in, we can see whether we might be able to help. A very good day to you.'

Johnson's the butcher's were more helpful. Mr John Johnson told Johnny Fitzgerald that he was the third John Johnson to hold the post. The second one was still here, working out the back.

'Mrs McQuaid, you say. Well, well. She's the old lady who works in the Close. I think I can remember when she first came to Lynchester, ten or fifteen years ago. But where she came from I have no idea. Let me ask my father.'

The third John Johnson pulled back a curtain to reveal the second, preparing meat to go in the shop window.

'Pa,' shouted Johnson Mark Three, 'Pa!'

'There's no need to shout,' said Johnson Mark Two, abandoning a side of beef in favour of conversation. 'I heard you the first time.'

'Can you remember where Mrs McQuaid lived before she came here?'

'Old dear who looks after the people in the Close?'

'That's her,' said Johnny.

'Let me think,' said Johnson Mark Two.

He put down a couple of steaks nearly ready for display in the window.

'Salisbury,' he said finally. 'She came here from Salisbury originally. I remember her telling another customer who was new to Lynchester. That's where you want. Maybe she likes living next to cathedrals.'

'I know this is a bit of a tall order, Mr Johnson, but she didn't mention any particular district, did she?'

'That's going too far for me, Mr Fitzgerald. All I can remember is that she said Salisbury. I'm sure of that.'

'Thank you very much,' said Johnny. He wondered if by some happy chance she had worked for Mr Freebody the auctioneer, but he rather doubted it. He wondered too where she might have lived before Salisbury. Yet another cathedral city, perhaps.

Powerscourt was struck by a sudden desire to see the Dean. So far, he said to himself, there have been three candidates on parade to take up the lease on Netherbury House. Were there more to come? Was there any link between these aspirant residents of the Close and the murders? For the life of him he could not work out what it might be, but it was a thread that seemed to run right through the case. He found the Dean staring moodily at a couple of large ledgers.

'Ah, Powerscourt,' said the Dean, 'take a seat. Any news from the battlefront? You find me surrounded by some of the trappings of finance, also known as the cathedral accounts.'

'I'm afraid we are still collecting our normal straws in the wind, Dean. There's nothing that I would call significant, not yet at any rate. But I have a question for you this morning about the interviews for Netherbury House. Am I right in saying that there have been three so far?'

'You are,' said the Dean, 'and candidate number four goes in to bat later on today. And that,' he glanced wearily at his ledgers, 'will be a welcome release for me from this financial assessment. I shall go into the meeting with a light heart, I can tell you. In our religion we don't believe in purgatory like our Roman Catholic friends, but if there is one, I expect there will be rooms and rooms of files to be sorted out before any final destination is decided.'

'Are there any more after today? Candidates, I mean, not files.'

'There is one more. I cannot for the moment remember exactly when he comes, but he is due fairly soon.'

Johnny Fitzgerald reckoned that the firm of Peabody, Auctioneers and Valuers, was a grander sort of business altogether from their colleagues in Lynchester. Mr Justin Peabody showed him to a seat in his impressive office near the local branch of Scott's Stores. He was in his early thirties, with a mop of curly black hair and wearing a well-cut suit. Johnny could just see the normal auction-eers' display through a pane in Peabody's door. The armoires and the chests, the commodes and the four-poster beds, the paintings and the drawings and the kitchen equipment were all waiting patiently for their new owners.

'Thank you for seeing me so promptly, Mr Peabody. I am much obliged to you. I am here as a colleague of Lord Francis Powerscourt, who has been asked by the cathedral authorities to look into the death of Mr Sandy Field.'

'That was a sad business, Mr Fitzgerald. I had hoped to be able to get to the funeral myself, but we had a valuation that couldn't wait. How can I help you? Sandy Field was a very popular visitor here.'

'I am particularly interested in some old drawings that he brought in to Gillespie and Crowther initially, and which then passed into your care.'

'I think we need to be careful about our definitions here, Mr Fitzgerald. My God, I'm sounding like a bloody lawyer. Sandy Field was anxious to get the best return for his clients. The drawings passed into our care, but Mr Field was still the owner, as it were, seeing as he represented the interests of the deceased. When he realized that these things might be valuable, he thought he would get a better price through us than through Gillespie and Crowther. So he was still the owner, or the man representing the owner, in legal terms. There were two drawings that were more or less worthless, but two that might have been old and valuable, I seem to recall. One showed a naked lady, possibly a goddess, reclining under a group of trees with a town on a hill in the distance. The other showed a group of elderly men apparently holding a meeting.'

'And did you put them up for auction in the normal way?'

Justin Peabody laughed. 'I did and I didn't. I like to think that we have a more sophisticated clientele here than Gillespie and Crowther's, but there aren't too many of our clients who know or care about drawings that might or not be Old Masters. So I invited two men from the leading London art dealers to come and have a look at them and, if they thought it appropriate, to put in an offer.'

'And what happened when the men from London came to inspect the goods, as it were?'

'Thank God I asked two of them, Mr Fitzgerald. Either one on his own would have fobbed me off with some artistic rigmarole about provenance and the nature of the pencil work. I had a sort of mini-auction here in my office, with the drawings on an easel in front of the men from London. I'm sure we could have obtained a much higher price for them than they would have raised in our standard auction.'

'How much did they offer in the end?'

'The first one, which the young man from Lonsdale's thought might be of the school of Titian, was valued at seven hundred and fifty pounds. The man offered to buy it on the spot.'

'And the other one?'

'Nobody tried any attribution at all with the second drawing, with the old boys holding a meeting. Maybe they both thought it was something special but didn't want to let the other fellow know what it was. Anyway, the other man offered about nine hundred pounds.'

'So would it be fair to say, Mr Peabody, taking into account the normal charges and so on, that Mr Field would have made his client or his estate about fifteen hundred pounds extra by coming to you?'

Mr Peabody paused for a moment. 'I haven't told this story very well. I haven't finished yet. I must say I was surprised at what happened next. Sandy Field refused both offers. He said he wanted the two gentlemen to take the prints away and put them up for sale at auction in London. He must have thought they would fetch a better price. Anyway, from that point, the drawings passed out of my sight. And out of Mr Field's sight, too. But it's not the end of the story. I have no idea what the two gentlemen finally sold them for, or to whom. You see, I thought they both had potential clients in mind when they agreed to sell them through their offices in London.'

'I don't think it's important for the murder inquiry,' said Johnny, 'but could you find out what they finally went for? Not if it involves a great deal of time and trouble, of course.'

'I'd be happy to do that for you, Mr Fitzgerald. I'll drop them a line.'

'There is one other question I would like to put to you, Mr Peabody, seeing as you have been so helpful. I have to track down a family who used to live in Salisbury many years ago. All I have is a name. I was thinking of starting out at the post office, but you might have a better suggestion.'

Justin Peabody laughed. 'Sorry, Mr Fitzgerald, I know this is a serious matter and a very serious case, but it just so happens that the man you want was in here yesterday checking through our latest collection of old books. He's the local historian and he's written two volumes so far on the history of Salisbury. He's a retired schoolteacher, and he says that the research and the writing keep him alive. He must be nearly eighty now, I suppose, so he may well be right. Walter Harrison is his name. He lives in Mitre Street round there at the back of the cathedral. Tell him I sent you.'

'Thank you so much, Mr Peabody. You've been very helpful. May I come back and trouble you further if I run into difficulties?'

'Of course you can, Mr Fitzgerald. Everything's for sale here.'

16

The hotel staff were capable and efficient in conveying Mrs Beatrice Field to her lunch in the King's Head. She was seated discreetly opposite Lady Lucy in a window table, inspecting a bowl of the hotel's finest vegetable soup.

'This is so kind of you, Lady Powerscourt. I cannot tell you how much it means to me to get out of the house.'

'Would you care for a glass of wine, Mrs Field? Perhaps that would make it a proper celebration.'

'Thank you so much. This soup is excellent, I must say. I haven't been here for a year or so. Sandy used to bring me here sometimes for Sunday lunch.'

It was towards the end of the roast lamb with mint sauce that Beatrice Field dropped her bombshell.

'You remember you asked me, Lady Powerscourt, if Sandy did any drawings or other sort of artwork? You'd been talking about his ability to forge signatures and I said, No, I didn't think so. Well, I was wrong.'

'What do you mean?'

'There is one big room up there in the attic. I had

never been there, but one of the young men from the solicitors' office came round to conduct an inventory of the place. Maybe they're trying to work out how much I'm worth, but that doesn't matter. He brought down a whole lot of art books and an easel where Sandy must have done his drawings. He can't have been working on anything when he was killed, as there was still a blank sheet on the easel. There were pencils and pens and drawing paper, and heaven knows what, all up there.'

'My goodness me,' said Lady Lucy, who could see all kinds of avenues opening out in front of her. 'Was there a folder or something up there that could have held the drawings he had finished?'

'The young man didn't say. He said he was just showing me the important things. He had to go off on another job. He says he's coming back tomorrow.'

A couple of helpings of apple pie with custard had just appeared.

'I'm not sure I can eat any more, Lady Powerscourt. You have been so kind. But tell me, do you think the drawings and so on are important? Surely they couldn't have led to his death?'

'I don't know how important they might be, Mrs Field. I shall have to ask Francis. Maybe it's just one of those harmless hobbies men have. You know, some of them collect books and stamps and things; others are never happier than when they're on the cricket pitch or the hunting field. It's all perfectly harmless unless you're a fox.'

'I wonder why Sandy never told me about it. He told me about lots of things, but never about the easel on the top floor.'

'I'm sure there's a perfectly reasonable explanation, Mrs Field. You mustn't worry about it. One of the other solicitors may be able to help.'

'Do you think I could be taken home now? Thinking about this again has made me rather upset, I'm afraid. It's not the drawings or paintings or whatever it was, it's the fact that he never told me about it, you see.'

Lady Lucy made a sign to the head waiter, and in a couple of minutes Mrs Field was taken back to her house in the terrace as discreetly as she had been brought.

The fourth candidate for the vacancy in Lynchester Cathedral Close was a man well known to the four clerics conducting the interview. Paul Jenkinson was in his middle thirties, wearing his best dark grey suit with a blue tie over a white shirt. He was clean-shaven, with dark brown eyes and a habit of brushing his light brown hair across his forehead. He was a history teacher in the grammar school in the Close and had been in post for eight years. In that time the fabric of his life had become so wrapped up in the life of the cathedral that he was virtually a part of it. He led his charges across the Green to services in the cathedral. He cheered on the cricket and football teams in their matches within sight of the cathedral itself.

'Good morning to you, Paul. Please sit down,' said the Dean, waving the young man to the empty chair. 'Thank you for coming. I have to say that we on this side of the house have found it difficult to know what to ask you. We know so many of the answers already. Some of the questions may seem unnecessary to you. We ask your forgiveness for that.'

The Dean did not say that the clerical gentlemen had asked the youngest of their number, librarian Timothy Budd, to ask the more difficult questions.

The Bishop opened the batting and made it clear that it was going to be a formal affair.

'Mr Jenkinson,' he began, 'perhaps you could tell us why you want to come and live in the Close?'

'Of course,' replied the young man. He had the sense, well known to teachers after indifferent homework had been handed back, that his audience were not with him. If not exactly hostile, they were certainly reserved. He felt, quite strongly, that so far the clerics were not on his side.

'Of course,' he said again. 'In a way I already live here in the Close, as you gentlemen well know. My work is here. A few of my pupils live here already. At present I live in the town. I could not pretend that my journey to work is either long or difficult. I want to come and live here because it would bring me into full communion with this institution. At present I am part of it, but I do not entirely belong. I would like to make the bonds that bind me to this place tighter still. I should feel, if you will forgive me, more fully a part of the cathedral family if I lived here all the time.'

'That is all very commendable,' said the Dean. 'Tell us if you would, your opinion on the central purpose of this cathedral, the belief in God. Where do you stand on that?'

'I think you know perfectly well where I stand on that, Dean. You must have seen me attending services here: communion on Sunday mornings, evensong once or twice a week. I have been a believer for as long as I can remember. I was taught my religion by my parents in the same way they taught me to walk. I still say my prayers every night. I think I am fortunate that so many of the doubts that cause others to abandon their Christianity have not come to trouble me. The cynics no doubt say that it is perfectly possible to go through the motions of belief, the daily rituals and so on, but still not believe. That is not so in my case. I believe my faith would be strengthened by coming to live in a community such as this. I am sure of it.'

Rupert Digby was next into the ring.

'Church music, Mr Jenkinson; perhaps you could tell us your position on that?'

'I enjoy it very much, Precentor. But I have a confession to make. I am virtually tone-deaf. My wife has been known to ask me not to sing at all at important family functions like christenings and funerals. She says it would put people off the service. So while I sometimes come to the concerts and so on, you will not find me queueing up to sing in one of your choirs. I would be an embarrassment to you.'

The clerical gentlemen smiled. 'That would never do,' said the Dean. 'Discordant notes in the choir stalls indeed. The Precentor's predecessors would be turning in their graves. Mr Budd, our librarian.'

Timothy Budd was not entirely happy to have been chosen as the man who puts the difficult questions. He felt that the task should have fallen to one of his elders and betters.

'Your application and your answers here this afternoon have been exemplary, Mr Jenkinson. I am sure that you are doing an excellent job teaching history at the grammar school. By your own admission, you live within walking distance of the Close here. Why should we give you a house inside the Close here when your own house is so near?'

'I expected somebody would ask me that question,' said the history teacher, 'and it is difficult, I grant you. I think you have to ask yourself one question, Mr Budd. Would you prefer to bring up a family inside the Close or out of it?

'I have no doubt that it is perfectly possible to bring up a family outside this inner circle, if you like. Most of the children in the town are brought up in the town rather than the Close. But I have no doubt about it. I have two children, a boy and a girl aged five and seven. I am sure they would derive enormous benefit by being brought up here.'

'Are you saying, Mr Jenkinson, that your principal reason for wanting a house here is that you would have a bigger playground for your children?'

'That is unfair, and you know it,' replied the teacher. 'There are many reasons why I would want to come here: for reasons of belief, for reasons of history, for reasons of continuity. I have never thought of the Close as a playground.'

'Perhaps I could put the question a different way, Mr Jenkinson. Why should you want to come and live here now? You are only in your thirties. You have years ahead of you. There will be further vacancies in the future.'

'I have thought about that question, too. No doubt you gentlemen could preach an elegant sermon round the question of whether pleasures should be enjoyed now or stored up for the future. For myself I prefer to seize the day. You ask me why I should want to come and live here now. I put the question back to you. Why not?'

'The reason for Mr Budd's line of questioning,' said

the Bishop, 'is that there are always a large number of suitable applicants for the vacancies when they arrive. The competition is usually pretty intense, as it is on this occasion. In these circumstances it is difficult to weigh up the differing merits and qualities on offer. Choosing the right man is never easy, as I am sure you realize.'

'Of course, Bishop,' said Paul Jenkinson. He was still smarting from the earlier line of attack. He was drawing his hair across his forehead at a fairly rapid pace. 'I would like to repeat my earlier question. Why shouldn't I come and live here in the Close?'

Even as he asked it, he knew that it was probably a mistake. Whatever you do, his wife had told him that morning, don't get argumentative. Don't start a row. Don't lose your temper. The Dean was of the opinion later that – whatever chance he'd had before he started – the history teacher had effectively blown his chances by asking the question twice. The Dean hoped that he wouldn't ask it a third time.

The Bishop smiled. 'I feel, Paul, that we have already gone over that ground, the number of candidates and so on. I don't think it would be fruitful if we were to carry on down that road. There is no question in any of our minds that you would be a suitable candidate for the vacancy. Otherwise you wouldn't be here. The question for us on our side of the table is how many other such candidates would also be suitable. Now, it is my turn to ask a question. Is there anything you would like to ask us?'

Paul Jenkinson smiled at his interrogators. 'I am sorry if I sounded rather petulant just now, gentlemen. I feel rather like somebody who has just failed a test he hoped to pass. I have only one question for my examiners. Will there be an opportunity to resit the exam in the future?'

'Of course there will be a chance to do that,' said the Dean. 'There's always a second chance.'

'Thank you very much,' said the young man, and fled into the sunshine on the Close.

17

'Mr Harrison?' said Johnny Fitzgerald, 'Mr Peabody at the auctioneers' said you might be able to help me. My name is Fitzgerald, Johnny Fitzgerald.'

'Well, you'd better come in, Mr Fitzgerald.' Harrison was a small tubby man with white hair and a white beard. He was permanently attached to a pipe, which seemed to have a serial habit of going out, causing frequent recourse to matches and bad language. Walter Harrison looked to be in his seventies if not more. He looked as though he enjoyed his work. He showed Johnny into a room that was entirely lined with files. They ran right round the room and over the door, so that the place looked rather like a womb, with Mr Harrison's desk in the centre.

'Forgive me for butting in on you like this, Mr Harrison. I work with an investigator called Lord Francis Powerscourt. We have been asked by the Bishop of Lynchester to look into a couple of murders that have taken place there. I have been charged to find out as much as I can about a lady called Mrs McQuaid, who now lives in Lynchester but used to live in Salisbury. We think she left here some years ago.' Johnny remembered Powerscourt giving him the maiden name, extracted from the files in the cathedral office. 'She was called Armstrong, Bertha Armstrong, before she was married.'

'Is this woman a suspect for the murders, Mr Fitzgerald? Is that why you are here?'

'I wouldn't say that exactly. We just need information about her. Before we go any further, Mr Harrison, can you tell me something about this room? I've never seen anything quite like it before.'

If the old man had reservations about telling the story of his study, yet again he didn't show them. 'Since you ask, Mr Fitzgerald, I'll tell you now. It started when I was coming up to retirement at the grammar school. I must have been close on sixty-five. I'd taught there for nearly forty years. In my last couple of terms I wrote an article for the local library about street names here in Salisbury and said that I wanted to spend my retirement writing more local history. The head librarian here was very keen – more so than his successor, damn his eyes. Anyway, the carpentry teacher and some of his more proficient pupils came and rigged up the room with all these shelves. They were all empty then, of course. It was a leaving present and I couldn't have asked for a better one. Since then I've written two volumes of local history which are available in the library. I'm just starting on the third. I've nearly got to the end of Victoria's reign now. That's what I was working on when you called. I should tell you there's another room upstairs full of copies of the local newspaper.'

'And are all these files full, Mr Harrison?'

The local historian laughed. 'No, they're not. I can't think what I would do if they were all full. This is the third filing system I've used since I started. I had one earlier where the Bishop got filed in the turf accountant's folder. They did share the same surname, mind you. Now then, Mr Fitzgerald, let's see what I can do to help. You said your woman was called McQuaid, and Armstrong before she was married. Do you know by any chance if she came from Scotland originally?'

'I'm afraid I don't know the answer to that.'

Walter Harrison rose from his desk and proceeded to bring back a file labelled McA on the front cover.

'Let's see what we've got here. I can't make any promises, Mr Fitzgerald. There are plenty of people walking the streets of the city here who never feature in my files at all. Maybe she was one of them. I'll give you the short version of my file entries.

'McAllister, George, deported for sheep stealing. He won't help us now. McCardle, William, city councillor in the 1850s, later served as Mayor. McFadden, kept a grocer's shop, fathered nine children; he's no good. MacParland, Anthony, farmer famed for his cattle, whatever that means. McQuaid, Horace, merchant seaman, married Bertha, née Armstrong, marriage notice in the local paper, in St Giles's Church, May 1883. There you are, Mr Fitzgerald. Further entry for Horace McQuaid, lost at sea in a terrible storm off the Scilly Isles six months after his marriage. There she is, poor woman.'

Harrison looked up. 'There are no records of any children. That could have been the time when she moved away.'

'Your excellent records don't have a street name, by any chance?'

'No they don't, they just give the name of the city, that's all.'

'Mr Harrison, I know this is asking a lot, but do you think you could try the file with Armstrong in it?'

'The difficulty about local history, Mr Fitzgerald, is the way one thing leads to another. Of course I'll bring down the file labelled "A" and we'll see what we can find. Maybe there'll be an address in there or something useful like that. Do you know how they say your memory begins to go as you get older? Names floating clean out of your brain, that sort of thing? Well it hasn't happened to me yet, I'm glad to say. When it does, that'll be the end of me. You can't commit a city and its people to memory if you haven't got any yourself. Now then, people beginning with A.'

The historian began rummaging through his collection of As. He stopped suddenly. 'Something tells me there used to be a family on the High Street who ran a butcher's shop called Armstrong's. I'll have to have a look in my business file. Hold on a second, Mr Fitzgerald, and I'll check.'

Walter Harrison set off on another journey round his filing system, and came back with another file labelled 'Shops A to M'.

'Would I be right in thinking, Mr Harrison, that you have in that file a list of all the shops that have been here right up to the present?'

'You would, Mr Fitzgerald. Most of the city's in here in one way or another. I try to be accurate in all my volumes of local history. Now then, Adkins, funeral directors. They're long gone. Amiss, general stores, they closed down about twenty years ago, proprietor more interested in the drink than in his other wares. Anson, greengrocer, he sold up and moved away. Doesn't say where. Armstrong, William, butcher's, sold out to the other butcher in the city called Shawcross, 1897. Wife Harriet, two boys and two girls, no names unfortunately – don't suppose the girls would have been much good in the butcher's shop.'

'Any sign of an address perhaps, Mr Harrison?'

'I'll have to go back to the other file for that, Mr Fitzgerald. You're not too bored with all this local news?'

'On the contrary,' said Johnny, 'I'm enjoying every minute of it.'

'Now then,' said Harrison. 'Apthorp of Mafeking Street, prominent member of the local cricket team, he's no good. He's dead these ten years. Armstrong of Silver Street, Salisbury. There's no mention of a butcher's shop, and no mention of any children. Maybe the family are still there, or some of them.'

Johnny Fitzgerald suddenly realized that this might be a good place to stop. He didn't want to get too close to Mrs McQuaid or her family, in case word was sent back to Lynchester about his activities. He didn't want even a hint of his inquiries to get back to Lynchester. After all, if Powerscourt really wanted to talk to the lady in question, he only had to walk a couple of hundred yards to her little house in the Close. He wouldn't want her to know he had been investigating her past history. He wondered why his friend hadn't done so already. There must be a reason, he said to himself. He would report back and await developments.

'Mr Harrison, when I came to see you today I only had a name. Now I have a late husband, a family, an occupation for her father, and maybe even the street where they live or lived. A remarkable performance, sir. I congratulate you. Could I just ask you one thing? I am staying at the King's Arms in Lynchester for the present.

If anything else occurs to you, or some other file has yet to yield up its secrets, I would be most grateful if you would get in touch. It's just possible that something will occur to you.'

'You're quite right, Mr Fitzgerald, that's often how things work out. I shall certainly contact you if anything comes to mind.'

Lord Francis Powerscourt was on his way to talk to the Bishop. Johnny Fitzgerald was back in town and told him what he had discovered in Salisbury. Powerscourt had telephoned ahead to the Bishop's Palace to give notice of his arrival. This was a call he should have made long before, and he knew it. Indolence, he said to himself, sheer bloody indolence. The Bishop was in his study, staring at a blank piece of paper.

'I've got to write another sermon, Powerscourt. You can see how far I have got. What can I do for you today? Is there any news?'

Powerscourt suspected that the Dean and the Bishop were almost in a competition to be the first with the latest news of the murder inquiry.

'It's a delicate matter, my lord. I should have mentioned it before, but you know how it is. You will remember the matter you first came to see me about in London?'

The Bishop looked as though he would rather not have been reminded about that earlier conversation. 'You mean Mrs McQuaid and the first death in Netherbury House? Of course I remember. I am not sure how that bears on our present inquiries.'

'It does and it doesn't,' said Powerscourt, delphically. 'I have no wish to go back over the question of the administration of the sleeping pills. I do wish to talk to Mrs McQuaid about Sir Edward Talbot; whether she knew him earlier in her life, maybe even long before she came to Lynchester. As long as we don't know if there is any connection or not, we can't rule Mrs McQuaid out of our investigation. It is, as I don't need to tell you, a long shot, a very long shot.'

'You're not suggesting the poor woman is responsible for the murder of Sir Edward Talbot, for heaven's sake?'

'I certainly am not, Bishop. I just think we need to clear up a few loose ends, that's all. A great deal of time on investigations like this is spent eliminating people from the inquiry.'

'Very good, Powerscourt. I see what you mean. I shall take you over and make the introductions myself.'

Ten minutes later, Powerscourt was sitting with Mrs McQuaid in her little sitting room. The Bishop had declined the offer of biscuits and departed back to his blank page.

'You must forgive me, Mrs McQuaid, for barging in on you like this. I'm sure you're very busy. There is really only one question I would like to ask you. It may surprise you. Did you know Sir Edward Talbot in the years before you came here?'

Mrs McQuaid looked at him very carefully. Then she began to cry.

'I'm so sorry, Mrs McQuaid, I had no intention of upsetting you.'

Mrs McQuaid rummaged round in her bag for a handkerchief. She wiped her nose. The tears began to dry up.

'I've known for days,' she said, 'that somebody was going to come and ask me that question, Lord Powerscourt. At least you're not a policeman.'

'Take your time, Mrs McQuaid, there's no rush.'

Mrs McQuaid poured herself another cup of tea. 'I always find tea very helpful at times like this. Another cup, Lord Powerscourt?'

'No, thank you.' Powerscourt would have preferred something stronger himself. He felt something very surprising was coming his way.

'I haven't spoken to anybody else about this for years and years, Lord Powerscourt. You must be patient.

'I was brought up in Salisbury. There were two brothers who went away to London and my elder sister, Winifred. My father was a butcher and we had no worries about money. When she was in her early twenties – she was two years older than me – Winifred began walking out with a young man who worked in the grocer's shop in the city. He was handsome, he was well spoken, and he seemed to grow madly in love with Winifred. My father thought he had prospects – I think he checked with the proprietor of the grocer's shop. Thirty-eight years ago they became engaged at Christmas time. The marriage was to be just before Easter. The church and the choir and all that was arranged. Five days before the wedding, the young man disappeared. The wedding was off. He left his job at the grocer's and vanished – presumably to London. I've always thought London must be full of people who ran away from something. The place is so big it could absorb them all without anybody knowing anything about their past misdeeds.'

Mrs McQuaid paused. Her hand began to hover over her handkerchief again. Powerscourt waited.

'It was a terrible time for the family. Winifred never got over it, being jilted at the altar. Early the following year she caught a very bad dose of influenza and died.

That was even worse, especially for my mother. I married a man who was a merchant seaman. At least he managed to turn up for the wedding. Not long after that, my Horace was drowned in some terrible storm off the Scilly Isles. I was so unhappy, I decided the only thing to do was to leave Salisbury. I knew I could never be happy there. I came here to Lynchester and found work in the cathedral. They've been very kind to me. I've been here ever since.'

Powerscourt waited to see if there were fresh disasters to come. Mrs McQuaid had fallen silent. At last he spoke. He thought he already knew the answer.

'And the young man? The young man from the grocer's?' He thought it might be better if the name came from her.

'The young man's name was Edward Talbot, Lord Powerscourt. Now he's dead too.'

'Did you recognize him when he came for his interview?'

'I'd have known him anywhere, even now. I kept well out of his way while he was here, I can tell you. I made sure I performed my duties in the house while he was talking to the clergy or taking his dinner. I never actually spoke to him. I kept well clear of him.'

'So you never talked to him at all?'

'I certainly did not. One look was enough to bring it all back. My poor sister. My poor mother having to bury her. Even now, some years later, I still want to cry sometimes because of what happened all those years ago.'

'But you didn't kill him, Mrs McQuaid?'

'I certainly did not. I was never even in the same room as him.'

'I'm so sorry, Mrs McQuaid. One load of grief is bad

enough. To have it brought back again must be very hard.'

'I think I'd like to stop now, Lord Powerscourt. I can feel myself getting upset again. Come back to ask some more questions if you have to. You've been very kind.'

Powerscourt collected Inspector Vaughan from the police station and told the sad story of Mrs McQuaid and her sister to him and to Lady Lucy in the private sitting room at the King's Arms.

'My God,' said Inspector Vaughan, 'that's put the cat among the pigeons all right.'

'Poor woman,' said Lady Lucy, 'and there weren't any children, is that right, Francis?'

'If there are, she didn't mention them. I'm sure she would have mentioned any offspring if she'd had any.'

'This is the first hint of a motive we've had since the case began,' said Inspector Vaughan.

'Come, come, Inspector,' said Lady Lucy. 'Where did she get the cider eau-de-vie and the strychnine? Is she supposed to have had them both stored up for a rainy day?'

'I don't know the answer to that, Lady Powerscourt. I do know it's a motive and it's the only one we have.'

'All we know about Mrs McQuaid is that she keeps herself to herself. She attends the services in the cathedral every day.'

'Praying for forgiveness perhaps,' chipped in Inspector Vaughan. 'I agree that there may be motive, but it is hard to see how she could have got hold of the murder weapon. It's even harder to see how she could have a motive or a gun to kill Sandy Field. Nevertheless . . . '

The Inspector stopped suddenly and stared at a picture of the cathedral on the wall. 'I'm just thinking about how it might go with Mrs McQuaid if she ended up in court, my lord. "Please tell the court, if you would, Mrs McQuaid, how you felt when your sister was jilted at the altar all those years ago. Now could you tell the court how you felt when you saw the man who had abandoned your sister after all that time?" With a really hostile barrister cross-examining her, things could look bad, really bad, for her.'

'You have spoken to her, Francis,' said Lady Lucy. 'What do you think?'

'Well, I don't think she killed Sir Edward Talbot. She had the motive. But I don't think she killed Sir Edward, and I don't think she killed Sandy Field. I can't see her out on the Close late at night with a gun in her hand. I think we may just be getting overexcited about the arrival of a motive.'

'What about the old gentleman who lived and died in Netherbury House, before the arrival of Sir Edward and the other candidates for the vacancy?' said Lady Lucy. 'Maybe it was he who had the eau-de-vie and the strychnine in his cellar and Mrs McQuaid was looking after them for him.'

'We'll have to search her little cottage, that's for sure,' said Inspector Vaughan.'Perhaps you could arrange for the old lady to be out while we go about our business, Powerscourt. We wouldn't want to upset her any more than we have to.'

'I shall see to it tomorrow. I don't think she would welcome any more visitors today.'

* * *

Inspector Vaughan set out for London early the next morning. His interviews round the Close with the husbands of Sandy Field's previous lovers had yielded three out of five with alibis, loyal wives prepared to say that their husbands had been at home all evening on the night Field was killed. The Metropolitan Police, acting on his request, had checked the London alibis of the husbands of the more recent mistresses of Sandy Field. Both Mr Deacon and Mr Brooks had watertight alibis about their presence in London on the night in question. Two of the latest husbands, a Mr Aldridge from the crescent and a Mr Smythe from one of the terraces, had both been working late in their London offices. Both claimed to have been working with a colleague who could back up their stories. The last train that could have brought them back to Lynchester in time to kill Sandy Field left shortly after seven o'clock. If they were still in London after that, Inspector Vaughan reckoned they were probably in the clear.

'I could have asked the Met to carry out these interviews, but I felt I had exhausted my credit there. I could have sent my Sergeant, my lord,' the Inspector had said to Powerscourt the evening before, 'but something tells me I should go myself. I don't care for London at all so I'll try to get away as soon as possible. My office made the appointments yesterday.'

Mr Aldridge's office was near London Wall. Inspector Vaughan was shown into a large room that he thought must be the partners' room. There were a lot of magazines on coffee tables and the inevitable hunting prints on the walls.

'Good morning, Inspector,' said John Aldridge, 'I see you have decided to come in person. Hold on a moment

223

and I'll fetch Robbie Collins who was working with me that night.'

He disappeared into the main body of his office and came back with a short chubby man who looked about fifty years old.

'Inspector Vaughan of the Lynchester Police. Mr Collins, senior clerk here.'

'Thank you very much, Mr Aldridge. Would you mind popping out for a moment while I talk to Mr Collins?'

'Not at all,' said Aldridge, and he disappeared into the outer office.

'Now Mr Collins, this shouldn't take long. I'm sure you know what we are looking for. It's just a question of confirming Mr Aldridge's alibi. You know the day we're talking about. There was a murder committed late that evening in Lynchester. Mr Aldridge tells us that he was not in Lynchester that evening. He says he was working late with you here in his office. Is that true?'

Inspector Vaughan had spent years of his adult life weighing up witnesses: who was telling the truth, who wasn't telling the truth, who was telling a pack of lies.

'That's right, Inspector. Mr Aldridge was here. I don't know if you are aware of it, but our firm specializes in organizing marine shipping, goods being transported from one part of the world to another. We had a big order on that day and we didn't finish it until well after eight o'clock. I remember looking to check the time as I went home.'

Listening to Robbie Collins, Inspector Vaughan thought he was probably telling the truth. The evidence could have been written down beforehand and learnt off by heart. But the policeman thought that no amount of questioning would make him change his story. The

224

chubby little man would stick to his guns all the way to the Central Criminal Court at the Old Bailey if he had to.

'Thank you very much, Mr Collins. That all sounds satisfactory. Thank you for talking to me.'

Powerscourt was also in London that afternoon for a meeting in Markham Square with Mr George Chambers, General Secretary of the Amalgamated Union of Shop Assistants, Warehousemen and Clerks. He had sent a very polite reply to Powerscourt's letter and made an appointment for four o'clock in the afternoon in Markham Square.

Powerscourt was feeling slightly nervous. He had never talked to the general secretary of a leading trade union before. George Chambers was feeling slightly nervous too. He had never had a conversation with a member of the aristocracy who was also an investigator before.

'Mr Chambers,' said Powerscourt, 'how good of you to call. I'm sure you must be a very busy man. Make yourself comfortable. Tea should be here in a minute.'

'Thank you very much, my lord,' said Chambers, perching on the edge of the sofa. He was in his middle thirties, with a respectable suit and a small, well-trimmed moustache. The most remarkable thing about him was his red hair. Powerscourt was in his favourite seat by the side of the fire.

'That was a bad business down in Lynchester, my lord. Our local secretary went to the funeral as a mark of respect. We may not have cared for Sir Edward Talbot very much, but he was fair most of the time. He realized early on, I think, that a happy workforce will always produce better results than an unhappy one.'

'Thank you for that,' said Powerscourt. 'I mentioned in my letter that we have heard a lot of rumours about Sir Edward's intentions in his last days. Not that he knew they were his last days, if you see what I mean. There was one rumour that he was to mount a takeover bid for his rival Scott's Stores. Then there was another rumour that he was going to close down all the Scott's Stores that were near his own. I'm sure those rumours have reached you too. Do you have fresh information on that score?'

'I think I'd like to answer that question in two parts, my lord, if I may. On the rumour front we have heard exactly the same as you. But we haven't heard a thing since Sir Edward died. It's as if someone put up a brick wall in the middle of the road. Nothing can get past it. It's not surprising, really. Everything will have to wait until his affairs are sorted out.'

'And your second part, Mr Chambers?'

'Well, I'm not quite sure how to put this, my lord. I'm not an investigator myself, I'm a union official. But I did wonder about how your mind might be working, my lord. You have been summoned down to Lynchester to sort out the murder – or murders, if you include the later one. Sir Edward hardly spends any time in Lynchester. I think he only arrived for his first visit the day he was killed. Why would somebody want to kill him? Is there a chance that it might be someone from one of the Scott's Stores that might be closed down, worried that their job and their way of life might be destroyed?'

'You have read my mind very well, Mr Chambers. I didn't want to spell it out precisely in a letter. I thought it might be misunderstood.'

'Let me put your mind at rest as far as I can, Lord Powerscourt. Our shop assistants are not violent people.

Think about how they spend their days, serving the public, on their feet all day in many cases. Imagine spending your days selling shirts in a big store on Oxford Street, my lord. If you were a violent man, you just couldn't do it. You might lose your temper four or five times a day. The employers are looking for placid people, not violent ones. If you worked in a different occupation, like coal mining, it would be different. Some of those miners hate the owners so much they might well contemplate killing all of them if they could. But shop assistants, I don't think so, I'm sure of that.'

'So you don't think it likely that any of your members, even those who might lose their jobs if Talbot's closed down some of Scott's Stores, might get violent?'

'That is correct, Lord Powerscourt.'

'I'm very relieved to hear it, Mr Chambers. I don't quite know how I could have questioned thousands and thousands of your members.'

'Well, I am glad to have been of service, Lord Powerscourt. I wish I could help you in some way. If I hear anything relevant to your inquiries, I shall certainly get in touch.'

Robert C. Smythe and Co., Solicitors, was the nameplate on the Georgian house off Chancery Lane. Mr Smythe was expecting him. He was tall and thin and smoking a cheroot. 'Good day to you, Lord Powerscourt. You've come about the death of Sandy Field, I understand. I'm not sure how we can help you here. I gather you want to speak to my colleague who was with me when we were working late that day. I presume this is to confirm my alibi. I shall fetch the young man who was working with me that night. His name is Perkins, Albert Perkins.'

Perkins was a small young man, barely over five feet

227

tall, with a regulation solicitors' office suit and a mop of dark brown hair.

'Mr Perkins, Inspector Vaughan,' said Smythe.

'I'd be grateful, Mr Smythe, if you could leave us alone together, just for a couple of minutes. It'll be easier to conduct the interview here than down at the police station.'

Smythe looked rather cross. He stalked out of his office, banging the door behind him.

'Now, Mr Perkins, you know the evening we are talking about, I presume.'

'Yes, sir.' Inspector Vaughan thought the young man was very nervous. Still, not everybody welcomed an interview with a senior policeman, even if they had nothing to hide.

'Could you tell me what happened on the evening in question?'

Albert Perkins paused. He looked as if he were trying to remember his lines from the school play. He was blinking rapidly as he spoke.

'We have a big case coming up, sir. The paperwork wasn't finished by closing time, sir, so Mr Smythe asked me to stay on to help him finish the work. I was here till eight o'clock, sir.'

Inspector Vaughan stared at the young man. He was still blinking.

'I don't believe you, Mr Perkins. I think you learnt your lines before I came. Perhaps you'd like to try again.'

'We have a big case coming up, sir. The paperwork wasn't finished by closing time, sir, so Mr Smythe asked me to stay on to help him finish the work. I was here till eight o'clock, sir.'

'Word-perfect, Mr Perkins. You have learnt your lines well. I still don't believe you.'

Inspector Vaughan realized that his witness was caught between the Scylla of his employer and the Charybdis of the forces of law and order. What had the young man to hide? Was this the breakthrough in the case? At last?

'Perhaps you'd prefer to come down to the station, Mr Perkins. All police stations have a good collection of cells.'

The words 'police station' and 'cells' seemed to have a dramatic effect on Albert Perkins. He stopped blinking. He looked rather faint.

'Perhaps you'd like to sit down and consider your position?' said Inspector Vaughan, moving a chair in the young man's direction.

'It's like I said before,' he began, stumbling over his words. 'We have a big case coming up, sir. The paperwork wasn't finished by closing time, sir, so Mr Smythe asked me to stay on to help him finish the work. I was here till eight o'clock, sir.' With that, he sat down.

'You must learn to vary your lines a bit, Mr Perkins. That's the third time you've told me in exactly the same words. I didn't believe you the first time, I didn't believe you the second time, I don't believe you the third time. Do you know, Mr Perkins, that you can be sent to jail for obstructing the police in the course of their duty?'

The young man was trying to compose himself. He was breathing deeply. He didn't speak for a moment or two.

'Very good, Inspector, I'll tell you the truth this time.'

'Please do, Mr Perkins. I'm waiting.'

'Mr Smythe asked me to say all that stuff about working late.'

'Did he write out the lines for you to remember?'

'He did, sir. I can see now that I shouldn't have gone along with it.'

'So what did happen on that evening, the one we're talking about?'

'Nothing happened as far as I'm concerned, Inspector. We do have a big case on at the moment, but that was all finished by five o'clock. I went home to my mother about half past five and we spent the evening together. She was turning the collars on some of my shirts, sir, and she likes me to be there when she does it, for some reason.'

'I see. Did all the others in the office leave when you did?'

'Yes, they did, sir. Only Mr Smythe was left, but he's often the last to leave.'

'So, just to be sure, when you left, Mr Smythe was the only person still in the office?'

'That is correct, Inspector.'

'I see,' said Inspector Vaughan. The last train to Lynchester leaves London at seven o'clock. Smythe had plenty of time to catch it.

'Could I ask you a question, Inspector?'

'You can.'

'You're not going to send me to prison, are you? For lying to the police, I mean?'

'Of course not,' said Inspector Vaughan. 'You told me the truth in the end. Now then, you pop outside and ask Mr Smythe to come in. I don't think I shall need you any more for the present.'

Robert Smythe was looking rather flustered when he came back to his office. 'I presume that's all cleared up now, Inspector. What else can I do to help you?'

'You can do a great deal to help me, Mr Smythe. Perhaps you could start by telling me the truth.'

'What do you mean?'

'You know perfectly well what I mean. Your man here has been instructed to tell me a pack of lies about what was going on here that evening. I didn't believe his story. He was a most unreliable witness, I'm afraid. The fact that he repeated his pack of lies word for word was pretty suspicious, for a start.'

'Are you saying, Inspector, that you didn't believe my alibi?'

'That is correct. Now, perhaps you could tell me the truth about what happened that night.'

Smythe sat behind his desk and lit another cheroot. He was staring out of his window.

'Could I ask, Inspector, that what I am about to tell you should remain confidential?'

Heaven knows what's coming next, Inspector Vaughan said to himself.

'I'll be the judge of that, Mr Smythe, when I've heard what you have to say.'

'Very well. I'm in your hands. Everybody had left the office by about six o'clock that day. I had some papers to tidy up, so I locked up about a quarter past. I then spent the evening with a friend. I returned to Lynchester the following evening.'

'The friend, sir – male or female?'

'Female.'

'And did you spend the night there?'

'I did.'

'And would you be able to give us the name and address of your lady friend, Mr Smythe?'

'Mrs Letitia Danvers, Argyll Street, South Kensington.'

'Perhaps you could remember the number, sir?'

'Number seventeen.'

'Could I make a somewhat unorthodox suggestion, Mr Smythe? Could you telephone the lady right now in my presence and ask her to come to your office immediately? If she says you were where you say you were on that evening, the matter would be cleared up. Once I know that you were in London that night, I can leave you in peace.'

Thirty minutes later, Inspector Vaughan had spoken to Mrs Danvers. She had had no time to confer with Mr Smythe. She confirmed what he had said. Robert Smythe might not have been where he said he was originally, but he had not been in Lynchester on the night in question.

It was only on the train back home that the Inspector saw the funny side of things. He had heard of this kind of behaviour before. Robert Smythe was just following in the footsteps of the late Sandy Field.

18

Johnny Fitzgerald was waiting for Powerscourt in the hotel bar. 'I've got news for you, my friend. It's not going to solve the mystery, but it opens up further inquiries all the same.'

'Tell me all, Johnny. I could do with some interesting news.'

'You will remember, I'm sure, that Sandy Field had two drawings that might have been Old Masters. One showed a naked lady, possibly a goddess, reclining under a group of trees, with a town on a hill in the distance. The other showed a group of elderly men apparently holding a meeting.'

'Yes, I remember. What happened to them?'

'Sandy Field took them to an auctioneer called Peabody in Salisbury. The good Mr Peabody brought a couple of experts from London down to look at them. They offered about fifteen hundred pounds on the spot. Sandy Field refused the offer and said he wanted them to go for auction in London. They were sold recently in a sale of Old Master drawings for eighteen hundred pounds and three thousand pounds, over three thousand more than the two gentlemen had offered in Salisbury. The one with the naked lady was sold as a Titian, the other one as a Rembrandt.'

'Correct me if I am wrong, Johnny, but are these not the two that might have been created on the top floor of Sandy Field's house in the Close?'

'You are absolutely right, Francis. If they were forgeries, he certainly had a lot of nerve. He was offered well over a thousand pounds for them in Salisbury and turned it down. The London people could have gone back to their offices and got their experts to say they were worthless fakes.'

'But that wouldn't have made the art dealers all that money. I seem to remember, Johnny, that they take a substantial cut – handling charges, storage charges, and so forth.'

'Even so, Francis, he made a lot more money by sending them to London.'

'I don't suppose we will ever know if they were Field forgeries or works by Titian or Giorgione or Rembrandt or God knows who. But they're probably Fields, as it were. Either the art dealers thought that they were genuine, or that they would pass muster as genuine. They'll have had some expert on the payroll to tell them what to believe.'

Johnny Fitzgerald ordered another two pints of beer.

'Thanks, Johnny. Two things occur to me. The first does not have an answer but it relates to the psychology of forging, if you like. It's not just about the money, though that would probably be the main thing. A man from the Royal Academy told me last time round with a forger that the forger wants to know he has been successful; that his works, masquerading as Titians or Rembrandts, can take in the greatest experts in the land. That might be why Sandy Field took them through so many hoops, if you like. He wanted to know that he had won, that he had deceived everybody.'

'I can see that, Francis. Do you think he would have been satisfied with one success story? Or did he turn out yet more that we have not yet heard about?'

'That is my second point, Johnny. I think you need to broaden your field of inquiry, as it were. Would the auctioneers here in Lynchester or the fellow in Salisbury get suspicious if he kept turning up with a whole series of Raphaels or Leonardos? Maybe he went further away and took his wares to other dealers, or even straight to London? Who knows? We are thinking that this recent effort with the Rembrandt and the Titian was the beginning. It could have been the last, rather than the first, if you see what I mean. What do you think of that?'

'I fear, as usual, Francis, that you might be right. How many auctioneers do you think there are between here and London? But hold on a minute. Do we need to make further inquiries? I don't suppose for a moment, and neither, I suspect, do you, that the forgeries are linked directly to the murder. Nobody's going to blow your brains out for a dodgy Canaletto or a fake Caravaggio, for heaven's sake.'

'That may well be true, Johnny; it probably is. But we're in the dark as long as we don't know. I think you should press on. We will never know what's under the stone until we turn it over.'

'Did you notice, Francis, the way Inspector Vaughan's mind seemed to be working the last time we talked?'

Powerscourt and Lady Lucy were in their room at the hotel.

'I'm not sure what you mean.'

'I just wonder if Inspector Vaughan is going to arrest Mrs McQuaid on a charge of murder. He seemed very keen on the motive. I just don't believe you could kill somebody because of something that happened all those years ago. And from what I've heard about her, I don't think she is the murdering kind, if you know what I mean. As you said before, I can't see her out in the Close in the middle of the night with a gun in her hand.'

'Well, my love, I have no idea what kind of pressure the Inspector may be under from the Chief Constable. The authorities must be wondering when there is going to be an arrest.'

'You're not suggesting Inspector Vaughan would arrest somebody just to curry favour with his Chief Constable, are you, Francis?'

'The thing about Mrs McQuaid is that she had the opportunity and she had the motive. Everybody could understand such an arrest, even if they didn't agree with it. I'm sure the police often make arrests when they have no intention of charging the person at all. Maybe they get carried away in the heat of the moment. I suspect that they do it sometimes, even when they are sure the victim is innocent, so the real murderer may think he is in the clear and make a mistake.'

The most remarkable thing about the next interviewee for the vacant Netherbury House was his physical appearance. Gervase Crutchley was like a human pencil or a human telegraph pole, dressed up in a dark grey suit with a white shirt and the tie of his Oxford college. He had, appropriately enough, a small, thin moustache, perfectly trimmed. He was in his middle fifties. He had the air of one who finds the external world more difficult than that of the mind. But it was the sheer slimness of the man that was the overwhelming impression. The Dean wondered if he only ate once a day. The Precentor wondered if he ate once a week. The Bishop wondered if he ever ate at all.

'Mr Crutchley, please sit down.' The Dean made the introductions. Gervase Crutchley nodded deeply to each of his interrogators. 'You are at present a fellow of Emmanuel College Oxford, and a philosopher by profession. Is that correct?'

Crutchley managed the hint of a smile. 'That is correct, yes.'

'Could I ask you why you wish to come and join us here in the Close?'

There was a hint of a smile, then it was gone. 'Of course. I have spent my life in the study of philosophy. It is a quest, as you all know, where reliable answers and definite proofs are almost impossible to attain.'

The philosopher crossed his legs and flicked some imaginary dust off his knee.

'I am at present preparing a Life of Marcus Aurelius. My superiors' – was there a slight sneer on the word superiors, hinting at abstruse academic arguments, learned papers fired across the quad? – 'believe that such a biography, such a reassessment, is long overdue. They seemed to think that even members of the public might wish to purchase such a volume. I'm not sure I would like to go that far.'

The Dean had come across enough philosophers in his

time to know that they were best kept away from their special interests. Otherwise the whole interview could disappear into a discussion about the precise meaning of virtue or the ninety-nine names of God.

'That is all very interesting, Mr Crutchley,' he said; 'perhaps you could tell us why you wish to come and live here.'

The human pencil sighed. 'There are a number of reasons. The principal one is that I want to get away from Oxford and find the right time and place to work on my book. I know the world would say that there cannot be any better place than Oxford to write a book. I disagree. You could say that I am tired of Oxford. Perhaps that means I'm tired of life too, I'm not sure. I'm tired of the petty feuds that constitute college life. I'm tired of the undergraduates, writing notes to each other in my lectures, endlessly applying for postponement of tutorials because they haven't finished their essays, shouting to each other across my court, being sick in the fountain in the middle of the quad beneath my windows. I have been to Lynchester before to give a talk to the senior boys at the grammar school. They were well behaved and seemed genuinely interested in what I had to say. That was a refreshing change. I don't suppose you notice it if you live here, but there is a deep peace around your Cathedral Close. I would like to share it.'

'Would it be fair to say,' Timothy Budd, the librarian and archivist, threw his hat into the ring. 'Would it be fair to say that you have had a row or are in the middle of a row with your college authorities?'

'I feel that might be something of an exaggeration. Let me say that I have asked to be moved to a different set of rooms three times now and always been refused.'

'So would you be coming to us to make a fresh start, away from the noise and the troublesome undergraduates?'

'I feel that too might be an exaggeration, stretching the facts further than they can actually bear. Of course I could continue living in my college. I would much prefer to come and live here.'

'Thank you,' said the Dean, sensing that the Oxford conversation was something of a blind alley. What mattered was not how the pencil-shaped man was getting on in Oxford, but his reasons for coming to the Close.

'Precentor,' the Dean went on, 'perhaps you would like to take over?'

'Thank you, Dean. Mr Crutchley, I am responsible for the music here in the cathedral: the choir and its anthems, the services that are spoken, and the concerts and so on. Would that side of life interest you at all?'

'I enjoy church music. I would certainly come to some of the services and concerts. But I have a great difficulty with the theological underpinning of church music. There is, as far as I know, no reference in the four gospels to singing and choirs and similar activities. These activities might have been added on at later dates to impress the devout and attract new members into the faith. But I cannot forget that they could not be described as the authentic voice of God's message. They are appendages to Christ's teaching.'

The Dean thought that each avenue of questioning seemed to produce a querulous response, as if there were pitfalls everywhere.

'Perfectly reasonable point of view,' said the Dean, anxious to close this line of argument down before it descended into metaphysical and theological thickets he had no wish to visit. 'Perhaps I could ask you for your attitude to the Christian faith in general. Don't get me wrong, Mr Crutchley, we have unbelievers as well as believers in our little community here. Scepticism is no barrier to entry.'

Gervase Crutchley paused. He stared for a moment or two at the plate of biscuits in the centre of the Dean's table, as if they might provide him with enough sustenance for a week or so.

'I think I would say, Dean, that I adhere to the Christian faith. I attend the services. My particular favourite is evensong – spoken not sung. There are a number of things in the Apostles' Creed I simply don't believe. I don't think that Christ is coming at the last day to judge the quick and the dead. There are simply too many of us. I don't believe in the Virgin Birth – the whole thing could be due to a mistranslation of the word "virgin" in the original Greek. I would not go so far as to say that I don't believe in miracles, but I am deeply suspicious. They might have been stories invented after the event to impress the doubtful and dumbfound the Pharisees. But if you are going to have a religion, and I think mankind has a very deep need for religions, you may as well have this one. If that makes me sound a rather sceptical Christian, so be it. I cannot pretend to believe in some of the tenets of Christianity, that's all. It might have brought peace to the cathedral and its Close, but the Church militant also brought us the wars of religion and the Crusades.'

'Thank you, Mr Crutchley,' said the Dean. 'Bishop?'

The Bishop himself had dabbled in philosophy at university. He gave it up, as he said to himself at the time, because it could never make up its mind. He decided to bring the conversation back to more mundane matters.

'Forgive me, Mr Crutchley, could I ask if you are a family man, if you would be bringing other people than yourself to the Close?'

'I have a wife and two grown-up children, Bishop. The boys are no longer at home. My wife's father was an Archdeacon in Rochester, so she has some experience of Church matters. She was brought up in this life here.'

Looking again at the extraordinary thinness of the man, Timothy Budd wondered how many meals a day were served in the philosopher's residence. One? Two when the children came to visit? Three on a birthday?

'Thank you, Mr Crutchley,' the Bishop carried on. 'Perhaps you could tell us what you would bring to our little community here?'

Crutchley flicked another speck of dust off his trouser leg. He stared, almost hypnotized, at the plate of biscuits.

'It depends, Bishop, on what you mean by "bring". I assume you are not referring to material possessions, but to more general questions of character. I think I would bring an inquiring mind to Lynchester. I might or might not bring it a certain amount of fame when my book on Marcus Aurelius comes out. I know my publishers have high hopes of it. Honesty – I could bring some of that. I would hope to participate in the life of the cathedral and the Close. I can bring little in the way of athletic pursuits, but I have a certain reputation as a scorer and as an umpire at cricket. I would do what I could to live a life of virtue. Do I make myself clear?'

'Umpires and scorers are always a blessing at cricket,' said the Bishop, thinking suddenly about philosophical arguments and what you meant by 'leg' and what you meant by 'before' and what you meant by 'wicket'. 'We have a good cricket team at present playing for the Close.

I'm sure they would welcome you with open arms. Is there anything else you wish to say, Mr Crutchley?'

'I don't think so.'

'Very well. Thank you so much for coming to see us. We shall be in touch.'

'Have you heard the news?' A distraught Inspector Vaughan burst into the Powerscourts' quarters at the hotel.

'You haven't arrested Mrs McQuaid, have you, Inspector?' said Lady Lucy.

'It's worse than that, Lady Powerscourt, much worse. Mrs McQuaid was murdered this afternoon. Smothered with one of her own cushions, according to the doctor.'

'Please tell us all you know,' said Powerscourt.

'Very well,' said Inspector Vaughan. Outside, the first shadows were beginning to appear on the street. 'This is what we know from the interviews we've done so far. I've tried to arrange the evidence in time order. The times are largely taken from the sundial, as most of our witnesses didn't have watches of their own. So all the times are approximate.'

'That must have taken some time,' said Lady Lucy.

'I've left gaps all the way through to put in the later witness statements. Nothing much happened between two and three. Various gardeners were passing to and fro. Shortly after three o'clock, Mr Puckeridge was seen passing the sundial. He had a sheaf of papers in his arms, as if he was going to a meeting of some sort in the cathedral. Nobody seems to have seen him returning to his office, so he must have gone back to his office by the path round the back. About twenty past three, two builders

– Johnny Smith and George Gardiner – passed by on their way to make repairs to the choir stalls. The wood has been chipped in places, apparently. Mrs O'Keefe from number twenty-eight West Terrace was seen heading off towards the shops just before half past three. At about twenty-five to four, one of the schoolteachers was also seen going towards the cathedral, but they're going back and forth all day, those people.'

'Did most of the people take their time from the sundial?' asked Powerscourt.

'Some of them did and some of them remembered what time they'd left home.'

Inspector Vaughan sounded slightly cross at his narrative being interrupted.

'At twenty to four, a delivery man appeared on his afternoon rounds. At a quarter to four, the supervisor in charge of the building work in the choir stalls came past. At ten to four, one of the kitchen staff from the cathedral was seen heading off to the High Street with a large basket, presumably to buy some more provisions. By four o'clock a man from the stationer's was seen making a delivery to the cathedral. At ten past four a couple of porters removed some chairs from the nave and took them round to the workshops at the back. At twenty past four, one of the porters from the cathedral headed off towards the shops. And about half past four, Mrs Pettigrew from the crescent pops round to see Mrs McQuaid. She finds her dead in her little chair by the fire. She'd been strangled.'

'How terrible,' said Lady Lucy.

'Fortunately the doctor was not far away. He arrived in about fifteen minutes. He said that Mrs McQuaid hadn't been dead very long. He put the time of death between three and some time after four o'clock, maybe earlier. The body has been moved by now, I hope. In a moment I must go back to the station and fill in some of the gaps.'

'There doesn't seem to be anybody who didn't have any business in the Close at all,' said Powerscourt.

'I don't think there usually is,' said the Inspector. 'These movements are exactly what you would expect.'

'Your account is very full, Inspector. Your men have done well. But I cannot for the life of me see how it takes us any further forward.'

'I must get back to my men, my lord. It doesn't do to leave them on their own too long at a time like this.'

19

Earlier that afternoon, the four clergymen who were to decide the ownership of Netherbury House were back in the Dean's dining room to award the prize. The Dean was presiding, the Bishop on his right hand. The Precentor and the archivist were below the salt, as it were, on his left.

'Thank you very much for coming, gentlemen. This is a sad occasion and I suggest we spend a moment or two in silent prayer for the deceased.'

Timothy Budd, the archivist, stared out of the window at the Close beyond. He thought it slightly hypocritical to mourn for the three people, including a man they had met for less than half an hour, but the Dean must have his way in his own house.

'Now then,' the Dean was in businesslike form today. 'I don't think this decision should take us very long. I suggest we hear each member's views before we make our final choice. Mr Budd, if you please.'

For Timothy Budd this was only the second of these occasions he had attended. He knew what he wanted to say was controversial. That, for him, was part of the appeal.

'Thank you, Dean. I suspect that my choice will not find favour with any of the rest of you gentlemen. Let me, if you will, run through the four remaining candidates. Captain Chapman is, on the surface, if I could put it like that, the outstanding candidate in my view. A distinguished man in his own field, he is playing a vital role in the defence of our country. We should all be grateful to him and hope he has success in his career. But I would draw your attention to what he said towards the end of the interview. Even now, in peacetime, he has to spend most of his time aboard his ship. If, heaven forfend, war with Germany were to come, he would be at sea virtually all the time. I suspect that as the Captain is meant to be the last man to leave the sinking ship, so the Captain may be the last man to be granted shore leave. We would be making Netherbury House over to his wife and children, who would of course be welcome, but the main participant could be away for years at a time. I do not believe the statutes, if there are any for this procedure, would approve such a choice.'

Glancing to his left, Timothy Budd could see the Dean beginning to glower. The Bishop seemed lost in thoughts of another world.

'I come now to the academic gentleman. He too is in many ways an admirable candidate. He would, no doubt, have to spend some time giving lectures and so on at his place of work, but so do many of our other residents, in the law courts or the counting houses of London. But I doubt that he would be happy here. There are no other philosophers here for him to talk to. I think he would feel like Ruth, lost amid the alien corn. So I do not think he is suitable for our purposes.

'As for the army gentleman, I just do not believe he would fit in. His thoughts would be far away – as indeed he might be – in the intrigues of army policy and army conduct and army strategy. I do not think we want to enlist such a man in our Close here. And the Colonel would be another absentee landlord.

'My own choice goes to the candidate who seems to have the least appeal on the surface. Our schoolteacher friend is the youngest candidate. He bears no scars of battle won in the heat of the day. His only distinction is the quality of his teaching, which I am told is first class. He has, through the school, the strongest links with the cathedral and our little community here. He has a young family. And he has one other advantage. He would be here all the time. When you look at the residents of the Close, it seems to me that too many are chosen because they will bring distinction to Lynchester because of their past records. They are, if you like, prize candidates, the prize for them being residence in this beautiful place and, for us, the distinction of having them live here. Most of them are not here very often; they are away in the great world adding further lustre to their record. So I would favour the schoolteacher.'

The Dean looked more and more uncomfortable as the archivist proceeded, as though he had just eaten something rather disagreeable. Was it for this that he had favoured Timothy Budd over five other candidates for his post? Was he to be rewarded now by what he regarded as a form of treachery? When the Precentor was invited to speak, the Dean realized that his troubles were only just beginning.

Rupert Digby, the Precentor, glanced down at his note-pad before he began.

'In many ways,' he began, 'I agree with our young colleague here. We should be taking a view on the candidates, not on the record of their careers, but on what they would bring to us here in the Close. I do not feel I can support either the naval gentleman or Colonel Colquhoun. Their business is killing and, as Mr Budd said, the killing may increase if war comes. I do not think we should welcome such people into our community, however successful they are in their activities. In time of war, Lynchester should be a haven of peace, not a rest home for soldiers and sailors taking a break from the slaughter.

'I do not agree with our archivist about the school-teacher, although I can see why he might appeal. I think he is too young at present. He can try again.

'My own preference is for our philosopher. I think he would be an admirable candidate. He would bring a whole new dimension to the composition of the Close.'

Out of the corner of his eye, Rupert Digby could see that the Dean was beginning to turn red. If affairs did not go his way, he had been known to reach purple.

Aylmer Fettiplace Jones, the Dean of Lynchester Cathedral, was breathing heavily.

'My dear Bishop, what are your views in this matter?'

The Bishop looked like a man who has just returned to earth from a long journey through the stars. 'I find these thoughts most interesting. They are well worth considering. My own preference is for the naval gentleman. I thought he was the most distinguished of the candidates by some distance. He may not be here a lot of the time, I grant you. There has been a lot of talk of war. I do not think it will come myself. In that case, if there is a sort of stalemate in the North Sea, the demands on the Captain's time will not be so time-consuming. He will be able to join our community here and I am sure he would bring a lot of qualities with him. That is why I am supporting him for the lease of Netherbury House.'

'Three members of our little committee,' said the Dean rather crossly, 'and three different candidates. I am afraid that I am about to bring a fourth into play. I agree with the Bishop when he says there has been a lot of talk about war. The Precentor seems to believe that we in the Close should steer clear of any involvement in any particular conflict. Myself, I take the contrary view. I believe that it is our duty to support our armed forces in every way we can. Patriotism is not only the preserve of the ungodly. It is also the cause of the righteous. That is why I am supporting Colonel Colquhoun. If we can offer him a haven of peace while his life is filled with the manoeuvres and the disposition of the forces of the Crown, we should be doing our nation a service. I believe the naval gentleman is too far away. I believe the philosopher would not be an appropriate candidate at this time. The same applies to our young schoolteacher friend, who can, as the Precentor pointed out, try again.'

The Dean glared round at his colleagues, as if daring them to disagree with him. Timothy Budd, the archivist, looked across to him.

'What are the procedures, Dean, when there is no agreement among the members of the committee? Has anything like this happened before?'

'I am glad to say there has never been a disagreement like this before. I would ask you to reconsider your positions for the sake of harmony. Mr Budd?'

The archivist felt that he would probably lose out on the final decision. But he decided that he would not go down without a fight.

'I have given this a lot of thought already, Dean. I do not want to change my mind.'

'Precentor?'

'I am of the same view as the archivist.'

'Bishop?'

'As ever, Dean, I remain firm in my beliefs.'

'Could I ask a question, Dean?' Timothy Budd was girding his loins for battle.

'Of course.'

'There are four of us here. Do we all have a vote?'

'A vote, young man? You did say "vote", didn't you? Did the disciples have a vote?'

'I'm not sure we have enough evidence to say whether they did or not. The fact there is no mention of a vote in the Four Gospels doesn't necessarily mean that they didn't have one.'

'I would have thought, young man, that your study of our ancient manuscripts would have taught you something about the nature of authority in our Church. It will always attempt to respect the opinions of its congregations while reserving to itself the right of supreme authority in matters of doctrine and policy.'

'I repeat my question, Dean. Do we have the vote or not? This seems to me to be another example of the Church pretending to be democratic with one hand while being authoritarian with the other. Is that not so?'

'I do not agree, Mr Budd. What would you have us do? Where would we be without authority, rule, precedent? Would you have us elect the ministers of the Church like the unfortunate Presbyterians? That way chaos lies.'

'I still don't think you have answered my question, Dean.' Timothy Budd was delighted to see that the Dean's face had turned from a red to a sort of mild plum, well on the way to purple.

'I am trying to make you understand the nature of authority in the Church, young man. You must see how necessary it is. Without authority, the Church would dissolve into a number of competing sects and factions. It would be chaos. You might not like the concept of authority in Church affairs, but you must recognize that it is there. I have always thought the Church is like some great tree. The Vicars are the leaves, the Archdeacons are the twigs, the Bishops are the branches and the Archbishop of Canterbury is the trunk. I cannot put it more simply than that.'

'Do I assume – as we are, at best, leaves on your tree – that we are not to have a vote in this particular question of who comes to live in Netherbury House?'

'If you want a definitive answer in this particular case, I cannot give it to you now. I would have to consult my files and the statutes. The decisions have always been unanimous in the past. I hope that we can reach unanimity again in this particular case.'

'Could I make a suggestion, gentlemen?' The Bishop didn't want this spat to go any further. 'I think we need time for reflection. Could I suggest that we meet again tomorrow and see if we can reach some measure of agreement? I don't think it would be fair to delay the appointment any longer. We need to have the matter settled quickly.'

Lord Francis Powerscourt was pacing up and down his sitting room in the hotel. Lady Lucy was sitting by the fireplace, staring at the wallpaper as if she thought it ought to be replaced immediately with something more suitable.

'Listen to me if you would, Lucy, while I take a walk round the remains of my brain. I am trying to pull these various deaths together to see if there is some pattern that eludes us so far.'

'Imagine I'm walking by your side, Francis. Please carry on.'

'The first death was that of Mr Simon Jones, the man the Bishop came to see me about. It's plain that there are only two possibilities here: that the man took the overdose himself, or that Mrs McQuaid administered it to him. I've always thought it likely that she did it, but I don't think there was ever enough evidence to convict her in a court of law. Now, we know that there was a connection between Mrs McQuaid and Sir Edward Talbot in that he jilted her sister at the altar all those years ago, but I think that was just an accident, one of those strange coincidences that come to make life difficult. I don't believe she had any connection with Sandy Field, except for being a neighbour in the Close. So I don't think she could be the link that ties all the murders together. Are you with me so far?'

'I agree, Francis. I must say I cannot see that there is any link that connects all four people together.'

'For the purposes of this conversation, Lucy, I think I want to leave the first death out of it. I cannot see how it has any bearing on the other three.'

'I'm not sure you can do that, Francis. I don't for a moment think that Mrs McQuaid killed Sir Edward Talbot, but she did have a motive.'

'But the motive was decades old by now. If she'd wanted

to kill him, surely she would have tried for a position with him or near him years before this. And how did she get hold of the poisoned eau-de-vie?'

'How did any of them get hold of the poisoned eau-de-vie, unless it was in Simon Jones's cellar? We just don't know.'

'Well, let's leave Mrs McQuaid to one side for now,' said Powerscourt. 'We are still with the first murder that can definitely be called a murder, that of Sir Edward Talbot of Talbot's Stores. We know he had a connection with Mrs McQuaid, but that was all a long time ago. And, apart from the application to take on the lease of Netherbury House, are there any links that connect the other murders?'

'Surely there is one thing that links two of the others, Francis. That application for the lease. Sir Edward Talbot was a candidate. Sandy Field looked after the legal side of things.'

'Surely people don't go round committing murder for a house, even if it is a very beautiful house in beautiful surroundings. And none of the candidates knew anything of their rivals for the position. None of the other four, as far as I am aware, could have known the names and occupations of any of the others. It's not possible that one of the other candidates could have killed Sir Edward because they wouldn't have known about him and his application. So I don't see how that gets us any further.'

'How about blackmail, Francis? Nobody's mentioned that so far. Do you think there could be a blackmailer about somewhere?'

'I can just about see a blackmailer in the cases of Sir Edward and Sandy Field. Maybe somebody was blackmailing them, or one of them was blackmailing the other, who knows? Sandy Field's track record would have made him a ripe target for blackmail, but nobody here could have known enough about Sir Edward Talbot to blackmail him.'

'You don't suppose that there were two different murderers, Francis? One for Sir Edward and another for Sandy Field and Mrs McQuaid? That might make our lives easier. Maybe there is something in the rumour that Sir Edward was going to buy Scott's Stores and sell off the shops that were close to his.'

'I know little about shops,' said Powerscourt gloomily, 'and even less about shopkeepers. All I have to go on is what the general secretary of their trade union told me. He thought it highly unlikely that any of his members would get around to murder. They might be cross, but they wouldn't kill anybody.'

'Let's go back to blackmail for a moment, Francis. Suppose Sir Edward was being blackmailed. For some reason the blackmailer follows him down here, or – more likely now I think of it – he sends down a hired killer to finish Sir Edward off because he hasn't paid up, or has stopped paying up. He could have been the man in black who was never found. He disappeared somewhere into the rail networks of western England.

'Was he blackmailing Sandy Field too? Did he come back again to finish him off? You said yourself that Sandy Field would have been a prime target for blackmail.'

Powerscourt stopped walking up and down and sat down by the fire. 'I don't think the blackmailing route is getting us anywhere,' he said. 'Any possible motive seems to work for one death but not for them all.'

'There must be something that connects them, Francis.'

'Let's go back to the first death, Lucy. Suppose Mrs McQuaid did kill Sir Edward. Suppose that her former employer Simon Jones had a bottle of eau-de-vie and some strychnine in his possession. Don't even think of asking me how he got them for the moment. Maybe he liked going to France in earlier times and brought back the eau-de-vie with him. Mrs McQuaid pops round to Sir Edward and offers him a drink to celebrate his coming to the Close.'

'Why didn't she have a drink herself? How come she was still alive the next morning?'

'You are being practical and unhelpful, Lucy. Don't expect this narrative to be consistent in any way for the moment. She tells him that she doesn't like this particular drink. It makes her sick, or some such story. She says she only drinks a small dry sherry at Christmas and on her birthday. Sir Edward knocks his own drink back and that's the end of him.'

'And Sandy Field? How does he come to be killed?'

'Let's just bring the blackmail theory back to life. If there was any one person who was liable to be blackmailed in Lynchester, that was Sandy Field. He goes for a late-night meeting with the blackmailer or his representative. He refuses to pay – maybe he hasn't paid for a while. The man shoots him.'

'Two down and one to go, Francis. Why does Mrs McQuaid get killed?'

'God knows, Lucy. I certainly don't.'

Powerscourt brushed some crumbs off his jacket and began walking up and down again.

'There is one thing we don't know much about, Lucy, and that is the arrangements for the sale of the house, handled by Ardglass, Puckeridge and Ross. If there is anything untoward going on in that respect, I doubt very much if any of the Church brethren know anything about it at all.

I shall get the relevant addresses from the Dean's office tomorrow. I'm going to write a letter to all the candidates.'

Inspector Vaughan arrived and sat himself down by the fireplace. He was looking dejected. 'Well, my lord, the picture about Mrs McQuaid hasn't changed at all. We don't have any more witnesses with fresh information. I have spoken to three of the witnesses and I don't believe they were lying. I'll see the others first thing in the morning. We checked her cottage this morning while she was at a service in the cathedral. There was no sign of cider eau-de-vie or strychnine.'

'Lady Lucy and I have been talking through the various possibilities, Inspector. We are no more cheerful than you appear to be at present. The only hint of a conclusion we came to was that the only thread linking some of the murders together is the question of Netherbury House and who should live in it. As I said to Lucy before, I'm going to write to all the candidates and ask them if they have seen anything odd about the proceedings. I hold out very little hope, I must say.'

Later that day, the Dean summoned Timothy Budd to a meeting in his study. The young man had only been in here once before.

'Mr Archivist and Librarian, please take a seat.'

Timothy Budd was relieved to see that the Dean's face had returned to its normal colour. The files were still mounting around his desk in well-ordered rows. Charm rather than menace seemed to be the order of the day.

'I have been meaning to ask you about the progress of your work with our ancient manuscripts, Mr Librarian. We all look forward very much to seeing the fruit of your labours and the translation into English of some of the more obscure sections.'

'The work is going well, Dean, but more slowly than I expected. My progress with some of the material is not as fast as I would like. My colleagues in other places tell me that is only to be expected.'

'Quite so, quite so,' said the Dean. 'I suspected something of this sort might happen. But the completion of the work must take precedence. I have been checking the details of your appointment here and I see that you are due to complete your work by Christmas. Do you think you will be able to meet that deadline?'

'I very much doubt it, Dean. If you pressed me hard I would have to say no.'

'Well then,' said the Dean, smiling at the young man in the manner of one who brings good news, 'other things being equal, what say you to the prospect of us extending your term of employment with us here until next summer, with the option of a further period until next Christmas?'

'That would be very kind indeed.'

'Consider it done, and a very good afternoon to you. May your work go well.'

With that the young man left the Dean's study, wondering about which other things might be equal and in what way.

'Dear— ' Powerscourt began, leaving the addressee blank until he had finished his draft.

> Please forgive me for writing to you out of the
> blue. I am an investigator, based in London.

The Bishop invited me down to Lynchester
to investigate the recent deaths here. I am
working with Inspector Vaughan of the local
constabulary.

Sir Edward Talbot, of Talbot's Stores, the first
candidate to be interviewed, was poisoned.
The lawyer Sandy Field, who looked after the
legal side of things was shot. Mrs McQuaid,
housekeeper to Netherbury House, was
smothered. I regret to say that this is proving a
difficult assignment.

I am writing with what may seem to be a
ridiculous question. In your negotiations with
Ardglass, Puckeridge and Ross concerning the
lease of Netherbury House, was there anything
that struck you as unusual? I know this must
sound a bizarre query but it may have some
slight bearing on our inquiries here.

My apologies once again,
With best wishes
Powerscourt

The Dean had an impromptu meeting with Rupert
Digby, the Precentor, in the choir stalls just after evensong.

'What a fine service, Precentor, and the choir were in
good heart. I have often thought that evensong is my
favourite service of all our devotions here.'

'Thank you, Dean. We aim to please God and man in
all our services.'

'Now then, I have been looking at the accounts for the
choir.'

The Precentor closed his eyes. He was no good at
arithmetic or accounts, and handed the whole question

over to the Bishop's Chaplain, who had been awarded a first-class honours degree in mathematics before he was called to the Church.

'Do not be alarmed, my dear Digby. The accounts are in much better shape than I expected. The reason I wanted to speak to you today is that I am virtually certain that we should be able to increase the annual subvention to the choir in the next financial year. Other things being equal, this should enable you to conduct a short tour with the choir, as well as buying some more sheet music. That should all be in order.'

'Thank you very much, Dean. That is excellent news and I am very grateful.'

'You will see,' said the Dean, leading the way towards the West Door, 'that we don't have to put these sorts of questions to the vote.'

The Precentor smiled as he emerged into the light. He didn't feel it was very difficult to work out which other things might or might not be equal. He headed off in the direction of the archivist's quarters.

Part Three
Action Stations

20

Inspector Vaughan and his colleagues spent the following morning checking through the notes of all their interviews, looking for a clue they might have missed. Powerscourt was busy with his letters. Johnny Fitzgerald was still on his quest for any other auctioneers who might have handled Old Master drawings for Sandy Field. One of the Inspector's younger Constables, fond of reading American thrillers, suggested that Mrs McQuaid was obviously in charge of an international criminal gang, masterminding a wave of murder and mayhem from the Close. Inspector Vaughan told him to shut up and get on with his work.

The four clergymen filed back into the Dean's quarters at exactly eleven o'clock.

'Gentlemen,' the Dean began, 'I have checked through the records of all previous invitations to vacant properties in the Close, and I can find no directions anywhere about what to do in the event of a four-way split between the remaining candidates. There have been majority decisions in the past, where the dissident agreed to change his mind and voted with the majority. We, as you know, do not even have a majority. So let me ask you first of all if any of you has changed your mind.'

The Dean turned towards his left. 'Bishop, any change in your position?'

'No, there is no change in my position, Dean. I am still in favour of Captain Chapman of the Royal Navy.'

'Well, that leaves our two junior members. Mr Archivist, perhaps you have news for us?'

Timothy Budd had thought long and hard about his position. He had spent the better part of an hour, the evening before, discussing their options with the Precentor in the back room of The Mitre.

'I do have some intelligence for you, Dean. I have given the matter considerable thought. I realized that none of you gentlemen was likely to change your mind in the direction of my preferred candidate. He may be too young; it may be too soon for him to come and live in the Close. So I turned my attention to the remaining candidates. My objections to the philosopher are as strong as ever. By his own admission he is a man who finds it difficult to live in institutions. I feel now, as I did yesterday, that he would be a difficult and divisive character. My objections to the military gentleman, Colonel Colquhoun, also remain the same. He would never be here. He would always be up in London trying to influence the future direction of the war, if war should come—'

'Forgive me for interrupting,' said the Dean testily, 'but don't you think that we should be offering the man help and comfort in his hour of need by welcoming him to the Close?'

'I'm afraid I don't,' said Timothy Budd. The Dean was

glowering at his table. He felt that the decision and the choice of winning candidate might be slipping from his grasp.

'Please carry on,' said the Dean.

'Thank you, Dean. As you have probably worked out by now, I have decided to switch my preference to the Bishop's preferred choice, Captain Chapman, the naval gentleman. He is a distinguished man in his own field and I am sure he will be a credit to our community.'

'So you are content to offer him the comforts of the Close rather than to the army gentleman.'

'I am.'

'I see.' The Dean was beating his fingers on the table. Two for the Bishop, but only one vote – his own – for his preferred candidate. What was the use of offering inducements when the recipients didn't follow their instructions, even if they were never precisely spelt out? It was all down to the Precentor now.

'Precentor, perhaps you would like to share your thoughts with us?'

'Thank you, Dean. I too have given the matter some consideration. And I, like our archivist here, have decided to change my mind.'

The Dean looked more cheerful. Maybe the Precentor had taken his enlarged budget to heart.

'My objections to the schoolmaster remain the same. He is too young. Like my colleague, I could see little prospect of more votes coming to my philosopher. Like the archivist, I have decided to support the candidacy of Captain Chapman.'

In their discussions in The Mitre the previous evening, both men had agreed that they would support the Bishop rather than the Dean.

'Thank you for that,' said the Dean. He realized that he had been outmanoeuvred. Perhaps he had outmanoeuvred himself. He resolved to put a brave face on things.

'Very well, gentlemen. So be it. Captain Chapman is our choice. I shall add my vote to the other three so that we preserve that unanimity which has always been a feature of these proceedings in the past. I shall contact the lawyers at once and let them know our choice.'

As he left the room, the Dean was already thinking about possible revenge on the two who had let him down.

Johnny Fitzgerald caught up with Powerscourt at the hotel. He threw himself into an armchair and stretched his legs.

'I've been halfway round southern England on your behalf, Francis, and I've just had one hit, if you see what I mean.'

'Where was that?'

'It was in Winchester. There's a very expensive-looking auctioneer over there. He told me that a man called Field had dropped in what looked like an Old Master drawing about two or three weeks ago. He asked the auctioneer to send it to a couple of dealers up in London to see what it would fetch at auction. He was very specific about the auction, apparently.'

'Has the fellow had a reply yet?'

'He has not. I told him to get in touch with Inspector Vaughan or yourself or me when he had word from London.'

'Well done, Johnny. You have done well.'

'I'm not sure about that, Francis, not sure at all. You can

do a lot of thinking on all these trains. I've been trying to work out how these Old Master drawings fit in with the murder inquiry, and I can't do it.'

'You can't find any connection at all?'

'Not one that works. I can't believe anybody would kill you for a couple of forged Raphaels, I really can't. You may talk about blackmail but I don't think that can work either. If you were the blackmailer and you knew about the forgeries, you'd want to keep Sandy Field alive. You'd want him producing more and more of the things so you could keep on blackmailing him for ever. If you shot him dead in the dark, you wouldn't be able to collect any more blackmail money. And that's the last thing you would want. I just can't see why the blackmailer would want to kill the goose that laid the golden eggs.'

'Suppose this business of forging has been going on for a long time. Suppose there are other outlets we don't know about. Maybe the blackmailer got too greedy and Sandy refused to pay up.'

'Why should he refuse to pay up?' said Johnny. 'If the blackmailer knows what Sandy Field's been up to, then his whole career could disappear for a second time. Nobody wants to employ a solicitor who forges Old Masters in his upstairs room. What's he going to do to your will after you're dead? Rewrite the whole thing when you're safely in your grave? Anyway, forging Old Masters must be a crime.'

'What happens, Johnny, if one of the auctioneers is the blackmailer? Not necessarily the auctioneer himself, but an associate to whom he gives tasty titbits from time to time?'

'I've thought of that. I thought about it a lot in some bloody train that seemed to move at little more than walking pace outside Winchester. The same objections apply, surely? The blackmailing auctioneer and his companion in crime wouldn't want to stop the supply of forgeries. And Sandy Field seems to have taken a lot of trouble to place his masterpieces in a whole lot of different places.'

'However the forgeries were working out, Johnny, it seems nobody can have wanted the supply of forgeries to stop. Heaven only knows, if we went through the Field household, we might find a secret place where Sandy kept his masterpieces – with a whole lot more stashed away.'

'Do you agree with me, Francis, that it's very difficult to see how the forgeries could have led to the murder?'

'I agree that it's very difficult, but I wouldn't want to rule it out just yet. We are as far off finding the murderer as we were when we started. And let's not forget, people might not kill for an Old Master, but they could certainly kill for the thousands of pounds it might fetch at auction.'

Inspector Vaughan was in sombre mood the following morning. 'I just don't feel we are making any progress at all.'

Powerscourt had decided on a new line of attack. 'Look here, Inspector, maybe we should try a different approach. Whoever the murderer is, he seems able to move about without being seen by any of the inhabitants of the Close.'

'I agree. What do you suggest?'

'I think we should try following the money. Take Simon Jones for a start. Do we know who he left his money to?

Did any of it go to Mrs McQuaid? And if so, how much? Then there's Sandy Field. We know he was anxious to leave enough money to look after his wife if anything happened to him. Where is it, this money? From my memory of your conversation with the bank manager, his account was in good order, but it doesn't sound as if he was building up a nest egg. Did he have another account in the same bank? Somewhere he put the money from the Old Masters, perhaps?

'Then there's the whole question of Ardglass, Puckeridge and Ross. You will remember that the other solicitor fellow claimed to have a number of clients who came to him precisely because their charges were so high. Could we find out how high they were, and if they were outside the recommended charges set down by the Law Society?'

'That's quite a shopping list, my lord. I can certainly deal with the first one about Simon Jones. His solicitors weren't in Lynchester at all, but with a prestigious firm off Chancery Lane. I shall write to them directly. And I shall call on the bank manager again to see if Sandy Field had a second account.'

'I think I shall drop a note to the widow Field and say I would like to talk to her again this afternoon.'

It was just after three o'clock when Powerscourt was shown into the Field drawing room in the Close. He realized that if he was going to talk to Mrs Field about her husband's state of mind in the weeks before his death, he would probably have to speak to the latest lover as well. He found it almost impossible to decide which one Sandy Field would have talked to about his problems at work.

'Lord Powerscourt, how good to see you again. Please sit down.' Mrs Field was wearing a long black dress and looked more composed than when Powerscourt had last seen her.

'Mrs Field, thank you for seeing me so promptly. I just have a few questions. It doesn't really matter if you don't know all the answers. I wouldn't want you to be worried.'

'The Bishop has been very kind, Lord Powerscourt. He has said that I can stay here for as long as I want. That was a great relief.'

'The last time I was here, you mentioned that your husband had been bringing a lot of papers home from work in the weeks before his death. Did he say what the papers were about?'

'No, he didn't, Lord Powerscourt. He did say once that things weren't right – but what things, I don't know.'

'Did he mention the firm he worked for at all?'

'He might have done, I'm not sure. I never really understood what Sandy did all day, if you see what I mean. It seemed to involve a lot of charging about. He was always a great one for going out and meeting people.'

'And you didn't have any idea about his concerns on this particular occasion?'

'There was one thing I'm trying to remember, Lord Powerscourt. I think he mentioned something called the Law Company, or something like that, but I wasn't really paying attention at the time.'

'Law Company or Law Society? The Law Society is the body that looks after the interest of solicitors in this country.'

'I'm afraid I can't remember.'

'Never mind, Mrs Field, you've been very helpful.'

Inspector Vaughan was closeted once again with Sandy Field's bank manager.

'How nice to see you again, Inspector. I presume you have come with further questions about Mr Field's money.'

'I have. The last time I was here you told me that his account was in good order with nothing out of the ordinary about it. My inquiry today comes from the fact that Mr Field appears to have been selling Old Master drawings and making considerable sums of money from them. Did he have another account here into which he deposited these funds?'

'I presume you are following normal police procedure in the case of deceased persons?'

'I am.'

'Very well then. I did not feel it appropriate to mention it the first time you called, as I knew Mr Field wanted this other account kept confidential. But, in our present circumstances, I have to tell you that he did indeed have a second account, solely for the use of his wife. It was, in fact, in his wife's name. It was into this account that the Old Master money went. There was a sum of between five and six thousand pounds in this account. No money was ever taken out of it to the best of my recollection. It grew steadily year by year as Mr Field deposited whatever surplus cash he had into it. He told me – it was in confidence, but I am sure he would want me to break it at a time like this – that the account was to look after his wife if he died before her. We also have a copy of his will here, in which he left all his worldly goods to his wife.'

'There was nothing untoward about this second account? No monies taken out of it at all?'

'Absolutely none,' said the bank manager.

'Thank you very much.'

Two hours later, Powerscourt was knocking at the door of Julia Brooks, last known lover of Sandy Field.

'Lord Powerscourt, I trust you are making progress in your inquiries.' She was wearing a dress of deep red. Powerscourt wondered if there were rules concerning the clothes and the colours appropriate to the mistresses of the dead.

'Mrs Brooks, I just need to ask you a couple of questions about Mr Field's state of mind in the weeks before his death.'

'Please carry on, Lord Powerscourt. Anything I can do to help.'

'We understand that there was something worrying him at that time. Did he, by any chance, mention it to you?'

'I remember him saying that there might be something odd going on at the solicitors', but he didn't say what it was. He hardly ever said anything to me about his work. He said he had to keep that side of his life confidential and he didn't want anybody else to get involved. He said it wasn't fair.'

'Did he mention the business about Netherbury House at all, Mrs Brooks?'

'Only to say what a nice house it was and that whoever was chosen would be a very lucky man.'

'He didn't mention who he thought the lucky man might be?'

'No, he didn't. I think he would have regarded that as out of bounds. There is just one other thing. I remember him saying that he might have to go to London soon on business and would I like to come too. He meant to London, of course, not to the business.'

'And did anything come of that?'

'No,' she said rather sadly. 'Do you know, Lord Powerscourt, I have never been to London with Sandy. I never will now.'

Johnny Fitzgerald had gone back to the offices of Gillespie and Crowther, the local auctioneers. He felt he could happily reach the end of his days without ever seeing an auctioneer's premises again: the worn carpets, the half-broken chairs, the over-elaborate curtains and the sagging settees. Mr Gillespie seemed pleased to see him.

'How good to see you again, Mr Fitzgerald. What can I do to help?'

'My apologies for troubling you once again, Mr Gillespie. I was wondering about the procedures you followed when Sandy Field was putting some of his clients' goods up for auction after their death.'

'Procedure? I'm not quite sure what you mean. We would make a note of the client Mr Field was acting for. He always dealt with us when there was a sale that involved his firm. When the goods were sold we would send the monies, minus our own account of course, to the solicitors handling the affairs of the deceased. That never varied.'

'And there weren't any occasions when the money went direct to Mr Field himself?'

'Only if he was handling the relevant account.

That sometimes happened, but it wasn't the normal practice.'

'If you were a very suspicious man, Mr Gillespie, do you think it possible that Mr Field could, as it were, have intercepted the money en route, so that it went to his own account rather than that of the client?'

'In theory that might have been possible. But we always sent the account to Mr Field, acting for the estate of whoever the dead person was. So I don't think it's possible. And I would never have believed that Mr Field was capable of such a thing. We get some people in here, Mr Fitzgerald, and you wouldn't trust them an inch. But Mr Field, he was a real gentleman. He would never have done anything like that.'

'Thank you very much,' said Johnny, and set off back to the hotel. They knew that Sandy Field had forged the Old Masters. The only question now was, what else had he been forging?

Powerscourt was checking his correspondence when a porter rapped on his door and announced that Mrs Field wanted to see him as soon as possible.

'Is there something the matter?' Powerscourt asked. 'Is the poor woman ill or something?'

'Afraid I don't know, sir. I was just asked to deliver the message.'

Mrs Field was sitting in her wheelchair by the window gazing out at the Close. She had tried to tidy herself up, but Powerscourt thought she had been crying.

'Lord Powerscourt, thank you so much for coming. I am so upset I cannot tell you.'

'What is the matter, Mrs Field? What's happened?'

'I don't think I've been in such a state since I heard Sandy was dead. It's too dreadful. I don't know how I'm going to get over it.'

'Perhaps,' said Powerscourt, 'it would help if you could tell me what happened.'

'I'll just have to compose myself for a moment, Lord Powerscourt.'

She turned her gaze from the grass and the early flowers of the Close and looked closely at Powerscourt.

'It can only be half an hour or so since it happened. I don't think it's any longer than that.'

She took a deep breath and checked her hair. 'I was sitting here, reading my book, when the maid showed a young lady in.' She stopped for a moment, as if her memory might be at fault. 'She wasn't very well dressed and she had a baby who seemed to be wrapped in rags at her hip. Daisy Cooper, she said her name was. Now I think about it, I don't believe she told me what the baby was called. It was a boy, I think. She had a simple story to tell. She lives in a rented cottage in one of those little streets down by the station. I think they were built for the original railway workers, I'm not sure. Her husband has been very ill. She said they had used what little spare money they had to pay for the doctor and the medicine. So she couldn't pay the rent. She was sure they would all be evicted. The husband still isn't getting any better. She's worried to death about his cough. It won't go away, apparently. He needs another visit from the doctor, only they haven't got any money. They'd have nowhere to go as their families all live up in the North of England. She was very upset about all that.'

'I don't see how you come into this sad story, Mrs Field.

How did the poor woman get in to see you in the first place? Why wasn't she turned away at the door?'

'Agnes the maid said she felt sorry for her.'

'I see. But what does it have to do with you?' Even as he asked the question, Powerscourt suspected he knew the answer.

'She said Sandy owned the house. The lawyers acting for him had told her when they moved in. She said he owned three of the houses in that street. She was coming to see me to explain why she couldn't pay the rent, you see.'

'She said what?'

'She said Sandy owned the house.'

'Did you know Sandy owned the house and rented it out?'

'I had no idea. That was what upset me – the fact that he hadn't told me about it before.'

'I see. Let me be absolutely clear about this. Your late husband had bought three houses in Lynchester, near the railway station, without telling you?'

'That seems to be the case.'

'God bless my soul. I don't think there's anything to worry about, Mrs Field. I suspect it was all part of his plan to look after you in case anything happened to him.'

'But something did happen to him, Lord Powerscourt. He's dead and he's never coming back.' She looked close to tears.

'I can see that this has come as something of a shock, Mrs Field. It would be enough to shock anybody. What did you say to Daisy Cooper, the woman with the baby?'

'I'm sure I did the wrong thing. I told her to forget about the rent for the time being. I gave her enough money to pay for the doctor to come again. What else could I do?'

'I'm sure the Church would be proud of you, Mrs Field. I'm certain that was the right thing to do.'

Powerscourt thought there must be thousands of tenants up and down the country who would wish they had Mrs Field for a landlady.

'I'm sure that was the right thing to do, Mrs Field,' Powerscourt said again. 'Would you like me to tell Sandy's firm of solicitors to look after things from now on?'

'Do you know, Lord Powerscourt, I don't think I would like you to do that. They might decide to play by the rules and throw them all out on the street.'

'Would you like me to talk to somebody from the cathedral? Maybe the Dean could help. It's the kind of thing the Dean is very good at. The Church owns all kinds of houses all over the place here.'

'I think I need some time to think about it all. I'm still so upset. Tell me again, Lord Powerscourt, why you think Sandy went in for buying up houses?'

'I can only guess at the answer, Mrs Field. But I think it was another way of trying to secure your future in case anything happened to him. You would have another source of income from the rent.'

'You don't think he was going to leave me?'

'I don't for a moment see how you could take that meaning out of it. You have told me before that he always said that he would never leave you, and I don't see how this changes that one little bit. Income from renting out houses is a reliable source of money as long as the houses don't start to fall down. You don't have to do very much, apart from repairs and maintenance. It would have been another kind of income for the two of you, or for you if anything happened to him.'

'I just wondered if he was building up other sources of income so he could have enough money to support himself in another establishment with another person.'

'I don't think that's true at all, Mrs Field. I'm sure of it. Now, is there anything practical you would like me to do now? I'm going to ask Lucy to come and see you later today. We can't have you getting upset over something like this.'

'That would be very kind of you. I don't think I want you to do anything at all until I've had more time to think about it.'

'Promise me you're not going to sit here all day wondering if Sandy was going to leave you. He wasn't.'

She managed a smile. 'You've been very kind, Lord Powerscourt. Thank you for coming so promptly. I look forward to seeing Lady Lucy later on.'

21

Inspector Vaughan groaned when Powerscourt gave him the news. 'What else do you suppose the bloody man was doing, my lord? One day he's forging Old Masters, then he's buying up houses, then he goes and gets himself killed. Still, it could have been worse, I suppose.'

'What do you mean?'

'Well, he could have put the houses in his wife's name. I'm sure that could have caused a great deal of confusion. He could just have popped a few documents down for her to sign – nothing important, dear, just routine business, you don't even need to read it. There we go. Thank you very much.'

Powerscourt laughed. 'Tell me, Inspector, do you think this takes us any further forward in the quest for his killer?'

'Not on the face of it, my lord. But I wouldn't rule anything out. Not in this case, anyway. I do have one fresh piece of news. I've heard from Simon Jones's solicitors. He left all his money to the cathedral to be used as they think fit. There wasn't a great deal of money involved, apparently.'

Powerscourt had a conversation with Dominic Porter, the hotel manager, later that day as he was taking tea on his own in the hotel drawing room.

'You've been working very hard on your investigation, my lord,' said Porter.

'I just wish we were making more progress,' said Powerscourt. 'Every time we think we've turned a corner, it turns into a brick wall.'

'I'm sorry to hear that, my lord. We were all very sorry to hear about Mr Field. He was a very popular man, well liked by everyone in Lynchester.'

Not quite everybody, Powerscourt muttered to himself. 'Was he a regular visitor here, Mr Porter?'

'Not so much as he used to be. There was a time a couple of years back when he was in and out of the hotel a lot.'

'Was he on his own?'

'Now I come to think of it, he usually had a young lady with him. Mrs Barker she was, Alexandra Barker, and pretty as a picture.'

'This is very interesting. Was she married, this young lady?'

'She was. Husband an architect or a surveyor or something like that.'

'How long did these visits go on for, Mr Porter? Days, weeks, months?'

'Do you know, I'm not quite sure. One day they were here as usual. The next they were gone. The lady moved away to a village called Thorpeville Barton, about seven or eight miles from here. They say the house is beautiful. The husband comes back here from time to time for his work.'

Does he indeed, Powerscourt said to himself. What sort of work?

'Do you know if the house had a name?'

'Anybody in the village could point it out to you, my lord. It's called the Old Rectory.'

Ten minutes later, a note was on its way to Mrs Alexandra Barker asking if Lord Francis Powerscourt could call that afternoon in connection with the recent spate of murders in Lynchester.

She answered the door herself. It was, she said, the maid's afternoon to spend time with her aged mother. 'Do come in, Lord Powerscourt. I have heard quite a lot about you from people in Lynchester and round about. How can I help?'

'Thank you very much for agreeing to see me at such short notice, Mrs Barker. I'm not really sure if I should be here at all. You see, I wanted to ask you about your friendship with the late Sandy Field.'

Alexandra Barker turned pale and stared out of the window for a moment to her lawn and her apple trees. 'I thought it must be that, Lord Powerscourt. I'm surprised you heard about it at all. It lasted such a very short time and it all happened such a long time ago. I hope we can regard this conversation as confidential.'

'Of course. Is it true that you and Mr Field were close friends for a while, Mrs Barker?'

She laughed. 'That would be one way of putting it. The more correct way would be to say that we were lovers. I don't suppose you are surprised at that.'

'Perhaps you could tell me a little about that time. And

perhaps also why you left Lynchester in what appeared to be a great hurry.'

'This is quite difficult for me, Lord Powerscourt.' She paused briefly and stared at a blue tit hopping about on her lawn. 'Let me put it this way. He was a very easy man to love, Sandy Field. He was good looking, he was charming, he knew how to talk to women. I don't suppose it lasted very long, our affair; only a month or so. It was springtime when it started. Then for me summer was cancelled. Autumn too, I suppose. It was winter for a very long time.'

Powerscourt waited for a moment. 'Forgive me for asking, but did the affair run its course, as it were? Did it just sort of stop, as these things sometimes do?'

She laughed a rather bitter laugh. 'No, it didn't run its course, as you so politely put it. It didn't end like that at all.'

Powerscourt waited again.

'We, I, both of us had to break it off. It was my husband, you see. I don't know to this day how he found out about us, but he did. My Johnny is a reasonable sort of man in most ways, fond of hunting and cricket, but he wasn't reasonable at all about this. I know as well as you do why you're here, Lord Powerscourt. You want to know if my husband could have killed Sandy Field. I have to tell you I don't think he did. He did get rather violent once he discovered our secret, mind you. He kicked quite a lot of furniture. He used to take himself off for very long walks on his own. He said it calmed him down. He wasn't sleeping well either. He was liable to bring the subject up all the time, like scratching at a wound. I really got rather worried about him.'

'Did your husband make any threats at all? That he

would like to punch Mr Field as hard as he could, that sort of thing?'

'There was a certain amount of that.'

'Might I ask how you resolved it?'

Alexandra Barker laughed. She pointed dramatically round the room and the gardens beyond. 'This is how we resolved it. I had to promise never to see Sandy again. I cannot tell you how difficult that was. We moved out of Lynchester so I would not be able to see him again. That's when winter started. That's when we came to this house. It's beautiful; it's all anybody could want in a house: it's old, it's got a history, it's got lovely rooms and gardens. It doesn't mean a thing to me. Sometimes I wonder if I shouldn't ask if we can move again. Then I think I would be miserable in another house, just like I am here.'

'I'd like to come back to your husband for a moment if I could, Mrs Barker. Would it be fair to say that his anger has grown less over time?'

She waited before she replied. 'You know as well as I do, Lord Powerscourt, what the real question is here. Did my husband kill Sandy Field? Well, I don't think wives are allowed to incriminate their husbands. The courts would never be empty if they were. He might have been capable of murder when he first heard of our affair, I don't know. It's not for me to say. As for now, I just don't know. I don't think so. I can't tell what's going on in his head any more. It's not my job to go around the place solving murders and other horrible crimes. It's yours.'

'Touché,' said Powerscourt. 'I'm quite prepared to admit that I'm not doing very well on that score at the moment. Let me ask you one final question, Mrs Barker, and then I'll be on my way. Did your husband have anybody he talked to in the difficult times? Any special friend?'

'Goodness me, Lord Powerscourt, you're like vultures you people. You're still feasting on one body when you start thinking where the next one's going to come from.'

'I would remind you, Mrs Barker, that I am trying to find out who killed Sandy Field. You might find my methods repulsive, but they are all I have. I repeat, was there anybody special your husband might have talked to in these difficult circumstances?'

'Since you ask, I think he talked to someone at the cathedral.'

'Do you know by any chance who that person might have been? The Dean? The Bishop? Some other member of the cathedral staff?'

'I'm afraid I don't know. And now, if you don't mind, I'm going to have to ask you to leave. I'm really rather upset.'

Inspector Vaughan had the air of a man who devoutly wished he was somewhere else, engaged on some different case. 'Is there no end to these women? This one didn't even appear in the little notebook Mrs Field gave Lady Powerscourt with the details of lovers past. Are they going to keep turning up at the rate of one every few days? I'll have to send my men over to that bloody village now. Did the man Field ever have time to do any work?' He got up out of his chair in the Powerscourt sitting room and went to stare out of the window at the shoppers and sightseers making their way up and down the High Street.

'How about this, my lord? We're looking not for one but for two murderers. Mrs McQuaid gave the overdose to Simon Jones, the old man with the terrible illness. In my book she did it out of kindness, but she killed him just the same. Thank God I don't have to decide whether to put her in the dock or not. Then she kills Sir Edward Talbot of Talbot's Stores. That's a revenge killing for what he did or didn't do to her sister all those years ago. Sandy Field was killed by the husband of this latest woman who kicked a lot of chairs when he was at home – Barker, I think you said the name was. He has to kill Mrs McQuaid because he thinks she might have seen him walking away from the scene of the crime. If she tells the police, he's in very serious trouble, so he gets rid of her before she can speak to me or one of my officers. Barker goes home to Thorpeville Barton, where he tells the wife that he has had a very good day at the office. How's that, my lord?'

'It's all very plausible, Inspector. If it were true you could wrap up the case now. But I don't think you believe it is true. I can imagine that Mrs McQuaid might have killed Simon Jones out of kindness, as you say. But I can't see her taking the poison and killing Sir Edward. I just can't. And for the time being I don't see how we can pin the murder of Sandy Field on the man Barker, any more than we can pin it on one of the other husbands who appear in this case. As for Mrs McQuaid seeing the murderer, she might well have done, but surely she would have come forward before she was killed. So I don't think your theory holds up, Inspector. Part of me wishes it did. But I don't think you're convinced either.'

'No, I'm not. As I said, I shall have to send my men out knocking on doors again. Would you like me to speak to Mr Barker, or will you do it yourself?'

'Why don't you speak to him, Inspector? You've had a certain amount of practice, after all. Let me tell you something else. I have written to the remaining four candidates who would like to live in Netherbury House. I was asking them if there was anything unusual about the procedure. I've had two replies so far. Both, and I find this rather odd, both say the matter is confidential. They don't quite say that they have signed something which indicates their agreement to confidentiality, but that's the implication.'

'Why on earth should it be confidential? It looks pretty straightforward to me. Sign here. Hand over the money. And the house is yours for the length of the lease.'

'Maybe it has always been confidential. That could be the way it has always been. The cathedral people might not want everybody in the Close knowing how much the new arrivals had paid for their house. Some of them might want reductions in their own rents. That's the best I can do. Perhaps I'd better go and see the Bishop. I could ask if the man Barker came to see him as well.'

'There's something not quite right about it, if you ask me,' said Inspector Vaughan. 'We'll have to wait and see what the other two have to say.'

Powerscourt secured an interview with the Bishop the following morning. He had breakfast with Johnny Fitzgerald. A whole new line of inquiry had occurred to him in the night.

'Johnny, I know you have been finding out a great deal about Mr Field and his forgeries – if they are forgeries. I think we've been too preoccupied with the Old Masters and the beautiful women. We've been far too preoccupied with the beautiful women.'

'You mean *you*'ve been too preoccupied with the

beautiful women, Francis. I haven't seen a single one of them. I've been stuck with a lot of dead Italian artists.'

'Fair enough, Johnny. I'll try and save the next one for you if you like. Tricky waters asking them if they think their husband could have killed their lover. Never mind. What I'm trying to get at is this. Did Sandy Field have any rich relations who might have left him a great deal of money? Inheritance, as we both know only too well, can often be a motive for murder by those who want to jump the queue. I'm going to ask Mrs Field, but if you could make some inquiries, that would be very helpful.'

'All right, Francis. I'll do it on one condition.'

'What's that?'

'That I get to interview the next beautiful woman who comes along. We can't have got to the end of them, not by a long way.'

'Done,' said Powerscourt.

22

Powerscourt found the Bishop walking very slowly round his cloisters. 'Good morning, Powerscourt. I try to walk round here two or three times a day. It calms me down. Maybe it's the presence of the dead trying to reassure the living. Come now, I can continue this another time. Come to my study.'

'There are two matters on which I would welcome your advice, Bishop,' Powerscourt began. 'The first and most delicate concerns a man called Barker who lived in Lynchester a couple of years ago. He discovered that his wife was having an affair with Sandy Field. He moved house very soon after this discovery. His wife believes he talked about the matter with somebody at the cathedral. I wondered if that might be you.'

The Bishop stared out into his garden A member of the staff was mowing his lawn. 'Barker, Nicholas Barker, would that be the man?'

'I'm afraid I don't know the Christian name and I didn't feel it appropriate to ask. My interview with the wife was a rather bumpy ride, if you follow me.'

'I see. I think we can assume that it was Nicholas Barker; he came to see me a number of times. I find it difficult to know what to tell you, Lord Powerscourt, because Mr Barker certainly did not intend the nature of our conversations to go any further. It's a bit like the confessional all over again, if you remember our earlier conversations.'

'I understand that, Bishop, of course I do. Perhaps you could tell me the general nature of your meetings.'

'Yes, I can do that. The poor man was having a lot of trouble with his anger. He couldn't control it. It would sweep over him out of the blue and leave him in a very poor state. He wasn't asking me to provide any answers – after all, I am a man of the cloth and not a doctor of minds; he just wanted somebody to talk to.'

'And did he continue to come and see you after he moved away?'

'He did, but less frequently than before. I think that as his anger ebbed, which it did with the passage of time, he no longer felt the need to come and talk to me. I think I was a sort of safety valve.'

'I see. Would you have said that Mr Barker was a violent man, Bishop?'

'My dear Lord Powerscourt, your good manners are sometimes too good for your own good, if you'll pardon that expression. There is really one question you want to ask me, but you can't quite work out how to phrase it.'

'And what might that question be?' said Powerscourt with a smile.

'You want to ask me if Nicholas Barker could have killed Sandy Field either then or recently. There, that wasn't too bad.'

'And what is your answer, Bishop?'

'Well, you won't be surprised to hear that we didn't

discuss murder or violence at any point. The thing that struck me about Mr Barker is that most of his anger was directed at himself rather than the other two parties. He was angry with them, of course, but the bulk of his wrath seemed to me to be directed at himself. He is a devoted churchman – not that that necessarily means you can't go round killing your fellow man – and I think that may have helped him. So, in answer to your non-existent question, Lord Powerscourt, I think the answer is no. I could be wrong, of course. I have probably given away too many secrets already. Let us move on to your other question, if we may.'

'My other query, Bishop, is very simple and quite trivial in comparison. I have been asking the candidates for Netherbury House a couple of simple questions about the arrangements for the purchase of the lease. The reason for my requests does not concern us here. Two of the gentlemen have replied saying that all the details are confidential. Is that the normal practice with these leases as they come up?'

'I believe it is normal. Certainly it has applied to all the leases I have been involved with since I came here. I shouldn't pay any attention to it. You obviously don't wish to discuss the reasons for your inquiries, but I find it hard to imagine how the details of those agreements could have any bearing on these deaths in the Close.'

'You have been very kind and very helpful, Bishop. Perhaps you have time now to return to your cloister walk?'

'I wish I did. I have always regarded that as God's work. I'm not so sure about my next engagement, a meeting with the diocesan subcommittee on Church stipends.'

* * *

Mrs Field was in her usual place, sitting in her wheelchair by the window, watching the birds hopping about on the lawns outside.

'Lord Powerscourt, how nice to see you again. I imagine that you have not yet solved the mystery or you would not be calling on me. What can I do to help?'

'It's very simple really, Mrs Field, and forgive me for asking it. Did your husband have any rich relations who might have left him some money?'

'Whatever will you think of next, Lord Powerscourt? There is a great-aunt somewhere in west London who was very rich. Aunt Euphemia, she was called. She was something of a family joke, really. My husband and I would have fantasies about what we would do with her money when she was gone. Go and live in the Danieli Hotel in Venice for a month. Sail round the world. Travel to China and see the Great Wall. There was no end to the fantasies we could rustle up. All a bit mean on the old lady, seeing that she was – and is still – alive, as far as I know.'

'How old is the lady?'

'She must be in her late seventies. Her husband made a fortune in the brewing industry – he invented some sort of machinery that makes the process more efficient, but I'm not an expert in that sort of thing.'

'Does the old lady have a lot of relations left alive, do you know?'

'I think there's another nephew somewhere or other, but I've no idea where he lives.'

'Forgive me for asking, but do you know how much money there is going to be in her estate?'

'We could only guess at that, Lord Powerscourt. Our ignorance meant that we could let our imaginations run riot when it came to spending this imaginary fortune.

I think I heard Sandy say once that she was worth well over ten thousand pounds when she was gone.'

'You could stay in a grand hotel for quite some time with that sort of money, Mrs Field. Even at the Danieli.'

Mrs Field smiled. 'Sandy always thought she would divide the money between her two relations, but we have no proof of that at all. I think he just felt it would be the logical thing to do.'

'Thank you very much, Mrs Field. If you could remember the address in London, that would be very helpful.'

'I'll send it over to the hotel later on.'

Johnny Fitzgerald looked round the houses in Belgrave Square. Great-Aunt Euphemia lived at number twenty-seven. An elderly butler showed him into the drawing room on the first floor. An elderly maid brought coffee. Johnny wondered if all the staff were as old as their employer. Mrs Ransome's hair was completely white and she was wearing a pale blue dress. She was carrying a diary in her left hand.

'You said in your note, Mr Fitzgerald, that you wanted to talk to me about my great-nephew Sandy Field. How very stupid of him to get himself killed like that. I presume that you and your colleagues don't know who killed him. Otherwise you wouldn't be here.'

'You are absolutely correct, Mrs Ransome. I have to admit that our investigation is not going very well at the moment. Perhaps you will be able to help.'

'I don't know how I can help you at all. I see – or I saw – Mr Field on a very irregular basis; maybe once or twice a year, at most. I was not a party to his way of life with all those married women down there in the country.

I suppose the only redeeming feature was that he didn't leave his wife, the poor woman with that dreadful disease.'

'Perhaps you could tell us something about Mr Field as a young man, Mrs Ransome?'

'I must say that I do not see for a moment how that could help you in your inquiries, Mr Fitzgerald. I did see him more often in those days, that is true. I do not believe that his behaviour as a young man has any bearing on his death. He was in his thirties when he met his end. I knew him well fifteen or twenty years before that.'

Johnny Fitzgerald was beginning to think that this interview was rather like drawing teeth. 'And what was he like as a young man?'

'He was very charming. Very interested in ball games – tennis, cricket, that sort of thing. He had one of those minds that absorbs information very quickly, so examinations were never a problem. I think he spent too much time enjoying himself at Cambridge to do well in the Tripos there. He was always very polite. He had a very strong sense of what was right and what was wrong.'

'Did he ever show any signs of being good at art?'

'Well, he did have this rather strange ability: he could reproduce anybody's signature whenever he felt like it. He once showed me a perfect replica of my own signature and teased me by saying he was going to make off with all my money. Not that he would ever have thought of doing such a thing – that would just have been wrong in his book. You see I think, Mr Fitzgerald, that I knew him before he set out on his life as an adulterer. I cannot think of another word that describes his conduct better.'

'How did you hear about his various escapades, Mrs Ransome?'

'Word gets round, you know. There was that business in Oxford, and I gathered from something his wife said to me that there hadn't been much change in that department since they moved elsewhere. It was as if he couldn't stop himself. He could never resist the challenge of a beautiful woman.'

'Might I ask, in the context of a murder inquiry, what you intend to do with your estate now he's gone?'

'I have suspected all along that this was the real reason for your visit here, Mr Fitzgerald. I can think of no reason, apart from cowardice, why you didn't mention it before.'

'It is not the only reason I came, Mrs Ransome. Your information about Mr Field as a young man has been most interesting.'

'What would happen if I refused to tell you what I mean to do with my money?'

'You have every right to keep quiet about that if you so wish, Mrs Ransome. I imagine that other people, police officers for example, might come and talk to you. Or they could talk to other members of your family. Or they could talk to your solicitors. It is very difficult to hide things in a murder inquiry.'

'Would I be right in thinking that, if I were to give you a name, you would go straight round and ask him or her a lot of questions?'

'That would be the case, yes, Mrs Ransome. I'm afraid you are absolutely right.'

'Very well then. At least you are an honest man. I shall give you a name. I intend – indeed I have for many years decided – to leave my entire fortune to the Church of England, to be used as they think fit in the alleviation of poverty in the East End. Even you, Mr Fitzgerald, are unlikely to accuse such an institution of murder.'

'I am much obliged to you, Mrs Ransome. A very good day to you.'

Johnny Fitzgerald whistled as he made his way back to the Tube station. Powerscourt, he suspected, would not be pleased to learn that a whole raft of potential suspects had simply disappeared from the inquiry.

Powerscourt himself was looking at a letter from Colonel Colquhoun, one of the candidates for Netherbury House. It confirmed that the whole question of the lease was indeed confidential. The Colonel regretted that there was nothing he could do to help, and wished Powerscourt Godspeed in his investigation. But his other letter from Captain Chapman, the naval gentleman, was rather different. He read it out to Lady Lucy.

> Dear Lord Powerscourt,
>
> Thank you for your letter. I have to tell you that the whole question of the lease is confidential. I have signed a document to that effect. However, I fully understand that murder makes its own priorities. I would be happy to discuss your investigation with you if you feel that might help in your inquiries. I have to be in London for a meeting at the Admiralty the day after tomorrow, and would be happy to call on you in your house in Markham Square at three o'clock in the afternoon. The Admiralty is notorious for meetings that go on far too long, but even My Lords should have completed their business by then.
>
> I look forward to seeing you then,
> Johnny Chapman.

'Well, Lucy, do you think this is a shaft of light, or just another door closing? This case is like one of those long corridors in official buildings, where the doors on either side keep closing on you as you get close to them.'

'The Captain still says that the question is confidential, Francis.'

'He does, but he also says that he is willing to meet and discuss it. Surely that's progress of a sort.'

'I shouldn't hold out too much hope, Francis. Maybe you will be able to convince him that the question of justice can outweigh the needs of confidentiality. Do we know, by the way, who the winning candidate is?'

'We don't. I think the men of the cloth have decided on their candidate, but he has yet to accept. We should hear in the next couple of days.'

Later that afternoon, Powerscourt met Johnny Fitzgerald with news of Great-Aunt Euphemia. Powerscourt was most interested in the details of their conversation, but did not seem too concerned that there was not another tranche of possible suspects. Johnny suspected that his friend was waiting for his meeting with the naval gentleman.

Two days later, Powerscourt was talking on the telephone to his brother-in-law, William Burke, while he waited for Captain Chapman to dock in Markham Square.

'William?'

'Burke here. That you, Francis? What can I do for you today?'

'I was just wondering if there was any fresh news about Talbot's Stores?'

'I was saying to myself only yesterday that there should be some news by now. But there isn't. There have been a whole series of meetings at Talbot's headquarters, but that's only to be expected at a time like this.'

'Nothing at all?'

'Nothing. Might I ask how your investigation is going?'

'Badly, William. I'm not much better off than I was before I started.'

'That's not like you. Let me know if there is anything I can do.'

'Thank you very much.'

Captain Johnny Chapman was in full naval uniform, all dark blue and gold braid, when he was shown into the Powerscourt drawing room.

'How very kind of you to come and see me, Captain,' said Powerscourt.

'I just wondered if I would be able to help in some way.'

'Let me just tell you about the murders, if I may. They all took place round about the same time as the interviews for the lease on Netherbury House. I am not saying they are connected, but I suspect very strongly that they are. Quite how they might be connected, I do not know.

'The first murder victim was Sir Edward Talbot, owner and patriarch of Talbot's Stores. He was also the first candidate to be interviewed. That took place in the afternoon. After a dinner with the clerical gentlemen, the Dean, the Bishop and a couple of others, he went back to Netherbury House where he was to spend the night. He had a meeting there with person or persons unknown. His visitor persuaded him to take a drink of cider eau-de-vie, which was laced with strychnine. We presume the killer left before the poison began to take effect. He would also seem to have avoided taking any of the drink on offer. Of the bottle or the poison we have no knowledge. They have not been found.'

'Did nobody see the killer make his way to or from Netherbury House?'

'By this stage it was quite late in the evening. Nobody saw the killer.'

'I see. How very difficult.'

'The second murder victim was Mr Field, the solicitor who was handling the transfer of the lease. I presume you have had some dealings with him. He was called out of his house in the Close late in the evening a couple of days later. He was shot at close range and died on the spot. Once again there were no sightings of the murderer.

'And the third person to die was Mrs McQuaid, who had been housekeeper to the previous tenant of Netherbury House. She was strangled in the middle of the afternoon. There were a number of sightings on this occasion, but there were no strangers spotted. Everybody who was reported as walking across the Close had a reason for being there.

'So, there we have the three murders. As you can see, the first involved a candidate for leasing the house, the second involved the lawyer who was handling the transactions with the various candidates and arranging the interviews, the third the old lady who had looked after the previous tenant while he was alive and kept an eye on Netherbury House. There, Captain. You now know almost as much as we do.'

Captain Chapman smiled. 'I'm sure there must be a great deal you are not telling me.'

'I wish there was, I really do. But I come now to the confidentiality letter signed by all the parties who were to come for interview with the Dean and his colleagues.

Could I ask you when you signed this document? Was it before any of the actual interviews? In other words, would the successful candidate have signed before he knew he had been awarded the lease?'

'I find all this very difficult, Lord Powerscourt. Forgive me if I sound unhelpful. I do not think I would be breaking any undertakings if I said that I signed mine some time before the interview. There was a slight hint that failure to sign might result in any interview being cancelled.'

'And the document came from the solicitors rather than the cathedral authorities?'

'Yes, it did. It looked like a pro-forma letter which might have been used on previous occasions.'

'Captain Chapman, I will be frank with you. Three people are dead. There may yet be further murders, I do not know. That, if you like, is on one side of the scales. On the other is a statement undertaking to keep the affair of the lease and all that pertains to it confidential. Three lives against a simple transaction involving bricks and mortar. I ask you if you would reconsider your position. There is, I believe, a naval tradition that takes in a Fleet Commander refusing to obey orders for the greater good of his country.'

Captain Chapman smiled. 'You mean Nelson at the Battle of Copenhagen looking at a signal through his blind eye, I presume. I can fully appreciate your position, Lord Powerscourt. I am finding this very difficult. Might I ask if you have been in touch with the other candidates?'

'You may, of course. I have been in touch with them.'

'And what did they say?'

'They all hid behind the confidentiality clause.'

'So I am on my own in this matter. I need time to think this over, Lord Powerscourt. An Englishman's word is meant to be his bond. I would not like to do anything which might touch upon my honour, if you will forgive such a pompous phrase. I have to return to my ship late tomorrow afternoon. Could I call on you again at the same time tomorrow?'

'Of course. I understand your difficulties, Captain. On my side I would urge you to reconsider. You know my reasons. It has been a pleasure talking to you.'

As Captain Chapman left, Powerscourt began walking up and down his drawing room, looking – as he put it to himself – rather like Nelson on his quarterdeck. At least he had both his eyes. He was searching for a key. After twenty-five minutes he went downstairs and left a message for the Bishop of Lynchester to call him at his earliest convenience.

23

Johnny Fitzgerald had been back to the only stationer's in the little city, the one where he'd bought his map earlier. He purchased a sketchbook and a selection of coloured pencils. He then set off for the Close, where he began making a series of drawings. Nobody paid any attention. If they had they would have seen that he was not drawing any buildings, but plotting the lines of sight between them. The cathedral to the Close, Mrs MacQuaid's house to the main entrance, Sandy Field's house to the main entrance, Netherbury House to the crescent and the two terraces, Mrs McQuaid's house to Sandy Field's house, the range of the view from the entrance encompassed in a V-shaped diagram, the front of the cathedral to the main entrance, the back route out of the Close to the river and the other one round the back of the cathedral. When he had finished, he made his way back to the hotel and inspected his work over a pint of beer. He began drawing coloured lines next to some of his original drawings. He ordered a second pint of bitter.

*   *   *

It was just over an hour later when the Bishop called Powerscourt in Markham Square.

'Bishop, I was calling to ask you a great favour. I have just been speaking to Captain Chapman, the naval gentleman who wants to rent your Netherbury House. I was asking him, in effect, to forget that he signed that confidentiality clause and tell me what it said. He has gone away to think about it. I do not think he will agree.'

'I don't quite understand where I fit into all this, Lord Powerscourt.'

'You told me yourself, Bishop, that the confidentiality clause was brought into play at the request of the Church authorities.'

'Broadly speaking, that is correct, yes.'

'I am sure that if you were to speak to Captain Chapman and relieve him of his confidentiality obligations, he would talk to me and tell me what it says. You could do this over the phone, although I suspect you would not feel happy doing that about such a sensitive matter. It would be much better if you were to talk to him in person.'

'Where are you calling from, Lord Powerscourt?'

'I am talking to you from my house in London, Bishop. Captain Chapman is due to call on me here again tomorrow afternoon.'

'Forgive me for asking, Lord Powerscourt, but why are you devoting so much attention to this confidentiality letter?'

'As things stand, Bishop, it might – I'm not saying it will – but it could prove important. We do not, at present, know what was going on about the lease of Netherbury House because of that confidentiality clause. It would be a help in our inquiries. I'm not saying it would make our difficulties go away; that would be putting it too strongly. I should add that, as a matter of course, people in my position and that of Inspector Vaughan and his men are always keen to find out what somebody doesn't want them to know.'

'But if the matter is not so important, why should the cathedral waive its normal policies in these matters?'

'It would help us in our inquiries, Bishop. If I did not think it was important, I would not be asking you to come to London tomorrow to speak to Captain Chapman in person.'

'I have a number of meetings tomorrow. I do not see how I could find the time.'

'You must make your own decisions about your time, Bishop. I would remind you that the Captain is due to return to the north of Scotland tomorrow. We may not be able to talk to him in person for some time if he sets out for the North Sea.'

'Tell me this, Lord Powerscourt. Do you feel that this question is of such importance that I should reschedule my diary for tomorrow and come to London?'

'I do.'

'What time?'

'Two o'clock in the afternoon.'

'Very good. I shall see you then. You are at the same address I came to before?'

'I am.'

'Until tomorrow then.'

The Bishop did not tell Powerscourt that the letter confirming Captain Chapman's successful application

303

for the lease of Netherbury House was in the post. Some things, he felt, could remain confidential until tomorrow.

Late that evening, Johnny Fitzgerald took himself for a walk on the Close. He was particularly active in the area around and behind Sandy Field's house. He checked out various views and proceeded to Netherbury House and Mrs McQuaid's cottage, where he seemed to check the line of sight from the front doors. He was not disturbed.

The Bishop was the first to arrive at Markham Square. 'This is really most irregular, Lord Powerscourt,' he said to his host as he made his way up to the drawing room on the first floor. 'If it wasn't for the fact that I can tell Captain Chapman the good news about his application, I doubt if I would have come at all.'

'You are most welcome, Bishop, and I am, as ever, very grateful for your assistance. It may be nothing at all, this confidentiality business, but I am keen to get to the bottom of it.'

'I did have one idea on the way up, actually. When the new arrivals are ready to move in, we shall hold a service of blessing in the house. It should help reassure the women who might feel reluctant to move into a house with such unfortunate associations.'

'Captain Chapman,' Rhys the butler announced.

'Bishop,' said the Captain, 'how good to see you. I hadn't expected to meet you again so soon. What brings you up to London today?'

'There are two reasons, Captain. The first – and this is at the suggestion of Lord Powerscourt – is that as the senior representative of the cathedral, I am waiving the confidentiality clause in your negotiations with the lawyers over the lease of Netherbury House. As far as the Church is concerned, it is at your discretion whether or not to answer Lord Powerscourt's questions about that matter. You may regard the confidentiality clause as null and void. I would ask if you could keep the details of any conversation you may have with our host here private. I could write you a letter confirming that if you like, but I would prefer not to.'

'I talked this over with Lord Powerscourt yesterday, Bishop, and I was coming to give my response this afternoon.'

Powerscourt noticed that Captain Chapman had not given any indication as to what his decision had been.

'But thank you very much, Bishop,' the Captain continued,'I am most grateful to you. And the second reason for your visit to London?'

'Why,' said the Bishop with a smile, 'there is a letter in the post, but I suspect it hasn't yet reached you, or it may be awaiting your return to Scotland. You have been selected as the next person to live in Netherbury House. You should be able to move in once the legal formalities have been completed. May I, as the Bishop, be the first to welcome you to your new home.'

'That is excellent news,' said Captain Chapman, and pumped the Bishop's hand. 'I am delighted. I can't wait to tell my wife and children. They will be thrilled, I'm sure.'

'I may say,' the Bishop replied, 'without breaking any family secrets, that the decision was unanimous. We are all so pleased that you are the winning candidate. I presume from your reaction that you accept the lease?'

'You may, you most certainly may.' Captain Chapman was still beaming.

'In that case, my work here is done. I shall leave you to the tender mercies of Lord Powerscourt. I must catch the next train back to Lynchester. I still have some meetings to attend there before the day is over. A very good afternoon to you both.'

The Bishop made his way back to his see. Captain Chapman was still beaming from ear to ear.

'Well, Lord Powerscourt, what a happy day this is.'

'Would you like a glass of champagne to celebrate? We should surely do something to mark the occasion.'

'That is very kind, but no. I too have another meeting to attend later this afternoon. Some other time, I'm sure.'

'Are you happy to answer my questions about the lease and the confidentiality clause?'

'I am. Perhaps it would be easier if I gave you a summary of my dealings with Ardglass, Puckeridge and Ross, and then you could ask whatever you like.'

'I'd be very happy with that.'

'I never had any dealings with Mr Ardglass, Mr Puckeridge or Mr Ross. I always dealt with Sandy Field, who was the acting solicitor. It seemed to me that the confidentiality clause had been put in originally to keep the cost of the lease a secret. I can imagine that the clergy weren't happy with the thought of the value of their properties being discussed around the Close. I would have had no trouble with that. The problem was that the confidentiality seemed to have been extended to cover all the work involved in the transfer of the lease, the conveyancing, and so on. And, quite frankly, the charges were outrageous.

'Once you were accepted for interview, there was an administration charge of two hundred pounds. After you were lucky enough to be selected, there was a management charge of some five hundred pounds. After that, there were further charges of one sort or another till the total bill for acquiring the lease – not the lease itself, you understand – came close to a thousand pounds. You may say that if a man is going to pay seven thousand pounds for the lease, the odd five hundred pounds more shouldn't matter, but the total bill was absurd. It was outrageous. I took the situation to one of London's most respected firms of solicitors, who handle similar cases here in London, and asked them what the total charge should have been. They said fifty pounds should be enough to cover it, and a hundred pounds would just be greedy. "Bloody greedy" were their words, Lord Powerscourt.'

'So, on this lease alone, the solicitors would have made well over a thousand pounds from the candidates and, because of the confidentiality clause, nobody would have been any the wiser.'

'I was going to raise it with Sandy Field actually. He was trying to arrange a meeting with me on the day of the interview. He always seemed to me to be a decent sort of fellow, but I didn't have the time when I came down to Lynchester for the interview. It was, he said the first time I met him, the first of these cases he had handled.'

'If you think that a couple of tenants may die or move away every year, it must be an absolute gold mine for Ardglass, Puckeridge and Ross,' Powerscourt observed.

But would it have been enough to kill people, he wondered to himself.

'I hadn't thought of that but of course you're right. The money must have been flowing in for years. And there was no reason why it shouldn't have gone on for ever. There was another deterrent to any client.'

'What was that?'

'Well, suppose you have just moved in to any new house. The last thing you want to do is to have a row with your landlord's solicitors. Especially when the landlord is a cathedral of the Church of England, well equipped with fire and brimstone and thunderbolts for the ungodly.'

'I understand. You don't know, I suppose, what Sandy Field wanted to talk to you about?'

'I assumed it was pure routine. There were always some little details that needed to be sorted out.'

'Could I ask if you have decided to take any action about the charges?'

'The position is somewhat different now I know that I am to be the new tenant of Netherbury House. The temptation is to say nothing at all and pay up.'

'You must do as you think fit, Captain. But I think you could leave matters as they are for a week or so. I think the position may become clearer by then.'

'Do you mean that you will have solved the mystery by then? Does the information about the confidentiality clause help you?'

'I'm sure it helps a very great deal, Captain. But, just for the moment, I'm not sure precisely how it helps. If I need to use the information you have given me here this afternoon, you can rest assured that I shall not mention your name.'

'That's very kind of you. But you can be sure that if you need me to go on the record, I shall be happy to do so.'

'I am most grateful. I just need to think about what you have told me today.'

'I would advise you to take great care, Lord Powerscourt. There have been three deaths in a very short space of time. You never know when or where the fellow may strike again. I should put your crew on action stations if I were you.'

24

Powerscourt took his pistol and a good supply of ammunition down to Lynchester. If a distinguished naval Captain told you to put yourself on action stations, it seemed the least one could do. A thin young man in a well-cut suit that had seen better days was waiting for Powerscourt in the reception of his hotel. He had fair hair and was inspecting the portrait of a Victorian patriarch on the walls.

'Are you Lord Powerscourt?'

'I am.'

'Allow me to introduce myself, my lord. Mrs Field sent me to speak to you. My name is Andrews, Robert Andrews. I'm an old friend of Sandy Field's. I couldn't get back here in time for the funeral, but I came as soon as I could. Mrs Field suggested I should come and talk to you about her husband. You see, Sandy and I grew up together.'

'We'll be more comfortable upstairs,' said Powerscourt, anxious not to conduct a conversation about Sandy Field's past in the reception area of the hotel.

Robert Andrews took a seat by the window. A print of Worcester Cathedral adorned the wall opposite him.

'We won't be interrupted here, Mr Andrews. Now then, you say you grew up with Sandy Field. Is that right?'

'It is. I don't mean we grew up in the same house, but we did grow up in the same street in Richmond – the one on the Thames, not the one in Yorkshire – and we were about the same age and went to the same school. Our house had a much bigger garden than his, so we usually played at my place. The usual things: bows and arrows, climbing trees, kicking a football. In the summer we had endless games of cricket with a dustbin acting as the wicket. I can still remember the day Sandy scored a hundred against me. We must have been about ten. You were only out if the bowler managed to hit the bin acting as wicket. I couldn't get through his defences. I was so cross I wouldn't play cricket with him again for a week.'

'But you recovered in the end?'

Robert Andrews laughed. 'I'm glad to say I did. I don't think we ever had another falling out, now I come to think about it.'

'What was he like at school? I mean, was he good at his work?'

'He was. He was very quick and he had a phenomenal memory. He always took the side of the underdog in history lessons. He was with Wat Tyler in the Peasants' Revolt, and with the ordinary Parisians in the French Revolution. I remember him telling me that one of his teachers suggested he should go into politics when he grew up. Sandy just laughed. He went off to learn the law at a local firm of solicitors after university, and I went off to be taught how to be a teacher, so our paths didn't cross as often as they had in the past. We still managed to play in the local cricket team in the summer holidays. Sandy could bat and bowl and I was rather an indifferent wicketkeeper. Those were happy days.'

'Do you know, Mr Andrews, I don't think I know anything at all about his parents.'

'They were very respectable people, my lord. His father was some sort of manager on the railways, always complaining about head office, and his mother kept house for us all. I sometimes think I must have eaten more often in their house than I did in my own.'

'I see. Did you keep in touch when he went off to the solicitors' firm in Oxford?'

'We did, but mainly by letter. We still saw each other in the holidays. I was working at a grammar school in Hammersmith by then, so it wasn't like seeing each other every day. There was one incident I should tell you about, I suppose. It was at the height of the difficulties with the colleague's wife in Oxford. We went for a long walk along the river. His wife was already very ill by this stage, and she was almost confined to the wheelchair. She could just about manage to walk upstairs hanging very tightly onto the banisters. She can't even do that now. That's why they converted the dining room downstairs into a bedroom for her.

'Anyway, he told me about his difficulties that day. I think I knew already about the affairs with other women. Maybe my parents told me, I can't remember. At this stage it was touch and go whether he would be fired or not. Sandy maintained that even solicitors couldn't include a clause about dismissal for carrying on with other people's wives in their employment contract. He said that he always felt guilty about his affairs, but he couldn't stop. He said it was probably like a disease that doctors would be able to cure one day, but they couldn't do it yet.'

'Did you get the impression that he felt he would still get away with the affair with the colleague's wife?'

'I didn't like to ask him, but I would say, looking back on it, that he did. I bumped into him again a week or so later and he told me the story. He was to leave the Oxford solicitors' immediately. He was not to mention the scandal to another living soul. In return, the senior partner would write a letter of recommendation to another firm if Sandy wished to stay in the legal profession. He was not to mention it to anybody in his new position if he decided to stay in the law. The senior partner apparently said that he was a competent and promising member of his team. Sandy thought he had got away with it by the skin of his teeth. I always remember something he said that day. We were walking past Richmond Bridge at the time. "Robert," he said, "never underestimate the power of the threat of scandal."'

'What did you think he meant by that?'

'Oddly enough, I don't think he meant the power of scandal as far as he was concerned. I don't think he was very bothered about that. It was the threat of scandal that might surround the solicitors' firm if it came out. Articles in the local press, a whispering campaign amongst the clients, perhaps; a feeling that your wife might become involved in the firm's affairs, that sort of thing. The solution they came up with had one main objective as far as I could see, and that was to draw a veil over the whole affair.'

'Thank you for that, Mr Andrews, you've been very frank with me. Tell me, if you would, how you would describe Sandy Field. Not physically, but as a man.'

Robert Andrews paused. He stared at the print of Worcester Cathedral for a moment. 'That's a difficult question. I suspect that it would be easier to give a description of somebody you weren't so close to.' He stopped again.

'Sandy Field was a man who loved life. He loved living it, if you know what I mean. He had a great capacity for enjoyment. I'm sure that however abstract the legal questions, the participants would always feel better for having dealt with him. He had a great sense of fairness as well as a sense of fun. He would always own up at school if he had broken the rules in some way. It was as if he had decided to live life to the full every morning when he woke up. If you bumped into him in a pub, he was the kind of man you'd arrange to meet again. You might even invite him home for supper if it was that time of day.'

'Did he ever mention his affairs here after he moved down from Oxford?'

'Not to me, he didn't. I think he might have talked about it to my wife. He was very close to her. I think he probably talked to her more than to me about that sort of thing. She's with Mrs Field now. I expect she'll be along directly.'

'I'm very grateful for all you've told me, Mr Andrews. Is there anything you would like to ask me?'

'Only this. I'm still feeling guilty that we couldn't get here for the funeral. My wife was ill and we just couldn't get away. My question is very simple. Do you know who killed him?'

'I don't know who killed him. I feel guilty about that in my turn. I have been here for a while now and I have no more idea than I did when I started.'

'Do you think his death has anything to do with the affairs he had been conducting while he's been here?'

'As a matter of fact I don't. I'm not absolutely certain about that – just at the moment, Mr Andrews, I'm not very sure of anything to do with this case – but I don't think so. Your information has been very helpful. If your wife can spare me the time, I would very much like to talk to her too.'

'She may be waiting downstairs in the reception area. I'll send her up if I may. Just one last question, my lord, if I may?'

'Of course.'

'If some angry husband didn't kill Sandy, then who the hell did?'

As Andrews set off to look for his wife, Powerscourt began looking at Johnny Fitzgerald's drawings. There was something in them he had not noticed before.

Mrs Andrews was blonde, her hair cut quite short. She was wearing a long dress in dark grey. Her most noticeable feature were her eyes, which were a pale blue colour.

'Lord Powerscourt, how nice to meet you. Mrs Field has been singing your praises to me just now.'

'That's very kind of you, Mrs Andrews. Please take a seat. Your husband tells me that you were close to Sandy Field. Is that right?'

'Well, I didn't see him all that often. But I suppose you could say that we were close when we were together.'

'Could I ask what brought you together?'

'I think it was because I was a woman, actually. I think he found it easier to talk to me about certain matters than he did to my husband or other men.'

'Did you have these sort of conversations every time you met?'

'No, we didn't. We had one long conversation about his other women when we met a couple of years ago. Sandy used to call me his mother confessor afterwards, but that was the only time he was really open about things. I think I only understood what he meant when I thought about it later. I'm sure other people must have mentioned this to you already.'

'Mentioned what, Mrs Andrews?'

'Sorry, I wasn't making myself clear. Sandy had made a deal with himself, if you like. This deal took in both sides of his life. He had to look elsewhere for some of the consolations of marriage, if I could put it like that. I don't think he was very happy about it, but he kept his spirits up. Sandy always did. That was on one side of the page. On the other side was the fact that, whatever happened, he would never leave his wife. And he would provide for her. He was always worried that the illness might get worse still and he would have to employ full-time nursing staff. He was prepared for that. He was quite careful with his money, even if he did throw it around from time to time on a new conquest. So that was it. One half of Sandy had affairs all over the place. The other half was planning ways to look after his wife. Is that clear, Lord Powerscourt?'

'It is very clear. It leads me to another question, one you may not feel able to answer. Did the ladies he was involved with know any of this?'

'I doubt it very much. Sandy understood women too well to tell them they had only half of him, if you know what I mean.'

'And what happened if the women got too involved?

316

What happened if they grew so attached to him that they wanted him to divorce his wife and marry them instead?'

'I'm sure it must have happened once or twice. He did tell me that he had ended one affair because the lady concerned got too emotionally involved. Divorce is always difficult, but I'm certain Sandy would never have thought about leaving his wife.'

'Would it be fair to say that the women may have cared for him more than he cared for them?'

'I don't know the answer to that, Lord Powerscourt. There's sometimes a fine line between being infatuated and being in love, isn't there? Sandy was the sort of man who fell for somebody very quickly, just as they could fall for him. Maybe the women crossed the line between infatuation and love rather faster than he did, I don't know.'

'I've asked other people this question, Mrs Andrews, and I know it's virtually impossible to answer. Do you think Sandy would have behaved as he did if his wife had been well?'

'I can't answer that, Lord Powerscourt. I've no idea. Probably not, I would guess. I know that's a totally useless answer, but there it is.'

'I have asked this question before too, Mrs Andrews, I'm afraid. What do you think the secret of Sandy's appeal was?'

'You must have heard all this before, Lord Powerscourt. He was good looking. He was very charming. Even if you met him at a party after a cricket match or something, he could always convince you that you were the only person in the room. In earlier times he might have been a knight in shining armour, come to rescue the princess trapped in a dark tower. He was very interested in politics; he always knew what was going on. I think Sandy would have been a supporter of Lloyd George if he had tried to get into Parliament. He couldn't have done that, of course, with a wife and a mistress to run at the same time.'

Powerscourt suspected that if the Westminster rumours were true, Sandy Field might have had more in common with Lloyd George than he realized.

'You must have heard the details of these three murders by now, Mrs Andrews. Is there anything, from your knowledge of Sandy Field, that would help me solve them?'

'I've thought about that ever since I first heard about the murders. I don't think there is. You see, I only saw one side of him – the man as husband and lover, if you like. I have no idea what he was like at work. You would have to ask other people about that.'

'Is there anything I should look into which might help me?'

'I'm sure you have looked into all the dark corners you can think of, Lord Powerscourt. I just pray that you can find the answer soon.'

Powerscourt escorted Mrs Andrews back down the stairs to reception. He returned to his sitting room and stared out of the window for a long time, thinking about knights in shining armour.

25

Powerscourt went to the police station and told Inspector Vaughan as much as he could without betraying any confidences. He had decided on another line of attack.

'Inspector, I think I have been rather slow about one aspect of this case. I think we need to know a lot more about Sandy Field's job with Ardglass, Puckeridge and Ross. I think we need all his correspondence from the last three months. And his diary. We might then be able to piece together a more accurate picture of his activities in the time before he died.'

'Very good, my lord. I'll ask my Sergeant to go down and pick up the papers. They told us just after he died that they were going to lock all his stuff away until further notice in case they were needed.'

'Let's hope they haven't tampered with them in any way.'

'I don't think they would do that, my lord. They usually play things by the book.'

Two hours later, Powerscourt took delivery of a large cardboard box full of papers. Looking at them, he thought that Sandy did not seem to have been very assiduous at filing. Perhaps he did it every few months. Powerscourt had a lot of sympathy for a man who wasn't fond of filing. He had, from time to time, sorted out his own affairs by arranging his papers into bundles right across the drawing-room floor in Markham Square. It sometimes took all weekend.

He began by separating the letters into sections. He had a pile called 'Conveyancing', about the sale and purchase of houses in and around Lynchester. He had a large pile he called 'Rental agreements'. There was another section he labelled 'Wills and Probate', which seemed to have accumulated an enormous volume of correspondence. There was a section on 'Agriculture', involving the buying and selling of agricultural land and boundary disputes. There was a section he called 'Miscellaneous', where he put things that didn't fall into any of his other categories. And there was a section called 'Cathedral', which he put to one side.

He then put everything else onto the floor and spread his 'Cathedral' file out on his little table. He began sorting the letters into chronological order, which took him a lot longer than he thought it would. Here, he realized, was the entire history of the sale of the lease of Netherbury House. The candidates were all here: a couple of retired businessmen, three former Bishops, a rural Dean who thought the cathedral should sell off all its property and give the money to the poor, a retired Colonel who believed the inhabitants of the Close should form their own Conservative Club to influence party policy, and an author who believed the lands around the Close should be given over to cattle and sheep as they had been in the past. Here was the whittling-down process, with the selected five sent off to the Dean for approval and the dispatch of letters inviting them for interview. Here too were the charges that annoyed Captain Chapman so much.

In the end it was Sandy Field's diary that proved to be the most interesting. He seemed to have organized interviews with all the candidates around the time of their visit. Here were entries for an interview with Sir Edward Talbot on the afternoon of the day he came for his meeting with the Dean's committee. There were further interviews lined up with all the other candidates. Looking back at the correspondence, Powerscourt thought that this must be perfectly normal. There would have been a lot to talk about.

Lady Lucy brought him a cup of tea. 'Any inspiration in these files, my love?'

'I wish I could say there was,' said her husband.'There were meetings planned with all the candidates for Netherbury House, some of which obviously never happened. But that must have been routine. It was quite a complicated business, after all. The stuff about the money is in there. I just need to read through it all again to see if I can find any inspiration. I think I shall ask the Dean if Sir Edward Talbot mentioned an interview with Sandy Field on the day he came down to see him and his colleagues.'

Early the next morning, Powerscourt received a message at his hotel. It invited him to a meeting at three o'clock with somebody called Nathaniel Ford, who was the owner and manager of the local abattoir. The note said that he, Ford, had something to tell Powerscourt that might help in his investigations. In the meantime he called on the Dean.

'My dear Powerscourt,' the Dean began, looking rather pleased with himself this morning. 'Is there any news about your investigation today?'

'Good morning to you, Dean. I have just called with a couple of minor queries about Sandy Field.'

'I shall do my best to answer you.'

'You don't happen to know if Sir Edward Talbot spoke to Sandy Field on the day he was here for his interview, do you? And you wouldn't know if he arranged to see you or the Bishop the morning he left?'

'My goodness, let me think for a moment. He didn't mention it during the interview, that's for sure. I wonder if he spoke of it before or during the dinner. Now I come to think about it, I think I heard him mentioning that he'd seen Sandy Field to the Bishop while we were having our glass of sherry, and that he – Sir Edward – would like to see the Bishop the next morning before he went back to London. I'm afraid you won't be able to check with the Bishop as he's not here at present. He's had to go up to London for a couple of days for a debate in the House of Lords.'

'Does that mean that you're in charge, Dean?'

The Dean smiled. 'I suppose you could put it like that, my lord. Yes. For the time being, I am. I think you can take it that Sandy Field did meet with Sir Edward Talbot on the day before he died, and that Sir Edward asked to see the Bishop the next morning. I have to say I don't quite see how that would help you with your inquiries.'

'I have to say, Dean, that I'm not quite sure about that either. But it's useful to know, all the same.'

As he left, Powerscourt wondered if the reason for

the Dean's good humour was the fact that he was, for the time being, the senior ecclesiastic in Lynchester Cathedral. Next stop God.

Powerscourt left his note from Nathaniel Ford on the coffee table in his sitting room. Remembering what Captain Chapman had said about action stations, he took his gun with lots of spare ammunition in his jacket pocket. There was nobody there when he arrived at the premises. The office was empty and the door was locked. Powerscourt was growing suspicious about Mr Ford, and tiptoed very slowly into the area of the abattoir itself. The place was very dark, apart from a couple of skylights with filthy windows at either end. Everything in the middle was nearly dark. There was a terrible smell. It was very cold. There was a low hum of machinery somewhere.

The first shot echoed round the building and passed well wide. Powerscourt fired back in the general direction of the skylight at the far end and rushed further into the building. He would have been a sitting duck if he had stayed by the door. Somebody at the other end, possibly the elusive Mr Ford, was trying to kill him. He thought his opponent must be at the far end of the building. Powerscourt had rows of sheep carcases lined up in front of him on a trolley. Further lines of trolleys stretched out in front of him down into the main body of the shed.

The floor was so slippery, Powerscourt decided to crawl. He knew there would be complaints about his suit but he didn't care. Lying on the floor, he realized, should mean that most of the shots ought to pass clean over him. He wondered if there was a back door and decided there must be, a very large one, so the staff could bring the animals in. Round the corner, in a little alcove, he discovered a group of four or five empty trolleys. He realized that he could send one of them down the abattoir towards the far end and try to get back to the entrance. He wondered if his assailant was intending to come down and finish him off. He decided to fire one round in the general direction of where he thought the back door must be. That, at least, should let the enemy know that an advance might prove to be a fatal proposition. He sent his second shot down the building, slightly to the right of the first one. He sat up with his back against the wall, put all his strength into his legs, and shoved one of the trolleys down the abattoir. It hadn't got the momentum to move any of the trolleys laden with carcases very far, but it did move them a little bit. Powerscourt fired off another bullet. He had only three left for now. The gunman fired again. Two rounds gone. Powerscourt wondered if the man had any spare ammunition, or if he had only four bullets left. He checked in his jacket pocket that he had a good supply of extra firepower. Who was this man? Who had brought him here? Surely he wasn't local? Then he remembered that Sandy Field had been shot. Maybe the gunman was local, after all. Powerscourt suspected that it couldn't have been the man who ran the abattoir, as he had no connections with his current investigation up until now.

Being close to the ground – Powerscourt was crawling everywhere now – meant that the stench was even more appalling; the unmistakable sweet, noxious smell of blood mixed with effluvia, disinfectants, and the all-pervasive aroma created by very large numbers of dead animals strung up ready to be butchered.

Powerscourt realized that he didn't have a plan. He was operating purely on the defensive. How could he bring the battle to his enemy without endangering his own life? He wondered about a headlong charge down the centre of the building, firing as he went. He loosed off another round to let the man know that he was still in business and not writhing on the floor. Another shot flew past. He wondered if he could turn the man's flank by hugging the wall nearest to him and inching his way down the abattoir, but he couldn't tell if that route would be blocked by fully laden trolleys that he might not be able to move. Over to his right, he could just make out another trolley, which seemed to have three or four carcases on it, not the full load. He crawled over to it. He sent it down the bloody corridor with all his force. There was an almighty crash as it careered into the other trolleys. It was hard to tell if any of the fully laden ones had moved at all. Another shot rang out. Powerscourt fired back, trying to aim at where the sound had come from. He too had missed again.

He wondered suddenly if he could ride down the passage hanging on to the back of one of the trolleys, but decided it would be too dangerous. He retreated for a moment into the alcove with the empty carts, dumb waiters for dead animals. Another shot ended up in the wall behind him. Powerscourt had one round left in his pistol. He fired it and reloaded. He still had plenty of spares. There was no scream from the other end of the building.

He wondered again about the man at the other end of the abattoir. Was he a hired killer brought down to Lynchester for the day? Was he one of the locals, a man who worked in the abattoir perhaps? One of the solicitors? Now was not the time to be thinking of these things, he told himself. Now was the time to get out of here alive, rather than end his days hung on a trolley and carved up like a dead cow.

He dived out of his alcove and came to a full stop halfway between the door to the office and the wall. He wondered about making a dash towards the door and back out into the street, where he would surely be arrested as a vagrant or a burglar. He decided it would be too risky. He reloaded his pistol. If he sprayed the back of the abattoir with all six bullets fired in slightly different directions, he might get his man. He wriggled himself round until he was facing where he thought the back door was. He reminded himself of the pistol firing lessons he had attended in India all those years before. One, two. Three. No joy so far. The Sergeant's dummy target hadn't received a blow yet. Four, five, six. On the fifth shot there was a shout of pain from the far end. Powerscourt could hear footsteps squelching through the mess on the floor. Which way was the man coming? Towards him, or towards the back door? Surely he wasn't heading for the front. Powerscourt slid his way back to his alcove and reloaded his pistol. He thought another round or two might finish the man off. The noise of boots didn't seem to be growing any louder. Was he going towards the back door, or up the passage towards Powerscourt? He fired off another three rounds and the noise of the gaps between the sounds of the boots grew shorter. Perhaps he was trying to run. There was a great bang from the far end of the abattoir. The gunman had closed the door. Powerscourt was too old a hand to fall for that one. The fellow could have closed the door inside just as easily as he could outside.

He waited. It was too gloomy to tell the time on his watch. He loosed off another couple of shots. He listened for the squelch of shoes or boots. Nothing happened. He waited for what he thought must be a full five minutes and began crawling down the passageway. He thought he could see a shape that might be the back door. He fired off another round. There was no reply. He was over halfway down in the direction of the door now.

'At last,' said a voice close by. 'You have fallen into my trap.' Powerscourt crawled as fast as he could for the cover of a very full trolley, leaning against the side of the building. He felt a shot pass over his head. He suspected the man had heard him coming rather than seen him. Powerscourt was swearing at himself under his breath. You've fallen for the oldest trick in the book. The smell, he noted, seemed to be even stronger at this end of the building.

The voice? Where did the voice come from? It didn't seem to have the rural burr of Lynchester. It sounded to him like the voice of a man from London.

He wondered again about the possibility of a rescue party. How would they know where he was? Maybe somebody might have read the note that summoned him here, left in his hotel sitting room. Maybe Inspector Vaughan and his men were even now circling the building, preparing a mission of mercy. Maybe they weren't.

The abattoir was about fifty yards long, a bit more than the length of two cricket pitches. Now the gunman was about one cricket pitch away. Reaching behind him, Powerscourt found a number of iron bars of differing lengths leaning against the wall. He grabbed one and hurled it over the top of the trolleys at where he thought the gunman was. He followed it with a barrage of further iron bars. They bounced off the trolleys as they landed. There was no noise in reply. Powerscourt wondered if the wound had proved more serious than he first thought.

All he wanted to do now was to escape. He inched his way back towards his earlier position, hurling iron bars as hard as he could on the way. He had decided not to fire his pistol for the moment. Still there was no noise. Maybe the gunman was waiting for Powerscourt to loom into view before despatching him. He was now three-quarters of the way back to the office. He was still crawling. A small part of his brain was thinking about a very long, very hot bath. There was still no sound from the gunman. Maybe his ammunition was running low and he only had enough bullets left to finish Powerscourt off. That might explain the silence. He could now see the opening of the abattoir and the office of its master. Should he rise to his feet and run as fast as he could across this slippery floor? In this world where sound rather than sight told you where people were, he decided to crawl as quietly as he could. He would have to cross the width of the building.

He grabbed a last couple of iron bars and sent them hurtling down the abattoir. Then he was off. Inch by inch, elbow by elbow, he crept across the floor. Halfway now. Still no gunfire from the far end. Just a little bit further. Three-quarters of the way now. The smell was nauseating. Powerscourt had great trouble not retching as he made his way across the last few feet to safety. There was another shot from the far end of the abattoir. It missed. Powerscourt used a doorknob to pull himself up and rushed out of the front door, still open, as it had been when he arrived.

He fell directly into the arms of Johnny Fitzgerald,

with Inspector Vaughan and a couple of Constables. 'I've told you before, Francis. You're not allowed to go off on these dangerous missions by yourself. Look at the state you get into when I'm not there.'

'We've only just got here, my lord,' said Inspector Vaughan. 'Lady Powerscourt saw the note asking you to come to the abattoir. She thought it was suspicious, so I collected all the Constables I could find.'

'There's a gunman in there. Right down at the other end. He very nearly finished me off. If you're quick, you might stop him before he makes his getaway. I wouldn't recommend going through the abattoir. He might shoot. But if he's still there, you could probably rush him from the back.'

'Very good, my lord.' The Inspector left one officer on guard duty at the front door. He and his companions and Johnny Fitzgerald set off at a run for the back door.

A familiar figure greeted Powerscourt on his way back to the King's Arms.

'Aha! said Simple Simon the human scarecrow. 'Aha! You look as if you've been crawling round inside that terrible abattoir, haven't you? Perhaps you've turned into a snake, looking for clues in the entrails of dead animals.'

Powerscourt couldn't deny it. He had been crawling round inside the abattoir. His clothes were covered in slime. He knew that he smelt appalling. Maybe he was only fit to be hung up on one of those terrible hooks inside. Simple Simon seemed lost in thought for the moment. 'I have a message for you, Lord Powerscourt. From the good book.

'"And the Lord God said unto the serpent, 'Because

thou hast done this, thou art cursed above all cattle, and above every beast of the field; upon thy belly shalt thou go, and dust shalt thou eat all the days of thy life.'"

'That's not all the good book has to say to you, Lord Powerstake, or whatever your name is. Look what you've done now.

'"And the Lord said, 'I will destroy man whom I have created from the face of the earth; both man, and beast, and the creeping thing, and the fowls of the air; for it repenteth me that I have made them.'"

'The creeping things salute you. Shall we meet again in the cemetery, the land of the dead?'

Powerscourt later described it as his Archimedes moment, inspiration in the bath. He was soaking in very hot water when he realized he had forgotten something. He had checked out Sandy Field's appointment book up till the present. What he hadn't done was to look forward. He got dressed quickly and shot through to his living room, where the papers sat still in their piles. He thought for a moment that they were reproaching him for his failure to unlock all their secrets.

He flipped through the pages. It didn't take long to strike gold. Ten days from now, Sandy Field had an appointment with the Law Society in London. Why on earth was he going to the Law Society? Powerscourt spent some time looking at Johnny Fitzgerald's drawings of the lines of sight around the Close, and then went for a long walk round the Close. He tried out various explanations for the murders. None of them seemed to fit. There was just one theory, but he thought it too fanciful to be true.

Powerscourt organized a tea party the following afternoon. It was to be held in the small private dining room on the ground floor. The hotel manager promised two sorts of scones with jam and cream, brown bread and butter, crumpets, cucumber sandwiches, three different sorts of cake and three different sorts of jam, all made locally by the hotel suppliers. Lady Lucy and Johnny Fitzgerald and Inspector Vaughan were to be the guests at the feast.

'Some of what I am going to say may seem pretty bizarre, Lucy,' Powerscourt said to his wife beforehand. 'Just bring me back to the straight and narrow if you can.'

'Are you going to go out on a limb, Francis?'

'Yes I am,' said Powerscourt, 'a bloody great big one, and I might fall off at any moment.'

'This is all very fine, my lord,' said Inspector Vaughan, tucking into his second fruit scone with strawberry jam and cream. 'I don't see why you haven't been providing this every afternoon.'

'Maybe you should lay it on every day from now on,' said Johnny Fitzgerald. 'A council of war with the crumpets at four o'clock.'

'I'll see what I can do,' said Powerscourt, waiting for the first wave of attacks on the food to die down. Lady Lucy was talking to the Inspector about the merits of round-the-world cruises. Powerscourt tapped his teacup with a spoon.

'Please carry on eating this delicious tea. I just want to share a few thoughts with you.'

'Have you solved the mystery, Francis?' asked Johnny Fitzgerald.

'I don't know,' said Powerscourt. 'I would like to try out a theory on you, if I may.' He poured himself another cup of tea and set out on his voyage of uncertainty.

'The first death in this case took place a couple of months ago. I refer, of course, to the overdose of Simon Jones, the old man who used to live in Netherbury House. The question was: did he take his life himself, or did Mrs McQuaid administer the overdose to put the old boy out of his misery? The Bishop, you will recall, came to me for advice. I think he was sure that Mrs McQuaid was responsible, but he couldn't bring himself to report to the police that she, out of the kindness of her heart, had committed a murder. We may never know the answer now, as all the participants are dead – except, of course, for the Bishop. Personally I thought that Mrs McQuaid did it for the best of motives, the relief of suffering. But I think we can leave it to one side when we come to consider the recent spate of murders.'

Johnny Fitzgerald was on to his third crumpet by now. The Inspector was wrestling with a large slice of chocolate cake. Lady Lucy was dallying with a cucumber sandwich.

'The first murder took place in the same house some time later: Sir Edward Talbot, killed by strychnine contained in an unusual drink, cider eau-de-vie. We have not found any trace of the bottle or the strychnine. There is, I suspect, a chance that the poison may have been originally intended for gardening purposes. Any great industrialist must have collected a number of enemies during the course of his career but, as a body, industrialists do not go round killing each other. There was a possibility that he might have been killed by a man in danger of losing his job through an amalgamation of

Talbot's Stores with Scott's Stores because Sir Edward might have intended to close down some of those branches. I don't think that very likely either. There was the extraordinary coincidence that Sir Edward as a young man had left Mrs McQuaid's sister at the altar all those years ago. It seemed to provide a motive for murder, but I don't think Mrs McQuaid killed him. She would have known, of course, if her employer had cider eau-de-vie and strychnine in his cellar, but I do not believe she would have used them. She might have been a mercy killer earlier, but I don't believe she killed Sir Edward Talbot.'

26

'The second murder was that of Sandy Field. On the face of it, there was no lack of suspects, as the man was a serial adulterer with affairs across the Close and beyond going back a number of years. Looking back at it now, I think we were dazzled by all these women – begging your pardon, Lucy. We were dazzled for far too long. We looked for an aggrieved husband, thinking that when we had found a man totally consumed by jealousy and anger we would have solved the mystery. Well, we didn't find one and we haven't solved the mystery.'

Johnny Fitzgerald had finished his assault on the crumpets and was staring into his tea. Inspector Vaughan had moved onto the fruit cake.

'The third murder is the most inexplicable. Why would anybody want to kill Mrs McQuaid? We haven't found a trace of motive anywhere.'

Powerscourt paused for a sip of tea and a mouthful of Dundee cake.

'There is a spine running through this case and it concerns the houses in the Close, all of which are owned by the cathedral. It is their policy to select all those who come to live here in these beautiful surroundings. The cathedral people conduct the interviews. They have the final say. I haven't counted all those houses, but there must be over a hundred of them. Some of the leases run out, some of the people decide to move away, some of them die, so there must be a traffic in them, on average, of three or four a year or more. New tenants must be as much a part of the life of the Cathedral Close as Harvest Festival and the annual carol concert. Ardglass, Puckeridge and Ross have been handling these leases for many years. Their charges, as we now know from Captain Chapman, are quite outrageous – far, far above what a London firm would charge for the same services. In a given year, I suspect, the charges would be more than enough to pay the wages of all the policemen in the county.

'This was Sandy Field's first outing as solicitor in charge of recruitment. He hadn't done it before. And the key phrase I would like to put in your minds is "knight in shining armour". It was mentioned to me by the wife of a very old friend of Sandy Field's, who was using it in a different context of accounting for his success with the ladies.

'But I wondered if it might apply to other areas as well.' Powerscourt took a sliver of his cake. 'This is the point where you may think I am losing my mind. Please feel free to tell me that I have taken leave of my senses. I have virtually no evidence for what I am going to say here this afternoon. This is guesswork from now on. I think Sandy took great exception to the fraud being carried out against the candidates for the vacant position at Netherbury House. As he polished his shining armour one day, I think he decided to stop it. Perhaps he had a conversation with Mr Puckeridge and asked him to change his ways. I think Puckeridge told him to mind his own business and let the partners decide such things. But I am virtually certain that he told Puckeridge what he was doing, and that Sir Edward was due to see the Bishop the morning after the dinner with the clergy. We know that Sandy Field talked to Sir Edward the day he came down for the interview. The Dean is fairly sure that Sir Edward had an appointment with the Bishop the morning he was killed. Sandy Field – in the best traditions of knights in shining armour who want their virtues to be known – told Puckeridge what he was doing, and must have mentioned that Sir Edward was going to tell the Bishop what was going on. Puckeridge, on this version of events, took the law into his own hands. If the size of these charges came out, there would be an outcry from all those members of the Close who have already paid over the odds. Other transactions would come under the microscope. I remember the only other solicitor in Lynchester telling me about people who came to him complaining about the exorbitant fees. At the time I thought it was sour grapes from a less successful rival. Now I'm not so sure. Ardglass, Puckeridge and Ross could be finished in a great cloud of scandal. All that money, coming in every year without fail, would stop as they would lose the contract.'

'Do you think that accounts for the death of Sandy Field too?' Inspector Vaughan had been taking notes on the last sections of Powerscourt's address.

'I do, Inspector. I do. You see, I don't think knights in shining armour have any brakes, if you see what I mean. He must have told Puckeridge that he was going to carry on regardless and expose the size of the charges. That was the end of him. Puckeridge lured him out of his house one night and finished him off.'

'And poor Mrs McQuaid, Francis? Why did he have to kill her too?'

'We know from Johnny's drawings in the Close that you could see Sandy Field's front door from Mrs McQuaid's house.' He rummaged about in his jacket pocket and put Johnny's drawings on the table. 'I think Puckeridge may have seen her the night he came to kill Sandy Field. Or, more to the point, he believed she might have seen him knocking on the door. Perhaps she heard something. We don't know. She could be a witness. She had to go.'

Powerscourt paused and polished off his Dundee cake. 'I have only one other piece of evidence, and it comes from Sandy Field's appointment book. In a week or ten days' time he had an appointment in London with the Law Society, the body that looks after solicitors. I believe he was going to make a formal complaint. I don't know what he was going to say, but I doubt very much if he was going to tell them about the progress of the flowers in the cathedral gardens.'

Powerscourt took a sip of tea and waited for a reaction. Johnny Fitzgerald was just coming to the end of a cucumber sandwich.

'You're right on top of your form, Francis. Theories pouring out of you like the butter from one of these crumpets here.'

'I do like this theory,' said Inspector Vaughan, 'I like it very much. I have only one problem with it. You know as well as I do, my lord, that we can't prove a single word of it. I can't see anything we could use to arrest Puckeridge. My Chief Constable would refuse to issue an arrest warrant – and he'd be quite right. And I don't think Mr Puckeridge is going to confess to his crimes – if he has indeed committed them – the moment we pull him in for questioning.'

'I see I am surrounded by doubting Thomases of one sort or another,' said Powerscourt with a smile. 'Perhaps we need our own knight in shining armour. Lucy, what do you say to my house of cards?'

'I think it all depends on how seriously we take your thoughts, Francis. There is one thing that occurs to me, mind you. If you are right, then this Mr Puckeridge is a very dangerous man. He or his agents may already have had a crack at killing you in the abattoir. Maybe they just wanted to scare you off. But what of the other women in the case, Mrs Brooks and Mrs Field? Surely Puckeridge must wonder if Sandy had told them about his concerns. They might know about his plan to go and lay the matter before the Law Society in London. They might not be safe at present. Puckeridge may come out again to kill them too.'

'By God, you are right there,' said Powerscourt. 'Do you think we should post a guard outside their houses?'

'It sounds rather melodramatic,' said Inspector Vaughan, 'but I'm sure you're right, Lady Powerscourt. I shall go and organize it when we've come to the end of our meeting.'

'I've just thought of something,' said Powerscourt. 'I think I should take myself back to London and see what I can find out at the offices of the Law Society. Sandy Field was going to see a man called Thompson. With any luck, he may show me what Sandy wrote in his letter. That might give us some evidence.'

'I doubt if that would do us much good in court,' said

338

Inspector Vaughan, who was looking at the last slice of fruit cake with hostile intent. 'Man goes to complain about high charges. Happens all the time, I'm sure. The solicitors will be keen to look after their own, and their own in this case happens to be a live Puckeridge rather than a dead Field.'

'I have had dealings with the Law Society in the past,' Powerscourt put in, 'and they are indeed determined at all times to protect their own. That's what they're there for, after all. We shall just have to see whether the defence of their own ranks higher than possible murders. It's all done with large helpings of charm, of course. You see, I suspect this theory won't travel well. It sounds pretty outlandish here in Lynchester, even though all the murders happened here. God knows what it would sound like in Lincoln's Inn Fields.'

'Have you caught the man in the abattoir yet, Inspector?' asked Powerscourt. 'Maybe he will have something to tell us.'

'We've got the fellow in custody, my lord. He had a small shoulder wound which should heal up in no time at all. I should have told you before. My men picked him up coming out of the abattoir with a gun in his pocket. Thank God they had the presence of mind to inspect the abattoir and make sure nobody else was there. William Farmer's a local thief who specializes in not getting caught. Heaven knows how many unsolved crimes could be laid at his door. Yet again we don't have any witnesses, except yourself, my lord, but you said you never saw the man in daylight. That might not go down too well in court.'

'You don't happen to know who his solicitor is off the top of your head, Inspector, do you? I know I've tried all of your patience with my theories this afternoon, but here is one more theory for you. I wonder if his solicitors, who may have helped him get off in the past, aren't Ardglass, Puckeridge and Ross, and if the particular solicitor who deals with him isn't Mr Puckeridge himself?'

'Do you mean that he may be repaying a debt, as it were, to the solicitors who have kept him out of jail in the past? It wouldn't be the first time such a thing has happened. I'll check it out when I get back to the station.'

Inspector Vaughan succumbed to the last available sandwich. 'Let me ask your advice on one important matter. When I first heard Lord Powerscourt's theories here this afternoon, my first thought was to bring Mr Puckeridge in for questioning. If he knew we were thinking about his role in the case, he might stop going round killing people, if indeed he has been going round killing people or trying to kill them. But he would be on his guard. He would be careful not to incriminate himself, as solicitors always are. I now think it would be better to leave him in peace for the time being until we can come up with more evidence, if there is more evidence to be found. Perhaps we should keep a watch on him, too.'

'Could I ask,' Johnny Fitzgerald put in, 'why you are certain it is Mr Puckeridge who is the guilty party, and not Mr Ardglass or Mr Ross?'

'Sorry, Johnny, I should have said,' said Powerscourt, 'both Mr Ardglass and Mr Ross are old now, and almost completely retired from the business. They look in a couple of times a month, that's all.'

'Keeping watch on Mrs Field and Mrs Brook would be a good plan,' said the Inspector. 'I can't see any point in arousing Puckeridge's suspicions when we have so little hard evidence. Heaven knows where we're going to find it. Any other comments?'

'Only this,' said Johnny Fitzgerald. 'Will you look at this chocolate cake here. There's only one slice left, for heaven's sake. I think the cook might be distressed if we didn't polish it off like we have the fruit cake.'

They might not have solved the mystery, but they had done considerable damage to the hotel tea. The sandwiches were all gone and only a couple of crumpets remained unloved and uneaten.

27

Julia Brooks was intrigued by the thought that there was going to be a guard on her house.

'The poor man stuck out there all evening and all night, Lord Powerscourt, it's like something out of a mystery story. Should we feed him with tea and buns from time to time?'

Lady Lucy had gone to tell Mrs Field.

'Dear me, Lady Powerscourt. Are your husband and the policemen sure that this is really necessary?'

'They are.'

'It looks as if Sandy is causing as much trouble dead as he did when he was alive. Don't worry about me. I shall sleep more soundly in my bed now.'

Nothing happened the first night. Mrs Brooks and Mrs Field lived to fight another day. On the second day, Powerscourt went to London to see Mr Thompson of the Law Society. Thompson was wearing a regulation dark blue suit and was beginning to go bald. He greeted Powerscourt warmly in his office looking out over Gray's Inn.

'Lord Powerscourt, have you come all the way from Lynchester to see me? The matter must be serious indeed.' He waved Powerscourt to a seat opposite his desk, piled high with files and papers. 'I looked out the letter from Mr Field yesterday afternoon. It looks at first sight like a perfectly normal letter of complaint from one solicitor about another, but that would not have brought you here today.'

'Let me explain the context, if I may, Mr Thompson. The background to this case concerns the lease of a very desirable property in Lynchester Cathedral Close called Netherbury House. The previous incumbent died some months ago. All the houses in the Close are owned by the cathedral. When a vacancy occurs, a firm of local solicitors called Ardglass, Puckeridge and Ross organizes the advertising with the local estate agents and the legal management for the new client. The cathedral people conduct interviews with the shortlisted candidates for the house. In this case there were five people summoned for the last round of interviews. Are you with me so far, Mr Thompson?'

'Everything is very clear so far.'

'There were five candidates. The first, Sir Edward Talbot, boss of Talbot's Stores, came for interview, took dinner with the cathedral people, and returned to Netherbury House for the night. There he was poisoned and died very shortly afterwards. Shortly after that, Mr Field was lured from his house in the Close one night and shot through the head. He died instantly. And, to make matters worse, an old lady who lives in a cottage near the house was also killed. We have three murders and we have no idea who committed them.'

'I see. How very dreadful. I think I may have seen

something about it in the papers. Let me tell you about the letter. It was a letter of complaint about the charges made on the various candidates for interview and the final impost on the winner. Mr Field thought the charges were far too high and, looking at the examples he gave, he was absolutely right. He went on to say that the practice seemed to have been going for a number of years, and gave an estimate of how much money Ardglass, Puckeridge and Ross must have made from these leases over the past ten years. I thought the figure was too high until I did the calculations myself. I then found that, if anything, his figures might have been an underestimate.'

'Forgive me for interrupting, Mr Thompson, but did he mention the firm as being responsible, rather any particular individual?'

'It was always the firm. I don't think he referred to any of the three partners by name. That was the prudent thing to do.'

'What else did he have to say?'

'He was asking the Law Society to investigate. As is normal in these matters, he wanted his own name kept out of it. Complaining solicitors nearly always want their own name kept out of it. I presume they think they might be fired on the spot if their employer knew who had blown the whistle. Why don't you read the letter for yourself? It's quite short.'

Powerscourt found that Mr Thompson's summary was totally accurate. He handed the letter back. 'I'm sure, Mr Thompson, that you will keep the letter safe.'

'Of course. We have already made a copy of it. But tell me, Lord Powerscourt, you said in your letter to us that you were investigating these killings down in

Lynchester. Do you think there may be a link between this letter and the murders? I am assuming you do, or you would not have come all this way?'

'You are quite right, of course, Mr Thompson, but I am reluctant to go into details.'

'I understand. You need time to reflect on the meaning of the letter and what bearing it has on the case. But tell me this, Lord Powerscourt. We pride ourselves here on the speed of our investigations in matters of this sort. I could send a reliable man down to Lynchester in the next couple of days to look into the affair. Or we could wait a little longer. Which would you prefer?'

'That is very kind of you, Mr Thompson. I think a pause might be the better option. Any immediate action might be like adding fuel to the fire. I just hope Ardglass, Puckeridge and Ross don't take to burning a lot of files.'

'I don't think they would dare do that. The Law Society takes a very strong line about evidence being destroyed. Is there anything we can do in the short term to assist you in your investigations?'

'It may, under certain circumstances, be useful to let it be known that a complaint has been launched and that one of your people will be coming to investigate.'

'Feel free, Lord Powerscourt, to use the information in any way you think fit. I shall await your instructions about our own inquiries into this matter. Is there anything else we at the Law Society can do to help?'

'You have been more than helpful already, Mr Thompson. For the moment, I don't think there is.'

'Then I wish you Godspeed. And good luck. It sounds to me as though you are going to need it.'

* * *

345

Powerscourt thought of two devices that might speed things up on his train journey back to Lynchester. He wasn't sure about either of them. One might provoke the killer to strike again. The other one might be illegal. He decided to tell Lady Lucy about the first but not the second.

Lady Lucy met him in the hotel reception. 'Francis, how good to see you. I thought you'd be on that train. You're a man in demand today, my love. The Bishop wants to see you as soon as you come back. And Inspector Vaughan wants a meeting immediately – if not sooner.'

'Now then, before I go to see those people you mentioned, Lucy, I want some advice.'

'I'll do what I can.'

'Suppose Inspector Vaughan puts it about that Mrs Field has just remembered some vital piece of evidence that puts the whole case in a different light.'

'How would he do that?'

'I'm sure he could manage it, Lucy. Drop a line into the local pubs, that sort of thing.'

'The intention being, I presume, to make the killer even keener to get rid of Mrs Field?'

'Exactly so. The killer pops round to the Field house and runs straight into the arms of the Inspector's men.'

'I can see the appeal, Francis, but I don't think it is a good idea. The killer – Puckeridge, we suspect – would already have a motive for getting rid of Mrs Field: the fact that he doesn't know what her husband may have told her. He doesn't need another motive. And what happens if he does go round there and manages to kill her? It would, in a way, be your fault for propagating this rumour. You would never forgive yourself. You could end up reproaching yourself for the rest of your life.'

'What would I do without you, Lucy? You're absolutely

right. I'll put that idea straight into the bin. Now then, I'd better set off on my travels.'

Powerscourt decided that the Bishop would have to come first. The Bishop, after all, was – as it were – his employer on this case.

'Lord Powerscourt, how good of you to call.' The Bishop was writing at his desk, looking troubled. 'My question is this. Should we proceed with the arrangements about the lease? It only occurred to me this morning that perhaps we should wait until things are a bit clearer. Captain Chapman would still be the winning candidate, of course.'

'Are you asking me, Bishop, if you should postpone the awarding of the lease to Captain Chapman?'

'I am.'

'My advice to you and your colleagues would be to press on. I can see little point in delaying things. Much better to have the matter settled.' Powerscourt thought that any deferment might make the murderer wonder if the authorities knew about Sandy Field's activities and Sandy Field's letter to the Law Society.

'I see,' said the Bishop rather sadly. 'I hope and pray that you will get to the bottom of it all soon.'

'There is one rather important development I should tell you about. Ardglass, Puckeridge and Ross have been overcharging all the candidates for their services relating to new leases in the Close. That, for the moment, must remain confidential.'

'God bless my soul,' said the Bishop.

* * *

Inspector Vaughan was in a good mood. 'The man in the abattoir was called William Farmer, my lord, as you know. I've interviewed the fellow once so far and he said absolutely nothing, apart from confirming his name.'

'Have you charged him with anything?'

'No, we haven't, not yet.'

'Does the man have a criminal record?'

'He does: a number of burglaries and a couple of cases involving violence. And heaven knows what all else that we don't know about, or that never came to court.'

'Do we know who his solicitor is?'

'You'll never guess, my lord.'

'Let me try. Mr Puckeridge, of Ardglass, Puckeridge and Ross.'

'Absolutely right. They say Puckeridge managed to get him off a number of charges a couple of years back.'

'I see. And what would you charge him with, Inspector, if you were in a charging frame of mind?'

'I'd charge him with attempted murder.'

'Of course you would. With me as the victim.'

'That is correct. You're plotting something, Lord Powerscourt, I can tell.'

'This is all rather unorthodox, Inspector. I advise you to treat my plan with caution. It may be illegal. Suppose the man appears in court and gets sent down for attempted murder. How long a sentence would he get?'

'I gave up trying to estimate what length of sentence anybody would get years ago, my lord. I could never get it right. Ten years? Maybe more and maybe less.'

'And do you think it likely,' asked Powerscourt, 'that he would tell us the name of the person who hired him to do the job?'

'I presume you are referring to Mr Puckeridge?'

'I am.'

'No, I do not think he would tell us that. Honour among thieves, and all that. He may have been paid on condition that he keeps his mouth shut. Puckeridge is a thief, too, come to think about it. All those five hundred pounds and all the rest of it.'

'So we would still have absolutely no evidence against Puckeridge at all.'

'That is correct. It's just like the murders. No evidence at all. My lord, I don't see what you are driving at.'

'It's this. What happens if I refuse to give evidence?'

'Then we couldn't charge him with attempted murder because we wouldn't know who the intended victim in the abattoir was. We could only accuse him of breaking and entering. He'd go to prison, but for a much shorter term. I'm lost, my lord, really lost.'

'What I'm suggesting, Inspector, and I'm sorry if I haven't made myself clear, is that you offer this man Farmer a choice. It depends on whether I decide to give evidence against him. If I don't, then he can't be charged with attempted murder because there was no victim to appear in court and give evidence. If Farmer refuses to tell you who hired him, then he is charged with attempted murder and I give evidence against him. But if he tells you who put him up to it, I don't give evidence and then he goes to court on the lesser charge of burglary, or what you will, and gets a much shorter sentence. Then it would be Puckeridge in court on a charge of conspiracy to murder, with Farmer as the chief witness. We suspect that Puckeridge was responsible for the other three murders but, apart from a couple of resurrections, I can't see how we could bring him to trial with no witnesses. But I'm

349

sure a jury would convict on that charge of conspiracy to murder.'

'Of course, my lord. Now I see what you're driving at. I'd have to talk to the Chief Constable, and I'm not sure the Chief Constable would approve.'

'That must be a matter for him. If you decide to tell him.'

'You're not making my life any easier today, my lord.'

'I think I am, Inspector. This way we get Puckeridge locked up for a long time. A clever prosecuting counsel could work in all that stuff about the leases. He could say that Puckeridge suspected you and I might be onto him for his outrageous fees and that he decided to have me killed in the abattoir. That should lengthen his sentence a bit. At least he'd be behind bars rather than free to carry out any more murders. Think of me as the magic witness, Inspector. Now you see me, now you don't. It'll be Farmer's choice, of course. He could refuse to tell us about Puckeridge and receive a long sentence. He tells us and he gets a much shorter one. I may be committing a crime by refusing to give evidence, but I don't really care. On the train I thought, we want success, not victory. Victory would be Puckeridge convicted of all three murders and, perhaps, the hangman's rope, God help us all. But I don't think we're going to get that. With the magic witness we get a measure of success: Puckeridge behind bars, probably for a long time.'

'I can see all that, my lord. It's certainly very ingenious. Let me think about it. I'll make an appointment to see the Chief Constable first thing in the morning.'

Inspector Vaughan saw the Chief Constable at nine o'clock the following day. The Chief Constable summoned Powerscourt to his office at ten.

'Lord Powerscourt, how good of you to come. I have been talking to Inspector Vaughan. He filled me in on the latest developments in the case – the Law Society and so on. I really want to ask you about your ingenious scheme to drop the charge of attempted murder against this man, Farmer. Tell me, if you would, the advantages and disadvantages of this plan. It seems to me that there is danger of the police encouraging a miscarriage of justice.'

'Thank you, Chief Constable. I think it would be useful if I were to outline what caused the suggestion. As things stand, we suspect Puckeridge committed all three murders. We could be wrong, of course, but I don't think so. We have no evidence. We have no witnesses. We have nothing that would enable your force to charge him with murder. The man looks as if he is going to get off scot-free, apart from whatever transpires from the Law Society, but that may not lead to a court case. One of the reasons, probably the main reason, I suspect, for Puckeridge to engage in this spate of murders, is that he can see his whole life falling apart. He was doing his best to stop it. I don't know if Sandy Field told him that he intended to approach the Law Society. I think he probably did. Sandy Field was that sort of man. But apart from a possible charge of professional misconduct and all that that entails, he might get away with it. He would still be at liberty to kill again if he decides somebody else holds the keys to his downfall.'

'That sounds perfectly reasonable to me. What of the other option?'

'Here again, we do not know what is going to happen. We do not know if William Farmer will agree to a lesser charge about the abattoir in exchange for giving evidence in court about who put him up to it. It would make a difference of years to the terms of his sentence. Indeed, I suspect, he could be a free man in less than a year. But if he does incriminate Puckeridge, then Puckeridge can be charged with conspiracy to murder. Not as good as being charged with murder, from our point of view, but at least it would put him behind bars for a number of years. He would not be walking the streets of Lynchester, able to kill again. If any further evidence were to turn up, which I doubt very much because I can't see where it might come from, then he could be charged with murder as well.'

'It's certainly ingenious, Lord Powerscourt. I don't like the idea of my police force conniving with criminals and offering false evidence in court about who was or was not in the abattoir. I don't like it at all.'

Powerscourt felt he had to intervene.

'Think of it this way, Chief Constable. If you decide to do nothing, a killer is still at large. If you engage on the other course, then at least he should end up in prison.'

'What happens if Farmer refuses to play ball?'

'Then the whole thing falls down. But I think he will decide to play ball. The difference in the length of any possible sentences should ensure that. And of course the whole gambit depends on his naming Puckeridge as the man who put him up to it. If he doesn't do that, then the whole scheme collapses.'

'I agree.' The Chief Constable paused and looked out at the view of Lynchester from his window. 'It's a very difficult choice, Lord Powerscourt. I shall consider it during the rest of this morning. I shall see Inspector Vaughan with my decision first thing after lunch.'

'Thank you very much.'

* * *

Lady Lucy had gone to talk to Mrs Field. Powerscourt paced round the Close and was back at the hotel for lunch. He suddenly realized that he might, quite soon, if all went well, be a free man, able to return to London.

It was four o'clock before Inspector Vaughan appeared, grinning from ear to ear. 'My lord,' he said, 'I have excellent news. The Chief Constable approved the plan. He wanted me to talk to Farmer immediately. I think the Chief Constable is now as keen as the rest of us to draw a line under this case. Once he knew the nature of the offer, Farmer confirmed that Puckeridge had asked him to go the abattoir and kill the man he would find there. I said that we might only charge him with breaking and entering. Just to make sure he doesn't change his mind, I said Mr Puckeridge would come to trial first. If he backtracked on his evidence, then he, Farmer, would face a charge of attempted murder and be sent to prison for a long sentence. I thought that was the way to secure his evidence, to hold his trial up until after Puckeridge's. I'm going to talk to Puckeridge tomorrow when Farmer's witness statement has been typed up.'

'Well done, Inspector, well done indeed.'

'The Chief Constable sends his thanks for all your work on the case. He said he didn't think you would find it amiss if he said he hoped not to see you professionally in Lynchester for the foreseeable future. I am going to continue the watches on Mrs Field and Mrs Brooks for the time being. I think it would be premature to call them off at this point. And now, if you will excuse me, I have a lot of business to attend to.'

* * *

Early the following afternoon, Inspector Vaughan decided that the time had come to interview Puckeridge. He and Powerscourt set out for the offices of Ardglass, Puckeridge and Ross. The receptionist told them that he was not in the office at present.

'Maybe he's working at home, sir,' she said. 'He does that sometimes when he's got a difficult case.'

'Could you show us to his office, please?' Inspector Vaughan was taking no chances.

The girl looked at them as if they were madmen come to call.

'Of course, if that's what you want.'

Puckeridge's office was empty.

'His house is on the crescent, is that right?' said Inspector Vaughan.

'Yes, it is, sir. Number thirty-four.'

The Puckeridge housekeeper told them her master had gone away. She thought he had been carrying a suitcase when he set forth about twenty minutes ago.

'I'm not absolutely sure about the suitcase,' she told them. 'I only caught a glimpse of him going out of the front door.'

'Thank you very much,' said Powerscourt.

'If you are going away from Lynchester, my lord, there's only one way to do it, and that's by train. We'd better head for the railway station.' Inspector Vaughan was now walking at top speed. Ten minutes later they were talking to the man in the ticket office.

'Mr Puckeridge?' he said. 'Why, he was here a few minutes ago. His train's just left.'

'Where was he going to?' asked Powerscourt.

'He took a first-class ticket to London, sir. He always travels first class when he's going there. Is there anything the matter?' He was looking suspiciously at Inspector Vaughan's uniform.

'Where does the train stop en route?' Powerscourt was trying to work out if they could head him off along the way.

'Next stop Prestbury, change for Reading, then straight through to London.'

Inspector Vaughan bought a pair of first-class tickets to London and moved to the rear of the reception area.

'How long does it take to get to Prestbury, Inspector?'

'It's about forty-five minutes.'

'Could we get there before that train if we took my car, Inspector? My chauffeur brought my wife down in it the other day. It's parked outside the hotel.'

'I didn't know you had a car down here, my lord. Let's try it. I could ask them to stop the train in Prestbury, but it's a long and complicated process. The train would have gone before we got authorization.'

Ten minutes later, the Powerscourt Rolls-Royce was on the Prestbury road.

'There are a couple of places where the road runs parallel to the railway track, my lord. We might even get a glimpse of it,' said the Inspector.

Powerscourt was driving as fast as he dared. He was hunched forward over the wheel, concentrating hard. Inspector Vaughan was peering out of the window in case the train was visible. He felt sure that they were travelling faster than the train. Then they met a farm cart. The road was going up a hill at this point, with a long succession of bends. Powerscourt didn't dare to overtake until he had a clear road ahead of him.

'There's the railway!' Inspector Vaughan shouted. 'And there's the train, by God. We could do it yet!' The bends going down the hill were exactly the same as those going up. Their speed dropped to a little below five miles an hour.

'I wish this bloody cart would get out of our way, my lord. If it goes on like this for much longer, we're going to lose him at Prestbury.' Inspector Vaughan was scratching his head now. The road cleared. It was clear for some time. Powerscourt pushed the speedometer back upwards. There was another sighting of the railway line, but no sign of the train.

'How far is it to Prestbury now, Inspector? I fear we may have lost too much time. And the car will be running out of petrol soon. I'm going to need a garage.'

'It can't be much more than a couple of miles now. Will the car take us there without running out of fuel?'

'It should do,' said Powerscourt, peering at his dials. 'But I can't be certain.'

They were on a long, straight stretch now. Powerscourt picked up speed again. Scattered groups of houses marked the outskirts of Prestbury. A smaller motorcar, travelling at ten miles an hour or less, blocked their progress.

'The station's on the other side of town, my lord. We need to turn left in a minute or so.'

The other car turned left, too. There was not enough clear road to overtake.

'There's a pedestrian bridge in the station, my lord. You have to cross over it to pick up the London express. Next turning on the right.'

There was the station. Powerscourt parked the car to one side of the entrance. They sprinted on to the platforms. The train from Lynchester was on the far side of the tracks. About fifty yards away was the pedestrian bridge. Two or three elderly passengers were coming down the steps and climbing aboard the London train. There was no sign of anybody else. All London passengers were now safely aboard the express to the capital. A whistle blew. The guard on the platform waved his flag. The three twenty-five for Reading and London Paddington began to move slowly out of the station. Powerscourt and Inspector Vaughan ran at full speed towards the front of the moving train where the first-class passengers were seated. They only had time to look in one first-class compartment before the train pulled away.

Puckeridge was not to be seen.

'We need to have another plan, my lord.' Powerscourt and a panting Inspector Vaughan were having a cup of tea in the station buffet. 'I don't think we could attempt to catch that London express by car, however hard we tried. It goes pretty quickly on that leg of the journey. Do you think we should just take the next express?'

'Is there nothing you can do to delay that train, Inspector?'

'I'm not sure. I think I'll have to go and have a chat with the stationmaster. We could ask them to hold it up outside Paddington, I suppose. It all depends on how cooperative the railway people are. I've done this once before and it took the Chief Constable in person on the line before they would agree to it. Let's hope he's in his office and not out playing golf. Why don't you come with me? A peer might work wonders on the railway mind.'

The stationmaster lived just behind the ticket office; a portrait of the King hung on his wall.

'This is most irregular,' he said. 'I shall have to consult my superiors.' A long series of telephone calls went forth from Prestbury Station. There seemed to be little progress. Powerscourt was growing anxious. The next express was due in less than half an hour. Once Puckeridge got to London, he could go almost anywhere.

A name materialized out of the phone calls. A Mr Samuels in head office was the person who was able to give authority. He was currently engaged on the telephone. Inspector Vaughan gave the stationmaster the name and telephone number of the Chief Constable to pass on to Mr Samuels. At last he came on the line and asked to speak to Inspector Vaughan.

'You want us to stop the train now en route from Prestbury to Paddington via Reading. Is that correct?'

'It is, sir,' said the Inspector. 'I have the phone number of our Chief Constable to hand.'

'Thank you very much. Let me speak to him and I will call you straight back.'

There were now ten minutes to go before the arrival of the next express. The stationmaster and Inspector Vaughan were staring hard at the telephone. It did not ring. There were five minutes left to go. At last. It rang. It was a purely local inquiry about trains running on Sunday. The stationmaster got rid of his caller as fast as he could. It rang again.

'Inspector Vaughan? Samuels here. I have spoken to your Chief Constable. We shall divert the train outside Paddington. We shall hold it there until you are at Paddington and report to the stationmaster. His office is on your right as you enter the main ticket hall. The man on duty will be James Gault. Have you got that?'

'Yes, sir. Thank you very much, sir. We must go to catch our train. I'm very grateful.'

Powerscourt and Inspector Vaughan had to run to board the train. They collapsed into a first-class carriage. Inspector Vaughan was looking cheerful. Powerscourt was not. There was something at the back of his mind; some piece of information that might be relevant to the case that he couldn't put his finger on.

'Let's try to put ourselves into Puckeridge's shoes, Inspector. I think we can safely assume that he must have suspected we were going to call. So he makes his getaway. But think of this. Does he have a plan? Or did he just catch the first train he could? My reading of him is that he would have some scheme or other up his sleeve. What might that scheme be? He must know that he might have every policeman in the country looking for him in a day or two. But he presses on. Desperation or cunning? What do you think?'

'I agree with you that he must have a plan. But for the life of me I cannot see what it might be.'

'If you want to disappear in this country, it is virtually impossible. It could be done, but with a lot of personal inconvenience, staying indoors, all that sort of thing.'

Inspector Vaughan had a brief meeting with the stationmaster at Paddington. He was told that the train would be released from its siding and would arrive at Platform Four in twenty minutes. Powerscourt and Inspector Vaughan took up their positions on either side of the exit where the passengers handed in their tickets. Powerscourt was still searching in his brain for the fact that was eluding him. Inspector Vaughan was thinking of yet another train to take the three of them back to Lynchester.

At last the train pulled in to the station. The passengers were grumpy, complaining about the delay. Some of them were definitely going to write to the railway company. There was a crush at the beginning of Platform Four as the passengers filed through. Powerscourt could not see any sign of Puckeridge. If he had been in the middle of the crowd, he might just have got away. The queue was thinning out. Puckeridge was not one of the stragglers. A mother with a couple of fractious toddlers brought up the rearguard. Powerscourt looked across for Inspector Vaughan. He was not there either. Powerscourt found him inspecting the taxi queue. He was on his own.

'Goddammit, he can't have been on that train at all.'

'Perhaps he got off at Reading. He could get to London by a roundabout route. Do you think he could have seen us at Prestbury? If he did, that would explain his changing trains.'

'It's possible,' said Powerscourt.

'I need to speak to the Metropolitan Police and to my Chief Constable. I suspect that the people I need to talk to will have gone home by now.'

'Why don't you come to my house and we can plan our next moves? I had high hopes that the whole case might have been over before the end of the day.'

It was in the taxi on the way to Markham Square that Powerscourt finally remembered what had been eluding him all afternoon.

'Let me put an outrageous theory before you, Inspector,' said Powerscourt when the two men were safely ensconced in his drawing room.

'It's that cider eau-de-vie that was used to kill the first victim, Inspector. I think we assumed that the bottle was in the cellar. But how would Puckeridge have known that? He wasn't a close friend or anything like that. It's much more likely that Puckeridge brought it with him and that he had the poison as well. He mixed the lethal cocktail in the kitchen before he brought it out. "Just give me a moment while I get the drinks sorted out", that sort of thing. Sir Edward Talbot wouldn't have known a thing. But the question is, where did Puckeridge get it from? He couldn't have got it in Lynchester because it's not for sale. I'm going to find out a lot more about cider eau-de-vie from my wine merchant's in the morning. I wouldn't be at all surprised if it's not for sale anywhere in this country. Which means, that Puckeridge must have picked it up in France. I think it may have a fairly restricted circulation there, too.'

'Are you saying that Puckeridge may be going back to where he bought the stuff? What on earth for?'

'Suppose he has a house in France, near a place where they make the cider eau-de-vie. That's how he came to hear about it. He brought a few bottles home with him. And it would be much easier to disappear in France than it would be in England.'

'I see,' said Inspector Vaughan, who wasn't entirely convinced. 'We'll have to wait until the morning.'

28

Powerscourt left Inspector Vaughan on the telephone the following morning while he made his way to Berry Bros and Rudd at number three St James's Street. He was shown up to the office of a Mr George Berry, who was an expert on the wines of France. Powerscourt had known him for years.

'Lord Powerscourt, how nice to see you. How can I be of assistance this morning? We always aim to help our old customers.'

'I'm in the middle of a rather difficult investigation, Mr Berry. I want some information on a drink called cider eau-de-vie.'

'Do you indeed. I don't believe we offer the stuff in our catalogue. I don't think I've ever heard of it being on sale in an English wine merchant's. There's no demand for it, or people aren't aware of its existence. It's very strong, even more potent than Polish vodka. Normandy, that's where it comes from, but I'm not sure how many of the cider firms sell the stuff. Hold on a minute and I'll consult the "bible". This lists all the major wine and spirits producers in northern France. That includes cider and the related products.'

George Berry brought down a thick volume from the shelves behind his desk. 'Cambremer in Normandy,' he said. 'They definitely make it there. And Belleville and St-Sulpice. There may be more but the catalogue doesn't say. The modern name for the most common type of cider eau-de-vie is Calvados, but some of the cider makers keep the old name and leave it to mature for longer, and still call it cider eau-de-vie to distinguish it from Calvados. It's also more expensive. Would you like me to ring the Cambremer people up?'

'God bless my soul,' said Powerscourt. 'I hadn't thought of that.'

'They have a phone number listed here in my book.'

'If you have the time, I'd be most grateful.'

'It may take some time. The patron might be out in his orchards. Is there anything you would particularly like me to ask?'

Powerscourt was tempted to ask if there was a connection with an Englishman who bought a bottle of cider eau-de-vie recently, but thought better of it. If his theory was right, a casual word might send Puckeridge off on his travels again. 'I think you should ask if they or any of their colleagues send the stuff over here. That would be helpful. And could you ask if the cider eau-de-vie is for sale in the shops attached to their works, like their cider or their Calvados are.'

'I could say we are thinking of selling some of it ourselves. We would like to know if we would have any competition.'

'Splendid,' said Powerscourt.

George Berry picked up his phone and asked if they

could connect him with Fadieres, the cider makers in Cambremer. He gave the French number. The girl protested that her French might not be up to it.

'Just let me know when the operator gets through,' said Berry.

'We'll just have to wait for the French connection, my lord. Could I ask if you have sampled some cider eau-de-vie yourself? I'm told it can be quite addictive.'

'I haven't had that pleasure yet, Mr Berry. Maybe some time soon.'

The telephone rang.

'Mr Fadiere, a very good morning to you. My name is Berry, from the London firm of Berry Bros and Rudd. We are one of the leading importers of wine and spirits in this country.'

There was a torrent of French from the other side of the Channel.

'You have heard of us, monsieur, that is most gratifying. We are not only interested in your excellent cider, but also in your cider eau-de-vie. We have heard good things about it.'

Powerscourt was trying to imagine what sort of Frenchman Fadiere was. Tall? Short? Smoking a Gauloise, perhaps?

'I see. So you say the cider eau-de-vie is not generally sold in the shops. The people prefer ordinary Calvados. But it is available from the shop attached to your works. Is that right?'

M. Fadiere was now going through a coughing fit.

'It is? How very interesting. So the only way for a tourist to buy a bottle would be to call in person to your shop?'

'That's right,' said M. Fadiere. 'I happen to know that

our colleagues in St-Sulpice and Belleville make a very limited quantity of cider eau-de-vie, but it is not for sale in their shops attached to the cider works.'

Powerscourt was staring out of the window at a traffic jam along this end of St James's Street.

'Thank you very much, Monsieur Fadiere. I shall write to you about our possible purchase of some of your cider eau-de-vie, and of course of your excellent cider. What was that? You are sure your cider is superior to that made in England? You put it down to the climate? Very good. Thank you very much. We shall be in touch, and many thanks for your time.'

'Are you actually going to buy some of his produce, Mr Berry?'

'I don't see why not, my lord. Maybe your investigation will end up all over the papers and there will be great demand for it.'

'Stranger things have happened.'

'Now then, my lord, I expect you picked up most of that. Yes, they do make cider eau-de-vie, but it's only available from their shop. There are – to the best of his knowledge – no other outlets in Normandy that sell it over the counter, as it were. Nor are there any firms that export it to England. He said they sell a number of bottles to English tourists every year, that's all, apart from the locals.'

'Well done, Mr Berry. You'd better put me down for three bottles of the stuff when it gets here. Thank you very much indeed.'

Inspector Vaughan whistled softly when Powerscourt told him about his conversations with Mr Berry.

'What do you think, my lord? Should we head for France?'

'I don't think our friend has any plans to come back here, do you?'

'I'll have to ring my office, my lord.'

'Carry on, please. You know where the phone is.'

One train ride to Dover, one cross-Channel voyage and a tortuous route across the railway stations of northern France brought them to Caen, the nearest train station to Cambremer where the cider plant was to be found. Powerscourt hired a taxi for the rest of the day.

'Should we ask at the cider place if they know anything of Puckeridge?' said Inspector Vaughan.

'I think we should try the post office first, if they have a branch here.'

Cambremer boasted a town hall, a baker's, a butcher's, a couple of bars, a newsagent's and tobacco shop and a miscellany of small shops clustered round the main square. The post office was right in the corner. Powerscourt took a deep breath as he went to the main counter.

'Good day to you, madame,' said Powerscourt in his best French. 'I come from England and we are looking for a friend who we believe has a house here. He is called Puckeridge, Mr Puckeridge. Could you give us some advice as to his address?'

'Good day to you too, sir. I am quite new here and I don't know the district very well. I could ask in the main office behind me, if you like.'

She disappeared into the interior. 'Do you think he has many letters here?' said Inspector Vaughan. 'I've not heard of him being in France before. You know how word gets round if people have property overseas.'

The lady came back. 'The person who would know is

366

not in the office at the moment. He should be back in an hour or so. Perhaps you could call back then?'

'Of course, madame. We shall come back in an hour. Could you tell us how to find Monsieur Fadiere's place in the meantime? I've been told he makes some of the finest cider in France.'

'That is true; their cider is famous here in Normandy. Go left out of here, follow the street up to the crossroads and turn left. It's just on that corner there.'

'Thank you so much,' said Powerscourt. 'We shall come back.'

Their driver had repaired to the bar in the centre of the square, where he would wait for further instructions.

'I'm losing hope, my lord. Surely Puckeridge can't have a place here in the back of beyond.'

'We shall find out very soon,' said Powerscourt.

The cider shop had walls lined with shelves and different varieties of cider. There was an elderly man behind the counter, smoking a pipe.

'Good day to you, gentlemen,' he began, 'how can I be of assistance?'

'Good day to you, sir. I wonder if you can help us. We recently enjoyed some of your cider eau-de-vie and wondered if we could buy some to take home?'

'Of course, one bottle or two?' said the man. 'We only sell it here in this shop.'

'One, please.'

'There you are, monsieur.'

'As a matter of fact, the person who bought the cider eau-de-vie was English. Would he have had to come here to buy it?'

The old man banged his pipe on the counter in front of him. Powerscourt paid for the bottle.

'We don't get many English in here, and that's a fact. The last one was some time last summer. The person who bought it said he had a house in the town. Now I come to think of it, he told me where it was.'

'Can you remember where his house is?'

There was a long pause. The old man was refilling his pipe.

'I've got it. Go back to the main square and take the road with the baker's shop in it. The house is two from the very end with a black door.'

'I don't suppose he told you his name?'

'No, he didn't. We don't normally ask customers for their names. I don't know what they do in England.'

'Thank you very much. One last question, if I could. Can you remember what he looked like?'

There was another pause. 'I can't remember. Middle-aged maybe? Well dressed? I'm not sure.'

Powerscourt and Inspector Vaughan set off for the house with the black door.

'Pity the old boy couldn't remember what the man looked like,' said the Inspector.

'At least he was helpful. He could have told us to mind our own business and gone back to his pipe.'

'Do you think Puckeridge is in this house with the black door?'

'I still think the odds are very heavily stacked against us. But it could have been Puckeridge who bought the eau-de-vie in that shop.'

They were passing the baker's shop. A few tired baguettes were sitting in the window, along with an elaborate apple tart.

'I think you had better do the talking to Puckeridge if he is there, Inspector. The long arm of the law, and all that.'

They were at the house now. Inspector Vaughan knocked on the door. A middle-aged woman, who might have been the housekeeper, opened the door.

'Is Mr Puckeridge at home?' asked Powerscourt with a smile. 'We are friends of his from England.'

'I'll just see if he's here. He might have popped out.'

She knocked on the door at the corner of the hall. There was a grunt from inside. Powerscourt was beginning to hope. Inspector Vaughan was twisting his hands together. There was a regular tick from the clock by the front door.

The door opened. Puckeridge came out, still dressed for a day at the office.

'My God!' he said. 'Inspector Vaughan and Lord Powerscourt! The last people I would have expected to see!' With that he pushed his housekeeper into Inspector Vaughan and fled towards the back of the house.

'After him!' shouted Inspector Vaughan, disentangling himself from the housekeeper.

They shot through the back corridor, past the kitchen and a couple of storerooms. Puckeridge had a start on them of about fifty yards. He was running along a minor road that ran parallel to a field on one side and a river on the other. A couple of cows observed their passing. The river made its way to the sea via a series of bends. Inspector Vaughan was in the lead, Powerscourt close behind.

'Damn you! Damn you to hell, the pair of you!' Puckeridge seemed to pick up a burst of speed as Inspector Vaughan began to close the gap.

Puckeridge was about twenty yards ahead of them. Inspector Vaughan shouted ahead.

'Stop, man! For God's sake, stop!'

Puckeridge twisted round to see how close they were. He tried to accelerate. As he turned back he must have tripped on a smooth stone. He fell into the river, his momentum carrying him away from the edge. Two things were obvious. The first was that the river was very deep at this point. The second was that Puckeridge couldn't swim. The speed of his run had carried him well away from the side where the water was shallower. He was floundering about – now rising, now falling back beneath the water.

'Help!' he spluttered. 'Help!'

Then he disappeared from sight once more. Powerscourt flung off his jacket and jumped in after Puckeridge. The water was very cold. He managed to get an arm around Puckeridge's shoulder. He tried to pull him back to the surface. Puckeridge was gasping for breath. Inspector Vaughan seemed to be having a wrestling match with a low branch on one of the trees.

'Get a hold of me. Under the armpit if you can.' Powerscourt was panting heavily. Puckeridge was just about able to do that when the current pulled him down once more, holding on to Powerscourt's shoulder. Powerscourt tried to keep the two of them afloat. It was very hard work. Puckeridge seemed very heavy here in the dark water. The bank was not very far away, but Powerscourt was not sure they could make it. The current had brought them close to the middle of the river. Something told Powerscourt that the two of them were quite likely to drown now. He could keep Puckeridge afloat some of the time, when his face came out of the water, but he did not see how he could reach the bank. He tried to swim as best he could, but he was making little progress against the current.

Inspector Vaughan had won his battle with the branch. It was long enough to reach the middle of the river. He threw one end as hard as he could into the river, holding on to the other one. Twice he tried, but his branch landed too far in front or too far behind.

'Get a hold of this, my lord,' he panted. 'I'll see if I can pull you both in.'

The next throw landed the branch right in front of Powerscourt. He had Puckeridge holding on to his right arm now. He grabbed the branch with his left hand. The Inspector began to pull. Powerscourt began to move, but he had great difficulty holding on to Puckeridge. Just when it seemed that they might make it to the bank, Powerscourt felt Puckeridge's arm slip on his shirt and he was gone. Powerscourt lost his hold of the branch at the same time. He swam the few yards that separated him from Puckeridge. He took hold of him once more. The branch was coming back. Powerscourt grabbed it again. He wasn't sure how much longer he could continue. His arms ached. He was very short of breath. He could see now that the two of them might be swept away to their deaths.

Puckeridge rose to the surface once more for a few seconds, spluttering. He tried to speak but the current dragged him down again. Inspector Vaughan was pulling as hard as he knew how on his branch. Then Puckeridge lost hold of Powerscourt. When Powerscourt tried to find an arm or a hand, there was nobody there. Puckeridge had been carried away by the current. He disappeared. In vain did Powerscourt try to find him, making little sorties in all directions. It was as if Puckeridge had never been there at all.

'Come back, my lord! Come back, for God's sake! You don't want to drown in this bloody river.' Powerscourt tried one last time to find the solicitor, but he was gone. By now he could be yards away, or even further. Powerscourt swam slowly back across the current to the bank.

'God help us all,' he panted as he stretched out on the path. 'I should have held on to him tighter. Maybe we could have made it. What a way to go.'

'You mustn't reproach yourself, my lord. You couldn't have done more.' Powerscourt got up and stared at the swirling waters of the river. 'We'd better follow the side of the river and see if he has managed to get out of the current. I very much doubt it, mind you.'

They patrolled the side of the river for an hour and a half or more, but it was no good.

'It's over now, Inspector, this investigation. We've just been part of the last act.'

It took two days to sort out the details with the French police, and with the undertakers, who were going to arrange the transport of the body back to England. It was found early that evening by a fisherman, a mile or so from where it started.

'Francis,' said Lady Lucy, 'welcome back. Are you all right? Thank you for the telegram with the latest news.'

'I'm fine, my love. I missed you. Do you know I've left my bottle of cider eau-de-vie on the riverbank in Cambremer? I've only just remembered.'

'Isn't it terrible about Mr Puckeridge? Can you now tell me, Francis, what you think he has been doing?'

'I can only guess. And even then I'm not absolutely sure about the details.'

'I'm all ears.'

'A lot of this is conjecture, Lucy. I fear that the people who could correct me are all dead now. I think Sandy Field raised the question of the exorbitant charges with Puckeridge some time before the first murder, that of Sir Edward Talbot. And I think Puckeridge told him to go to hell. Then I think Sandy told Sir Edward about the charges. And I think he told Puckeridge that Sir Edward was going to raise the matter with the Bishop the morning after the dinner on the day of the interview.

'That was the end of Sir Edward. Once he had seen the Bishop, the whole question of the high charges would be out in the open. Puckeridge took his bottle of cider eau-de-vie – which he must have brought home from his place in Normandy – and his poison round to Netherbury House, and that was the end of Sir Edward.

'I think Sandy must have talked to Puckeridge again the day after Sir Edward's murder. That was when Puckeridge realized that Sandy Field was too dangerous to be left alive. There was no knowing when he, Sandy, would tell the cathedral authorities about his suspicions. He lured Sandy out of his house on some pretext or other and shot him. I think he must have suspected that Mrs McQuaid might have seen him with Sandy as they walked across the Close or came out of Sandy's house. We all know what happened next – the sad end of Mrs McQuaid. Puckeridge would have said that she was alive when he arrived and alive when he left.

'I think Puckeridge panicked after that. He engaged the man Farmer to meet me in the abattoir. Obviously I was never meant to come out alive. I don't know if he realized that Farmer might talk if he was arrested, and that he would incriminate Puckeridge in the killing.'

'What about the Law Society and that man you saw in London, Francis? What was Puckeridge going to do about that?'

'I'm not sure about that. I don't know if somebody had tipped him off that there was trouble ahead. I would assume, I think, that he would have tried to mount some sort of defence for those high fees. Or he could have repented and offered to pay back some of the money to the residents who had paid his charges. I don't know the answer. If Puckeridge hadn't grown so greedy about the charges, those three people would still be alive today.'

The next morning, Powerscourt was planning to go and say his farewells to the Bishop and the Dean and to Mrs Field. Inspector Vaughan came round with news about the case.

'What do you think will happen, Inspector,' said Lady Lucy, 'about the overcharging?'

'Do you know,' replied Inspector Vaughan, 'I'm not sure that it is a matter for the police. It'll be up to the Bishop and the cathedral people to sort that one out. I'm not sure the police need to be involved at all.'

'I expect the Dean will have to sort it out,' said Powerscourt. 'I know it's a rather uncharitable thing to say, but I suspect he'll rather enjoy unravelling all that.

He can feel even more important while he's sorting the problem out.'

'Really, Francis,' said Lady Lucy, 'I'm not sure that this is the most appropriate time to be voicing such thoughts.'

'I think we can let him off,' was the Inspector's verdict.

Powerscourt set off once more to the cathedral to bid his goodbyes. 'What an unfortunate end to this business,' was the Dean's reaction. 'I feel rather sorry for Puckeridge, you know. Greed carried him off in the end. I suppose I'll have to sort out the mess he's left behind with all these people he's overcharged in the Close. God's work never stops.'

The Bishop was rather less worldly. 'What a terrible business. All these people gone to meet their maker before their time. And in such violent circumstances. I shall pray for them all, wherever they are.'

Mrs Field was more personal. 'I do hope we shall see you back in the Close very soon.'

On the way back to London, Powerscourt turned to Lady Lucy sitting by his side. Rhys, the Powerscourts' butler-cum-chauffeur, had retrieved the car from Prestbury Station and was driving them back to London.

'When you came down here, Lucy, did I see that you brought those brochures about the round-the-world cruises with you?'

'As a matter of fact, I did.'

'Why don't you bring them out when we get back? I think we'd better have a good look at them.'